THE ODDITIES

MURDER ONCE SEEN

J.T. HALL

RIPTIDE
PUBLISHING

Riptide Publishing
PO Box 1537
Burnsville, NC 28714
www.riptidepublishing.com

Murder Once Seen
Copyright © 2016 by J.T. Hall

Cover art: Kanaxa, kanaxa.com
Editor: Carole-ann Galloway
Layout: L.C. Chase, lcchase.com/design.htm

ISBN: 978-1-62649-429-9

First edition
December, 2016

Also available in ebook:
ISBN: 978-1-62649-428-2

THE ODDITIES

MURDER ONCE SEEN

J.T. HALL

RIPTIDE PUBLISHING

TABLE OF
CONTENTS

CHAPTER ONE

A TERRIBLE NIGHT

Derwin Bryant never quit in a chase.

A light rain was falling on the city of Nis, turning the neon lights of the porn shops and drugstores into pretty reflections on the asphalt. Derwin avoided a puddle as he ran down an alley and then swerved around an overturned trash can. He grimaced at the stench of rotting food and old beer. It'd be nice if his heightened senses blocked unpleasant things like that.

Up ahead, the alley was a dead end. No way would ol' Jack escape this time.

The fugitive Derwin was pursuing was an Oddity—annoying because the guy could read minds. He knew exactly where Derwin was. Derwin's own unusual abilities couldn't compensate for such an advantage, even though he'd powered up before heading out.

Derwin slowed to a walk to check the shadows in doorways. He lifted lids of garbage containers to be sure Jack wasn't hiding there, and kept his pepper spray in his left hand, ready to fire at the first sign of the mousy guy. Jack Rapper was short, only five foot two, with dark skin and a gold-capped tooth. He was also quick, but Derwin was quicker, thanks to his own Oddity. And with his larger size and muscles honed daily at the gym, Derwin was a match for just about any criminal in a fight.

Satisfied that Jack couldn't be hiding nearby, Derwin broke into a run from the last garbage canister to the brick wall at the end of the alley. No Jack Rapper. He turned and cursed. Where had the guy gone?

He scanned the closed doors, wondering if Jack had managed to get one open. As he reached to try the first door, his cell phone buzzed in his pocket, the single pulse of a text. Swearing under his breath, Derwin pulled out his phone with one hand while he jiggled the doorknob with the other. The door was locked.

On a whim, he glanced up, in case his skip had suddenly developed the ability to climb walls, but there was nothing above him other than a laundry wire several stories up, where an abandoned T-shirt dripped in the rain. It appeared Jack had managed to escape. Not surprising for a guy who had managed to hide his special powers from police. Derwin probably should tell the cops about Jack's Oddity, but he couldn't do it. Couldn't betray a fellow Oddity, even a low-life, criminal one like Jack.

Derwin flipped open the phone and tapped on the text, just in case it was important. In his line of work, anything could happen. He didn't recognize the number, but he recognized the tone and the awful spelling: Lloyd Brunson, one of his past fugitives out on parole again.

You fucker. I shuld kill you and yur pretty boyfriend fur putting me away like dat.

Derwin shook his head, fuming. It wasn't right that Lloyd had threatened Grady, who had nothing to do with Derwin's job. Lloyd had been a good chase as well, mostly because the guy had a knack for stealing fast cars. He had a temper too, but as far as Derwin knew, he wasn't the violent sort. Derwin shoved his phone back in his pocket; he'd warn the guy off later, once he was certain Jack was out of reach or in custody.

Cans crashed at the other end of the alley. He crouched, mentally cursing Lloyd for the interruption. Had Jack managed to trick him somehow? Maybe he hadn't gone into this alley at all. Derwin began walking toward the noise, readying his pepper spray once more.

His phone buzzed again.

He was going to kill Lloyd for the stupid interruptions, and then shut off his phone. Yet when Derwin glanced at it this time, he recognized the number.

It was from Grady.

Come home. Hurry.

Derwin halted in alarm. He ran a hand through his wet hair, pushing the long strands out of his eyes so he could verify what he'd read. Grady wasn't the type to send a cryptic message.

Cursing under his breath, Derwin tapped the button to call his lover. One ring, two, three, and then it went to voice mail. Coldness spread from his gut up his spine. After a text like that, he couldn't imagine why Grady wouldn't answer. *Unless he can't.*

"Call me," Derwin growled when the voice mail beeped, and then put his phone away. Still no sign of Jack, but he couldn't worry about that now. With one last look at the alley's dead end, he ran back toward his car. Grady had to be all right. Even if Derwin called the police for help, what would he tell them? Plus, working as a bail bondsman had taught him that the cops would only screw things up, and anyway, he didn't have a lot of friends on the force.

Ten feet from his upgraded black muscle car, Derwin clicked the little key fob to turn off the alarm and start the engine. It paid to have a ride ready to go when his fugitives fled.

It took only a second to climb into the seat, strap himself in, and shift into drive, stomping on the gas to blast forward into the empty streets. Over the rain-slicked asphalt, past hookers on street corners and young men hanging out near liquor stores, Derwin headed east, away from the seafront and toward the less crime-ridden areas.

The broken-down stores and apartments soon gave way to modest condos and shops wedged between large financial buildings and parking garages. Each red light taunted Derwin, whispering to him: *You'll never make it in time if he's in trouble.*

His hands shook on the wheel, though he fought to remain calm. Maybe it wasn't an emergency. But the fact that his phone hadn't rung yet made him step on the gas harder, urge more speed out of the vintage car.

It took twenty-two minutes to reach his condo. It seemed like an eternity.

He swerved around another car, ignoring the blare of horns as he pulled into an open space in front of the brownstone building he called home. It wasn't a huge place, just one bedroom and a moderate-sized kitchen and living room, but it was his. Theirs, actually. Grady had moved in a year ago, after they'd been dating for almost three years. Grady, with his open smile and his hair like sunshine. He was one of the best things that had ever happened to Derwin.

Derwin fumbled his car door open and got out, grasping for the gun at his hip—no bothering with pepper spray this time. The little window beside the entrance was broken. Glittering shards of glass littered the ground. The front door hung slightly open.

He ran to the door and took the steps two at a time. His hand touched the doorknob, then he stopped. Should he call out for Grady? Or would that warn the intruder? The seconds ticked by while he stood undecided.

Better to call out, on the chance that Grady was hurt or in a hostage situation.

"Grady!" He shoved the door open and pressed his back to its solid surface as he scanned the hallway, where a potted plant had been knocked over, its soil spread across the carpet. He couldn't hear anything from the living room beyond. To his right, the kitchen was undisturbed.

Gun raised and ready, Derwin crept down the hall. "Are you okay?" There was a small click and then a hiss—the slide of a window, perhaps. He rushed around the corner to find the living room empty, though in disarray. A chair lay overturned, next to a bowl of popcorn that had been spilled onto the floor. And something was missing from the entertainment center—Grady's gaming system had vanished, the cords left hanging loose. There was still no response from Grady. Derwin's heart pounded in his ears.

He quickly crossed the room to put his back to the wall and check the stairs, but the silence continued. The little downstairs toilet was empty as well, but its window was open. Should he check to see if a possible burglar had escaped? Or find his lover?

There was no choice really, although frustration tore at him. Derwin glanced out the window, but there was no one there. He hurried up the stairs, keeping his gun ready in case it should turn out that the intruder had tricked him. The bedroom door was closed. He didn't bother shouting this time, but kicked it in.

It took a second to process the sight: blood on the carpet, a ransacked room, papers littering the floor from the computer desk. And finally, slumped in the desk chair in front of the bed, his boyfriend, throat slashed, with a knife stuck in his chest.

Derwin's vision darkened; he couldn't breathe. A moan escaped him, a painful sound, like a wounded animal. "Grady . . . No. No!" He pounded his fist against the doorframe, closing and then reopening his eyes, but the sight in front of him remained the same. *Too late. I got here too late.*

He approached the chair slowly, forcing himself to hold back and not touch the knife, even though he longed to gather up Grady into his arms and pull out that knife. Gently, even tenderly, he placed two fingers at Grady's carotid artery, checking for the pulse he knew he wouldn't find. What tore him the most was that Grady's skin still felt warm. He counted the seconds, waiting, hoping despite the evidence of his eyes. Rage and anguish combated inside him, making his vision blur. Not even a hint of life.

Grady—he'd been alive this afternoon! He'd been alive to send that text. And now Derwin would never hear him laugh again, never look into those intelligent blue eyes. Never hold his willowy frame in his arms once more.

With a shaking hand, he trailed his fingertips over Grady's cheek. Grady's eyes were already closed, thankfully. Derwin clenched his hand into a fist, backing away so that he didn't disturb anything, stepping over the slowly spreading red stain. He dropped to his knees on the soft carpet, shuddering with sobs. He'd been too late. His special strength, his speed, so good for catching bad guys, hadn't helped him at all. Had Grady called out for him? Had he suffered, hoping to be rescued in time?

Blinking away tears, Derwin grabbed his phone. The silence in the room was deafening. He'd be alone tonight. Alone, for many, many nights.

He even laughed at my stupid margaritas joke. Tears choked Derwin, but he couldn't mourn just yet; he had to function a little while longer. Hands shaking, he dialed the emergency services.

Whoever had done this was going to pay.

CHAPTER TWO

THE RETURN OF JACK

Derwin parked on Twelfth Street, being careful to remain inconspicuous as he left the car. Today was the day. A fugitive could run. He could even hide. But eventually, Derwin would find him.

Two years had passed since Grady's murder; two fucking *years*, and he was still dealing with the same shit. The cops had caught Jack Rapper days after Grady's death. Then they had chased their tails for six months looking for Grady's killer, before pursuing Lloyd Brunson, whose shoe size matched prints found at the scene. But all for nothing. There hadn't been enough evidence to take him to trial. The case had gone cold, and while Lloyd Brunson had gone to jail eventually, it had been on an auto-theft charge, not for murder.

During that time, Jack had served six months for burglary, been released, been arrested again for grand larceny, and returned to Bob's to post bond. Which he'd promptly jumped bail on a few weeks ago. Why old Bob's Bonds had given the guy another chance, Derwin didn't know, nor did he care. This time, Jack wasn't getting away.

Scanning the expensive cars along the street, Derwin kept an eye out for Jack. This was a wealthy part of the city, close to a three-story mall for the elite. People strolled the streets dressed in designer fashion, their woolen coats and furs wrapped tight against the cold ocean wind.

The city of Nis was one of the largest ports on the west coast of the United Federation of America. The country wasn't like it had been eighty years ago, before the demons and monsters started appearing, and the damn wars. The United States had crumbled to dust sixty years ago. Out here in the West, the capital Los Fuegos (formerly Los Angeles) ran the show now, with a lot of military might and not a lot of civil liberties. That was probably why car theft was so popular here. Thieves could load up the cars on the dock and sell them overseas in Asia.

Derwin walked, aware that people were staring at him. Dressed in jeans, a T-shirt, and an army vest, he didn't really blend in with the higher fashion styles. A woman wearing a floral silk skirt and walking a Pomeranian stopped short and glared at him. He gave her a nod. She'd thank him when her car was where she'd parked it—if she even drove herself.

Up ahead on the other side of the street, he spotted Jack strolling with his head down, wearing a leather jacket and slacks. His dark hair stuck out at odd angles under his woolen cap, and his hands were shoved into his pockets. His stride was casual, but he was clearly nervous, looking over his shoulder repeatedly. He didn't seem to have spotted Derwin.

Derwin couldn't waste time; any second now Jack would sense him with that damned psychic gift of his. He crossed against traffic, narrowly avoiding a delivery truck. Fortunately, the driver didn't honk.

With a burst of speed, Derwin ran to the sidewalk and ducked behind a group of women standing with open shopping bags, comparing their purchases. He tried to think of nothing other than how one of them reminded him of his mom. The woman wore her dark hair plaited with a mother-of-pearl comb in the back. *Mother-of-pearl . . . mother-of-pearl . . .* he used that image as a shield against a foreign mind that might be sensitive to his focus.

He peeked around the women to see if Jack was running yet.

Jack wasn't, but as Derwin prepared to sneak up behind him, Jack glanced back once more. His eyes widened, and his mouth made a horrified O.

Inside Derwin's head, someone screamed, the sound reverberating between his ears. He stumbled, vision darkening, and was just able to see Jack taking off. Around him, people walked on, oblivious. Derwin rushed after him, trying to focus past Jack's mental attack.

Even though he wasn't charged up enough to use his own power, Derwin was still faster. He dodged an elderly man with a silver cane and a couple pushing a stroller, then grabbed Jack by the arm. With an almost savage fury, he slammed the fugitive face-first against the brick wall of a nearby bookstore. Jack cried out, and the mental scream stopped.

"You failed to appear for your court date, Jack—*for the second fucking time!*" Derwin snarled, clamping on the cuffs. Once the cuffs were on, he readied the pepper spray. People stared and gave them a wide berth.

"I was hungover," Jack said, throwing Derwin a glare over his shoulder. One look at the pepper spray, and he submitted, holding still with a hangdog expression. He might have been forty, or he might have been half that age and just weathered from street life. Three days of scruff on his cheeks showed he hadn't been taking care of himself lately.

"Of course you were." Derwin took him by the arm and led him back to the car. The last thing he needed right now was for a cop to show up and steal the arrest from him. Funny how in the good parts of town, cops were everywhere.

Derwin opened the car's rear door and helped Jack climb in, leaving him cuffed and not bothering with the seat belt. He needed to deliver Jack quickly; the local police station was a few miles away, but he was worried about getting him there. Not because of Jack's agility or strength, but because the guy was likely to try to fuck with his mind.

You hear me? Stay out. Derwin growled as he sat in the driver's seat and turned on the engine, listening to the sputter of the muffler as the engine struggled to find its pace. He'd neglected the poor car over the last couple of years. Maybe with today's check he could give her a tune-up.

"You don't seem to ever learn, do you? Bob's been good to you." He pulled into traffic.

"Better than most," Jack agreed, voice raspy, probably from years of smoking. The guy had been in and out of prison much of his life, but while he was a pain to catch, once he was in custody, he always seemed polite. Maybe that was why Bob kept helping him.

Derwin headed downtown, the wide tree-lined lanes and flashy shops transforming to shiny financial skyscrapers and then to apartments and public offices. The streets narrowed, became dirtier and less cared for. The buildings grew shabbier as well, red brick crumbling at the corners from the salty ocean air, vacant lots ringed by chain-link fences, concrete split by encroaching weeds. No fancy fashions here; those who walked the streets wore faded, threadbare clothes from several seasons ago.

He checked on Jack regularly through the rear-view mirror, expecting at any moment a remark about some deeply buried secret of his, or a mental assault. Jack seemed worn out, possibly from making his earlier mental assault. He was staring out the window, a lost look on his face. Derwin almost asked what he was thinking, then decided it didn't matter.

At the back of the police station, near the general lockup, Derwin pulled into a parking space. "Don't fuck him over again, or I'm going to bring you here in pieces next time. And don't miss your court date or you won't have a bond company left to work with."

"Yeah, got it," Jack murmured, as Derwin climbed out and opened the car door to pull him out. "You know, you were a lot more fun when you were getting laid."

He smirked and a shiver went through Derwin. Was the telepath rifling through his thoughts?

It was best not to rise to the bait. Silently, Derwin led the man inside.

It took far too long to get Jack booked and for Derwin to return to Bob's Bail Bonds to get his cut of the money. Most fast-food joints were closed by the time he got back to his little brownstone and parked on the street. It was going to be peanut butter and jelly sandwiches for dinner. Again.

From force of habit, Derwin checked out the condo as he walked up the steps. The door was locked, lights were off, just as they should be. Derwin opened the door and sighed when a plaintive meow came from behind the potted palm. His mother had suggested that a cat would help with the loneliness. She'd been partly right. But it was like feeding crackers to a man starving for steak. Having a pet was nice, but he needed a real connection. Human companionship.

"Hey, Colonel Bickering. Find yourself a lady yet?" He closed the door and crouched down to scratch at the cat's ears. The name was a play on words from a character in a musical, one of his favorites. It fit the feline well. Often when Bickering mewled, he sounded like he was complaining.

At the moment, however, Bickering was all purrs, rubbing against Derwin's hand, his flattened Persian face ecstatic. Derwin scratched the thick black and gray fur, earning an especially blissful purr from the usually grumpy cat. He had to admit that tonight, having Bickering helped. After catching Jack, the last thing he needed was to sit in a silent townhouse and remember that night.

After attending to Bickering, Derwin made himself a sandwich and sat down in the living room, turning on the television to the local news. Most of the stories aired were propaganda; if he wanted real news, he'd search the internet. But the noise made the place less oppressive. He ate slowly, trying to focus on the prattling newsreaders.

It didn't work; it never did. His body ached with something that wasn't fatigue or strain. Since Grady, he hadn't had a lover, and every night he felt the same. His Oddity was sexual in nature; while he wasn't like the Enticers who fed off lust, he wasn't that far off. Pain was his elixir, his steroid. Dad got his fix roughing up unruly prisoners and participating in a local boxing ring. For Derwin, trouncing the skips helped the craving a little, like a piece of candy. However, his main meal had always come from sadism in the bedroom.

Leaning back against the buttery leather of the sofa, he closed his eyes and tried to push down the electric tingles creeping up and down his body. He'd been able to hold the hunger off for a few months now, but he was paying for it; the emptiness churned in his stomach. Before Grady, he'd always had a steady stream of guys to fuck. Why couldn't he go back to a casual lifestyle?

Derwin knew the answer. After love, after a relationship, one-night stands didn't compare. Which wouldn't have been a problem, except he couldn't consider dating anyone seriously again. Everything was too raw. Even thinking about the love they'd shared made his heart ache with the void, the loss. *Grady. It was all my fault. I wasn't fast enough.*

After a half hour of trying to watch TV, Derwin gave up. His body burned from the inside, taut and demanding. He craved touch. He craved a hell of a lot more, like a lover who was also a masochist, but that wasn't likely to happen. Still, he'd held back the need for too long to continue functioning. He'd pay for sex tonight just to shove down the urges to do something worse to feed his power. All he had to do was pick up a rentboy, let him know there would be some kink and pain play, then shove him out before dawn. It was what Derwin'd been reduced to.

Derwin headed up to the bedroom to change into a black T-shirt. He laid aside most his bond enforcement gear, save for one knife hidden in an ankle sheath. A quick comb through his hair, and he was ready, if not enthusiastic. Perhaps he'd go over to Club Demon, one of the darker gothic hotspots in town. Maybe he'd even find a date, and not just a drug-addicted whore.

He hopped into his car and drove off into the deepening night.

CHAPTER THREE

ELLIOT LEED

Elliot Leed stared into a cracked mirror, carefully applying black eyeliner to accentuate his blue eyes. Somewhere else in the building, a factory machine was pounding and a stray cat let out a yowl. He smirked. One could almost make a heavy metal song out of that. The noises might be annoying, but he'd grown used to them.

This room had once been a storage closet, but part of a wall had caved in, rendering it useless to the factory owners. At the moment it served as his home sweet home.

His stomach growled rudely; he'd only eaten a breakfast bar today. He'd planned to use a dramatic yet wide-eyed look to bring him customers tonight at Club Demon. Dressed in black leather pants and a pale-blue silk shirt that had cost him a week's earnings, he hoped the clothing would attract a richer clientele and hide his thinness. Maybe he could even earn enough from such patrons to get him out of this hellhole.

He closed his eyes. *How would I survive if I stopped selling myself? I don't know a fucking thing about how to live like a normal day-jobber.*

Elliot took a moment to check his wallet—no ID, because he didn't drive and hadn't been in the system since freshman year of high school. Instead, he had few dollars that he was saving for the bar, a handful of condoms and packets of lube, and a business card or two of clients he could count on if he couldn't find anyone tonight. Those clients gave him the creeps, however, and they were cheap. He needed to find new options. His other pocket contained what he hated but needed the most: his gloves. His Oddity was one of the worst ones a rentboy could have, but since his parents had kicked him out, he hadn't had much choice in careers. At least he wasn't dead. And the government hadn't found him yet.

After locking the door to his room, Elliot headed out to retrieve his bicycle from the warehouse's main room. He longed to have a real bike—a motorcycle. His good friend Stefan, a retired rentboy, had started to teach him how to ride one, but there was that whole problem of having no ID and not existing in the system. Elliot laughed to himself. *Face it. You're just scared to live a normal life like everybody else.* Having wheels would be a big step in that direction, and the idea of a regular job and life terrified him. Still, it was good to have a goal.

It was drizzling outside as he pedaled past factories and warehouses out to the main road. He darted between parked cars and through the light traffic, scanning the area for any dangerous *yokai* from the docks. Nothing would end his night sooner than a smoke spirit or sea dragon looking for prey.

Few of the streetlights worked near the docks, but as soon as he passed into the lower-income residential sections, Elliot encountered more traffic, and more people. His nerves settled a bit. Theresa's little apartment was one street down—Theresa, his Madame, and best protector. She had plucked him from the streets when he was fourteen.

It had been raining that night as well.

And it had all started with a kiss.

Jake Townsend had been the school heartthrob, with adorable scruffy blond hair, brown eyes, and perfectly defined brows. Their eyes had met during Biology, across the classroom. He'd had not one girlfriend but three already during their freshman year. That was why Elliot hadn't thought much of the look at first. But then he'd caught Jake staring again. There had been weight to his gaze. Heat. Each time he'd glanced Jake's way after that, he'd found the young man staring at him with an intensity that conjured butterflies in his stomach. When Jake eyed him like that, Elliot felt like he could fly.

During lunch Elliot tried to convince himself that he shouldn't get his hopes up, that a stupid glimpse shouldn't affect him so much.

Yeah, he found guys attractive, and his fantasies were often filled with scenarios of this boy or that boy shoving him up against a wall and taking him, right in front of everybody. But those were just fantasies.

The reality was that he had to be careful around others, because his Oddity could get him in real trouble if discovered. Why he was the only one in his family with one, he didn't know; his sister liked to tease him that he was the milkman's son. Sometimes he wondered if something like that was true.

He always wore protection against the visions that had started when he was eight. These days that meant fingerless gloves, which he liked to say were his fashion statement against the majority. Since he needed full hand contact to read objects, the gloves protected him but didn't look as strange in warm weather. Luckily, most objects didn't hold psychic imprints, and flesh didn't hold them at all.

Standing in line at lunch later that day, he felt a hand on his shoulder and turned to find Jake standing behind him. Soft brown eyes regarded him with curiosity, and a shock went through him.

"Jake?" He held his empty tray almost as a shield between them. What could Jake want with him?

Jake said nothing. His eyes narrowed, not in anger, but in interest, the pupils widening. A hot flush started from the back of Elliot's neck, then spread to his cheeks. His dick hardened. It was tempting to lower the lunch tray to cover his crotch, yet he seemed unable to move, unable to speak. He swallowed, and Jake's eyes flickered to catch the movement. Jake was seriously too gorgeous. And too near.

Elliot's heart pounded in his ears, even as Jake's arm stretched toward him. *I'm going to pass out if he—* Then Jake reached past him and retrieved a salt shaker from the counter behind him. Elliot released the breath he'd been holding, as Jake turned and walked away.

I'm such an idiot. Trying to hide his discomfort, Elliot quietly took his plate of food and headed to an empty table.

He thought what had happened at lunch had just been another trip by his overactive imagination, but when he encountered Jake after school that day, it became clear that he was wrong. Elliot emerged from the bathroom, shaking his hands dry, to find Jake putting books into his locker and shutting it. Elliot stepped up beside him, intent on putting away his own books before catching the bus, when Jake grabbed his arm with surprising force. Elliot stared up at the taller boy. Was he about to be punched for what had happened earlier? Maybe Jake had seen his blush—or worse.

Elliot opened his mouth to ask what was the matter, to beg Jake to let him go, but again, he froze.

With a flash of movement, Jake pulled Elliot close and slammed his back up against the lockers, the bang echoing down the empty hallway. Elliot gasped, but the impact almost felt good. His thoughts were too scattered to question why.

This is it. He's going to hit me.

Instead, Jake kissed him.

Heat filled Elliot. He could smell the clean, herbal scent of Jake's cologne. A little moan escaped him as Jake pressed a thigh to his groin, rubbing the erection that had appeared. *He likes boys too,* Elliot thought, light-headed even as they paused for a breath.

Jake leaned in for another kiss, moving slowly this time, his fingers clenching on Elliot's arm. It started out tentative, but then he began exploring deeper, using his tongue. Elliot could die right there, and it would be a good death. He kissed back, nerves on fire, certain that he'd fly apart if Jake let go now.

He placed his hand on Jake's shoulder as Jake nipped at his bottom lip. Elliot's hands brushed the cotton of Jake's T-shirt. Instantly, he realized his mistake.

Images bombarded him—*Jake's father shouting, "You'd better win this basketball game!" A fist struck him in the gut. He looked at himself in the mirror, only to find Jake's face staring back, a bruise under one cheek.*

Elliot heard himself babbling, but the sound was far away. It was like when Elliot's own father beat him. Then more images: *Jake's younger sister crying, a stash of porn under his bed.* Then echoes of something dark and secretive, something Jake's father demanded. Something to make Jake a man—

"Steroids. Steroids." Elliot couldn't stop saying the word, couldn't break free from the visions. He was Jake, and then abruptly he was himself again, aware that Jake had moved away. A female voice was shouting down the hall. He blinked, trying to get his bearings, and found he was slumped on the ground. It hadn't happened at school like this. Not ever. Elliot stared up at Jake dumbly, still feeling the sensation of Jake nibbling his lower lip.

"You bastard," Jake hissed, and kicked him in the side. Elliot cried out, curling in to protect himself.

"Jake Townsend! Elliot Leed! Both of you in my office, now!"

Jake swore under his breath as he turned to Ms. Fenwick, the vice principal. Elliot groaned and struggled to regain his feet, hot and cold running through him. How much had she seen? The kiss? The vision? Both?

Jake feinted a punch, but then he walked over to where Ms. Fenwick stood. Elliot grabbed his gloves from his pockets and his backpack from his locker, then followed behind. Together, they headed for the admin offices, while Elliot's stomach churned in fear as he pulled his gloves back on. How many times had his mother warned him? He couldn't let people know about his Oddity. People with Oddities tended to get drafted into the military. Or worse.

Once they reached Ms. Fenwick's cramped little office, Elliot and Jake had to wait while she sat down and began typing something on the computer. Five, maybe ten minutes later, she paused and looked at them over the top of her steel-frame glasses. "Care to explain yourselves?"

Elliot opened his mouth, but Jake answered before he could utter a word. "He hit on me—he tried to kiss me. That's why I kicked him. He was acting all crazy. I think he's been stalking me."

Elliot glared at Jake, his astonishment turning into anger. "I did not! You kissed me!" How would his father react if word got out about this?

Ms. Fenwick shushed them. "I don't care who started what. There is no fraternizing or fighting in the halls. Now sit down, you two, while I call your parents." She glanced at Elliot. "Did he hurt you?"

Worse and worse. He shook his head—the last thing he needed was for her to call the nurse, or send him to a hospital. "I'm fine. It won't happen again. Can we just go home?" They'd both missed the bus by now, and it wasn't safe to walk, but Elliot dreaded the idea of asking for a ride. Putting his mom out would only make his punishment worse.

Jake ran a hand through his hair, pushing it out of his eyes. "Yeah. This was only a stupid prank. You don't need to call anyone. We've learned our lesson." He sounded as scared as Elliot, which wasn't surprising, given what Elliot had just seen of his home life. They'd probably both get beatings tonight.

Ms. Fenwick ignored their pleas, and pointed to the two chairs by the wall. Sick to his stomach, Elliot sat down and didn't even glance at Jake.

She did the calling from the principal's adjoining office, which meant that Elliot couldn't hear what was said. By the expression on her face when she returned, however, he knew that his parents' response hadn't been good. She instructed them to wait at the front of the school for their mothers. Dejectedly, he headed there and did so, aware only that his secrets had been laid bare—Jake had seen him having a vision, on top of the kiss. Would he tell people?

Ms. Fenwick stood a few steps from where they waited, watching Elliot and Jake carefully, though they maintained several feet of distance from each other and kept their eyes on the parent drop-off point.

Elliot's mother was the first to arrive, which spared him from having to watch a confrontation between Jake and either of his parents. It was just her—Dad was still at work, then. Hopefully Mom hadn't called him yet.

He climbed into the four-door sedan's front passenger seat and buckled up, shame turning his stomach sour. His mom waited until they pulled onto the street before she cuffed him on the side of the head. He winced.

"Idiot!" she swore.

He nodded, but stayed silent. It was better to let his parents take out their anger in silence first. Talking back only made things worse.

Her breath hissed between her teeth, and her knuckles were white where she clutched the steering wheel. "So now you like boys." It wasn't a question.

Elliot considered lying, but what was the use? If he ever wanted to live his own life, they'd find out sooner or later. "I swear he approached me." It was his only defense.

She slapped him again, this time on the cheek, and the car swerved a little. Elliot bit his lip. "I don't give a damn what he did! That's in your record now, you know—that you're a sexual deviant! Do you realize what this means for your future?"

He wanted to keep quiet, he really did. But he couldn't stop the rage, or the words that spilled out. "It's not like that anymore, Mom. More people are coming out. It's not going to change anything like colleges or jobs."

Like his dad, Elliot had a head for numbers and computers. Unlike his dad, however, he wanted to go into something fun, like software development—games, maybe. Not be a boring analyst for some financial firm.

His mother made a hard right onto their street, passing by the security guard at the gates of the walled community with a quick wave. Her tone dropped to ice-cold. "It changes everything. You don't know about how the world works, Elliot. You're supposed to hide your sexuality, just like you hide your ability. Those who don't hide things don't make it far."

"Why—"

"Because some consider homosexuals to be expendable. As for your Oddity, there are powerful people out there, corporations, who keep the rest of us safe. They'd snatch you up in a heartbeat for the war against the demons. You've never been in the wilderness before, beyond our neighborhood walls. You've never seen a *yokai*."

Elliot shivered. He'd heard tales about the demons and spirits and the way they fed on humans. The gate and the wall around their neighborhood weren't just for show. His family lived on the outskirts of Nis, in the suburbs. Other fortified neighborhoods surrounded them, but beyond those was the city wall, and then the great forests. Few dared to venture out there without a guard escort or combat training. Few without that expertise or escort came back.

She pulled into the driveway and shut off the car, turning again to look at him, but Elliot stared straight ahead. He was probably in for the beating of his life once Dad got home.

Abruptly, his mother opened the car door and got out. She slammed the door behind her, and Elliot blinked in surprise.

No lecture? No more ranting? He wasn't sure whether to be grateful or worried, as he watched her stalk toward the front door.

Elliot hesitated for a moment. Would he be better off waiting outside until supper? It would give her time to cool off. On the other hand, he'd rather get the lecture now. Get it over with. Groaning, he opened his door and grabbed his backpack, then walked to the front door, entering slowly. He paused when he heard his mother's voice in a heated argument.

"Yes, that's what Ms. Fenwick said she saw. I don't know. *I don't know.*" Her voice grew more and more agitated as she spoke. Elliot shut the door behind him and crept across the living room to his room, keeping clear of the kitchen, where pots and pans were being slammed about. "He's *your* son!"

Elliot winced at her words as he hurried the last few steps and closed his door. For the next half hour, he tried to do his homework, but his concentration kept slipping away. How was he supposed to focus? *Tomorrow will be another day*, he reminded himself. Nobody at school would know what had happened, outside of Jake, himself, and the vice principal. Things could go back to normal.

He'd just assured himself of that for the hundredth time, when his mother opened the door. Her eyes looked dead, and her face was expressionless, even slack. Elliot shivered.

"Pack your things. You can't stay here anymore."

"What?" He stared at her, dumbfounded. He'd expected a beating. A lecture. Cold silence for a week. Not this.

His mother crossed her arms over her chest, not meeting his gaze. He'd always thought she was beautiful with her raven hair, her azure eyes—features he'd inherited. Right now, though, she could have been a statue. "Your father said to get out. If you're here when he gets home . . ." She took a deep breath. "He's getting the shotgun."

Elliot's legs felt like water, and he was thankful he was sitting. "Where am I supposed to go?"

She shook her head. "A friend. The military. Wherever you people congregate—it's your problem now." She swallowed. "It's too much. Your Oddity . . . and now this. I won't risk Clara and Bobby over you. You figure it out. Your father wants nothing to do with you anymore." With that, she turned and walked away, leaving the door half-open behind her.

You people . . . did she mean Oddities? Or gay people? He waited several minutes for her to return, for Clara to come in and ask what was going on. He could hear his mom in the kitchen again, hear her snap at Clara. Shotgun . . . was that for real? The room spun, out of control.

She didn't return, and Elliot realized he was losing time. He pulled out his backpack and emptied his school things. Would he need them? He settled for keeping a few of his books and some paper and pens, then stuffed in two pairs of jeans, three T-shirts, a jacket, underwear, and socks. It was too bad he wouldn't be able to take his desktop computer, and he didn't know how long his phone would work before they shut off the service. The only other stuff he could think of was food and money. Did he dare enter the pantry?

"Ten minutes!" His mother shouted from the kitchen. Elliot's heart raced, and he couldn't help double-checking the clock.

He quickly threw in a few electronic items—calculator, watch, a music player. He looked around his room. Would he ever see it again? Taking a deep breath, he slung the backpack over his shoulder and exited. In the living room, he found Clara reading a book. She didn't glance up at him. Bobby was probably at a friend's house, which was good. He loved his little brother. Saying good-bye would be another wound.

He headed for the door, but before he could open it, his mother cleared her throat from the kitchen doorway. She held out a twenty.

Elliot swallowed. There was so much he wanted to say, so much emotion trying to burst out of his chest. But he said nothing. She'd made her choice. He snatched the money, turned, and walked out of the house.

For a week after his parents kicked him out, Elliot had stayed close to home. He slept in a neighbor's doghouse the first night with a mutt who adored him. The next day, he visited his friends' houses to see if anybody would take him in, but gossip had spread not only about the kiss, but about his Oddity as well. He suspected Clara. She'd always been jealous of his visions, though he'd told her they were a curse, not a gift. Besides making his current predicament harder, this meant he couldn't go back, even if Dad allowed it—no way was he taking the chance of a government recruiter "visiting" him and hauling him off to the military.

The second night, he ventured past the subdivision's security gates to sleep on his school's grounds, but had to flee when someone called the cops. By the end of the week, he'd taken to digging in restaurant dumpsters and sleeping under bushes. The threat of police constantly plagued him, and it wasn't long before he left the gated suburbs and headed downtown.

That was where he met Theresa.

He'd been trying to pull the remnants of a burger out of the dumpster when four teenage boys approached him.

"Loser!" one hollered, as another yanked on his backpack.

Elliot snarled, holding on tight to it. He wasn't letting go without a fight. He'd already sold off his electronics, but there were still some items of worth in there, including his high school math book, his favorite subject.

"He's not even that," another boy said. As Elliot faced him, they shoved him hard against a wooden bench, knocking him down. They started kicking him, and he yelped, curling in on himself. The blows continued, hard and fast, as it began to drizzle.

Then a shadowy figure materialized out of nowhere. It— She gave a shriek, and whacked one of the boys with a cane. The rain shower became a torrential downpour, as she rounded on another boy, swinging. Cursing, they backed off, shielding their faces from the rain and her fury.

"Not fucking worth it," one boy whined. He took off running. The rest followed close behind.

He could never recall later what she'd said. All Elliot remembered was her face as she'd bent down to examine him in the gutter of the street. Her eyes were almost as blue as his, though her hair was steel gray. She was beautiful, despite her age.

Theresa took him to her apartment where she kept beds for others just like himself, young boys and girls lost to the streets of Nis. She told him he could stay two weeks for free, but then he'd have to find a way to contribute: by joining a gang and running or selling drugs, by becoming a thief, or by becoming a whore. If he chose the last, she could be his Madame and set up safe contracts.

He chose whore.

It actually wasn't as simple as that. He tried his hand at thievery for a while, but the danger of arrest proved too great for him, and his Oddity made him a liability. As a rentboy, he could wear latex gloves in the name of hygiene and nobody thought twice about it. The cops used Theresa's services, so they left her boys and girls alone. It was a decent arrangement, all things considered.

So when he turned fifteen, he'd started selling sex, and he'd learned more than he cared to know both about himself and other people. She'd set up his clients for the first few months. After that, it had been up to him.

Now, at nineteen, he was an old pro, but still young enough to attract the good clients—ones who wouldn't try to kill him. If he continued on this path, he might expect to become like Theresa and take younger boys and girls under his wing.

He hoped to quit the streets before that happened. His friend Stefan had done it—at least mostly. He was an erotic dancer now, no Madame, no debts to Theresa. For Elliot, it was more about fighting his own insecurities than simply finding other work.

I've lost out on so much in life. How do I overcome that?

CHAPTER FOUR

CLUB DEMON

Elliot reached Club Demon as the rain let up, and chained his bicycle to a light post a few buildings down. No point in advertising his lack of wheels. He waved to the bouncer and got in without charge—another perk of being one of Theresa's boys—before heading to the restrooms to do damage control on his wet hair. Thank the gods his eyeliner was waterproof.

Once he'd perfected the "wet, sexy look," Elliot went to the bar and sat down, giving Neil, a jovial bear of a man, a smile. The place was busy, the dance floor crowded. Just the way he liked it.

Neil returned the smile and came over. He leaned in close, his smile turning to concern. "Haven't seen you in a bit, E. Take care—the Tatsu boys are here tonight." He glanced over at one of the pool tables, where a few men stood around, wearing leather jackets with water dragons emblazoned on them.

Elliot's heart sank. He'd entertained the Tatsu boss before, but preferred to keep his distance from gangs in general. Each time he'd entertained the boss, he'd been in fear for his life, though he trusted the higher-ups more than their lower thugs, like the ones playing pool here. They had something to prove.

"Thanks. I'll try to stay clear."

Neil nodded and left to wait on another customer. Expelling a breath to calm his nerves, Elliot scanned the place for past clients or possible new customers. It was difficult to tell who was paired with whom on the dance floor, but as soon as he got out there, the guys seeking his type of fun would find him.

Sitting alone at a bar without a drink in his hand was a cue for the buyers. Elliot stretched a little, catlike, and gave one fellow a lazy smile. He got a wink back, but that was all. Pity. He enjoyed being pursued.

A brief rise in the noise level by the pool table caught Elliot's attention. But as he turned to look, a hand gripped his arm. He tensed up. The guy holding him had a crew cut and wore the water-dragon leather jacket with black denim jeans.

Pushing aside his nerves, Elliot managed to conjure up a sweet and innocent smile.

It wasn't returned. "I've seen you around before. Looking for a little rough play?" Dark eyes swept over him, measuring, and the guy smirked. The tough ones often liked Elliot. They figured since he was small, he'd be easy to shove down and take advantage of. He'd had to break a few bones before to prove such types wrong. Noses were easy to break, for example.

The trick with the Tatsu, though, was to be polite and tread carefully. Elliot shrugged nonchalantly. "Maybe a tearoom set or two," he drawled, nodding toward the bathroom. "Nothing too heavy tonight; I'm just browsing." That was true enough. He didn't know if Mr. Crew Cut knew the boss Elliot had visited, but it was best not to admit to someone as disrespectful as this that yes, he did enjoy pain play—emphasis on the word *play*. A trip to the hospital afterward cut the fun out of it.

Crew Cut leered, sliding a hand down Elliot's side to rub his thigh through the soft black leather. "Nah—not one for baring my dick in public. You'll come with me instead, to my place. Give me a freebie for your security, whaddya say?"

Elliot leaned back, shaking his head. "You'd have to talk to Theresa." In his peripheral vision, Crew Cut's friends were still shooting pool, but they'd be over in one word if their gang pal called them.

"Come on. A freebie. No one has to know about it." Crew Cut's fingers were digging in. Elliot tried to think of something diplomatic to say, some way to refuse without pissing the guy off.

Before he could open his mouth, however, another hand—this one large and attached to a bare muscular arm—knocked Crew Cut's away from his thigh. A deep voice cut in. "Is this guy bothering you?"

Crew Cut scowled, baring his teeth. Elliot craned his neck to peer back at his rescuer.

A handsome, chiseled face. Light-brown eyes that had a sparkle of amber to them, medium-length brown hair tousled like the guy had just gotten out of bed, and the kind of physique that reminded Elliot of a soldier. The man's manner instantly warmed Elliot, reassured him. The combination of good looks, broad chest, and muscular arms was devastating. Plus the guy *smelled* good. Like soap. He didn't even seem stoned or drunk.

"I— Yeah," Elliot fumbled, trying to recall what the guy had asked him.

Crew Cut hesitated, his eyes narrowing.

Some confidence crept back into Elliot as he smiled at the newcomer. "Yeah. A little."

This was probably going to get him into trouble later, but fuck that. Right now, he was taking a gamble on Mr. Rescuer.

"Who the fuck are you?" Crew Cut let go of Elliot's arm to take a step forward. Elliot had to push back the urge to leave the place to let the two of them fight. He scooted to the side instead, so that he could see both of them without having to turn.

Mr. Rescuer crossed his arms and stared down the less-muscular gang member. "Your worst nightmare if you ever become a fugitive."

Elliot's blood went cold, but it was Crew Cut who asked, "You a cop?" He didn't look scared. Not yet, anyway.

Mr. Rescuer shook his head. "Bounty hunter. However, I'm real friendly with the cops. Want me to call them and have them bust your ass?" He brought out his phone and tapped on the contacts icon. Elliot's eyes flicked up to meet Crew Cut's. Cops would pretty much wreck the evening for both of them.

"Asshole," Crew Cut muttered, but he stepped back. He pointed a finger at Elliot. "We're not done. I'll see you later." With that, he turned and walked over to his friends.

That might be a messy meeting. Still, Elliot was relieved. Maybe Theresa could apply pressure to the gang lords, keep his skin safe. He flashed Mr. Rescuer a smile. "Thanks."

The guy chuckled. He had a nice laugh. "No problem." He arched an eyebrow, his eyes traveling down Elliot's body. "You even old enough to be in here?"

Ouch. While his young appearance helped score some clients, it hindered him with others. Elliot shrugged, trying not to feel deflated. "I'm old enough. Ask Neil." He nodded at the bartender, who gave Mr. Rescuer a thumbs-up. They had an understanding that Elliot could drink what he liked here despite his age. Theresa's boys were a popular attraction in clubs like these.

"Uh-huh." Mr. Rescuer gave Elliot another appraising look, then shrugged, holding out a hand. "Derwin Bryant." He glanced at Elliot's gloved hands before they made contact. Probably thought he was a biker. Well, a wannabe, anyway.

Elliot shook hands with him, and melted inside at the sheer *strength* in that grip. "Elliot Leed. New here?" Surely a body like that would have stuck in his memory.

Derwin shook his head sheepishly. "I've been here before, but it's been a while. I don't get out much." He chuckled, nodding at a group of young men wearing makeup and dressed in black. "I think it may have changed a bit since the last time." Derwin's eyes flicked down, and Elliot realized with horror he wore a gold ring on his left hand. Aw shit. The guy was married?

Before Elliot could think of something to say to cover up his surprise, Derwin seemed to notice Elliot's attention and stuck his hand in his pocket sheepishly. "Whoa—sorry. I still wear it. He, um. He died two years ago." Derwin laughed bitterly. "That's why I haven't been out much. Figured I should, though."

Derwin was actually blushing. It was cute, particularly from someone so physically imposing. Elliot suspected that under other circumstances Derwin could be lethal. He had that feel to him.

"Well anyways, guess I'm lucky you picked tonight." Elliot turned on the charm again, smiling in a manner that was both innocent and inviting. It usually did the trick with sensitive johns like this. The fact Derwin was both easy on the eyes *and* seemingly a nice guy could make for a lucrative and enjoyable evening.

"Are you trying to pick me up?" Derwin sounded more amused than interested, but his eyes drifted over Elliot's body. Too soon to reel him in, but it wouldn't take much.

Languidly, Elliot rose from the stool, leaning closer. "Maybe. Want to dance?" If Derwin didn't want to buy him a drink, then perhaps he'd at least indulge Elliot in that—and then enjoy it.

Derwin's eyes narrowed. "You're legal?"

Elliot smiled and took his hand. Morality. Wasn't that a refreshing change? "I'm legal. Definitely legal—I'm nineteen." As he pulled Derwin over to the dance floor, the guy offered no resistance.

Bait taken.

CHAPTER FIVE

DEVIL WITH THE BLUE SHIRT ON

So Elliot was old enough to fuck and not old enough to drink—Derwin just didn't care. As they headed over to the small and crowded dance floor, he spared a glance to see if their good friend the gangbanger would be trouble. The guy was talking with his friends on the other side of the bar. He seemed to have given up on Elliot, thankfully. Then Elliot's lithe body pressed against Derwin's, and he lost track of what anybody else was doing.

He hadn't intended to do more than rescue the kid. But, oh, something about Elliot's small, fit build, his curly black hair and deep-aqua eyes that were too wise for his age . . . something about him called to Derwin. Grady's social awkwardness had attracted him, but Elliot seemed anything but awkward, despite his youth. He *felt* good. Derwin couldn't explain it better than that. And the young man was beautiful in his blue shirt and leather pants. Grecian-statue beautiful.

The song morphed into a techno beat that pulsed around them. Derwin gave in to the music, resting his hands on Elliot's hips as they danced in the tight space. Elliot gave that knowing smile again, the one that made him look like a cat that had swallowed the canary. Wasn't Derwin supposed to be the dominant one here? At the moment, it didn't feel like it. "I'm so out of practice at this," he said, just to get past his ridiculous nerves.

Elliot laughed, wrapped his arms around Derwin's shoulders, and ruffled the hair on the back of his neck. The damp leather gloves rubbed Derwin's heated skin, and he wondered why the guy hadn't taken them off. Fashion statement, most likely, to go with the black-outlined eyes.

"You're doing great," Elliot said, grinding up against him. Derwin sucked in a breath as his body instantly responded, cock hardening in his jeans. He needed this. *Craved it.* It had been too fucking long since he'd relaxed and just let himself have what he wanted. Elliot leaned up to whisper in his ear, his lips brushing the sensitive skin there. "It's only a dance."

It felt like so much more to his oversensitive abilities and hungry libido.

And if he didn't get some control soon, they'd be doing a whole lot more than dancing.

"Right. Hey—this might be a stupid question, but last time I was here, this seemed like a lifestyle-oriented club. Did that change?" With all the punks and goths, it looked like a fashion show rather than an actual leather-and-whips group.

One of Elliot's brows raised. "You mean BDSM? It still is. Maybe you meant the leather crowd? They moved to the Hammer Bar a few blocks over. Less dancing and music." His hand slid down into one of Derwin's back pockets, and Derwin's cock twitched in response. By now Elliot had to be aware of his erection.

Derwin wasn't sure how to respond to Elliot's words, and the hand in his pocket was distracting. He growled in the back of his throat, frustrated. His fingers clenched, digging into Elliot's hips.

Elliot's eyes twinkled, and he gave a crooked smile. "Yes, I do play."

The words brought a surge of desire almost too strong to push back. Derwin lowered his head, needing proof. His lips grazed the skin of Elliot's throat. He sensed a shiver go through the young man.

He gave Elliot a kiss on the neck, tender and inviting, lightly scraping with his teeth. Testing. The young man sucked in a breath, arching, his body demanding more. Derwin nipped at where neck met shoulder, then as Elliot moaned, he couldn't help it. He bit down, sucking at the skin, hard enough that he surely was leaving a mark. Elliot trembled, and thrust up against him. The guy was stone-hard, and the pain that emanated from him was like honey to Derwin's special senses. *Gods and demons. So perfect.*

The music changed to a soulful pop tune, but Derwin couldn't pay attention. It was imperative to get himself and Elliot somewhere private, fast. He panted, forcing down the hunger that was even more insistent after that little taste of Elliot's pain.

"Come on." Derwin took Elliot's hand and nodded toward the door, turning to face it.

Elliot resisted. Derwin blinked in surprise and then focused on his face. The young man wasn't smiling. "There's something I need to tell you."

Those were never good words.

Derwin nodded and began to lead him away from the dance floor toward the club entrance. It would be quieter out there. Private. But before they had taken more than a few steps, the guy with the crew cut and dragon leather jacket strode up. This time he had a couple of buddies with him, one on either side. They walked with their hands down, fingers splayed as if ready to grab for something—like a gun.

"Nuh-uh," the guy said, shaking his head at Derwin. His companions moved forward, and one revealed a blade in an inside pocket of his jacket. Blades Derwin could deal with. Guns would be trickier.

Derwin started to position himself to disarm them, when Crew Cut's next words brought him up short. "I saw the whore first. He's coming with me."

Beside him, Elliot winced. "That's what I needed to tell you."

Derwin stared at his companion. "So you're a—"

"Rentboy, yeah." At least Elliot had the grace to seem apologetic about it. Except . . . that connection on the dance floor. That hadn't seemed fake.

"Come on." Mr. Gang Leader grabbed Elliot by the arm, pulling him toward the exit with his goonies in tow. Derwin watched, bemused. While Elliot didn't physically resist, his shoulders slumped, and worry was plain on his face. He looked like a fox in a trap.

So the rescue had been real.

Maybe the young man had turned on the charm for Derwin, tried to seduce him a little. But fuck, on the dance floor, it had felt good. His Oddity meant that he could read people's responses to pain. Elliot had enjoyed it. That had been real too.

So he could forgive the little shit for playing with him and not telling him from the start.

Better to get out of the club before he got into it with the gang, though. Derwin followed and waited until they'd reached the sidewalk. Only a light drizzle was falling, covering everyone in a fine sheen of moisture.

He checked to be sure nobody else was nearby, then cleared his throat loudly. "Excuse me. He's not some fucking coin on the pavement. Did you ask him if he wanted to go with you?"

As one, they all turned, the leader glaring in fury. "You really want to fuck with us?" Spittle flew with his words. "Do you fucking know who we are, pussy?" He jerked Elliot's arm, and Derwin didn't have to see the kid's grimace to know it hurt—he sensed the pain, not sweet and consensual, the way he liked it, but bitter and unwelcome, the way his dad usually took his. Derwin's Oddity still drank it in—he couldn't stop that if he wanted to.

Then he punched Gang Leader in the throat.

The fellow gagged, his eyes bugging out in surprise as he let go of Elliot and doubled over. Derwin turned, ready for the two other goons. His kick knocked the knife out of the first guy's hand. He side-stepped to give the tall, gangly fellow a blow to the solar plexus, but held back at the last moment when Elliot pounced on him like an alley cat in full fight mode, bowling the gang member over.

Derwin shook off his disbelief. Though he still was choking, Gang Leader was trying to pull a handgun from his jacket, so Derwin grabbed his wrist with superhuman speed and wrenched, breaking it. This time the guy fell down, crying out and curling up in pain. The first guy was the only one left standing, a younger kid with a scar on his lip.

Scar Lip backed up, shaking his head. "There's something weird about you."

Derwin gave him credit for not abandoning his buddies, eyeing Gang Leader with concern. Elliot had jumped off Gangly Fellow, but only after punching him in the face a few times. All of them would bear bruises from this little encounter.

Gang Leader staggered to his feet, cradling his wrist and glaring at them. "Big mistake," he hissed.

"Mess with the gang—*no bueno*." Gangly Fellow stood up slowly, clearly just as pissed. He spat blood and wiped at a scratch across his tan cheek, then eyed the knife lying at Derwin's feet, though he made no move to try for it.

"Yeah, I know," Derwin shot back, tallying up in his head how many times he'd heard similar talk from a fugitive. "Better hope I'm not the guy assigned if you ever get arrested and have to make bond." They were low in the ranks, or they would've been packing more heat. He just prayed they weren't siblings with anyone big in Tatsu.

Elliot kept an eye on the gang members as they stalked off, then wiped mud off the knees of his leather pants. "I'm going to have to tell the other whores about them," he muttered under his breath. He rubbed at a scratch and glanced at Derwin uncertainly.

Derwin waited until the three turned a corner and were out of sight. He doubted he'd run into them again. But Elliot was another matter. "You going to be okay? You have friends who can watch your back?" Hopefully Elliot didn't live on the streets.

The smile returned to Elliot's face, although this time it had a bitter edge. "Yeah, I've got friends, and some of them are connected to the Tatsu. I should be fine." Derwin couldn't tell if that was truth or bravado. But what was he supposed to do about it?

It started to rain a little harder. Elliot scowled at the sky and stepped under the awning by the doorway to the club. He ran a hand through his already wet hair. "So . . ." Cautiousness had come over his features—not dread, but apprehension. "What now?"

Derwin paused. When he'd come here tonight, he'd been seeking sex, yes—and he'd been willing to pay for it. Only earlier, when they'd been dancing, the thought of something *beyond* a one-night stand had entered his head.

Well, that wasn't to be.

Elliot was into BDSM, and he was obviously a masochist, so he'd be able to derive pleasure from hurt. And Derwin still needed pain to feed his inner beast; he just wished it didn't make the rest of him feel so empty.

"How much?"

CHAPTER SIX

UNCOVERED

The relief Elliot felt at hearing those words was potent enough to frighten him. In the back of his mind, he knew he should have gone with Crew Cut and his gang. Fighting them was asking for trouble later. But for once he didn't want to be used callously and tossed out with his pay. At least Derwin seemed to have some respect for his well-being.

It was dangerous to want someone like Derwin. Every time he'd wanted something in his life, the world had given him a kick in the nuts.

"It depends on what you'd like," he answered, figuring he'd be able to get a ride back to the club for his bicycle later. Otherwise he'd have to find another way to his part of town. He wondered where Derwin lived. It had to be the inner city. Derwin didn't look like the walled-community-suburbs type of guy.

Derwin frowned, pursing his lips. *Gorgeous lips*, sensual, with just a slight curve. He had to mentally tear himself away from them.

"Simple scene—percussion play or a lashing, maybe clamps. Sex afterward. I'm not sure what else."

Elliot gnawed at his cheek, trying to hide his excitement. Percussion play, as in spanking? He hoped so. "I'll give you a deal tonight since you helped me. Basic scene with sex, two hundred." He charged other men twice that. "Limits for me include no scat, no bondage for the first session, no marks that'll last more than a week. No drugs, and no breath play."

When Derwin nodded, there was no hesitation. "Do you have a safeword?"

Elliot smiled. "Yeah, it's 'sapphire.'" Theresa had suggested it to go with his eyes.

"Hmm." Derwin bent over to retrieve the knife and gun dropped by the gang members. Then he held up a finger. "Hang on—I'm going to give these to the club owner. In case they want them back, you know." He smirked roguishly. "You're not going to kill me in my sleep or rob my apartment, are you?"

Elliot gave him a withering look. "I'm a little classier than that."

Derwin grinned and stepped inside. While he was gone, Elliot tensed every time someone came around the corner where Crew Cut and his companions had departed. He breathed a sigh of relief when Derwin reemerged.

"I'm parked down the street," Derwin said, scratching his head nervously, even bashfully. Elliot blinked at the change in demeanor. *Maybe he's shy.* With a smile, he took Derwin's arm, coaxing him along.

He couldn't figure Derwin out. During the fight, Elliot had been sure he must be ex-military. Nobody moved that fast, with such precision, without formal training. Put that together with the near-perfect physique, and it seemed a given.

Despite his combat skills, the guy seemed socially as awkward as a middle schooler. It was kind of charming, actually.

He tried to think back to their earlier conversation, and then his attention was pulled away as they came upon a black Ford Galaxie, restored and in prime condition. Elliot whistled as Derwin opened the door for him.

"Classic," he murmured, climbing in. Derwin sat in the driver's seat and turned the key in the ignition, pumping the gas twice to bring the motor to life. A car said a lot about a man. This one seemed old-fashioned, but in a good way. "You said you're a bounty hunter? How long you been doing that?"

Derwin shrugged, pulling into traffic as Elliot buckled in. He drove like he fought—fast and sure of himself. "Since I was eighteen. My dad's a correctional officer out in Mephist." He made a face. "I didn't want to do that, but you could say roughing up criminals was kinda in my blood. So the bond-agent thing made sense."

That brought to mind all sorts of questions, but Elliot stuck to what he wanted to know most. "You ever in the military?" Correctional officer and bond agent was close enough to law enforcement to make his nerves itch. It would be ironic for him to avoid the government this long only to be snared by a gorgeous hunk of a customer.

Again, Derwin made a face. "Nah. Not for me."

"How'd you learn to fight?" The edge of a tattoo was barely discernable under Derwin's short sleeve. Elliot wondered what it was.

"The usual. I worked out at the gym and took martial arts classes." Derwin chuckled. "Since I was eight."

Well, that explained it. "Wow. It shows." Elliot had to admit it made him feel better *not* to be bunking up with an ex-soldier. They'd passed the entertainment district now and were headed into the lower-middle-class apartment buildings and condominiums.

Derwin raised an eyebrow at him as they waited at a red light. "And you? Lemme guess—orphan, been on the streets your whole life?"

Elliot snorted. "Hardly." He looked down, not wanting to see Derwin's reaction. "Parents kicked me out at fourteen. They're both still very much alive." Not that he checked on them.

"Damn. Why?"

Bitter sadness ate at Elliot, but he tried to smile again anyway. "Because I like guys."

The light changed, and Derwin returned to driving. "That sucks. I was lucky. My parents are fine with it. A little too fine sometimes— my mom tries to set me up with the weirdest people. But I'd prefer matchmaking over nothing."

They made a right, and Derwin pulled into a space on the side of the street, across from a brownstone building.

Derwin didn't speak as he led Elliot to the apartment and produced a key to unlock the front door. He turned his back to Elliot for a moment to punch in a security code on the alarm panel, then gave him a half smile. "It's not fancy—I don't know what kind of clients you're used to. But it's private. Generally quiet, as well."

He was right. The apartment wasn't grandiose, but Elliot immediately liked its simple design. Pale-mocha carpeting, a white leather sofa, and a glass coffee table in the living room, with a decent-sized flat-screen TV. A mewl at his feet alerted him to the cat before it began rubbing against his legs in greeting. Elliot laughed, bending over to pet it.

Derwin shut the door. "Meet Colonel Bickering. Present from my mom." He chuckled as Bickering arched and bit at Elliot's fingers. "He's temperamental."

It was just a love bite. Elliot pulled his hand away. "Doesn't accept affection easily, huh?" He understood how that felt.

"You could say that." Derwin paused a moment, looking him over. In the heat of the gaze, Elliot felt like a prime rib, freshly served. And yet the man hesitated.

Elliot licked his lips. Even though he preferred his clients to take charge, he knew how to get the shy ones motivated. "Downstairs or upstairs?"

Derwin blinked. "Upstairs. Bedroom." One hand curled into a fist—anxiety, Elliot realized, not anger.

"Take me there." Elliot thought he might have to lead the way, but at that instant, whatever had been holding Derwin back seemed to vanish. With an expression of pure lust that made Elliot's stomach flutter, Derwin began walking. Elliot followed him up the stairs, to a spacious bedroom with a king-sized mattress, an antique chest of Asian design at the foot of the bed, and a small computer desk and chair. A few well-placed eyebolts were affixed to the walls; perfect spots to chain up a lover for a beating. Inside Elliot's leather gloves, his palms began to sweat; his nerves were an old friend and part of the thrill. He wasn't surprised when Derwin led him over to where the bedroom opened up into a master bathroom. At this juncture, there was even enough room to use a small whip.

He was about to ask if he should undress, when Derwin pressed him up against the wall. Derwin captured both Elliot's wrists with one hand and pinned them above his head, using his body to keep the rest of Elliot in place. Elliot's pulse stuttered, and he was reminded of his first kiss up against the lockers. At this point, Derwin could have asked anything of him, and he would have done it. Something about that kiss to the throat at the club had rattled him to the core. No, perhaps not the kiss. Perhaps more the emotions in Derwin's eyes. Pain and want. It spoke to Elliot, reminded him of himself.

When Derwin captured his mouth in a searing kiss, Elliot struggled to keep his knees from buckling as his bones turned to water. There was no artifice in the desperate mewl that escaped him; he kissed and pushed back, loving the resistance. To surrender would drop him so deep into subspace that he'd never return. The kiss seemed to go on and on, Derwin's grip bruising him, but Elliot didn't care. Nobody had kissed him like this before. Nobody had made him want to let go, to submit, not since he'd become a rentboy. There had always been that little corner of his mind keeping an eye on things, making sure he was safe, helping him to act the part.

That corner of him was shutting down right now. The kiss, the strong thighs, the muscled chest against his, and the hips grinding up against him took over everything. Elliot sighed, letting it sweep him away, and sucked at Derwin's tongue.

Dimly, he was aware of Derwin unbuttoning his pants and pulling the zipper down. Derwin's hand worked its way inside, stroking him through his briefs, and Elliot gave a soft cry. He squirmed, gasping for breath.

"Nobody's done this to you properly, have they?" Derwin asked in a low voice. He nibbled at the side of Elliot's throat.

Elliot struggled to think. "Not sure," he admitted, then felt a pang of loss when Derwin let go of his wrists. That was replaced by panic when Derwin tugged at his gloves, pulling them off. "Wait—need those," he pleaded, closing his hands into fists, but it was too late. The first glove was already off. "Hygiene." It wasn't always successful. But he'd managed to only have a couple of visions during jobs so far. "I can wear latex ones if you prefer."

Derwin snorted. "I prefer you a hundred percent naked." He pressed on a nerve between Elliot's thumb and forefinger, forcing his hand open. The second glove followed the first to land at his feet. Derwin began to work on his jacket. "It'll be okay. I promise."

You can't promise that. Elliot said nothing. He considered safewording, but . . . *Eh, I'll be fine without my gloves for this one scene.* It was all too good to resist.

The shirt went next, and then Derwin's mouth was on him, moving from Elliot's neck down his chest, finding a nipple and then sucking on it hard. The pleasure came so sharp it was painful; Elliot gasped, grasping Derwin's shoulders. Before he could push him away, a growl stopped him. "Put your hands where I had them. If I can't restrain you, then you'll have to restrain yourself." Derwin glanced up, with fierce lust in his eyes. Elliot bit back a moan.

How could he know I like that? Bondage was actually one of Elliot's biggest kinks, but it was also one of the most dangerous things to trifle with, especially with uncaring, paying strangers. Biting back a whimper, he obeyed, crossing his wrists over his head and trying to hold still as Derwin turned to the other nipple, lavishing it with the same attention. Elliot shuddered, hips thrusting out, seeking contact of some kind, any kind.

Derwin put a stop to that, grabbing the waistband of Elliot's pants and yanking them down. He quickly removed Elliot's shoes and socks, then the pants came off, followed by his black cotton briefs.

Naked, Elliot stared through a haze of lust at the man who had hired him for the night. In turn, Derwin was studying him, intently.

"Gorgeous," Derwin murmured. Elliot knew he must be quite the sight right now, pale-skinned and languid, nipples standing erect from the attention they'd just received, cock jutting out.

But he was more interested in seeing this bounty hunter who had saved his ass twice this evening. And luck was with him. As Elliot watched, Derwin slowly took off his shirt, and laid it on top of the chest by the bed. Shoes and socks followed next, but he left his jeans on, to Elliot's disappointment.

Still, there was plenty to see. Defined pecs, nice muscular arms, and a lean stomach. A tattoo of a snarling panther on his biceps, another tattoo on his stomach—a ring of intricate runes. There were scars as well. The largest, across his chest, looked like claw marks. Demon, perhaps? There was a pucker along Derwin's collarbone, which had to be from a gunshot wound. Small white lines decorated his forearms, telling the tales of countless fights, possibly with knives.

Dangerous and gorgeous: a heady mix, as far as Elliot was concerned.

Derwin stared at him a moment, then crossed over to the Asian chest. He opened it and pulled out something—a pair of clover clamps. Elliot bit his lip, and Derwin grinned as he returned, holding them out.

"Those are going to hurt," Elliot said, half in acknowledgment, and half in excitement. Anticipation tightened his gut.

Derwin chuckled. "That's the plan." He began to rub one of Elliot's nipples between his thumb and forefinger. Elliot gasped.

Derwin tortured that one for a bit before gently placing the clamp on it. Elliot closed his eyes as the pain set in, low and deep. It wasn't much now, but it would grow worse. Clamps probably had the most bang for the littlest buck; he knew that from previous experience.

The other nipple received similar treatment from Derwin's mouth, then the clamp, and somehow the pain from the first nipple merged into pleasure from the second, making Elliot's head spin. When he opened his eyes again, he caught a peculiar expression on Derwin's face. It reminded him of junkies shooting up. His smile was ecstatic.

Their eyes met, and awareness seemed to return to Derwin; he faced away, gathering his belt in one hand. There was another tattoo on his right shoulder: a little girl with wings—an angel. Derwin turned back and held up the belt, a look of promise on his face. "Turn around. Keep your wrists up."

Elliot did so, careful to keep his hands clasped, palms to each other so that they wouldn't touch anything. While the wall might not hold potent memories, he wasn't taking any chances, especially given those eyebolts. Scenes could be quite intense. He sensed rather than saw Derwin take hold of the belt buckle and then felt the strap graze his leg. This would definitely hurt.

The first strike didn't disappoint. Pain, sharp and clear, burned across his back. Elliot hissed, arching as he adjusted his stance, widening his legs. Apparently Derwin didn't believe in a warm-up. No worries; he could take it.

A second strike blazed warmth across the shoulder blade, and then Derwin leaned in close, nibbling a trail up Elliot's neck. Elliot shivered and gasped, once again caught between sensations. Derwin spoke at his ear. "I'm not usually this . . . impatient."

If that was supposed to be an apology, it was all Elliot received. Derwin stepped back and laid four blows in quick succession, each more powerful than the last, until Elliot cried out, clenching his hands and pressing himself up against the wall. Derwin stopped, allowing him to breathe, letting the pain settle into something a little easier to bear. The clamps burned as well, heat slowly building upon heat on his chest.

As soon as the fire from his back started to ebb, Derwin began again. More lashes, each stronger, alternating sides on Elliot's upper back, on his ass at times. But never the lower back. He avoided the kidneys with expertise, and never wrapped around. The blows came until Elliot was almost sobbing, but then they would stop, allowing him time to recover.

He could take a lot. But it had been a while since he'd played with this kind of intensity without slowly building to it. The catharsis was wonderful, and Derwin was a master sadist; he had to give him that. Derwin knew how to bring a person to the edge of agony, but not beyond. Pain, and yet pleasure at the same time.

After another long pause, Derwin's finger traced one of the welts. His voice was low and heated. "Three more. Then I want to fuck you."

Elliot winced as his sore, clamped nipples brushed against the wall. "The clamps . . ." The longer they stayed on, the worse they would hurt coming off.

Derwin reached around to fondle and tug at them. Elliot whimpered. "In good time. When I'm ready." He turned Elliot's face from the wall, so they were eye to eye. "I haven't heard a safeword yet." He paused. Giving him the chance.

Elliot took a deep breath, sinking with the pain, riding the wave. The endorphins would come soon, and then he'd be flying high with it. "I'm fine."

Derwin kissed him on the lips, softly. "Good boy." He raked a short fingernail over a welt, making Elliot gasp once more.

It was hard to think, hard to focus. Elliot whispered, after more tender kisses, "What do I call you?" They hadn't exactly established protocols.

A shadow passed over Derwin's face. He took a step backward. "Just my name. Nothing else. Unless we become . . . more than we currently are." He raised the belt, and Elliot took a deep breath.

Three strikes, each a blazing fire. Elliot screamed, his back raw. Then strong hands eased his arms off the wall, guided him toward the bed, laid him down. Elliot hissed as the sheets brushed against his sore skin, but allowed himself to be positioned, putting his hands behind his head. After a minute, the submissive position felt natural. The endorphins were kicking in. He drifted, floated, aware that Derwin was spreading his legs, pushing his knees toward his chest.

Derwin's mouth on his, and then traveling lower, across his belly, lips ghosting over his cock, reviving his flagging erection. Elliot moaned.

Derwin took him into his mouth. As wet heat enveloped him, Elliot bucked up, pleasure overcoming the ache from the clamps. How long since someone had done this for him? He couldn't remember. Couldn't focus on anything at the moment, except the feel of Derwin's mouth, slick tongue and scraping teeth, coaxing him quickly to the edge. The finger rubbing at his asshole, exploring.

Abruptly, Derwin stopped. Elliot shivered, dangling on the thin wire between pleasure and pain. "Condom?" Derwin asked, sheepishly. "Not sure if mine are still good."

"Back pocket," Elliot answered, glad he was coherent enough to say that. His lack of concern with his own safety should have frightened him. With the expertise that Derwin was handling the scene with, however, he just couldn't bring himself to care. The comforter beneath him rubbed at the welts left by Derwin's belt, a pleasant reminder of the earlier sharper pains.

It only took a few seconds for Derwin to find the little packet, along with the lube. Elliot enjoyed the view as the man finally shed his jeans, revealing yet another large scar on one thigh that might have been a knife wound. But at the moment, Elliot's eyes were focused on something else. Long and slim, Derwin's cock jutted out from a dark nest of curls, looking eager and ready to play. Elliot squirmed as Derwin knelt, this time to spread lube over his hole.

"Please," he moaned unashamedly, widening his legs even farther.

A harsh exhale was Derwin's response. "Damn. You are so . . ." He shook his head, fumbling to roll on the rubber. Elliot saw that internal struggle again in Derwin's furrowed brows, his warring between lust and hesitation. Elliot smiled.

"Don't need prepping. Fuck me. *Please.*" His nipples were in agony at this point, but he'd never been so aroused.

Derwin's growl was more like a purr. Then he was on top of Elliot, spreading the lube around with the head of his cock, pushing in slowly. The stretch burned as Elliot had known it would, but he wanted that as well. He arched his head back, whimpering, and was rewarded with an affectionate bite to the sensitive area where his neck met his shoulder. Another thrust, and Derwin was deep inside.

Elliot's body clenched, and he rode the pain until he relaxed, extending his arms above his head. Derwin groaned, as if in sympathy.

Elliot leaned up to kiss him, wanting that, needing it, as Derwin began to move, shallow at first, getting settled in. Derwin's eyes were almost all pupil, glazed, and there was a glow to them that Elliot couldn't explain. *Like a fully charged laser beam.*

Soon the thrusting became smooth and easy. Derwin raised up on one elbow and reached for the first clamp. "Taking these off now. They're going to hurt. A lot." He nuzzled the hollow of Elliot's throat. "I would love to hear you scream."

Elliot's breath caught, but he gave a nod, preparing himself. The first clamp came off, and blood rushed back to his nipple like molten lava. He did scream—he couldn't help it. The intensity was nearly enough to make him pass out.

Afterward he lay panting, as Derwin returned to stroking his cock, slowly fucking him. Pleasure coiled up through him, surpassing the fading ache, though he knew the other clamp would have to come off, and soon.

Derwin began pumping harder, and Elliot detected a shudder go through the man, a stutter in his rhythm that warned he was near to losing control.

God damn, but it all felt so good.

Elliot's hands clenched and unclenched. Hard to think, when Derwin was pumping his cock with a fist, a hard, insistent pace that demanded he give in to the impending climax. "Close," Elliot warned, unsure if he was supposed to beg or ask permission.

"Good." Derwin's voice was rough and guttural. He adjusted his position again so that Elliot's ass hung off the bed, and fucked him while standing, placing his left hand near the remaining clamp. "Let it come."

"Oh demons," Elliot moaned.

CHAPTER SEVEN

VISIONS OF THE PAST

I t felt so good to bury himself in Elliot's sweet ass. With Elliot lying faceup on the bed and Derwin standing, he was in the perfect position to fuck him deeply. While part of him wanted to see the marks he'd left, it was enough to recall Elliot's back against the wall, the red welts from his belt against the pale skin.

If Derwin were a lightbulb right now, he'd be glowing at a hundred watts.

He'd rarely found a submissive so enticing and satisfying. From the moment he'd first coaxed pain from Elliot, the energy pull had been incredible. It wasn't a big surprise that after being famished for so long and denying himself for weeks, so much sweet pain would be intoxicating. In such a state, he was only glad that Elliot had been able to answer him about the condom. Stupid mistake, not to have basic things like protection at hand before he started. He was out of practice.

He'd loved how Elliot had arched and cried out when he removed the first clover clamp . . . the second one would catapult both of them over the edge. It was hard enough to keep his climax at bay when Elliot's ass was clenching around his cock. He slowed his thrusts even as he pumped Elliot's dick harder with his fist, wanting, needing the young man to find his pleasure before Derwin lost the last shred of control.

Just watching the pulse beating at Elliot's throat, the way he thrashed his head from side to side, was pure beauty, pure torture. *His body was made for this kind of treatment.* Suddenly it wasn't so strange that Elliot had become a pleasure worker. Grady had enjoyed their sessions, sure. But not like this.

Derwin plunged deeper, feeling the first shudders going through Elliot, who bucked and cried out, his seed spilling over Derwin's hand. Elliot grabbed at Derwin's arms, clutching him as he trembled. Time to plunge forward.

Just a quick pinch to the clamp released it as he began thrusting in harder, and then Derwin was engulfed in a euphoric rush of energy. His cries joined Elliot's moans as Elliot's pain poured into him. He came deep inside, hips pumping furiously. Elliot let go, but Derwin couldn't register much else beyond the white-hot heat of the orgasm, wave after wave, until he was panting and shaking all over. Unable to help himself, Derwin rolled his hips a few times after the last wave, basking in the aftershocks. He supported himself on his elbows, head bowed over Elliot's throat, breath gradually slowing. Everything tingled, leaving him in a postorgasmic haze.

Elliot, however, seemed to be in trouble.

His eyes had rolled up into his skull, showing only the whites. He was clutching the comforter in a death grip as tremors wracked his body. Alarmed, Derwin pulled out, cradling Elliot's head and nudging his side to wake him from the seizure.

It didn't work. Elliot began breathing hard. "Grady," he said, his voice toneless and far away.

"What?" Alarm gripped Derwin's chest. "Hey—snap out of it!" He slapped Elliot's cheeks, but to no avail.

"Grady," Elliot said, louder this time. The tremors continued, and his eyes remained closed. "Love you. So much love."

Derwin glanced around, half expecting to see his deceased lover. Was Elliot a Ghost Talker? Those were incredibly rare; he didn't know of any in Nis. One thing was certain: he had some kind of Oddity. Derwin swallowed back the grief—Grady was gone; he'd never get to see his face again. What if this was Grady sending him a message from beyond the grave? That he loved Derwin? Or that he was angry with Derwin for letting him die? Guilt made his heart pound and his throat close up.

Derwin leaned in closer, forcing himself to speak. "What do you see? What is he saying?" He didn't know if what Elliot was experiencing was visual or auditory, but that didn't matter. Any details he could get about Grady right now were precious.

Elliot's features contorted. "So sad . . . so sad . . ." He sobbed out a breath. Tears glistened at the corners of his eyes. Next Elliot moaned, and for a second Derwin thought that was it, end of seizure. Then the moan turned into a ragged keening.

"My fault." Elliot shook his head, brows drawn together in distress. "It was my fault."

Now how was that possible? "Elliot?" Derwin asked, hoping to get some sense out of him, something he could use. "What's going on? What are you talking about?"

Elliot's breathing quickened again. "Grady," he pleaded, arching up. "Grady . . . Grady . . . no . . ."

Derwin gripped Elliot's shoulders, shaking him. "Who are you?"

For the first time, Elliot seemed to hear him. "I'm Grady—love you," he said, eyes still closed. His knuckles had turned white with the power of his grip on the covers.

It finally dawned on Derwin. *You're an Object Reader.* It was too freaky, hearing those words from a man he'd just met, echoing the love that he'd lost. He pulled Elliot's hands away from the comforter, moving them to grip Derwin's arms instead. The tremors stopped, and Elliot drew in a deep breath, letting it out slowly. Fuck. An Object Reader. *And I took away his gloves.* Derwin mentally slapped himself. How could he have been so stupid?

"Who are you?" Derwin repeated.

The young man didn't answer immediately, still breathing deeply. He blinked. "Derwin?" His hands flexed, grasping at Derwin's arms.

Derwin's pulse began to settle. "Let's try it again. What's your name?" He spoke slowly and calmly, though he felt anything but that. Gods, the ordeal was giving *him* the shakes. *He's gone. I have to remember that Grady's gone, and nothing will ever bring him back.*

"Elliot," he replied, finally opening his eyes. He looked around, glancing at Derwin's hands holding him in place. "Oh damn." He shivered.

"You okay?" Derwin hadn't brought any water with him into the bedroom, another detail he should have remembered for a play scene. He'd worry about the vision in a minute; it was time to provide care. He tried to ignore just how sexy Elliot was post-sex, even rattled. In fact, he looked even sexier than in the club.

Elliot's hands closed into fists, and he drew them against himself, not meeting Derwin's gaze. "I'm fine."

Fuck, fuck, fuck. "Hang on."

Derwin crossed the room to grab the gloves, flipping them right side out. Both he and Elliot were smeared with come and needed a shower, but first things first. He grabbed Elliot's hands and pulled the gloves on, ignoring the young man's hesitant efforts to assist. Then he leaned back, resting his hands on his thighs to assess Elliot's condition. "Better?"

He only hoped his stupidity hadn't destroyed the trust they'd built up so far between them. A person like Elliot would be a perfect play partner for the future, if not more.

Was he kidding himself? The guy was a prostitute. It wasn't like he'd get to see him after tonight anyway.

The wariness left Elliot's face. "You don't care?"

Derwin smiled a little. "That you're an Oddity? You know how many Oddities I run into as a bounty hunter? I don't care." Derwin almost found himself telling Elliot the truth then, that he himself was an Oddity. But that would be crazy. People were distrustful enough of telepaths and clairvoyants who could read your mind or maybe your bank statement. Feeding on pain made his type one of the most hated Oddities out there. The Interrogators, people called them. Used in the military as soldiers and as inquisitors, they were usually experts at torture, given their ability to monitor pain levels in their victims, inflicting maximum agony with minimal damage. As soldiers, they could feed on every wound they inflicted on the enemy to increase their strength, stamina, and speed. From what Derwin had heard, the military excelled at conditioning his kind into merciless predators.

He lay down next to Elliot, sideways on the bed, their hips touching. "You scared the crap out of me. Can you tell me what you saw?"

Elliot rubbed his forehead. "Well . . . I saw that you used this bed. A lot." He blushed, which surprised Derwin. Up until now he'd seemed impossible to embarrass. "You and Grady—your boyfriend. You two loved each other. I saw that."

Derwin's heart felt two sizes too large, bleeding and raw. He took a deep breath. "Yeah. We did." But was that all Elliot had seen? Had he seen the murder? Or more importantly, the murderer?

"I saw lovemaking. A ton of it." Elliot shivered, and moved closer to Derwin. "And then you were sad, really, really sad. You thought his death was your fault. You had nightmares."

Derwin nodded, struggling to keep his emotions down and out of sight. Tonight was supposed to be about forgetting the past. "It was my fault. He texted me, but even though I rushed home, I was too late." All those nights, wishing he would die. Wishing the killer had stabbed him instead.

Puzzlement showed on Elliot's face, which answered one of Derwin's questions. He must not have seen how Grady died. "What— How was that your fault? Did he commit suicide or something?"

Grady had been too lighthearted for that, too sunny. "Somebody murdered him. Here. In this room." Derwin pointed over to the space in front of the bed where he still remembered the puddle of blood, by the doorway. "I found him slumped in the computer chair. The police said it was probably a burglary gone wrong." He didn't believe that. Someone had targeted Grady. Targeted *him.*

Elliot's eyes went wide with horror, flicking over to the place he was pointing. "Did they find out who did it?"

Suddenly all Derwin's weariness returned with a rush, the heavy guilt. The helplessness. He shook his head, numb. "The case went cold. They suspected it was one of my fugitives, a guy named Lloyd Brunson who I'd caught when he skipped bail for grand theft auto. He had a long arrest record—mostly property crimes. He's currently in jail for auto theft. But they never got enough on him to charge him with Grady's murder." It made him sick to his stomach even now.

Elliot touched Derwin's arm. The gloves were cool against Derwin's heated skin. "I'm so sorry."

Derwin shrugged. He was used to the condolences, the empty words. But the fact that Elliot had seen what he had . . . "Do you always get images? Feelings? From anything you touch?" New possibilities opened up for him, along with a dangerous hope. It wasn't fair to ask. He'd only just met the guy. *Still* . . . "Would you be able to do one more reading for me?" He hadn't gotten rid of Grady's desk or chair.

Partly in hope that there was some kind of evidence on them that the police had missed, that could help solve the case. Partly as self-punishment, a reminder of what he'd let happen.

Elliot's walls slammed up; Derwin saw it happen, but he couldn't proceed gently as Elliot shook his head. Derwin grabbed his shoulders, forcing him to keep eye contact. "Please. I'll pay you extra. Another hundred bucks."

Elliot's mouth curled with bitterness. "To witness a murder? To experience it? Because it's not just *visions*, as you say. When it happens, I'm *in* the memory. I *was* Grady. And you." He fixed Derwin with a glare.

No fucking way was Derwin letting an opportunity like this slip away. How many Object Readers was he likely to come across? Elliot was the first he'd ever met. "Two hundred—a total of four hundred for tonight. That's all I can pay." If it worked, he might request Elliot's special ability again. What might Elliot accomplish with a personal item off a skip? "Do you realize what this means? You could sell this service. You wouldn't have to sell sex."

Elliot clawed at Derwin's hand, forcing him to let go. He sat up, putting distance between them. "Yeah, and then one of my clients goes and tells the authorities, and next thing you know the police department owns me, or some corporate agency. They'd make me read all kinds of horrible things. Use me. You don't *get* it—right now they have no way of knowing that I exist. I don't have ID. *I don't exist in the system.*" Years of bitterness seemed to infuse that last sentence.

Elliot stood up, and Derwin knew he'd blown it—the young man was leaving. He couldn't let Elliot think his interest was just about some special ability.

"Wait." He stood up as well, and held out his hand. "It was rotten of me to ask. I don't know anything about what it's like. But I like you, and I'd like to know more about you. Will you please stay? Just for the night?" He felt raw, burned. Another empty night yawned in front of him, mocking his efforts to get past Grady's death and move on. Another night of loneliness and dreams of being loved again.

Elliot stared at him for a moment with narrowed eyes, then looked at the floor by the bathroom, where his clothes lay strewn about. Taking a deep breath, he raked a hand through his dark curls. "Fine. I need a shower." His voice was cold, businesslike.

Derwin sighed inwardly, but nodded. At least he'd salvaged this much. He'd have to be more patient to get Elliot's trust again. And then? Who knew? He wasn't ready to give up, either on solving Grady's murder or getting to know an intriguing person like Elliot. Such a perfect and willing masochist in bed, and smart too? Crazy not to explore that further.

He led Elliot into the bathroom, showing him the glass-walled shower and the deep-tiled bath. He'd upgraded the bedroom and bathroom shortly after purchasing the place. His kitchen might be twenty years old, but Derwin insisted on a bath that fit two comfortably. He glanced at Elliot's gloves and then at the shower. "Are those going to be a problem?" Hard to imagine being afraid to touch anything, lest you get a lot more information than you wanted.

Elliot smirked and pulled the gloves off, setting them carefully on the counter without touching the surface. "Showers, baths, and pools are generally fine. Water seems to erode some of the memories or something, though I've had visions from garments that have been washed, so it must take a lot of water. Touching people never gives me visions. And it's just my hands that trigger this. Not the rest of me."

Derwin nodded. After turning on the hot water for the shower, he quickly set out towels for the two of them, then stepped inside the shower, motioning for Elliot to join him.

As soon as Elliot came closer, Derwin pulled him the rest of the way in, firmly enough that Elliot brushed up against him with a slide of skin against skin. The hot water ran over their bodies, washing away the day's dirt and sex remnants. Elliot relaxed, the frown lines transforming into languid desire.

Derwin shared that lust. Maybe it had just been too long since he'd allowed himself pleasure, allowed himself to enjoy another's company, but oh, he wanted Elliot. He skimmed a hand down Elliot's back, enjoying the feel of raised welts, as he reached for the soap with his other hand.

"Let me take a look here," he murmured, gently turning him to inspect his work with the belt. The welts were good—very little broken skin. "These should be healed in a few days," he told Elliot, as he began washing, being careful of the damaged areas.

Elliot sighed as Derwin cleaned him, which made Derwin wonder how often others had offered him aftercare like this. Personally, he found giving care almost as satisfying as giving pain. He set the soap on the ledge and rinsed Elliot off. The idea that tomorrow he'd be letting this perfect sub out into the streets, back to who knew what, felt wrong.

After turning Elliot to face him, Derwin leaned in and kissed him.

Soft lips met his, and then there was the scrape of teeth, the slide of tongues. Derwin felt himself falling into a purely sexual need. He pulled Elliot up against him and kissed him harder, thirsty for him even though they'd just had sex. Neither of them seemed to have had enough. Elliot matched his ardor, kissing back fiercely, like the way he'd fought—such passion. Derwin's chest heaved with the force of it.

Part of him screamed out, *Don't fall for him! He sells sex.* But some deeper, more primal part didn't care. Elliot's hard cock rubbed against Derwin's thigh, and it was the most natural thing to reach down and stroke him, to feel the young man arch and thrust into his hand. Derwin captured in a kiss the moan that escaped, and exulted in the power. Was Elliot like this for every dom? For the moment, he allowed himself the fantasy.

Derwin stroked him a little harder, and then stuttered to a stop as Elliot's hand closed around his own cock, bringing a shock of pleasure. They shared more kisses, moaning as they jerked each other off. The water was beginning to grow cold, but Derwin didn't care. Elliot felt so right, filling his arms perfectly, a person he could cherish, protect. This was heaven.

His breath hitched as Elliot increased his pace, his thumb expertly finding the bundle of nerves by the head, rubbing them. When Elliot bit Derwin's bottom lip, it triggered something primal inside. Derwin's balls tightened up, and he shot off over Elliot's hand with a groan. A moment later Elliot came as well, sighing and leaning against him, almost peaceful in his release.

Once they were clean, Derwin shut off the water and grabbed the towels. He dried himself and helped Elliot too, and then led him back to the bed.

"I should go," Elliot murmured, even as Derwin pulled the covers down for him. But he climbed into bed without a fuss, donning his gloves. Derwin wasn't about to let him go anywhere right now if he was hurting or in subspace. He wondered what it would take to get Elliot to agree to breakfast with him.

He settled in next to Elliot, knowing that sleep was far away. After a session like that, he typically went out and spent some of the energy, catching fugitives. Since that wasn't an option, he took the time to enjoy having a warm body next to him, and to think about things that couldn't be.

He couldn't help also thinking about Elliot's ability, what he might see if he dared.

By the streetlight filtering in through the window, Derwin watched Elliot's eyes move beneath closed lids. His mouth was pouty at rest; errant curls half covered his face. Derwin sighed, resisting the urge to brush back one of those curls.

It was going to be a long night.

CHAPTER EIGHT

A CLUE

When Elliot woke, he found himself alone in the bed.

He yawned and stretched, more rested than he had been in days. It wasn't often that clients let him sleep in their beds. His own discarded mattress with its broken springs and smell of old cigarettes was a sad alternative. Maybe he could find a kind and rich sugar daddy to keep him as a permanent plaything with a bed as comfortable as this one.

Derwin wasn't rich. His place was nice enough, but hardly grandiose. Elliot liked how lived-in it felt though, how average. Too often his clients were wealthy and cold, their houses or suites pristine, tidy. Even fake. But not Derwin's.

Elliot remained in bed for a moment, wondering where Derwin had wandered off to, until the smell of bacon reached his nose. He groaned, half in pleasure, half in apprehension. He had a sense things were about to get complicated.

Maybe breakfast was a bribe to get him to do the object reading. The thought niggled him as he rose and got dressed, saving him from having to think too deeply about how amazing last night had been, what a perfect dom Derwin was. He could get used to someone like Derwin all too easily, and he couldn't afford to. The man was a bounty hunter, for crying out loud. One call to his cop buddies, and Elliot could find himself in jail. Or worse—pressed into service reading murder sites every day, pushing his Oddity to the limit until his mind broke.

After a quick check in the mirror to make sure he didn't have crusted drool on his face, Elliot descended the stairs and headed to the kitchen. He walked slowly, trying to plan how to play his role, what to say. Derwin's needing to know what had happened to his partner was understandable. If he were in Derwin's shoes, he'd probably be just as determined. But to sink himself in a vision that he knew would be violent, to open himself up like that . . . the idea scared him shitless. He rubbed his arms, and the feel of his gloves comforted him.

Pots and pans clattered in the kitchen ahead.

Elliot turned the corner, opening his mouth to make some witty remark, but he stopped as he spotted his client in front of the stove. Derwin was butt naked—except for one thing. A grill apron was doing a great job of covering his front side. His backside, however, was bare save for the tiny bow framing it.

Elliot couldn't help it. He laughed.

Derwin turned around, smiling sardonically, and immediately Elliot missed the sight of that glorious muscled ass.

"Morning," Derwin said, holding a pan of sizzling bacon. "I hope you're not vegetarian or something."

"No, I like my meat." There, his witty comebacks were still working. He shook his head, stepping into the kitchen. "You always cook in the nude? Why bother with the apron?"

"And get hot grease on my nuts? I'm not that crazy. I just didn't feel like pulling on dirty clothes, or trying to rummage around in the closet while you were sleeping. This gets the job done." Derwin set down the pan and used a spatula to lift off the bacon, transferring the pieces over to a couple of plates. "I've got eggs as well, and toast if you want. Anything more fancy than that, I'm afraid you'll have to go elsewhere."

Elliot's mouth was already watering. "Bacon and toast is good. I'll hold off on the eggs for now—they don't always agree with my stomach." The smell reminded him of simpler times, happier times, when he'd had a family, and a shiver went through him. He took a piece of bacon, and raised it to his mouth for a bite. He savored it, closing his eyes. So much better than cheap fast food. Or worse, dumpster diving.

Derwin stood by the stove and munched on his own slice of bacon, licking his fingers. Chewing slowly, Elliot watched Derwin, trying to read him. The man ignored him as he set about making the toast, buttered it, then sat down at the small dinette table to eat. He nodded toward an empty chair.

Elliot sat down, taking a piece of toast. "So is this an attempt to get me to do that reading?" Elliot's conscience gave a twinge at the flash of hurt in Derwin's eyes. It wasn't a kind thing to say, but Derwin's own kindness with the whole breakfast was threatening to make him like the guy. He couldn't let himself yearn for something he'd never be able to have, like a real relationship. He was a whore, and Derwin was just his client. Not only that, but Derwin was still grieving. Any kind of romance between them would be doomed from the start.

As quick as it had been there, the hurt was gone, and Derwin was all smiles again. "No. No strings attached. I just thought it'd be nice." His eyes flicked toward the door. "I didn't know what your living situation was." An indirect way of asking whether he was homeless, if Elliot ever heard one.

"I'm not roaming the streets, if that's what you're worried about. I have my own space." Elliot finished his toast. Of course, his space didn't have a kitchen. It didn't technically have a bathroom either, but he used the employee restrooms in the warehouse. It served. And it was rock-bottom cheap.

Derwin chuckled nervously and shrugged. "Okay. It just seemed like the proper way to end a date. And yes, I know it's not one, but I'm the customer, and I prefer to treat it like a date." He picked up a piece of bacon and ate it in two bites, looking smug.

The annoying thing was that Derwin was probably telling the truth. He was being so chivalrous, making sure not to send him off on an empty stomach. It made Elliot's insides twist with guilt. He really did sympathize with Derwin. What lengths would Elliot have gone to find the killer of someone he cared about? Someone like Theresa? He would have gone pretty far. Lied. Cheated. Manipulated someone like himself, perhaps.

The toast suddenly didn't taste as good. Why was he being so obstinate, when Derwin was treating him so well—like a person, and not some plaything?

"Hey." Derwin touched Elliot's arm. The concern in his voice and face didn't help with Elliot's guilt. "I'm being serious here. I can't imagine what it's like to have visions like you do. You don't have to do a reading for me."

"Don't. I'll do it." The idea still scared him shitless, but maybe he could do something good in his life. The gods knew he had few enough chances.

Derwin blinked and stared at Elliot. "I just said—"

"I'm doing it." Elliot took one last bite of his toast and set it down. Better not to have much in his stomach, considering how gruesome the images might be. "Let's get it done now. I may need some time to recover after." Hopefully not too long. Theresa would be expecting to hear from him before dark. She liked keeping track of her "children." It kept them all a bit safer, anyway.

He stood and headed upstairs to the bedroom, not waiting for Derwin. Once there, however, he paused, staring at the computer desk and chair. While he wanted this over, he needed to make sure he was reading the correct object. Derwin came up beside him, eyeing the chair as well as he pulled off the apron and slipped into some sweats.

Elliot took a deep breath and let it out slowly as he removed his gloves.

"So how do we do this?" Derwin asked, and Elliot had to smile a little.

We. Cute that Derwin included himself. And yet, Elliot felt more connected to him after one night's sex than he did to clients he'd seen a dozen times. *Not a good thing.*

"I think it'd be best if I'm sitting on the floor. That way I can't fall and hurt myself." He glanced at his feet. "It took place right here?" The idea creeped him out. He wouldn't have been able to stay in the same house.

Derwin nodded, and pulled over the computer chair. "He was sitting on this." Elliot moved aside as Derwin wheeled it across the carpet and in front of the bed. "Right here."

Chewing on his lip, Elliot carefully kneeled on the tan carpet, careful not to touch the chair or the carpet with his bare hands. "If I start having a seizure or if I'm, like, passing out or having a heart attack, yank my hands away and try to wake me up." While nothing physically bad had ever happened during a vision, he'd experienced some that had lasted for hours, until he woke up shaking and exhausted. He could vividly recall his first night at Theresa's place, on a cot where a dozen other unfortunate youths had slept before. It held some pretty intense memories.

Derwin sat down on the carpet next to him, his brows drawn together. Elliot glanced away; the concern made him quiver inside. He flexed his fingers and rolled his neck, trying to relax. The last thing he needed to do was pull a muscle. "Ready?"

Derwin chuckled nervously. "Don't ask me. Just try to describe what you're seeing. Anything." Blinking, he held up a finger. "Hang on. I'll get something to jot down notes." He dashed over to the night table and returned with his cell phone, sitting back down. "Okay. Now I'm ready."

Elliot grunted. At Derwin's nod, he reached out to grip the sides of the chair, wondering whether it would matter where he touched.

It didn't.

The room changed; suddenly, he was *in* the chair rather than on the floor. *A gun was pointed at him, held by a gloved hand. Fear squeezed his chest, and all his focus was on the gun; all he could think about was that he'd never seen this coming. A gold watch glinted on a masculine wrist, an expensive one, before it was covered by the dark sleeve of a sweatshirt. The gun swayed and dipped; the guy was frantically pulling at the cords of a laptop on the desk with one hand. Elliot couldn't see his face.*

"Said you'd regret this!" The exclamation, like the man's actions, was anxious. Panicked. "Tell me what you know!"

The vision dipped and swayed; one second Elliot was himself; the next instant he was Grady again. Elliot fought to retain his own thoughts, his own perspective.

Grady said in a weak voice, "You're right. I never should have looked in that damned folder. But he's coming—I'm sure he's on his way now." He'd sent the text, before the man had pulled the phone from him. Derwin would come for him. They both knew it.

"You fucking idiot! You could have avoided this!"

Suddenly in the other hand, there was a kitchen knife—but why a knife when he already had a gun? The gun lowered. Maybe it was a bluff. *Then the knife came up, slashing him across the throat. No time to plead, or talk. Pain engulfed him as warm liquid gushed down his front, spilling onto the carpet. He cried out.* I should have told Derwin.

He couldn't breathe. Was choking on his own blood. His vision darkened until all he could see was the knife, dripping, wavering. Beyond the knife, work boots. The boots were all wrong, somehow.

That was the last thought Grady had, as the knife plunged into his heart.

Darkness. Falling. Someone far away called out to him. He was spinning out of control, consciousness melting away . . .

Elliot coughed, unable to get air, unable to see. Derwin was there, holding him and calling him Elliot, not Grady. Elliot tried to suck in a breath and coughed again, shivering hard.

"Easy there. Breathe. Just breathe."

Elliot obeyed, although he couldn't seem to stop shaking. His heart was hammering in his chest, a testament to his fear.

"That was horrible," he whispered. He tried to pull air into his lungs, his eyes squeezed shut. Everything seemed to dip and lurch, making him nauseous. "I don't want to ever do that again." Elliot forced himself to open his eyes. He saw the chair, and for a second he saw the red stain on the floor. "Get that away from me!"

"Hang in there," Derwin consoled him, reaching over to get the leather gloves and pulling them back on Elliot's hands. "Okay. Just a second." He rose and wheeled the chair over to the computer desk. Elliot found himself looking at the desk with new understanding. There were cords dangling beneath.

"He stole the computer?"

"Um?" Derwin glanced over at the desk. "Yes. Along with Grady's phone, gaming console, and some jewelry and cash." His face darkened. "At first the cops thought that it was a home invasion gone bad. Later they thought it was a revenge attack and the stuff was just an added bonus. That's not what it was, huh?"

Elliot shook his head, still wobbly and disjointed. He'd *died*; it had actually felt like he'd died. Was that possible in a vision? If only he understood more about his ability. "No. Grady had information the killer didn't want him to have, and the killer seemed familiar to him. Grady texted you, right?" At Derwin's nod, he continued. "If he hadn't texted you, and if the killer had thought he had time—I think it was supposed to be an interrogation. The killer asked what Grady knew. He said something about Grady regretting this."

Derwin rubbed his hands. "Did you see his face? You said 'he.' It was a man?"

"It was a man." Better to get it all out now. Maybe then he'd never have to think about it again. "Boots—they just seemed like normal work boots to me, like a construction worker might wear. Something about them bugged Grady. He knew the guy, but didn't ever focus on his face." He shrugged. "I have no clue what he looks like."

Derwin jotted down the details. "And you said 'gold watch' while you were in the trance. So he was wearing a gold watch?" He frowned. "That doesn't sound like what a construction worker would wear."

"True," Elliot conceded, mystified by it all. If the cops hadn't solved it, how were they supposed to? "Yeah, black leather gloves and a gold watch, black hoodie, jeans. That's all I saw." *Other than all that blood, of course.*

Derwin nodded, writing. "Anything else you can remember? Who knows what could be a clue."

Elliot forced himself to think back. "Um, he slashed Grady's throat first then stabbed him, but you probably already knew that. Oh—and the man had a gun, but he didn't fire it, which seemed pretty strange. He just used it to threaten. Grady told him that he'd texted you. Not the best move, considering the outcome." Had there been anything else? "Folder. When the man asked Grady what he knew, Grady thought of 'some damn folder.' Like a manila one." Or had it been a picture of a folder?

"Got it." Derwin typed furiously. "We use manila folders to hold information about our fugitives, at the bail-bond place. The medical examiner said that the stab wound to the chest seemed almost like an afterthought—the knife was just thrust in and left. It was a cheap kitchen knife, available pretty much everywhere. There were no prints."

He looked up at Elliot. "Thanks. This is more than they've had to go on before. I kept thinking it happened because of me, something I'd done—revenge, you know. It sounds like that's not why." His voice was gruff, like it was nothing, but Elliot could see the emotion being held back in the deep lines between Derwin's brows, in his gaze.

Now that he'd shared the details, Elliot was starting to feel like himself again. There was an annoying headache, however, to remind him of the horrors he had just witnessed. He slowly stood up. "You're welcome."

It was probably best now that he moved on. Things were just going to grow more awkward the longer he stayed. Plus he needed to leave before the headache worsened, or he wouldn't be able to go anywhere for a few hours. "I have to go to Theresa's." She'd take care of him.

Derwin rose as well. "Let me drive you over to the club." He paused. "You have transportation there to get you back home?"

Presuming it hasn't been stolen. "Oh yeah. Don't worry about it." He waited for Derwin to change into jeans and a T-shirt. As Derwin grabbed his wallet and opened it, he couldn't help but notice the large bills. "Bail bonds mostly a cash business? You're lucky I'm an honest whore." He meant it to be a joke, but it came out a little weakly. Funny how now that it came to it, he didn't want to leave. Horrible murder scene aside, it had been nice.

Derwin was nice. Why couldn't he be rich as well? The cash looked good, but the apartment said there wasn't much more of that in the man's bank account.

"Four hundred—and yeah, I usually ask for cash. Just easier that way," Derwin said, offering him the money. Before he let go of it, he added, "You could help me. Be a consultant, or even a private investigator. I don't have extra funds now, but I could take some cases to help pay you. Might be best for you to lay low for a while anyway, right?"

Elliot shook his head. "I can't. I need to see Theresa—my Madame. She looks out for me and the others. Then I'll need to book a night with one of the Tatsu bosses to smooth things over with them." He chewed on his lip. *I should really leave it alone.* "You can drop a message with the bartender if you have any more questions." Or if Derwin just wanted to see him again. It was a nice thought.

"Good idea—I probably will at some point. Seriously, think about your options. I could use your help in following up on some leads, talking to people. Nothing as bad as this was, though. I hope." Derwin let go of the money, then stuffed his wallet into his back pocket with one hand as he grabbed his keys with the other.

Elliot followed him down the stairs and grabbed another piece of bacon as they paused by the kitchen, next to the front door. Every fiber of his being wanted to stay, slide up close to Derwin, coax him back into bed. What the hell was wrong with him?

"Okay," he finally said as Derwin opened the door. Was it just him feeling this powerful attraction? "What will you do next?"

Derwin ushered him out, arming the alarm system afterward. He didn't look at Elliot when he answered. "I'm not sure yet. I'll visit Lloyd Brunson first. He's the one the cops suspected—a former fugitive that I helped capture. I'm hoping I can rule him out before I start to list Grady's connections." He frowned. "The boots sound like him. But not the watch. He steals cars for a living—he would have sold something like that for the cash."

I have nothing to do with any of this. "I'm sure you'll figure it out." As good as last night had been, it was time to get back to reality. Already he felt the buzz of pain gathering in his temples, threatening like a storm. He smiled through it.

Derwin gave him a smirk. "I'm sure I will."

CHAPTER NINE

DEMON HUNTING

Derwin and Elliot drove up to the curb in front of Club Demon and checked for the gang who had harassed them, but the streets appeared empty. Elliot opened the door and an odd sense of emptiness gripped Derwin. He brushed a hand against Elliot's wrist, wanting—craving the contact. "You've got transportation?" He didn't know if the young man had been honest about having a place to live. Still, he appeared a little too well put together to be living on the streets.

"Yeah, I'm good."

"I'll leave a message with the bartender here if I need you." Derwin wished there were some way, any way to convince Elliot to stay with him, to continue helping him with the investigation. But it was like trying to pin down a feral cat. The sign on the door promised the club would open again at 8 p.m. Maybe he'd leave a message with the bartender then.

Elliot laughed and got out of the car. "Okay. I'll check when I can."

"Promise?" Derwin tried to infuse his voice with playfulness, but the tightness in his chest made it sound needy.

"Promise," Elliot said with a cocky grin, then he closed the car door and took a step back. Despite the somewhat rumpled appearance of his leather pants and uncombed hair, he still looked sexy as hell.

Damn. I sure don't need to be falling for someone right now. With a last peek at Elliot and a little wave, Derwin pulled away from the curb. Time to hit up Bob's Bail Bonds. He had to make more cash.

The bell above the door rang as Derwin walked into the bond agency, a cheery sound in the otherwise drab office. He spotted the secretary immediately. Connie was bent over examining the bottom drawer of a filing cabinet, her ample rear end jutting out. She liked to wear bright skirts a size too small for her frame and today was no exception. Her ass glowed fire-engine red.

Derwin cleared his throat.

She straightened and flashed him a winning smile with a gap tooth. She had dark skin and the shape of her eyes suggested there might have been some Asian heritage thrown into the mix. "Derwin, baby! Didn't expect to see you in here this morning." She set a couple of folders on the desk, looking him over. "Don't tell me you need another one already?"

He shrugged, smiling back. "What can I say?" He couldn't help but glance at the human skip folders, each with a photograph of the bonded party stapled to its corner. No new faces, at least as far as he could see. "Actually, I'm checking to see if there have been any bounties posted for demons lately."

While demon hunting was not strictly part of the bail-bond business, law enforcement agencies frequently sent out requests to bounty hunters via bond companies to capture or kill local *yokai*— demon spirits. Bond companies were a good way to alert people like him of reward notices.

Connie pursed her red-painted lips, frowning.

"Hmm. Lemme check. We usually have a few." She walked over to a smaller file cabinet by the front window. After searching, she returned to the desk with two new folders. "Got a couple here. One's not too far—over by the warehouses. *Nukekubi*." She shuddered.

Derwin grimaced. "Ugh. I hate those." The *nukekubi* was a demon who could detach its head from a humanlike body. The head would then sprout wings and fly. "They have a description? Male or female?"

She flipped open the file and glanced over it. "Female. Been feeding on dockworkers. You strapped for cash or just bored?" Turning the paper around, she let him read it.

The front sheet said the reward was two thousand dollars. That would go a long way to helping him out. "Yeah, something like that. Got a new lead on Grady's killer."

"Oooh." Connie drew out the sound, shaking her head. "Don't be getting yourself in trouble. I like you. You'd be hard to replace."

Derwin chuckled as she took the file to the copier and began photocopying pages. "Don't worry. I can take care of myself." He'd head over to the docks and interview some of the men. With luck, he'd be able to track the demon down while it was still daylight. The tricky thing about *nukekubi* was that both the body and the head had to be killed. Kill just the head, and the body would grow another.

She eyed him as she handed over the copies. "Mm-hmm. Even Superman has his kryptonite, you know."

He grinned but patted her on the arm. "I'll be careful. Is Bob in today?"

"He's at a doctor's appointment. Probably has lung cancer or something." Her cutting tone didn't throw him a bit. Derwin knew she cared for Bob like a favorite uncle, and his health worried her; the man did like to smoke. As for himself, he and Connie had been friends for ages. Connie tutted to herself as she returned the original files to the cabinet before sitting down at the desk.

"Let him know I stopped by. I won't be able to go after any skips tomorrow—I'm driving over to Mephist Penitentiary to interview Lloyd Brunson. I need to see if I can rule him out in Grady's murder." If only he could convince Elliot to come with him. Then again, Lloyd likely wouldn't have any personal items worth reading.

Connie huffed. "Lloyd. That man is more screwed up than a football bat." She peered at Derwin again, dark eyes meeting his. "Seriously. Watch yourself."

With a nod, he headed out of the office.

He glanced through the file before starting the car. Two days ago, a dockworker had encountered the demon and lived to tell about it. It was female, Caucasian, young and pretty, with black hair. Derwin checked the dock number and revved up the engine. He wanted to interview the witness. Hopefully the demon-girl showed her face in the daylight in some way, either as a dockworker's girlfriend or perhaps at a local business. If she hid inside until dark, that would make it a lot harder to hunt and kill her.

By closing time, he'd interviewed the shaken witness as well as a few other scared dockworkers. They'd only seen the demon after nightfall, which had led to bosses ending shifts before sunset. All of them agreed on the black hair, although from there the descriptions didn't match up. She might be young, middle-aged, or old. When a flying, screeching head was chasing you, details got fuzzy.

Derwin searched for the foreman before he left, an older guy by the name of Boots who claimed to have seen enough crazy creatures in his lifetime that one *nukekubi* didn't frighten him. By this time the sun had sunk low on the horizon, and Derwin feared he'd be meeting the demon on her terms rather than his own. It would be smarter to wait until morning, but that would give her the chance to kill again. He followed Boots to his truck as the guy packed up for the day.

"She's a streetwalker—or at least she poses as one." Boots set down his toolbox in the back of an old Ford truck.

That was the first solid lead he'd heard. "Do you know where she hangs out in the daytime?" If he couldn't locate her today, perhaps he could get her early tomorrow, before leaving for Mephist.

"Not far from the warehouses—on Oceanside and Sixteenth Avenue or thereabouts." Boots removed his baseball cap to mop sweat from his wrinkled brow. He blushed, grinning, and Derwin suspected Boots frequented the area often. "You know. The main drag for hookers." Oceanside ran parallel to the bay for several blocks. The demons and monsters tended to stick to the outskirts, and that section of the bay qualified.

Derwin handed the guy ten bucks. "I appreciate your help."

Boots grunted approvingly, and pocketed the money before climbing into his truck. Derwin headed back to his own car. If he hurried, he might still catch her on the street before she laired up for the night and detached her monstrous head to feed.

He really didn't want to see that.

On the drive, Derwin kept his eyes open for the black-haired woman, or a bunch of people screaming and running from a flying head. The sun hadn't set yet, but it was close. He spotted a cluster of female prostitutes standing at a corner and pulled into a not-so-legal parking spot. Maybe the demon was hiding among them, or they'd seen something.

"You're not a cop, are you?" A blond asked him as he got out of the car. She'd probably spotted his ankle sheath.

He smiled and opened his leather jacket to show his bounty hunter gear—and no badge. "Evening, ladies. Bond enforcement agent—not out for any warrants right now. I'm looking for a demon."

There were five women: two of them with obviously dyed blond hair, one redhead, one brunette, and one with sable-black hair. Three stepped back, eyeing him warily. Still, none of them had run, which was good.

Behind them, the sun was setting into the ocean.

They eyed him wordlessly, waiting for him to act, perhaps. He studied them, particularly the tall raven-haired woman, wearing a black corset top with black jeans and fishnet gloves, her hair falling loose. Around her neck, she wore a black, fringy scarf. If she was *nukekubi*, there would be a tattoo circling her throat, where she would detach herself.

"What's your name?"

She glared at Derwin with challenge in her eyes. "Maria." Was that a slight foreign accent? Derwin hooked a thumb in his belt, near his gun but not on it. Should he try to coax her scarf off, or grab it?

"Maria," he repeated, smiling at her. "That's a nice name. Seen anything strange lately?" He moved forward, but she took a step back. The other girls backed away as well, giving them space.

The red-haired one spoke up—she was both the shortest and the youngest of the group. "Maria just started working this corner." She took another step away from Maria.

Derwin couldn't help but smile. It was always useful when people ratted each other out. He grabbed at the scarf, but Maria ducked and began running, faster than a woman wearing heels could possibly run. He took off after her.

She raced across the street, vaulting over parked cars, but last night had charged Derwin up. He leaped the cars as well, keeping up with her. She shrieked at him, probably realizing that this was no mere human chasing her.

They ran past an alley, and abruptly she stopped and faced him. He halted just in front of her, hand near his gun. Above them, the streetlight flickered on in the settling dusk. "Let me see your neck," he ordered. If she didn't comply, he'd tackle her.

She growled, low under her breath, untying the knot in her scarf and pulling it open. Derwin had a second to see the red tattoo circling her throat like barbed wire. Then the tattoo stretched and ripped apart. Crab-like legs emerged from the holes, along with two dark-red membranes. He blanched—were those *entrails* dangling? He stared as the red things unfurled.

Wings.

Derwin had seen demons before—plenty of them. But he'd never seen a *nukekubi* in the process of detaching. Gruesome. Bile rose to his throat, and he stumbled back. Like a giant spider emerging from a crevice, the demon's head crawled out to perch on the shoulder of the body.

Maria's mouth opened in a scream as she flew at Derwin.

Derwin drew his gun and fired three shots, dodging as she tried to slice at him with razor-sharp claws. He prayed the blessed, cold-wrought iron bullets worked on this particular demon. Two shots only grazed the creature. The third hit right between the eyes.

Teeth snapped as the head hurtled past him. It landed with a crunch on the pavement. The wings flapped uselessly, then were still. Apparently the blessed bullets worked.

He nudged the head to be sure it didn't move, his heart pounding. Then he realized something was missing from the scene. The headless body was running away at full speed, as if it had eyes. Derwin cursed and took off, arms pumping. If it escaped, it'd find a hiding hole he'd never be able to locate, and grow another head.

The body turned a sharp corner, and Derwin ran harder, flying past parked cars and a bum with a grocery cart, who huddled against the building to avoid him. He hadn't run this fast in ages. Air burned in his lungs. There was nothing so good as a chase.

He turned the corner and caught sight of his quarry climbing up the side of the building. Derwin grinned. If the demon thought that would stop him, it was sadly mistaken.

He ran up and took aim at the leg, then shot. If he could bring it down this way, he wouldn't have to go up.

The bullet hit, but the demon continued to ascend. Derwin sighed and jammed the gun back in its holster. He launched himself up to grab hold of the crumbling brick, grimacing as he began to climb.

He was quick, but the demon was quicker. It made it to the roof, and he had to scramble to follow, muscles burning with the strain. Superhuman strength or not, it wasn't easy scaling a building like this. Just as he gripped the edge to pull himself up, the demon appeared above him and tried to wrench his fingers off with its clawed hands.

Pretty smart for a thing with no brain. Derwin frantically tried to find something else to grab on to. He managed to swing one leg up and used the leverage to haul himself to the roof, before the demon tackled him.

Derwin's body armor protected his chest, but his arms were bare and he cried out as the demon's claws raked through his skin. *Shit, that better not leave a scar. Must remember long sleeves next time.* Worse, his throat was unprotected as well. He grappled with it one-handed, reaching for his gun.

He succeeded in pinning the demon beneath him. Panting, he pressed the muzzle of his gun against fine breasts that looked grotesque without a face to go with them. *Bang*! He ducked a claw. *Bang*! The shots were deafening. One last shot, and the demon finally stopped moving. Black blood began to pool beneath the body. Derwin groaned and rolled away from the corpse, breathing heavily.

Gods, he hated demons.

After resting for a moment, Derwin rose and inspected the body to make sure the thing was dead. How far had he run from the head? The police would want all the demon's pieces as a matter of public safety, before they paid the bounty.

A quick search revealed a fire-escape ladder on the back of the building. He made sure to lower the ladders before dialing the police. As usual, they'd probably be surprised that he'd actually chased down a supernatural creature, but as long as there was a viable explanation, they wouldn't ask questions. That was how he'd made his living all these years. And how the cops cleared their workload.

Derwin sighed, glancing at his watch as he listened to the rings. It would be at least two hours before he'd be able to wrap up the paperwork and head over to Club Demon to leave a message with the bartender.

Would he hear back from Elliot?

CHAPTER TEN

RISK AND REWARD

When Derwin had pulled away from the club, it had left Elliot feeling strangely empty. Even though Derwin had kind of used him with the whole vision thing, he'd felt like he'd made a connection. For once the sex had seemed like more than just business.

It didn't help that Elliot had then found his bike frame with no front tire. He'd been in too much of a rush to remove the tire and lock it with the back one.

One trip to the bike shop later, Elliot was heading over to Theresa's place. He couldn't seem to shake his depression despite the sunny day. Derwin and he were from separate worlds. He needed to let it go. At the curb, he secured the bike again, this time correctly. Two children about eight and ten sat outside the dilapidated apartment building on the steps, wearing torn and dirty clothes. Their faces revealed their inner despair. *New kids.* Theresa's latest acquisitions. The young ones without parents often ended up here. The last place anyone wanted to go was the state-run orphanages, which promptly drafted those who aged out into the military.

He climbed the stairs to the third floor of the building and rapped on the door, wondering how to tell Theresa about his latest client. A boy of about fifteen opened it, giving him a sullen look with dark-brown eyes painted in eyeliner. Elliot blinked, swaying with vertigo for a second. It was like seeing himself a few years back.

Recovering, he peeked past the boy to where he could see Theresa sitting on the couch watching TV. She smiled and waved at him.

The boy grunted and let Elliot in, before heading out the door himself. Probably to meet with one of the clients who liked the underaged. Elliot tried not to think about it.

"There you are," Theresa said, patting the space beside her. "Come talk for a few."

Elliot flopped down on the sofa restless and out of sorts, his head aching. "Got some new kids, I see," he began, more to put off discussing his night than out of any real curiosity. When didn't Theresa have new children hanging about her?

Even though she was over fifty, Theresa still possessed a firm hold on her former beauty. She'd found a way to make her steel gray hair work, styling it around her face to set off her light-blue eyes. She wore red lipstick and dressed stylishly in loose tops and tight pants to show off the figure that might have been fuller with age but that was no less attractive.

She turned to scrutinize him, her lips thinning with concern. "Something's different. Bad night?"

He shrugged, an uncomfortable heat rising to his cheeks at her stare. "No—good night, actually. Made four hundred for some SM play." He smiled self-depreciatingly. "You know how I like that."

One of Theresa's penciled eyebrows rose. "Depends on how rough they are on you." As his blush deepened, she drew in a breath. "Ohh. You liked him." It wasn't a question.

Elliot didn't know how to respond. "Nice guy—knew what he was doing. Met him over at Club Demon." His stomach was slowly rolling over on itself. He looked away, the emptiness tugging at him again.

"Honey." A lifetime of experience, of disappointments were infused in those words. "You *really* like him." She patted his knee in consolation. He knew the unspoken message. *Don't fall for the johns. It only leads to heartache.*

He rocked back against the soft cushions, cursing his stupidity. "He's a bounty hunter. Found out about my Oddity, but he seemed okay with it. Even offered me some extra cash if I could read a few objects for him. He's trying to figure out who killed his boyfriend."

Theresa was probably the one person who knew everything about him. When he'd first arrived here, he'd been scared and helpless. It had been her shoulder he'd cried on, her face he had screamed at with frustration at his circumstances, at the lost opportunities. She'd seen him have visions before. Yet she'd kept his secret. Of all the people in his life, she'd been the only one who never let him down.

So when she rubbed his shoulder slowly, it helped to settle his nerves a little. "Be careful. I don't think I need to tell you, but all the same . . ." She sighed.

He smiled without humor. "I know. If it makes you feel any better, I don't think he'll call the cops. He seemed okay." He'd been awfully at ease about it, to the point of making Elliot wonder. Not to mention the way he'd acted during their session, the way his eyes had almost seemed to glow—there was something different about him. Elliot didn't know what.

Theresa looked doubtful. "Just let me know if you're ever in trouble. I won't give you any advice about using your gift for payment—that's entirely up to you. But guard yourself. And guard this." She touched the left side of his chest.

My heart, yeah. "I will," he said, but it already felt a bit late for that.

Her reference to guarding reminded him of the fight at the club, the gang members.

"Oh! I need to tell you something. While I was reeling in this guy, three members of the Tatsu gang gave me trouble. They actually tried to drag me off at gunpoint. The guy who seemed like their leader was a white guy with a crew cut. He had two companions. One had a scar on his lip, and the other was gangly, with black hair. Derwin—the bounty hunter—and I fought them off. We landed a few blows. They were pretty pissed." He tried to think of any other details that might help. He couldn't recall if they'd said their names. "I mentioned your name, but either they didn't know about you or didn't care. They seemed low in the rankings."

It occurred to him that it hadn't been such a good idea to use Club Demon as the rendezvous point for messages with Derwin. Crew Cut might be looking for him there. But now that Theresa knew, she'd fix the problem. Elliot had full faith in her.

She nodded, frowning. "You should let Roy Yoshiro have you for an evening, no charge. Tell him what happened, and why you were forced to fight. We can't have members of the largest gang in town disrespecting us. It puts us all in danger. He can deal with his boys however he likes, but I think we'll get better results if you 'sweeten the pot,' so to speak."

Elliot chuckled, but a chill went down his spine. Roy had rather brutal tastes. He trusted the man not to seriously injure him, but he'd be recovering for a few days after a booking with the Tatsu boss. Well, it wouldn't be the first time he'd be used to rein in the gang's violence against Theresa's whores. At least Roy preferred his boys—and girls— to be of legal age. Elliot had endured creepier clients in the name of protecting himself and others.

"That's fine," he answered, mentally preparing himself. "You might want to schedule it in a few days, though. Welts." He could imagine how the drug lord would react to them. Even though Roy knew anybody could have the boys he rented, he preferred the illusion of possessing them entirely. Much like his gang members.

"I'll make the call. Will you be here for a while?" Theresa stood, setting down the remote control.

Elliot stood as well. "I'm going to find something to eat and make a deposit. I'll stop by later." He patted his jeans pocket with the wad of cash Derwin had paid him, and pulled out a few bills for Theresa before tucking it back. Food would come first to help with the raging headache, but he'd have to stop by his place right afterward to hide his money. He wasn't walking around with cash like that on him.

Theresa nodded. "I'll see you later. And I'll let the others know to watch out for the Tatsu, in the meantime."

That settled, Elliot headed over to his place, stashing the money in his usual hiding spot—a locked box hidden behind a few loose bricks behind his dresser. It wasn't the best location in the world, but then what was? The important thing was that he'd soon have enough for a motorcycle. After he'd gotten that . . . he had dreams, if he could just get the courage to realize them.

If he could somehow create a new identity, he wouldn't be stuck on the streets for the rest of his life. He could start a career as a dancer, like Stefan. Maybe even build up enough cash to get his diploma. It was good to dream. But the lure of cash for sex, when he liked sex anyway . . . that would be hard to walk away from. Maybe when he aged out, when nobody wanted him any longer.

Afterward, he grabbed a burger, swallowed some aspirin for the headache, then walked to the closest laundromat to wash his clothes. He had no clients booked for the evening, so he debated between lazing around at Theresa's place, or hitting the streets to sell a quickie. Staring at his hands, he recalled what Derwin had said about earning money doing readings. It might not be so bad, as long as he screened his clients and the types of cases he would take. Using his ability was risky, but then again, so was whoring. Maybe he should leave word at Club Demon for Derwin tonight. How pathetic was it that he couldn't even wait a day? Was it better to cut his losses now and avoid the guy? Or take the job and risk growing more infatuated? The money beckoned; he couldn't deny that. But he wasn't sure it was worth the price.

He decided to hang out at Theresa's and watch TV. Once there, however, he couldn't seem to relax. Every time someone dark and handsome appeared on the screen, his heart skipped a beat, and he couldn't help rubbing the welts on his back against the sofa to feel the burn. Crap.

Theresa ordered pizza, and as the sun set and darkness settled outside, all her little foundlings came by for a bite. Elliot learned the names of the newest two—Sera and Jackson—and got to catch up with a couple of girls he hadn't seen in a while.

As they all ate, Theresa's phone rang. She excused herself to the kitchen. Elliot paused between bites to listen in, and by her tone, he knew she was talking to a client, a powerful one. When the call ended and she returned, he looked at her expectantly.

"I have you set up for this coming Wednesday." She jotted the date and pickup location on a scrap of paper for him. "His driver will pick you up at City Central Station. Dress nice."

"Did he say anything about talking to his boys?" At least he wouldn't have to worry about those idiots much longer. Today was Friday. Wednesday wasn't that far away.

Theresa shrugged, handing him the paper. "He said he'd pass the word around to 'be respectful.' Unless somebody gets hurt, I doubt he'll do more than that. But it's a start."

"Probably about the best we can expect." At least his skin should be safe now. He could only imagine what Roy would do if some young gangster fucked with his toy.

While it reassured him to have personal protection in the Tatsu ranks, he'd chosen whoring to stay as far from the gangs as possible—their members tended to have short life spans. The Tatsu situation just underlined how much he needed to get away from all this. He needed money. He needed a plan to get off the streets, and into a real job. Standing, he made a resolution. "I have an errand to run. Thanks for the pizza—I'll see you in a few days, okay?"

"Take care. And keep me updated."

With a wave and a smile at Theresa, who waved back, Elliot headed out.

Riding his bike, it only took a few minutes to get to Club Demon. It had to be close to 9 p.m., but that was the perfect time to let the bartender know that Derwin would be leaving messages there and to leave a quick note himself. It might be days before Derwin saw it, of course—depending on when or if Derwin stopped by. He had to take the chance. The Friday crowd was just starting to hit the place, and while there were no lines yet, the bass beat and chatter from inside made a low thrum in the quiet evening.

He'd forgotten to ask Theresa for a pen and paper to write the note, but he could sweet-talk the servers into lending him some. He didn't know what he'd write, other than telling Derwin he was interested and to write back with details. Maybe he should use some cash to get a burner phone.

He parked his bike across the street and down a little ways this time, hoping to thwart whoever stole his tire last time.

As he hurried over to the club, a familiar voice stopped him cold. "Hey! Asswipe!"

Should've parked closer, Elliot thought, heart racing as Crew Cut emerged from a dark alley. He had the same two goons with him, plus two more who looked barely legal. Elliot's gaze flicked over to the bar entrance, hoping to see the bouncer. But with no line, there was no reason for them to be standing outside, at least not yet.

They were *alone* on the street. *Not good. This is really not good.*

"I'm seeing Roy next week. Roy Yoshiro. If you want to book me after that, you'll have to speak with him," Elliot said loudly, to make certain they all heard the name. Surely that would make them pause.

"Nice try." Crew Cut brandished a tire iron.

Hope faded, rapidly replaced by foreboding. His breath coming in short gasps, Elliot scanned the area for help, any kind of help, but there was nothing. His only shot was to make a break for the club.

"I'm telling you, it's true! You're gonna be sorry if you do this!" He took off running, the gang close behind.

He didn't get far.

Pain exploded in his calf as Crew Cut swung the tire iron into it. Elliot had time to be grateful it hadn't been the knee itself before he hit the ground. He skinned his knees, and the grit of the road tore through his gloves into the flesh of his hands. Hissing, he tried to get his bearings. Then a strong hand hauled him upright, and he flailed as Scar Lip swung at him. The punch hit him in the gut. Elliot doubled over, wheezing.

Crew Cut seemed to be everywhere and nowhere. A fist caught Elliot's jaw, rattling the world even as pain struck his ribs, his back, and his stomach. He curled up, trying to protect his head and face, but that only encouraged them to kick instead of punch, with brutal blows that rattled his bones. Something cracked and he cried out, rolling to escape the booted feet.

A kick to the groin left him in the fetal position in the gutter, fighting not to puke. Blood was running down his neck; something sharp must have nicked his cheek. When nothing further happened, Elliot opened his eyes, but he had a hard time focusing. Gods, he *hurt*. Even breathing was a struggle, lying there.

"Piece of shit. I better not see you around again," Crew Cut hissed, then turned and walked away, followed by his buddies. Elliot moaned, shivering as the cold water in the gutter soaked into his clothing. He coughed, and agony exploded in his side. Mewling, he clutched at himself. *Fucking asshole cracked my rib!* His side burned as he fought against rising panic. *Should have fought back! Made them pay.*

But if he'd done that, he'd probably be dead now.

Spitting a wad of blood and phlegm, Elliot tried to roll over. He got halfway up before pain laid him flat again, sobbing. *Fuckers!*

Belatedly the gravity of his situation hit him—he was vulnerable out here, helpless. *I need help. Maybe I could crawl to the club. Safety.* His head pounded and the world spun, but he struggled to get up anyway.

He blacked out.

CHAPTER ELEVEN

PICKING UP THE PIECES

By the time the cops confirmed the demon slaying and hauled away the body, it was well after eight, and Derwin was starving. It had been too long a day after too long a night, and all he wanted to do was grab some pizza, eat it in bed, and watch TV. And sleep.

He would've driven right home, except he had told Elliot that he'd stop by Club Demon, to let the bartender know he'd be passing messages to Elliot. He didn't need an Object Reader to interview Lloyd in a place where he wouldn't have personal items. But then again, what if Elliot decided to leave him some kind of message? Derwin couldn't take the chance of missing anything.

Plus he craved more contact, any contact with Elliot. When the guy had looked right at Derwin and told him he loved him? Even though it had just been a vision, even though Elliot had been feeling Grady's emotions and not his own, it had shaken Derwin. Brought back that human connection.

This was the first time he'd felt a real attraction to someone else in ages. Why'd it have to be for a prostitute?

He didn't have time to contemplate further. It was a short drive from the warehouse district to the club, where dark, abandoned streets were busy and well lit. Derwin spotted a few rentboys standing along the curb near another club and caught himself searching for a familiar face, but Elliot wasn't among them. He drove by the club entrance, looking for parking. A ways down the street were two figures, one lying in the gutter, while the second was crouched over him, trying to rifle his pockets. A junkie and a thief, most likely. He pulled over and parked on the curb.

As he got out of the car, Derwin noticed the slightly curly black hair and pale skin. Icy panic gripped him; it felt like losing Grady all over again, finding him dead in the bedroom.

"Elliot?" he called, hoping—praying he was wrong, that it was some other kid in torn-up blue jeans and a shirt that might have been white but was now stained with blood. He ran toward the two figures, snarling at the thief, a kid not more than thirteen or fourteen. The kid hissed at him and took off into the shadows, leaving only the still form in the gutter.

Dreading he'd find the skin cold, Derwin reached out. *Still warm.* He turned the body over, and horror washed over him. Elliot's face was barely recognizable with all the bruises. Derwin gathered Elliot in his arms, his hands shaking. Was this because of him? Fear and guilt racked Derwin as he brushed a wet strand of hair from Elliot's face.

"Elliot?" His voice shook.

Elliot sucked in a breath. *Thank the gods.* As soon as Elliot moved, however, he cried out, flailing. Eyes widening, Derwin clutched him. Elliot's pain assailed Derwin like the buzzing of angry bees in his head, and he grabbed Elliot's wrists, noting the bruising along the jaw and temple, the bloody nose, the scrapes scoured into what was left of Elliot's gloves.

"Hey," Derwin said urgently, worried about injuries he couldn't see. A steady burn from Elliot's chest hinted at something fractured or broken. "It's me. Derwin."

Elliot pushed at Derwin, then stilled. He took another breath and coughed, then opened his eyes. His gaze was unfocused, his pupils blown. Concussion, maybe.

"Can you stand? We need to get you to a hospital." Derwin's mind was racing. Who had done this? Had to be more than one person. From what he'd seen last night, Elliot knew how to take care of himself in a fight.

Derwin mentally kicked himself. The gang members. They'd been at this club. The club where Derwin was supposed to leave Elliot notes.

This was all his fault. *I should have thought of some other way to keep contact.*

Elliot blinked and struggled to get up. "No hospitals! 'M okay." His slurred speech said otherwise though. He managed to get one foot under him, then bleated out in pain, falling. Derwin caught him again.

"You've got a concussion." Derwin picked up Elliot in his arms, inwardly wincing at the sharp gasp and the jolt of power from Elliot's hurts.

Elliot groaned and then coughed, holding his side. "Bastard broke my rib."

"Okay—just take it easy. We'll get you patched up," Derwin assured him, as he carried him back to his car. What if he hadn't decided to check here tonight? If only the cops had arrived sooner at the waterfront, though thank god they hadn't arrived any later or Elliot would be . . .

Trying to steer his mind away from gruesome thoughts, he set Elliot in the front seat. Elliot's face was even paler than usual, and Elliot was wheezing now. At least with the fight knocked out of him, he didn't resist as Derwin buckled him in.

"I can't afford it," Elliot got out between breaths. "And they're gonna want to know who I am."

Derwin hurried round to the driver's side and strapped himself in. "Don't worry about that. You think they don't see criminals coming in with gunshot wounds and all? They're not going to care who you are. And we'll figure out payment." He chuckled. "Not like they can send you a bill, right? Do you even have an apartment?"

Elliot groaned as they drove off, tenderly touching the back of his calf, where more pain blossomed, like sparks of lightning to Derwin. "Sorta—it's not technically an apartment. But it's a living space, and it's in a building. That's all you need to know."

"So don't worry about it," Derwin replied, being careful of traffic as they headed across town to the main hospital. "Was it the gang members again? Or do you have other enemies I should be aware of?" He glanced over, wishing he could differentiate more nebulous injuries, like internal bleeding or a ruptured spleen. "You're lucky to be alive."

Elliot hissed as they passed over a pothole. "Yeah. It was Crew Cut and his boys." He laughed without humor. "They're so dead. My Madame already booked me a night with their gang boss." He coughed. "Think I'll have to postpone it."

An ugly feeling sprung up in the pit of Derwin's stomach at the mention of Elliot's appointment. *Ignore it.* "I'm sorry I agreed to leave messages there. I should have known it was dangerous. I'm an idiot. Does your Madame have a phone? Can you reach her?"

Elliot's grunt indicated that he'd heard the questions, but he didn't respond. Sighing, Derwin concentrated on driving. He was about to ask something else when Elliot finally answered. "I have Theresa's phone number. I'll give her a call as soon as I can."

At least Elliot was coherent enough to make sense, though Derwin dreaded having to deal with the Madame if his condition worsened again. He hoped Elliot had never been picked up by the police before; even so, the hospital shouldn't have any trouble treating him. But then what? "I think you need to stay away from your usual haunts for a while. So that your Madame or their boss or whoever can clear all this up.

"Stay with me." The words were out before Derwin could rein them in, pull them back. His heart pounded. "Until things are safe, at least."

Another moment passed by in silence. They'd soon reach the hospital. Derwin sensed rather than saw Elliot squirm. "I thought about your offer. I was going to leave you a message that I'd do it—*within reason.*" Derwin glanced over—Elliot was glaring at him. "No more making me watch murder playbacks!"

Too grateful to protest, Derwin merely nodded.

In the ER, it took them over an hour to see a doctor. Once they finally did, the tests showed that Elliot's vitals were fine, and though he was still in pain and had multiple bruises and lacerations, the only worrying injuries were the cracks to his rib and his head injury. When the nurse pulled off Elliot's shirt, Derwin fought the urge to punch something. How many of them had there been?

He kept his distance, knowing that if he got close he'd want to wrap his arms around Elliot, hold him while the nurse cleaned the grit out of his scratches and applied gauze bandages. The Tatsu gang boss might not have time to do crap to those guys. Derwin would break every bone in their bodies for this.

Worse, he couldn't help continuing to drink up Elliot's pain. Even though, like milk gone bad, it made Derwin want to vomit.

Luckily Elliot had no difficulty giving his name, the president's name, and the year, and he claimed the dizziness had subsided. The CT scan didn't show a fracture or any trauma to the brain, which left Elliot with the basic diagnosis of "concussion, mild." When the hospital staff asked Elliot to stay overnight for observation, he refused.

Derwin instantly volunteered to watch him.

"You don't have to do that." Elliot was sitting shirtless on the small gurney, and the red and purple bruises stood out painfully on his pale skin. Derwin fought to keep his rage from surfacing.

"You should consider that offer—unless you have relatives who can monitor you for the next day or so?" The physician's assistant was young, male, and rather attractive, in Derwin's opinion. He was also insistent. "You don't want to take chances with a head injury. Brain swelling can lead to permanent damage. Even death."

"You're coming with me or you're staying overnight," Derwin stated in a voice rough with emotion. He could be a stubborn bastard, and he knew it. In this instance he didn't care.

Elliot stared at him. The heat in his gaze matched Derwin's, and the charge between them was palpable. The PA took a step back. "You two can discuss it for a moment. I'll return." He closed the curtains, leaving them at least with the illusion of privacy.

Derwin held up his hands. "I'm not trying to intrude in your life. Or your work. I just think you need to have someone who can keep an eye on you for the next few days. And no, it's not because you agreed to read things for me, though once you're feeling better, I'd still like your help. I'm not expecting anything near as intense as what you already saw." He fell silent, allowing the young man a moment to ponder things.

With a sigh, Elliot glanced at his hands, which were carefully clasped in his lap and gloveless—he wouldn't be wearing that wrecked pair of gloves again. He was clearly struggling, but with what? The young man probably had trust issues, not that Derwin could blame him. Would it have helped to admit that Derwin also wanted him close for selfish reasons? Just because it *felt* right, having Elliot around? Or would that scare him off?

Derwin wasn't sure, so he didn't speak.

Elliot clenched his hands into fists, scowling at nothing in particular, then looked back up. "Okay. For a few days. But I have to get in touch with Theresa. She needs to know what happened to me in case they decide to target anybody else."

The urge to wrap up this prickly but vulnerable man in his arms was getting even stronger, but Derwin settled for a terse nod. "Not a problem. You can use my cell phone." He handed it over, still not trusting himself to stand too close. He knew Elliot was hurting, but gods, he wanted to touch him. Wanted to just take him away, and—

Elliot was staring at him, and Derwin flushed. "I'll just pop out for a moment." Elliot probably needed a little privacy to talk.

Derwin took a step, but Elliot stopped him. "You can stay." He chuckled painfully, his shoulders slumped, his expression open and vulnerable. "Not like you wouldn't hear me in the hall anyway." He opened the phone and fed it a number, then lifted it to his ear. After a few seconds, he said, "Theresa? Yeah, it's me." He winced. "I'm in the hospital."

Part of Derwin wanted to turn away, not to witness the shame and guilt that was passing over Elliot's face. But that part of him was overridden by another, a part that wanted to know what made Elliot tick. *Take it easy. You'll have at least a day or two with him. Maybe more.* Still, he couldn't have torn his gaze from him for anything at the moment.

Whatever Theresa said must not have been pretty, for Elliot scowled. He scooted to the edge of the gurney, but then pain flashed across his face. "Yeah. Busted rib, knock to the head, big ole bruise on my leg. It was those fucking low ranks. I'm fine—" He grimaced, and Derwin did hear the woman this time, shouting about hurting somebody. He couldn't help but smile. Those boys were earning new enemies by the minute.

"I'm *fine*," Elliot repeated after a pause. "But the doctors want me monitored, you know, because of the head thing. The—uh—bounty hunter brought me, and he's offered me his place to hole up for a few days until Yoshiro gets his boys under control." Pausing, Elliot listened, and glanced at Derwin. This look wasn't like his others. He looked . . . sad?

Elliot eyed his ripped jeans again. "I know. And I will." He sighed. "I just need you to call Roy. I'm not going to be fit for, you know. Probably not for a couple weeks." He kicked at the gurney. "Yeah, I understand. He'll be *pissed*."

Who's Roy? Derwin mouthed, but Elliot didn't appear to notice him. Derwin had a feeling he knew the answer: The Tatsu drug lord, who was supposed to be fucking and laying his marks all over Elliot next week. Derwin turned to hide his grimace and tried to tell the ugly feeling in his stomach to go away.

Elliot wasn't his.

He studied the medical diagrams on the wall as Elliot promised to call her back later to check in, gave her Derwin's address, and then hung up. Derwin pressed the space between his brows with his thumb, trying to stave off the headache that was beginning to pound in his temples. Lack of food, undoubtedly. Either that or the rage that was still bubbling under the surface.

At Elliot's hiss, Derwin spun, and nearly had to catch him as Elliot tried to stand on his battered leg. If he held on to Elliot for a few seconds more than strictly necessary, it was only because he needed to know that Elliot was okay. This situation had become complicated very quickly.

Elliot looked up at him as he handed back the phone. "Theresa's going to send someone over to your place with a few things for me." He rubbed a hand up Derwin's stomach, sending a hot thrill through him. Something wicked danced in Elliot's eyes. "Take me there."

CHAPTER TWELVE

FULL DISCLOSURE

Elliot was lucky to be able to fill his prescription in the hospital pharmacy. They gave him acetaminophen and oxycodone, the latter to be taken only after twenty-four hours had passed. Once in the car, Derwin insisted on stopping by a late-night taco place. Elliot wasn't hungry, but he ordered some rolled tacos with guacamole just because it felt strange not to get something. Plus he really liked them.

It was nearly midnight when they reached Derwin's place. Derwin petted the cat as they brought the food into the kitchen and sat down to eat. Elliot bit into the greasy rolled taco, savoring the taste. Ironic that he'd wanted to stay before, and now Derwin had needed to talk him into spending another night here. Across the kitchen table, Derwin was wolfing down his second burrito. They weren't small ones; the guy must burn thousands and thousands of calories a day to stay in shape.

Derwin noticed Elliot watching him. "What? I haven't eaten anything since this morning." He took another bite and swallowed.

Elliot chuckled, wiping his mouth. "Sorry that I held things up for you." The evening had gone all wrong. His head hurt, especially at the back where he'd hit the concrete. Every breath sent daggers through his rib cage. Still, he was happy not to be in a hospital bed, and not just because of the cost. Places like that freaked him out, given the possibility of discovery, and the kinds of psychic imprints that must be there.

"Don't worry about it. I'm glad I found you when I did." Derwin polished off the last bite, licking his fingers. "Don't do that to me again. I almost had a heart attack."

Elliot blinked at the sight. Something about the unabashed openness really set his blood humming. He reached for a glass of water to ease his parched throat. "Oh come on. You barely know me." All this help and concern was freaking him out. When was the last time somebody had given a damn? Oh right. Theresa.

Derwin's eyes bore into Elliot's, all fun and games gone. "I'm serious. I don't care if we've only had one night together. I was worried. Be safe."

The moment stretched on, unbearably. This time Elliot couldn't blame his rib for the tightness in his chest. He coughed and grimaced, rubbing his side. When Derwin's intense look was replaced by concern, he was almost glad. Derwin's focus was both exhilarating and frightening.

Elliot peered down at his torn and bloody shirt. "I need a shower." *I really need you to fuck me again too, but that's probably not happening.* He resisted the urge to adjust his jeans that had grown uncomfortably taut.

"God! Me too. I had to wrestle with a demon today." Derwin stretched out his arms, joints popping. The motion also made the bottom of his T-shirt ride up over his toned abs, giving Elliot a glimpse of dark hair traveling down from his navel. That shower was sounding better and better.

Then Derwin's words caught up with him. "Demon?" Elliot realized for the first time that he wasn't the only one bearing scratches and signs of a scuffle. "What— You mean—"

Derwin laughed. "Yeah. I'm a bounty hunter, remember? I hunt bond jumpers and demons too. Good money. Lots of trouble." He stood and set about cleaning up the kitchen, wiping down a sparkling gas stove that looked like it'd never been used.

Elliot's mind whirled. Hunting demons went beyond most humans' skills. Again he wondered about that flash he'd seen in Derwin's eyes during their scene, his ease with Elliot's Oddity. "You caught it?"

Pouring out an old pot of coffee, Derwin smirked. "Sure did. Nasty little fucker too—*nukekubi*. The kind that detaches its head to feed." He sponged off the table and then held out a hand for Elliot's trash.

"Where was it?" Just the thought of encountering something like that made Elliot nauseous. He handed over his garbage, then watched as Derwin threw it away.

"By the docks and warehouses. I actually found it in its human form hanging out with some hookers on Oceanside Street. They had no idea."

Elliot stared at Derwin in horror. That wasn't far from his place. He might even know the girls. "Was anybody hurt?"

Derwin leaned back against the counter with a dishrag in his hand. "Couple of dockworkers killed over the past few weeks. That's all, as far as I know. Anyways, it's dead now."

"That's a relief." Elliot realized his hands were shaking. It was always scary to hear tales of demons killing people in his area, and the endorphins and adrenaline from earlier were wearing off. The acetaminophen hadn't touched most of the pain, which would likely be worse tomorrow. "I think I need to lie down." He just wished he could breathe properly.

Derwin moved quickly to his side, leaving the dishrag in the sink. "You can use the shower upstairs. And we're sleeping in the same bed since I'm supposed to wake you every few hours to check on you. Try to take shallow breaths—it may hurt less."

Nodding, Elliot eased himself out of the chair, too hurt and tired to argue. Plus, he wanted to sleep next to Derwin again, so any excuse was good. They headed upstairs, and when they reached the bedroom, he sat down gingerly at the end of the bed, careful not to touch anything but his own clothing. His calf throbbed just from the short climb up the stairs.

Derwin stepped into the bathroom, while Elliot started to undress. As he removed his shirt, pain shot through his ribs and he bit back a cry. *Fucking rib!* He let out a breath, and heard a hiss. Derwin was facing the running shower, tapping his foot, his arms folded. Elliot cocked his head. *Okay, that's weird.* And wasn't it funny how Derwin had mentioned his breathing, even though he hadn't said anything about the throbbing in his rib?

A wild idea came to him. He jabbed a finger into the bruise on his calf, sending pain flaring through it. Derwin clutched his stomach like he was going to be ill, his gaze still directed toward the shower.

That couldn't be coincidence. "What is this?"

Derwin looked back at him and frowned. "Excuse me?"

Elliot stood, even though the action made him hurt all over. He limped forward a few paces. "You. This." He jabbed at his rib this time, biting his cheek against the agony, and caught a slight hitch in Derwin's breath. "You're sensing my pain somehow. You're an Oddity." If he sounded accusatory, he was justified. He'd spilled his deepest secret to this near-stranger. Time for Derwin to reciprocate.

Steam began to rise from the shower; Derwin sighed and stepped over to adjust the nozzle before facing Elliot and pulling off his shirt. "Yes. I am." The shirt landed on the ground, quickly followed by his jeans. Elliot saw new scratches and bruises that hadn't been there last night.

His casual confession only incensed Elliot more. "Why didn't you say so earlier? What are you, an Empath?" He longed to undress and join the man, but felt betrayed. No wonder Derwin had said he was fine with Oddities!

Derwin's mouth made a tight line as he shook his head. "Not exactly." He stripped out of his briefs. "Can we talk about this later?"

"Why didn't you tell me before? When I told you?" Ire turned to concern as Elliot tried to see if there were any other injuries on Derwin that maybe the guy was trying to ignore. Elliot eased his own jeans down, steeling himself as he bent over to remove them. The pain nearly overwhelmed him, and he gasped, but before he could fall or lose his balance, Derwin was there to support him as he pulled off the torn clothing.

Carefully, Elliot straightened. This time he definitely saw a slight glow in Derwin's eyes before it faded. "What are you?" He looked normal enough. Gods, he looked like human perfection at the moment, all dusky skin, muscle, and the tattoos that Elliot so loved.

Derwin offered him an arm, helping him over to the shower. "An Oddity, just like you said. Only unlike object reading, mine runs pretty consistently in families. Sensing pain is part of it."

"Odd—ty," Elliot murmured, leaning against Derwin, unable to hold on to anger. Derwin had picked him up near-dead on the street and helped him instead of calling the authorities. He supposed he could give the guy a pass on not telling him sooner. Elliot stepped under the spray and whimpered as the hot water hit the scratches, before Derwin adjusted the temperature.

"The heat might be good for sore muscles, right?" Elliot asked, rinsing away some of the blood stuck in his hair.

Maneuvering into the shower, Derwin steadied him with a hand on his back, then closed the glass door. "Yes. But not too much heat. Here—you just concentrate on standing. Let me help you."

Elliot nodded, closing his eyes. The dizziness had returned. Derwin's touch was gentle but firm as he scrubbed the dirt from Elliot's back and his hair, taking extra care around the bruises and cuts. As Elliot allowed himself to be washed, he tried to force his brain to work. Derwin could sense pain. An Oddity that ran in his family. There was speculation that all Oddities were hereditary, but even with the Human Genome Mapping Project delving into the mysteries behind genetic code, science hadn't figured out what caused Oddities to manifest. Supposedly, however, some Oddities were more dominant in the population than others. His own talent was pretty rare.

Derwin knelt down and began working on his abused calf. Elliot whimpered, torn between the pain from his injuries and the arousal from being bathed so tenderly. When Derwin chuckled, Elliot opened his eyes and glanced down.

"That's much better." Derwin glided his hands over Elliot's ass, around to his hardening cock, his expression blissful. The pain *was* better, and Elliot wanted to enjoy what Derwin was doing, but he was so tired. He began to droop, his legs shaking.

Instantly, Derwin straightened, supporting him around the waist. "Hang in there. Let's get you rinsed off."

"But you need to wash off too." Elliot hated how weak his voice was, how far away.

"Just take me a second," Derwin assured him, swiping himself with the washcloth, keeping at least some part of himself in contact with Elliot the entire time. Elliot turned up the heat, letting it soak into his muscles as the water rinsed away the soap. Way too long a day.

If Derwin didn't like others' pain, why engage in sadomasochism? That didn't make sense.

Elliot's mind drifted, until Derwin turned off the water. Blinking, he let Derwin help him out of the shower and dry him off. Bedtime: it sounded so good right now.

"Why do you like pain play if you can sense pain?" He was hardly aware of asking it out loud until Derwin stared at him.

"In bed," Derwin ordered, guiding him. Elliot took the help gratefully, and soon found himself lying down on sheets that still smelled faintly of last night's activities. "Are you going to be all right without your gloves?"

Elliot nodded, wishing Derwin would answer his question. "If I get any visions, they'll be fainter than they were the first time. Little ones don't give me headaches." He yawned. "Besides, I liked most of those visions." The images of sex and lovemaking were a world better than torture and murder.

Nodding, Derwin slid into bed beside him, apparently comfortable in his nakedness. He rested on his side, facing Elliot but not touching him. "It's because I feed on it. Pain, I mean. You've heard of the Incubus Oddity?"

It took a few seconds for Elliot's brain to catch up. He stared at Derwin's muscled chest. If Derwin was a sexual Oddity, he fit the role well. "Yeah. They feed on lust and sex." He'd fantasized about being taken by one—or even a group of them. Supposedly they not only fed on pleasure; they increased it. Of course there were also horror stories about them actually killing people through sex.

Derwin seemed pleased. "Right. Well, my Oddity is like that. Only instead of my abilities being amped up by sexual pleasure, they're amped up by pain." He looked at Elliot meaningfully.

Amping up . . . Elliot's eyes grew wide. "So you're like superhuman."

He received a shrug in reply. "I'm faster, stronger, and more agile when I've recharged, so to speak. I wouldn't say superhuman. Bullets will kill me as easily as anyone else." He ran his thumb over the back of Elliot's hand.

As he did so, however, Elliot realized that he *had* heard of Derwin's kind before. *Interrogators.* Nightmarish tales from his parents. Interrogators sensed pain, and they fed on it. Everyone knew the government used them to torture and pull secrets out of people.

"Interrogators! You're a—" But before he could finish, Derwin rose up in bed, shaking his head vehemently.

"I'm not."

"But—" Elliot tried to say, but Derwin held two fingers to his lips.

"I'm not an Interrogator. Neither is my dad. Not all of us go into that line of work." Derwin's tone was completely serious. More than that, his mouth was drawn down in disgust. Elliot nodded, and swallowed as Derwin pulled back his hand.

"But it's the same Oddity." Elliot made it a statement, not a question. When Derwin's face darkened, he knew he was right.

Derwin returned to stroking up and down Elliot's arm, almost as if to calm himself. Elliot couldn't complain; it felt nice. Sleepiness dragged at his senses, lulling him, but he forced himself to stay awake.

"It's the same Oddity," Derwin confirmed, eyes down. Then he looked up. "But we're not all sick and twisted. Pain like that— unwillingly given, harmful . . ." He blanched. "It makes me ill. I find it disgusting." The stroking became a caress, moving from Elliot's arm to his back, then his hip. Elliot gasped as Derwin's fingers trailed over his thighs.

"I prefer my pain to be willingly given, and sexual in nature. I want it mixed with pleasure." Derwin's voice was low and heated, the vibrations traveling straight to Elliot's cock. "So maybe I'm a mixture of both Oddities. I don't know."

A sexual sadist who actually *fed* off pain. Yeah, he could accept that. No wonder they'd done so well during that fight with Crew Cut. Each wound Derwin delivered had strengthened him.

"Well that's not too bad," Elliot agreed, wanting him to do more. Sadly his body wasn't going to cooperate. His lids were closing, and he gave a huge yawn. "Sorry."

Derwin's hand shifted to his brow, brushing back his hair. "Hey, don't worry. I'm just trying to distract you a little. I'll be honest: I want you. But you're in no shape for anything at the moment." Elliot felt Derwin reach across him for the night table. "I'm setting an alarm for three hours. Get some sleep."

Elliot wished he'd go back to touching him, but supposed certain things had to be done. "Are you going to sleep with me?"

"I'll try. I'm tired, but you're sending me waves of energy." Derwin smirked, and his eyes crinkled. "Kind of makes it hard to sleep. Imagine drinking about ten cups of coffee and then trying to snooze."

If he did that, Elliot would be bouncing off the walls and jittery as hell. "Hold me?" He just wanted—needed contact. The attack felt too near.

He sighed as Derwin moved closer and wrapped his arms around him. *Yes. Better.* Even though he wanted to stay awake and enjoy being snuggled like this, his body was shutting down, exhaustion winning out.

Laying his head on Derwin's chest, Elliot slept.

CHAPTER THIRTEEN

PLANS AND DIVERSIONS

At about 4 a.m. Derwin's phone beeped, waking him from a light doze. He had to disentangle himself from Elliot to shut off the alarm.

Elliot didn't even wake up.

Not surprising after the beating he'd had, though. In the darkness, Derwin snuggled against him and allowed himself to exalt in the feel of him for the moment. Elliot had taken the news of Derwin's Oddity better than expected. So what happened now?

Stop fooling yourself. He's not going to turn into a tame pussy cat just because you're growing attached to him. Derwin sighed. The last thing he needed was to fall in love with someone he couldn't have. But when had his heart ever listened to logic?

It was his damned protective instincts. That had to be it. He saw in Elliot someone who needed to be rescued, someone who needed his strength. But that was no basis for a relationship.

As soon as he solved Grady's murder, his heart and brain would be normal again. Then he could start to look for someone new. Elliot had already stated that he didn't require Derwin to watch over him.

Except, of course, that he did.

Letting out a breath, Derwin nudged Elliot awake before his warring sides could duke it out any more. Long lashes fluttered, and with a groan, Elliot opened his eyes.

"Hey, gorgeous." A thrill went through Derwin as those deep-blue eyes fixed on him. Holy fuck, but the man was pretty. Unfortunately, he couldn't let himself be distracted, for Elliot's sake. Time to run through the doctor's checklist. "Tell me your name."

Elliot blinked. "Elliot," he said, and then tried to sit up. His face went white, and he clutched his side, hissing as he fell back against the bed. "Fuck!"

Derwin sucked in a breath as Elliot's pain struck him like he'd touched a live wire.

Definitely worse than it had been a few hours ago. "I'll get you acetaminophen in a moment," Derwin assured him. "Just a couple more questions. What day is today? And where are you?"

Elliot frowned. "May third," he said at last, craning to look at the clock. "Jesus, it's four in the morning? Really?"

Good enough. "Yeah. Your friendly three-hour wake-up call." He set his phone alarm to go off in another three hours and reached for the bottle of pills. "Your head is fine." The kid had a thick skull. But, oh, his rib and various bruises were not.

Elliot nodded, then grimaced. "Stomach's nauseous though. I don't know if it's the pain or what. Also, breathing sucks."

"Just a moment." Derwin left the bed and went to the bathroom to grab a cup, filling it with water. Returning, he handed Elliot a couple of pills, holding the glass for him. "Try taking those." As Elliot did so, he added, "You think you can sleep a bit more?"

With a sigh, Elliot stretched. "I'm sore. If I could get comfortable, then yeah. Maybe." He looked up at Derwin. "What's today's plan?"

Distraction. That was what Elliot needed. Happily, it was something Derwin could provide. Crawling back under the covers, he trailed a hand along Elliot's hip, down his thigh. He resisted the temptation to do more. "I'm driving out to Mephist Penitentiary later—it's a two-hour drive. You're coming with me. We're going to interview Lloyd Brunson, and then we're going to have dinner with my parents and stay the night there."

Elliot's eyes nearly bugged out. "We're *what*? Your parents? Why?"

Derwin fought the urge not to laugh. "You seem more afraid of my folks than the prison. It's because they don't get to see me very often. Plus it's dangerous to drive back here in the dark, and I don't feel like having to fight off demons on the road, especially with you injured. I'm supposed to be keeping an eye on you."

"What do I say to your parents? Are they going to make us sleep in different beds or what?"

It occurred to Derwin that Elliot had spent the last few years dealing only with the dregs of society, the outcasts and the criminals. Even his clients were breaking the law. He had probably forgotten how to function in regular company. "I already told you, they're cool with me, so you'll sleep wherever you want to sleep. It might be awkward to mention your occupation, but don't feel like you have to lie to them. They can deal with it." He took Elliot's hand and squeezed it. "My mom goes a little overboard sometimes. She'll try to stuff you with food. Other than that, they're cool."

Elliot's shoulders relaxed. "And your dad's . . ."

"Like me," Derwin finished for him, with a nod. "Yeah. He works at the prison as a correctional officer, so we may run into him there."

Elliot stared at him for a moment, but said nothing. Instead, he moved Derwin's hand to his crotch, where he appeared to be suffering with a case of morning wood. "Distract me," he pleaded, arching up against the touch. "I need more sleep, but I can't."

Derwin sucked in a breath, his own cock stirring as his hand explored the hard ridge under the sheets. Part of him balked at the idea, even though earlier he'd been for it. How was he supposed to remember that it was meant to be pure business with Elliot if they had sex at every opportunity? If he let the physical relationship continue, he'd want to have Elliot all to himself. Then again, there might not be another opportunity. He craved the sex. Gods, he craved *Elliot*, and whatever the young man was willing to give him. Maybe he'd have to be satisfied with just the occasional play session, allowing Elliot to keep his freedom, his work as a rentboy.

Then again, maybe something beyond play partner was an option.

Fuck it. Derwin pulled off the sheets and covered Elliot with his body. He pressed his erection against Elliot's, and their cocks rubbed and slid alongside each other. Elliot moaned, his eyes closing and head falling back. He opened his legs wider to give Derwin access, clearly begging to be taken.

It wasn't a good idea to do anything rough right now, unfortunately, but Derwin could still come up with something suitably distracting. He worked his way down, kissing Elliot's body until he was nestled between those slender legs with a hard, weeping cock in his face that was just begging for attention. Elliot kept himself shaven. Probably cleaner to play with, not that Derwin minded.

Elliot's cock slid down his throat so easily, so naturally.

Derwin enjoyed sucking cock. The taste of the pre-come. The feel of the flared head on his tongue; both sent his blood straight to his groin. The sighs Elliot made as Derwin licked from base to tip were pretty damned nice as well. Derwin wanted to push him over the edge, to drink him down, then to watch Elliot swallow him, watch those pretty red lips on his dusky cock.

Sliding a hand between Elliot's legs, Derwin played with his balls, and worked his tongue over and around the hood of his cock, moving the foreskin back and forth. Elliot grabbed Derwin's shoulder, as if anchoring himself. His breath was coming in harsh little pants. Briefly, Derwin wondered if the broken rib was going to mess with their fun. Still Elliot's sighs remained nothing but encouraging.

Derwin progressed from tonguing Elliot's slit to sucking on his balls, first one and then the other. There was a strangled groan in response.

"Derwin . . . you're killing me here," Elliot whined, his short fingernails digging into Derwin's shoulder.

"You don't need my permission." He slowly stroked Elliot as he lavished attention on his balls, before finally returning to his cock. He worked Elliot's cock deep into his throat, loving the feel of it, loving the little pulses in his own cock that reminded him he, too, was in serious need here.

Elliot's hands combed through Derwin's hair, urging him on. He didn't thrust, but his thigh muscles contracted and relaxed, as if he was fighting the urge. *Gods, that's hot.*

To tease him further, Derwin wrapped his fingers around the base, stroking there in time with his mouth. He could feel the vein on the underside pulsing. Concentrating on the head, Derwin pumped Elliot's shaft until Elliot came with a cry, grabbing handfuls of Derwin's hair. The first splash of come hit the back of his throat, then he went shallow to taste the next one on his tongue. Derwin sucked gently on the head until he'd gleaned the last drop.

As he let go and sat up, he felt a shudder go through Elliot, accompanied by a moan. He smirked, ridiculously pleased with himself. "Better?"

"Fucking hell. You're good at that." Elliot sounded both sleepy and satisfied.

Lazily Derwin stretched out beside him, sliding his hands down to his own erection, pulling on it. "I like to think so, thanks."

The sight of that lean, youthful body next to him, the bliss in Elliot's eyes, together with the memory of sucking him . . . it wasn't going to take much to reach his own peak at this point.

Elliot's gaze traveled downward. He tried to sit up, but then hissed and lay back down, grimacing. "I want to help."

"No," Derwin said immediately. The last thing Elliot needed was for the pain in his rib to flare up again and undo what Derwin had just done. "You can watch, and then you will sleep. And so will I." He pulled a little harder on his cock, groaning under his breath at the sharp, shooting pleasure it produced. "You're welcome to help another time, when you're not hurt."

Elliot pouted but complied, lying placidly with no attempt to cover himself or his slowly softening cock, and sighed as Derwin fisted himself. "I enjoy watching." He blinked. "I haven't been asked just to watch in ages."

Derwin had hoped to avoid the whole prostitution subject, at least for a little while. Given that Elliot was a rentboy, he could forgive him for making Derwin's words sound like a client request. Then again, there had been no mention of money for the sex this evening.

So he ignored the comment, focusing instead on stroking himself, and on watching Elliot's face, especially his eyes. Too often Elliot appeared jaded, but right now he wore an expression almost like awe. Derwin's breath caught in his throat as he increased his pace, his body demanding it. He imagined pounding into Elliot's sweet hole again, their faces close together, as Elliot tipped over the edge.

Derwin forced his lids to stay open as waves of ecstasy hit him and hot jism spilled over his hand; what turned the orgasm into something incredible was the excitement in Elliot's eyes. As his climax went on and on, Derwin finally had to shut his eyes, slowly pumping himself until the sensations passed. He let out a slow breath, shuddering.

When he opened his eyes once more, Elliot was grinning at him.

"Better?" Elliot asked, and Derwin nodded, smirking. He reached for a couple of tissues to clean himself up, then adjusted his position so that he was facing Elliot. Languor settled over him, along with a nice buzz. What pain Elliot was still experiencing was tinted with enough pleasure to make it palatable again.

"Think I'm ready to sleep some more. You?" Derwin asked, stifling a yawn. Outside, the streets would start to lighten soon, but with the curtains closed, it should remain dark in his bedroom for another couple of hours. No need to rise so early.

Elliot yawned as well and snuggled closer. "Think so. Tired." With an ease that Derwin envied, he drifted off, and it wasn't long before he began to snore.

It could only be good that Elliot'd grown comfortable enough to trust Derwin, right? Derwin would need that trust as they started searching through the list of possible suspects. He'd never done an investigation like this before.

As he tried to sleep, his thoughts were already on the following day. *What will I ask Lloyd?*

CHAPTER FOURTEEN

MEPHIST

In the morning, it took them two hours to haul themselves out of bed and get on the road. Elliot moved stiffly and complained of a headache, so Derwin allowed him half an oxycodone, though technically they were supposed to wait twenty-four hours before using it. Neither of them would be much good if he was walking around in agony. Derwin was already so wound up that he'd explode if he had to endure much more of the constant nourishment from Elliot's pain without expending the energy in some way. He knew he should be letting Elliot take it easy, wait a day before making the trip. But now that he'd learned additional details about the murder, he just couldn't wait. Still, he wouldn't have Elliot read any objects until he was doing better.

While they were packing an overnight bag, the doorbell rang, and Derwin found a boy on the porch with a small knapsack tucked under one arm—Elliot's things. The kid, no more than thirteen or fourteen years old, stayed long enough for Derwin to hand him ten dollars, then he ran off, waving farewell.

Elliot gratefully changed into a clean pair of jeans, a black T-shirt, and a fresh pair of leather gloves. Derwin decided on a button-down shirt to look more professional, and after much internal debate, he settled for jeans rather than slacks. Suits had never felt right to him.

After a stop to gas up and grab breakfast, they headed east toward the outskirts of town, passing gated communities and area watchtowers. They drove through a fenced checkpoint and left information with the Federation Security Force about their destination and expected return date.

Then Derwin drove into the thickly forested wilderness.

The way started out paved but soon became a poorly maintained dirt road; even that had cost men to build. One of the greatest achievements, as well as greatest hazards for the nation, was its road system built in the demon-infested wasteland between cities, which was only made possible through military escorts and support. They were fortunate to have the largest national armed forces in the world.

Though the government did a lot to protect the citizens from the demons that had overrun the world during World War II, he still wasn't comfortable about the power the administration had, and the way it sometimes used that power.

"I've never been outside Nis," Elliot said quietly as the vintage muscle car bumped along on the narrow street and up over a hill. Derwin kept his eyes open for anything unusual. Not all monsters were nocturnal.

"Yeah? I actually grew up in Mephist." Derwin turned the wheel sharply to make it around the curve of a hill. He spotted freshly cut trees and logger huts just off the road and was relieved. If there were loggers in the woods today, there would be an armed escort too. Added safety.

Though he remained focused on the winding curves, Derwin could feel Elliot watching him. "What was that like?"

Derwin shrugged. "Small town where you knew pretty much everyone. My dad was the star quarterback for his high school team." He smirked. "I preferred wrestling. Won a few tournaments."

That earned him an amused snort. "Wrestling. Yeah, I can see that. Wouldn't have to do with grappling sweaty male bodies, would it?" There was just a slight slur to Elliot's speech, and he sounded relaxed for once. The painkillers were working.

Derwin chuckled. "Maybe." Outside, the pine and fir trees flew past as they bumped and wound their way through the forested hills.

A few minutes later, Derwin forced himself to speak, though he dreaded Elliot's reaction. "My parents know how much I've gotten involved in trying to find Grady's murderer. You mind if I tell them how you're helping? You know . . ." he raised a hand, touching the dashboard with exaggeration.

Elliot eyed him warily. "It's safe?"

"My secret's been safe, right? Plus my dad's always hidden his Oddity as well. Trust me: you're safe with them. My mom would fight a mountain lion to protect me and my friends."

That got a laugh. "I think I already like your mom."

They reached Mephist at noon. Security was tight, but as soon as he mentioned his parents, the guards greeted Derwin with a smile. He and Elliot passed through the palisade wall, made of tree trunks sharpened to vicious points, that ringed the entire town, including the fields of cows and sheep, and the local water tower that stood upon the forested hill. It looked like the wall had been repaired since the last time Derwin had been there. He smiled in nostalgia at the wooden houses with slanted roofs, little cabins with neatly paved roads connecting them. They made a quick stop for pizza at his favorite hole-in-the-wall, then drove to the prison, which was a few miles outside the town and located within its own walls of concrete and barbed wire.

Two armed guards stood at the compound's electronic gate, the first of three checkpoints that needed to be passed in order to visit Lloyd. Derwin rolled down his window and nodded at the burly man in a blue shirt and security badge who was approaching the car.

"Visiting or— Hey," the man began, then paused, staring at Derwin. "You're Jerry's kid, aren't you?"

Derwin smiled. "Yep. I'm actually here to visit an inmate, though. Lloyd Brunson."

The man frowned and rubbed at his thinning hair. "Whatever for? Friend of yours?" He glanced at Elliot, who appeared ready to crawl out the window. Derwin threw him an encouraging look, then turned back to the guard. "No. He was one of the skips I caught. I have a couple questions for him regarding something else I'm working on."

"Uh-huh," the guy said, still clearly mystified. "Right—sign in at the Visitors Checkpoint up there." He chuckled. "Don't forget to say hi to your pops. He's in D wing today."

"Will do, thanks," Derwin replied, and waited as the gates opened for him to drive forward.

It only took a few minutes to park and check in at the main security office. They had to endure a body search for drugs and weapons and gods knew whatever else visitors tried to sneak to inmates. Derwin kept a hand on Elliot, who had hardly said a word from the moment they'd entered the compound. He was even paler than usual, and Derwin wasn't sure if it was from exhaustion or fear; he looked like an animal in a trap. When Derwin grasped his wrist, he found Elliot's pulse racing. He tried to communicate via the touch that everything was fine; he wasn't going to leave him here! But it didn't seem to register. Elliot kept his gloved hands clasped in front of him and avoided eye contact with everyone.

The guards led them to the visitation area and pulled up an extra chair for Elliot so that they could sit together, facing the glass window. Once they were both seated, the guards retreated. Derwin whispered in Elliot's ear. "Shouldn't take long—everything's cool, okay? If you happen to remember anything from your vision while I'm interviewing him, tug on my sleeve and tell me."

The timing of Lloyd's threatening text had been suspicious, and for a while he'd wondered if the guy really was guilty. Now, with Elliot's vision, things appeared different. It didn't sound like Lloyd could have held a gun to Grady and sent the text all at once; nor had Elliot witnessed such a thing. That meant it had been someone else. Maybe.

Elliot gave a stiff nod.

There was movement from beyond the glass, and two guards escorted his old fugitive in, wearing a bright-orange jumpsuit with wrist and ankle cuffs. Lloyd sat down slowly, glaring at Derwin.

The past year hadn't been kind to Lloyd. He'd shaved his head, but there was gray stubble along his jawline and his pale crown. Big and broad, he still looked like he could pick up and carry the cars he'd been known for stealing, but there was a gauntness to him now.

Dark hollows showed beneath his eyes. When Derwin had captured him for the grand theft auto, Lloyd had nearly broken his restraints. Now he seemed worn down, harmless.

Well almost, anyway.

Derwin picked up the receiver, and Lloyd did the same, glowering like he wanted to kill him.

"Been a while, Lloyd. How are things?" Derwin kept his tone neutral. Calm. Even if he was gazing at his lover's killer, he wasn't going to get anywhere if the guy hung up on him.

"What's it to you? I'm doing ten for auto theft and resistin' arrest. Your boys shook me up good, thinkin' I was a killer 'n' all. An' my heart's been actin' up. How you think I'm doing?" Lloyd seemed prepared to slam the phone back onto the holder, but Derwin held up a hand, leaning forward.

"Hang on. I can get you some cash, perhaps a favor or two if you answer a few questions for me. My dad works here, you know. You might have seen him." He'd heard enough stories from his dad to have an idea about how things worked in the prison, what the inmates wanted and tried to get away with. From what he was seeing, Lloyd wasn't high in the ranks. He was probably miserable.

Lloyd frowned, but returned the receiver to his ear. "Such as?"

"Lighter chores. Recreation time. Conjugal visit?" Derwin counted to ten.

One corner of Lloyd's mouth turned up. Slightly. "Maybe. This have to do with that stupid murder they tried to pin on me?"

Another ten, and then five more to keep his blood pressure stable. *Stupid murder* that fucking ruined his life. "Yeah. I'm thinking that maybe you didn't do it after all. But I need to ask a few questions to clear you for good." The carrot was there. Now Lloyd just needed to reach for it.

Settling in his chair, Lloyd nodded. "Fire away."

Derwin allowed himself a tiny breath of relief. Then he inwardly winced. He wished he had case files, police reports, anything. All he had to go on was his own memory of how things had transpired. "So I recall them saying you had no alibi."

"I had an alibi." Lloyd grimaced, rubbing at his split lip.

"What was it?"

Lloyd stared at him without blinking. "Doing my job."

This guy's going to give me a headache. "You had no job."

Lloyd grinned. "Sure I did. Stealin' cars. That's what I was doing."

"Seriously?" Elliot said under his breath. Derwin wasn't sure whether to laugh or cry at the thought that the police had suspected this guy.

But he couldn't count Lloyd out just yet. "That's not much of an alibi. Were you alone?"

"Well what you think?" Lloyd rolled his eyes. Then he leaned forward. "But here's the thing. They almost caught me that night—some witness called the cops. I know that because I heard sirens coming, and I had to run and hide. That was way over on Seventy-fifth Street. I thought it was 'cause I sent you that text, 'member? I was pretty mad about you catching me the time before. So how could I have been chased on Seventy-fifth if I'd murdered someone in some other place? I never even knewed where you lived."

That was a good question. Derwin looked Lloyd square in the eye. "And what did the cops say to that?"

Lloyd leaned back, wiping his mouth like there was a bad taste in it. "Well they didn't charge me with it, did they? But I don't like the boot-prints thing. Almost like somebody was trying to frame me for it." He chewed a fingernail, falling silent. When the police had picked him up, Lloyd had been wearing similar boots to the prints found at the scene, same shoe size. The boot prints hadn't matched exactly, however. Without any physical evidence, the police hadn't been able to press a charge for murder.

Maybe it was far-fetched, but Derwin had to allow that it was possible Lloyd had been framed. He glanced at Elliot. "Anything to add? Anything familiar about him?" He indicated Lloyd with a nod.

Warily, Elliot scooted forward, sizing up Lloyd. He shook his head. "That's not the guy I saw. He's too broad, for one. And the guy's voice is totally wrong. Grady's killer sounded more educated than that."

Derwin nodded. So that took care of this suspect. Still, Lloyd's comment troubled him. Had someone tried to frame him? If so, who would have the kind of information to even try? He recalled Elliot's words during his vision. *"Tell me what you know!"*

What secrets had Grady been keeping that were worth getting killed over?

They finished their talk, and Derwin arranged for Lloyd to have some extra time in the recreation area of his choice, as well as a conjugal visit, if Lloyd had anyone on the outside to take him up on that offer. It helped that his dad worked there, and that he'd grown up with others who worked at the prison. Then they left the main cell block area and walked to Cell Block D, Death Row, where his father was working. Elliot continued to stay close, and Derwin sensed that his rib was troubling him again, but it was too soon for more painkillers. "We'll just say a quick hello to my dad, then we'll go to my parents' place. You can rest there."

Elliot gave him a nervous smile in response. They lingered inside the visitor area as one of the guards paged Jerry, but before Derwin had time to ponder whether there was anything he needed to warn Elliot about, the wait was over.

His father was about an inch shorter than Derwin, but he was even more solidly built, with a square jaw, cropped light-brown hair graying at the sides, and the same dark-brown eyes. Derwin smirked and waved as his dad headed over, noting that he hadn't let up any on his weight-lifting regime: his biceps were practically as big around as Elliot's thighs. With a grin, Dad opened his arms, and they hugged, slapping each other on the back.

After the embrace ended, Dad eyed Elliot with curiosity, a muted glow flashing in his eyes; he had to be picking up on Elliot's pain. Derwin had to push down a ridiculous wave of possessiveness. His dad couldn't help feeding off the pain either.

"Good to see you, boy," Dad said, returning his gaze to Derwin. "What's the occasion?" He grinned, a little too exuberantly in Derwin's opinion. Probably already coming to conclusions about Elliot and him.

Derwin took a breath. "I got some fresh information on Grady's murder. I came here to follow up on it and speak with Lloyd Brunson."

Instantly his dad's face darkened. "Information?"

The familiar lump formed in Derwin's throat, the familiar ache in his chest from thinking about Grady's death. Meeting Elliot had been a wonderful distraction. But gods, he still missed Grady. "Yeah. Let me introduce you to Elliot here." He touched a hand to Elliot's shoulder, claiming him, then leaned in close and whispered in his dad's ear. "He's an Object Reader."

Even greater interest showed on his dad's face. "That so?" He reached out and nodded at Elliot's gloved hands as they shook. Elliot smiled cautiously. Inspecting him more closely, Jerry hissed and narrowed his eyes. "Busted rib?"

Elliot glanced at Derwin. "I— Yeah. Last night." He took a step closer to Derwin.

A million questions had to be bubbling in his dad's head. Derwin decided to address the first ones head-on. "Elliot's been on the streets most his life. I met him in a bar the day before yesterday. And he saw the whole thing, Dad. Grady's murder. You know, in a vision." *Yes, he's a whore. Yes, he was in my bedroom.* "I found him again last night after he had a run-in with the Tatsu gang."

Hs dad blew out a breath. "Rough bunch." He seemed to be taking things pretty well. The slight frown he gave Derwin said he'd want more explanation later, however.

Elliot on the other hand seemed about ready to crawl into a hole. "Um, yeah. Would've done better, but there were like six of them." He cast Derwin a pleading look.

His dad snorted good-naturedly. "You both staying the night?" He didn't have to say where. There was only one place Derwin would stay in Mephist if he didn't want hysterics from his mother.

"Yep."

His dad cocked one eyebrow. "Your mother know?"

Derwin bit his lip sheepishly. "I haven't called her yet."

This time both eyebrows went up. "You should. I think she's making stew for dinner. Hope there's enough."

This time Derwin grinned. His mother might yell at him for not telling her sooner, but she'd be happy to see him nonetheless. She always made enough stew to feed an army anyways. "I'll do that. You off at five?"

Jerry grunted and nodded, checking his watch. "Gotta get back. But we'll be talking." His tone allowed for no argument. He flashed Elliot another smile, more calculating than the first, and headed toward the cell security door. Derwin saw him pass through, then turned to find Elliot glaring at him.

"What?"

Elliot poked him in the chest. "First, you need to wait until you're in private to mention some things about me. You know what I mean. And second, you enjoyed that. Watching me squirm."

Derwin's grin was impossible to keep at bay. "Well I am a sadist, after all." When the ire in Elliot's features threatened to break loose, he hastily added, "You did great. I told you he wouldn't care about who or what you are anyway." He shrugged. "I think he was simply happy to see me with another guy, period." It had been a long two years.

Elliot didn't look swayed. "His eyes do the same glowy thing as yours."

"You're in pain. He senses it, just like I do. Nothing to worry about, trust me." He glanced to make sure no one was listening, but the guards were ignoring them, making their rounds.

Elliot let out a slow breath. "Okay. But I feel really weird here. Can we go now?"

The urge to put his arm around Elliot tugged at Derwin, but he forced it away. Even though his dad worked here, the prison was still a dangerous place to reveal secrets—of any kind. "We're going," Derwin agreed, and began leading him back toward the car.

One suspect down. Now he just had to figure out who the real murderer was.

CHAPTER FIFTEEN

HOME SWEET HOME

Elliot didn't relax until they exited the gate leaving Mephist Penitentiary, heading toward Derwin's parents' home. He cranked up the heat against the damp chill in the air that promised rain by nightfall. The lump on his head throbbed, and his whole side was burning. He dug into his pocket for the oxycodone and showed Derwin the half tablet before swallowing it, so that they could both keep track of his meds.

He wondered if the headache was from all the tension he'd been holding since they neared the jail. Of all the places he'd *never* wanted to see, a high-security prison in the middle of a demon-infested wilderness was up there at the top of the list. It came right after a government detention facility/torture chamber.

Shit, but that visit had rattled his nerves.

It wasn't just the possibility that he might someday end up locked away with the other criminals and likely passed around among them like a candy dish. That had been bad enough, but the measuring stares of the prison guards that had been on him wherever they went had been even worse. Derwin had seemed too preoccupied with his whole murder-investigation thing to notice, and Elliot had the feeling that if he hadn't stuck close to the man, a guard or prisoner would have found some means to force him to stay. To use and abuse him.

It didn't help that meeting Derwin's dad had left him with a few unsettling thoughts. "Your dad was feeding off me, wasn't he?" he asked as Derwin drove along the two-lane paved highway through dense forest. Morning had stretched into late afternoon, and lunch seemed far away. Hopefully they'd reach the house soon.

Derwin gave a shrug that might also have been a nod.

"Was it my imagination, or did he find me really interesting?" Interesting in the same way that one might find a new tech gadget interesting. Like he was an object, not a person.

Gripping the steering wheel harder, Derwin expelled a breath. "Yeah. He did." He squirmed in his seat. "Look . . . right now I'm so charged up that it's making me a little crazy. And cranky. Like I told you earlier, I usually go hunting after being exposed to your kind of pain. So, I know you have questions, but I'm not sure I can answer them at the moment." He grimaced, shaking his head. "There's something else I should let you know. My parents have been trying to get me to start dating again for the last year. Be prepared—they may give you the third-degree." He grinned awkwardly.

"I knew it." Elliot groaned. Still, while he wasn't looking forward to it, he appreciated that Derwin was keeping him filled in. He *liked* Derwin, despite this crazy trip and the prospect of nosy parents. Despite Derwin's warning, Elliot had faith that he'd intervene if things became too uncomfortable.

They drove in silence for a few minutes, then Derwin spoke up again. "So I'm trying to make a list in my head about who could have killed Grady. Sounds like he was hiding information, even from me."

Elliot didn't need a pain-sensing ability to hear the hurt in Derwin's voice.

"Must've been something really bad. Maybe he wanted to protect you?" It would have been great if Grady had just thought about whoever or whatever it was in the vision. "I could try to read other objects in your house. Stuff only he touched."

Derwin's eyes didn't leave the road, but he muttered, "Grady should have known that I could help him. He should have trusted me." Elliot remained silent, and after a few minutes, Derwin sighed. "The cops have his cell phone—evidence, they said, even though it was smashed to hell. His computer and gaming console were stolen. He often used the TV, but I've touched that too many times. Maybe the desk? I don't use it much. I only have pictures and a few personal items of his. His sister would have anything else." He blinked. "We should talk to his sister. She's a drug addict. Grady was always trying to get her clean, going on about her hanging out with some low-life guy. Maybe he had something to do with it."

Elliot tried to think back to the vision, to see if he could sense any connection. "Sounds like a good place to start. Did Grady have any possible criminal ties?"

"Not that I know of." Derwin seemed dejected. Small wonder, considering.

Elliot gently rubbed his shoulder. "We'll figure it out."

Derwin clearly wasn't going to have any peace until he had answers.

Derwin pulled in to the driveway of a simple wooden cabin with lace curtains on the windows and manicured juniper bushes beside a small bed of geraniums and tiny white flowers. As soon as they exited the car, the front door opened and a husky woman, possibly of Italian descent, strode up, wearing jeans and a Western-style shirt. She only came to Derwin's chin, but she cuffed him across the cheek with an angry glare. Elliot winced.

"That's for not phoning me ahead of time!" she announced, and then her demeanor changed completely. With a laugh, she grinned and hugged Derwin hard enough that Elliot expected to hear his ribs crack. "And that's for coming out to see us! You don't visit often enough!" She slapped him on the back, reminding Elliot of Derwin's father, then she turned to Elliot.

Derwin clearly took after his father physically, but his mother's impact was apparent in Derwin's emotions and his smile. Her exuberant personality made Elliot dizzy.

She stared at Elliot expectantly, shrewd eyes taking in everything. Elliot felt awkward in his tight jeans with scratches and bruises on his face. He opened his mouth, uncertain what to say, and then Derwin laid a hand on his shoulder, much like he'd done earlier when Elliot had met his father. "Mom, this is Elliot—Elliot Leed. He's working with me right now to hunt down some new leads on Grady's case. I know I should have called, but it all happened so quickly."

"Goodness' sakes." Derwin's mom took hold of one of Elliot's gloved hands, rubbing it as if trying to warm it. "And what happened to you? Find a lead that fought back?"

"Ran into some bad men." He blushed as she gently touched one of the bruises on his cheek. Did everyone in Derwin's family have such a lack of regard for other people's personal space?

"Mom, don't overwhelm him." Derwin stepped in between them, as if to protect Elliot. "He's been on the streets since he was fourteen. He was beat up by a bunch of gang members yesterday because he didn't want to play their games."

Well that was one way of putting it.

"The poor thing! I've got frozen peas I could put on those bruises—is he hurt elsewhere, Derwin? I also have some of that ointment—you know the one: your father uses it when he gets a little roughed up. Should help him heal faster." She raised Elliot's arms to inspect him as if she could see through his clothing. He blushed again and glared at Derwin.

Derwin gave him an apologetic look as he stepped out of the way. "That's actually a good idea. Oh—and careful. He's got a busted rib."

With that, Derwin reached into the car and brought out their overnight bag, leaving Elliot to his mother, who grabbed Elliot's hand and pulled him toward the house in a manner that allowed no argument. "On the streets since you were fourteen? Whatever went wrong? Here, I'll set you up in the kitchen. I just have to check the stew and get that ice pack and the ointment." She brought him over to the counter and pulled out a barstool for him, waiting until he sat down to bustle over to the stove. Behind him, Elliot heard the front door close as Derwin brought in their stuff.

He peered at the modest living space, and a thrill went through him. How long had it been since he'd been in a home like this? Not a downtown apartment, a cheap motel, or a tiny place like Theresa's, not even a penthouse suite like Yoshiro's, but a real home. Where families grew up and marriage actually meant something.

His chest grew tight, and he struggled to breathe against the sudden overwhelming memories: running through the house as a child, squealing with delight when his father chased after him only to grab him and tickle him on the floor. Mom baking cookies during the holidays. Arguing over the TV remote with his little brother.

He blinked away the burning moisture in his eyes as Derwin came up beside him, rocking on his heels. A glance at the man showed that

Elliot wasn't the only one having issues. That nervous energy was still there in Derwin's movements, as well as the telltale golden glow in his dark irises.

Derwin expelled a breath, wringing his hands. "Mom, you're going to hate me. But I've gotta run."

She turned from where she'd been stirring the pot. "You just got here!"

To Elliot's relief, she'd apparently forgotten her earlier question. But his heart lurched at Derwin's words. He was *leaving*? As in leaving Elliot to fend for himself with his overzealous mother?

Derwin's smile appeared almost sickly. "I know. But if I don't go running right this instant, I think I'm going to explode." He gave Elliot a beseeching look. "It's too much energy all at once. I've got to release some of it."

Comprehension dawned on his mother's face, and she frowned. "Okay. When will you be back?"

"Before dark."

She crossed her arms. "And am I preparing one bed or two for tonight?"

It was a perfectly reasonable question. And yet, the blood surged to Elliot's face. How would Derwin answer? On the one hand, if they kept separate beds, they could make the excuse that they were merely working together at the moment. On the other hand, he wanted nothing more than to fall asleep in Derwin's arms.

"One," Derwin said, but not without a glance at Elliot, who couldn't stop the smile that sprang to his face. Screw the "working" relationship. Literally.

Derwin's mom barely blinked as she returned to stirring the pot. "Right. And you've got your blessed blade with you? Just in case."

Were infiltrations so common here? They could be. It wasn't like Nis was all that safe either.

"In my ankle sheath," Derwin answered glibly. He half turned and patted his pocket, presumably to check his wallet or phone, then headed for the door. By the time he reached it, he was already half running.

Once he'd left, Elliot regarded Derwin's mother with trepidation.

She let out a sigh, her gaze still on the door. Then she smiled at Elliot. "Well you're obviously in more pain than I realized. So let's take care of that before either him or his dad gets back here. Were you looked at? And did they give you any painkillers?" She opened up the freezer, brought out a pack of frozen peas, and offered it to him.

He took it and applied it to what hurt most at the moment—the lump on the back of his skull. "Yeah, Derwin took me to the hospital. They gave me a prescription, and I took half an oxycodone earlier, but I'm not supposed to take a full one until tonight. Concussion." A thought occurred to him. "What should I call you?"

"Mom, if you like. Or my name: Myrna." She was digging into a drawer and pulling out a small tube of cream. "This stuff does wonders for bruises. Derwin said you broke your rib. Are there bruises under your shirt?"

Elliot nodded, and grimaced as she motioned for him to take it off. "You really don't have to do this," he said, but set down the peas and pulled off the T-shirt, wincing at her gasp. "There were five or six of them," he explained, not meeting her eyes. He shouldn't have fallen into their trap in the first place.

"Tsk." Myrna inspected the marks on him, most a dark purple or bluish color, but given a day or two, they'd turn green and yellow. Squeezing cream into her hand, she set to rubbing it on him, concentrating on the worst bruises along his sides. "What were they doing? Kicking you with steel-toe boots?"

"Maybe." He held the frozen peas to his head again. "I don't remember everything. They *were* wearing boots. And I know I ended up on the ground." Myrna's attention felt nice.

She shook her head. "How did this all happen? You're going to have to tell me your life story, you know." She poked at his gloves. "You gonna take those off and stay a while?" Her tone was chiding but gentle, and Elliot experienced another moment of painful regret for the home and family he'd lost. Not that they had ever been like this.

How much to tell? He considered his gloves, then shrugged. Derwin would probably tell her anyways, and at least he knew Derwin's dad would sympathize as a fellow Oddity. "I'm an Object Reader—the gloves protect me from having visions I don't want. As for my life story . . ." He sighed. "My parents threw me out when I was fourteen."

Horror crossed Myrna's face. "Whatever for?"

He felt safe answering, given how she'd asked about their sleeping situation with such ease earlier. Elliot had to admit he was envious of Derwin. His mother would have burst into flames if he'd brought home a lover. "Because I'm gay. And because of my Oddity."

She returned to dabbing ointment on his back. "Oh that's ridiculous. Fourteen? Did they try to find you afterward?"

"Not that I know of." Not that he'd really checked. Elliot had a feeling that if they'd wanted to find him, they would have. "So, you know, I lived on the streets."

She paused. "Doing what? Not dealing drugs, I hope."

Well, here it was. Derwin had already told his father, so there was no use hiding it. "No. Just myself. I met Theresa, and she took me in. She's my Madame." It took a second for understanding to dawn, then Myrna's eyes widened, and her mouth made a little O. He tried to ignore the nervous flutter in his stomach. Would she insist on the separate beds now? Or maybe that they shouldn't stay the night after all.

But Elliot had to give her credit: she recovered quickly. "Well I suppose that's better than drugs. I do hope you're protecting yourself and not risking your life or others." She gave him a stern look as she screwed the cap on the tube of ointment. Then she smiled. "If you've got bruises where I can't see them, you'll have to apply the rest yourself."

Elliot put down the peas and pulled his shirt back on. The frozen pea pack had helped, and the painkillers were starting to kick in; they were making him a little drowsy. He glanced at the clock and wondered how long Derwin would be. "I'm always safe. I don't want to live on the streets forever, after all." Derwin's mom was easy to talk to. Probably due to her lack of hysterics.

Myrna returned to the pot, tasted the spoon, then reached for the salt shaker. "Well that's good. Is Derwin helping you with that?"

"I'm not sure." Elliot chewed his lip. He remembered Derwin suggesting that he could use his Oddity to support himself. But he still wondered if he could handle reading multiple objects each day, even if the visions they yielded weren't intense. "I never graduated high school. I don't have any skills."

"You could always get your general diploma." Derwin's mother tasted the stew again.

The same arguments he'd heard from Derwin. How to tell her that the idea of trying to catch up was terrifying? "I don't even have a copy of my birth certificate. I don't know my Citizen's Number. My entire work history is whoring. Who'd hire me?"

She looked over at him and shrugged. "You never know. It depends on the industry. As for papers . . ." Myrna chuckled. "Derwin might know someone. Or his dad might. They've got their connections."

With that little quip, she herded him into the living room and turned on the TV. "Go ahead and relax. It'll be at least a couple hours before either of them get home, and you look exhausted."

Elliot nodded. It was probably the pain pills. At her urging, he lay down on the sofa and got comfortable, choosing a quiet nature show. A nap might make the time go by quicker.

Despite how nice Derwin's mom was, Elliot needed him to come back soon.

CHAPTER SIXTEEN

AN EVENING WITH THE FOLKS

The sun dipped behind the trees as Derwin returned to his parents' house. He stank of sweat and blood—the latter not his own—but it was worth it. He felt calmer, not supercharged anymore. While he'd managed to shed the excess energy, he was still a little nervous about stepping inside. Throughout his run, he'd thought about Elliot and his mom, wondering how they'd get along.

He jogged the last few feet up to the driveway just as his dad pulled in, driving his rugged, mud-covered truck that sported a dent on the front bumper. Maybe he'd hit a deer. Maybe something else. Derwin raised a hand to wave, the other holding on to the sack containing a dead *kasha*, a small catlike creature who loved to rob graves for food.

As he climbed out of the truck, his dad chuckled at the sight of the bloody sack. "You better not bring that in the house. Your mom will kill you." He shut the driver-side door, clicked on the alarm, and walked over.

"Freezer on the patio have space? I'd like to be compensated for my trouble," Derwin returned, smiling. In Mephist, it was open season on demons at all times, though the rewards were less.

"Yeah, it's empty. I'll come with you to the back patio. Give us a chance to have a few words."

Derwin sighed inwardly. Better to get it over with. Nodding, he fell into step, walking beside his dad toward the side gate that led to the backyard.

Once again, Derwin tried to forestall questions. "I only met him about forty-eight hours ago. Yes, he's a rentboy. Yes, I'm being careful. No, I don't know where this is going. I just know he's got an Oddity that may finally get me some answers about Grady's death."

Dad snorted. "Easy, boy. You're an adult. I'm not your mom, so I'm not going to tell you how to live your life." He opened the gate and held it for Derwin, raising an eyebrow at him. "On the other hand, do I need to tell Myrna to hide the silver while you two are here?"

Derwin shook his head. "He's had ample opportunity to steal from me, and he hasn't, so I think you're safe. As far as I'm aware, he keeps to escort services and prostitution. Not like he's had a lot of choices—he got thrown out of the house at fourteen." He went to the large freezer and placed the sack inside, thankful that it wasn't hunting season yet, and the freezer was empty.

"Hmm. I see you going into hero mode. Just watch out for that."

Derwin closed the freezer door. "I know. And I know I'll probably get butt hurt when he takes off again after this is over. But hey, it's better than me moping around at home by myself, isn't it? I actually came out to see you guys."

Dad sighed, smiling. "I'll give you that. At least you're walking in with both eyes open." He glanced at the back patio door. "Shall we see what the two of them are up to?"

If past experience was anything to go by, Mom would have Elliot in a full-body cast by now. "Yeah, let's go see."

Inside, Derwin found Mom in the kitchen adding the last ingredient to the stew. Elliot had fallen asleep on the couch with the TV on. He looked angelic, black curls falling into his face, a little pout on his lips. His pain was only a dim buzz in the back of Derwin's head now, thankfully.

Derwin gave Mom a hug, while Dad plopped down into his favorite recliner. The sudden throb in his cortex told Derwin that Elliot had woken up.

Mom glanced at him. "Go wash up before dinner."

He knew better than to disobey that tone. Hurrying toward the bathroom, he heard his father asking Elliot how he was doing, and then at Elliot's answer, about his family, where he'd grown up, and if he knew what their situation was now. Elliot mumbled out a few answers, most of which Derwin couldn't hear over the running water. While Derwin could tell Dad was trying to be friendly, as usual he was showing his cluelessness when it came to social interactions.

As soon as he'd scrubbed off the blood and sweat, Derwin headed over to rescue Elliot. He sat down on the couch next to him, and a shock of pleasure went through him when Elliot leaned closer, brushing legs with him. Elliot had his shoes off and a slight smile on his face. Things must've gone okay. "What'd I miss?" Derwin asked, looking between Elliot and his dad.

Dad shrugged, glancing at Elliot. "Just having a nice chat. I told Elliot it was a real shame what happened to him, and asked if he has any long-term plans for himself."

Derwin could only imagine how that conversation had turned out. The first time he'd brought up the idea of a normal job, Elliot had practically bitten his head off. "And?"

This time it was Elliot who shrugged. "He pointed out that my line of work doesn't have a long life span, and I argued that I don't know how to do anything else. I've probably forgotten everything I ever learned in school. And then he said there were jobs out there where I wouldn't need a formal education." He smirked. "Like yours. Or like, you know, becoming a private eye, with my Oddity and all."

Derwin resisted the urge to mention that he had said something similar. If Elliot was more willing to listen to his dad than him, so be it. At least it lit up a glimmer of hope that maybe, just maybe, he and Elliot could have a future together. That Elliot wouldn't run right back to his Madame and the gangs when the case was over.

"Okay," he said, trying not to let such hopes show. If he said the wrong thing now, they could all go away. "I guess you have some thinking to do."

"Of course there are details he'd have to work around," Dad interjected. "But it's something to consider. My dad—your grandfather—he was just the sort of thing that we've tried to avoid becoming. An instrument of the government. But I avoided it. It can be done. Hell, I even managed to do it right under the government's nose, working a regular job, living a decent life."

That was news to Derwin. Dad rarely if ever talked about his own father. Derwin had never even met the guy. He didn't know if his grandfather was alive or dead.

Before he could ask for further details, Derwin's mother announced, "Dinner!"

The three of them rose and headed for the table.

They talked little. Derwin hadn't realized how hungry he was until he started eating. Mom's stew was as good as always, hearty and filling, with a combination of herbs Derwin couldn't begin to guess. Elliot ate two bowls and then blushed before asking for a third. He ate like a starving man. Maybe he was one. That was an uncomfortable thought.

Again, Elliot reminded Derwin of a feral cat that he hoped wouldn't turn on him and bite.

Once dinner was over, Derwin spent an hour filling his parents in on his recent skips, how Bickering was doing, all the mundane stuff. Elliot listened in, lying back with his hands folded, more relaxed than Derwin had ever seen him.

An hour later, Derwin still had enough energy to talk through the night, but when he saw Elliot's eyelids drooping and felt his steadily rising pain level, he rose to his feet. "Time for another painkiller, Elliot." He didn't have to check his father to know that he was growing uncomfortable with the amount of energy flowing from him too.

Elliot held a hand to his mouth. "Yeah, good idea. I'm beat." He glanced from Derwin's mom to his dad. "Thank you, guys. I really appreciate the hospitality." He smiled, and for a moment, actually looked like a normal kid just barely out of high school. Which of course was what he *should* look like.

Why the hell was Derwin with this beautiful, young waif?

Elliot stood and flashed him another smile that warmed him clear down to his toes.

Oh yeah. That was why.

"I'll show you the shower," Derwin said, blushing and powerless to do anything about it.

He resisted the urge to take Elliot's hand, but led him to the spare bedroom where his mother had already turned down the sheets and stowed their backpacks by the closet. Just off from the bedroom was the bathroom, which had barely enough room to cram in the toilet, shower, and a pedestal sink. Derwin made sure there was a towel hanging on the rack and turned to Elliot, ready to ask if he needed help again.

Instead, he discovered Elliot staring at the bedroom, a stricken expression on his face.

What is he staring at? Used as a guest bedroom now, this had been his room growing up. Mom had tried to make it less "teenage jock," but there were still remnants of his childhood present. On a shelf next to wrestling trophies stood pictures of himself as a glaring young teen wearing a band T-shirt, and beside those, as a grinning little boy holding up his first kill, a hare that he'd trapped out in the woods.

Elliot swallowed, his attention fixed evidently on the pictures, fists clenched at his sides. When Derwin gently laid a hand on his arm, he jumped and turned to him, eyes suddenly bright with tears. Derwin's chest grew tight with concern. "What is it?"

Trying to smile and failing miserably, Elliot shrugged. "Told you, I haven't been in a real home since—since I got kicked out. Brings back memories." He swiped at his eyes, but not before the first tear slid down his cheek. "I'm okay. Really I am."

Derwin pulled him into a gentle hug, before Elliot crumpled entirely.

"Don't know what's wrong with me," Elliot said between sniffles, hands clenched in Derwin's T-shirt, face pressed against his chest. He gave a weak laugh that pierced Derwin's heart. "Not like I haven't had years to get used to things."

"I don't know how you could ever get used to being abandoned by people who are supposed to love you," Derwin returned, maintaining his careful hold. Elliot gave a broken sob, and Derwin sensed the accompanying stab in Elliot's chest.

"Damn it. Can't even cry without it hurting. I hope Yoshiro pounds Crew Cut and his dumb gang friends. All of them." Even through his tears, there was rage in Elliot's voice.

He gently tilted Elliot's face up and kissed the tear-stained cheeks. When Elliot's knees gave out, he held him up and led him over to the bed, then let him curl up against Derwin. He didn't say anything, but simply let Elliot cry out some of his grief and loss.

After a few moments, Elliot spoke again, his voice soft and bewildered. "You didn't have to do this. You didn't have to do any of this." He raised his head off Derwin's shoulder and looked at him. "Why are you doing this?"

That brought Derwin up short. "Because I like you," he blurted out. "I think you're insane for wanting to go back to your profession when you have other options. But I like you." He couldn't, wouldn't admit to the deeper feeling stirring within. It was too soon, and he was too unsure. Not to mention ridden with the guilt that he'd be betraying Grady if he actually moved on.

Elliot sat up a little, smiling bitterly. He brushed at his eyes as if surprised to find moisture there, then glanced away. His back straightened and his chin raised. Derwin's heart clenched, and he wondered if he should have said more. No, didn't wonder—he *knew* he should have. But it was too late now. Elliot's brief show of emotion was over.

"Well, I like you too. I'm sorry. It must be the painkillers." Elliot let out a slow breath. "I should take that shower now."

He got up stiffly, but waved aside Derwin's offer to help. "Won't take me long," Elliot assured him, leaving Derwin to pull on gym shorts and a T-shirt for bed. As he brushed his teeth a couple of minutes later, he tried not to stare at the pale beauty of Elliot's naked form in the shower, half-blurred by the patterns on the shower door. What did Elliot want? If Derwin confessed that he could fall for Elliot, would it convince him to stay? Or run away?

Derwin sighed and returned to the bedroom to slide into the full-sized bed. Despite the long run, he felt anything but tired. His body craved sex and that wasn't likely to happen, not with Elliot's injuries, not to mention his parents in the other bedroom. Stretching, he fetched Elliot's pain pills from his backpack.

True to his word, it didn't take Elliot long to shower. He emerged from the bathroom in only a towel wrapped low around his hips; even his hands were bare. The fresh bruises marred the view somewhat, but he was still gorgeous. Running a hand through his damp curls, Elliot crossed over to the bed and sat down. "Well, this looks awfully domestic."

He pulled out a T-shirt and briefs from his bag, then set them aside before letting the towel fall. Derwin couldn't help it; his eyes followed the movement to take in all of him. His cock came to life.

Elliot popped his painkiller and crawled over with an almost careless grace, molding himself against Derwin's body. It was probably yet another defense, a way for Elliot to keep emotions at bay by offering up his flesh.

Derwin couldn't help himself, though. When Elliot reached for him, Derwin wrapped an arm around him and drew him in for a deep kiss.

CHAPTER SEVENTEEN

SUPPOSED TO BE BUSINESS

Elliot knew it was a bad idea, even as he pulled down Derwin's shorts.

Sex was supposed to be for business. It was how he paid for food, clothing, and what little roof he had over his head. Unless he found a rich sugar daddy, free sex with a person wouldn't pan out.

That made no dent in his desire to be with Derwin, however.

Elliot yanked at Derwin's T-shirt, nearly ripping it in his haste to get it off. Once he had him bare, Elliot dove in, pressing, arching against warm flesh in a frenzy of need. Maybe it was being wounded and feeling useless. Maybe it was the reminder of a home he'd lost and could never have. Maybe it was just Derwin himself, that dark-tan complexion, the muscles and the scars and the tattoos, the demon hunting and the noble attitude.

All Elliot knew was that he craved Derwin right then.

Derwin's mouth closed on his, and Elliot kissed back fiercely, sucking hard on Derwin's tongue. He grabbed at Derwin's hips, heedless of the pain from his own rib and calf as he crushed himself against the man, rubbing their cocks together in a desperate attempt to quench his lust. When Derwin rolled them so that he was on top, Elliot bit back a curse and then sighed.

"Yes," he breathed into Derwin's chest, tracing the line of a scar with his fingertips. "Take me. Now." It wasn't the time or place for it, not with Derwin's parents near, but he didn't care.

Happily, Derwin didn't seem to care either.

"You're addictive," he murmured back, shifting his weight so that his hips held Elliot, keeping their erections pressed together. Such heavenly contact. It made Elliot feel grounded, secure.

Derwin tangled his fingers in Elliot's hair and feasted on his neck, a heady mixture of teeth and lips and tongue. Elliot kept his hands on Derwin's hips, kneading the flesh there, careful to touch only skin. Not that he worried about getting any bad visions in this bed, but he didn't want anything interrupting them.

"Just need you to fuck me," Elliot panted, sliding his hands down to squeeze Derwin's ass.

"Shh." Derwin reached for Elliot's backpack, grabbing a condom. "You don't want my mother hearing us." He sucked in a breath as Elliot took the packet from him and ripped it open, then slid the rubber onto Derwin with practiced ease.

"Why not? Would she be horrified?" Not that Elliot wanted to witness her reaction. But it was fun watching Derwin struggle to keep quiet, the way his features contorted as Elliot gave his cock a stroke . . . that was worth the risk of being caught at this.

"No. She'd ask a ton of embarrassing questions." Derwin closed his eyes, pumping his hips, thrusting into the tight circle of Elliot's fist. When he opened them again, the intensity in those dark irises pulled Elliot in, made him want to stay trapped beneath him forever. Derwin opened the lube and squeezed some over Elliot's cock, stroking him. This time it was Elliot's turn to lie back and close his eyes. Derwin nuzzled him. "You're sure you're up for this?"

"Oxycodone's starting to work." The pain had fuzzy edges now, and wasn't really bothering him anymore. He'd be drowsy later, but right now he was wide-awake. And horny. He slicked his fingers with the lube from his cock, intending to grease up his hole, but before he could do so, Derwin grabbed his wrist.

"Nuh-uh. I get to prepare you this time." Derwin worked a little lube onto his fingers, and slid them around Elliot's sensitive entrance, rubbing his perineum before pushing a single digit inside. Elliot moaned and scrabbled for something to hold on to, settling on Derwin's upper arms even though his hands were slick. Derwin chuckled. "You could stroke yourself for me. As long as you think you can hold off from coming." He wiggled his finger, and for an instant, Elliot saw stars.

Despite the shocks going through him, Elliot tried to keep his voice nonchalant. "You think I haven't learned control?" He returned one hand to his cock but only gave it a slow pull, reluctant to test himself in truth. Most of the time restraint wasn't that difficult. With Derwin, however, all his carefully honed skills slipped away. It wasn't right that he should want one person this badly.

Derwin chuckled, but Elliot couldn't muster up indignation as Derwin slowly fucked him with that one finger. Every time he almost drew it out, Elliot's body clenched, trying to keep it in, as waves of desire moved through him.

"For gods' sake, have a little pity!" He fisted his cock, squeezing it hard from base to tip.

"You are so much fun." Derwin snickered, obviously pleased with himself. He pushed a second digit inside.

"Mmf."

"Stop touching yourself. Play with your nipples instead," Derwin said in a low voice, his tone sliding from jovial to intense.

Elliot's eyelids fluttered as he pinched the sensitive nubs. He wanted to close his eyes and enjoy it, but he also wanted to watch Derwin, see the lust in his face. A third finger was thrust inside him, creating an intense burn from the stretch.

Elliot moaned, unable to keep silent. He slowly dragged a fingertip across his nipple, and a stab of pleasure went through him. "*Please,*" he begged, not knowing if that was what Derwin wanted. All he knew was that he needed more.

"What I wouldn't give for an entire weekend to tease and torture you like this," Derwin murmured, but he pulled his fingers out with a *plop*, and then wiped them off on a tissue as he settled himself between Elliot's legs. He pushed a pillow under Elliot's hips to raise him, then carefully lined up their hips. "I have patience."

With that, he began pushing in, one inch at a time.

But Elliot was fresh out of patience. "More," he said, resting his ankles on Derwin's shoulders, the better to open himself up. His rib hurt, but it was so worth the pain. It was hardly his first time for any of this, and yet somehow it all seemed different. There was a tightness in his stomach, a thrill, as Derwin made a shallow thrust and half pulled out to thrust in harder, deeper. Demons, but he was *good*. Elliot somehow managed to bite back a moan at the fullness in his ass.

Their eyes met, and the passion in Derwin's only made the sensations more intense. Even as Derwin began a steady rhythm, muscles contracting under Elliot's hands as he moved, his gaze never left Elliot's face. Consuming him. Daring him to look back.

For once, Elliot dared.

Pinned by the gaze, by the rocking motion of their bodies, Elliot succumbed to the connection between them, to not only being taken, but being cherished. He gritted his teeth, trying to hold back the cries that wanted to break free, his short fingernails digging into the cords of Derwin's arms. His nerves sang with every thrust, every time Derwin's cock stroked that inner part of him. The nagging soreness from Elliot's calf faded away under the pleasure spiking through him. His cock rubbed up against Derwin's belly, aching for attention.

If Derwin kept looking at him like that, like he wanted to stay with him forever, Elliot wouldn't be able to keep quiet. Derwin lowered his head and kissed him, teeth scraping as they fucked. Elliot mewled into his mouth and bucked up, wanting more, wanting everything. Derwin's much larger size made Elliot feel safe, secure. Derwin tasted clean and fresh, and their tongues dueled as they tried to get as much of each other as possible.

Derwin broke off the kiss, his lips trailing over Elliot's jaw, along his throat to the shell of his ear, panting as his movements grew more forceful, more rapid. "If you're going to scream, muffle it against me. Fuck, if you could see what you look like right now."

He reached down and wrapped his fingers around Elliot's shaft, stroking him.

Pleasure coiled up from his balls through to his cock, and Elliot knew he'd never last, that he'd never be able to keep the scream inside. He grabbed Derwin by the shoulders and arched up, pressing his mouth to the warm fluttering pulse at Derwin's throat, crying out softly as each stroke brought him closer to the edge.

Too much of everything he wanted. Yet he'd never be satisfied. Pleasure exploded in white heat as he came, biting down on the curve where Derwin's throat met shoulder, his screams muffled even as the climax swept through him. A hot splash of his own come landed on his belly. Derwin continued to fuck him as he milked every last drop, and Elliot sagged back against the bed, breath sobbing in his chest, bones going liquid.

Derwin let go of him to brace himself on his hands, pumping faster, his expression changing from near agony to ecstasy as his own climax hit. Elliot shivered at the burn, wishing he could feel Derwin's seed inside him. With a groan, Derwin jerked one last time and then settled on top of Elliot, slowly pulsing cock still deep in his ass. Elliot ran his fingers through Derwin's sweat-damp hair, content.

"Were we quiet enough?" Elliot murmured in his ear, after they'd rested for several minutes. Derwin laughed, and his cock twitched, making Elliot whimper.

Sighing, Derwin pulled out and grabbed tissues. "Dunno. If Mom starts waggling her brows at us and asking questions in the morning, then we'll know." He hesitated, looking at Elliot. Brows drawing together, he leaned in and kissed him with a mixture of passion and tenderness that set Elliot's emotions off-balance again. Thoughts of the future returned; the idea of leaving Derwin and returning to his usual clients sent uncomfortable flutters through his stomach.

Still, he couldn't help but kiss back with all his being.

Sighing, Derwin curled up and drew Elliot closer, wrapping his arms around him. The painkillers were making Elliot sleepy now, together with the post-sex haze. He yawned, and rested his cheek against Derwin's meaty biceps, lying spooned with him. In no time, he was fast asleep.

"So did you both sleep well?" Derwin's mom asked at breakfast. No eyebrow waggling, but there was a gleam in her eyes.

In truth, Elliot had, for he didn't remember a thing after dropping off. No dreams, no visions, which was surprising since he'd forgotten to put his gloves back on. He'd woken up sprawled across Derwin's chest, drooling on him. The guy hadn't seemed to mind.

"We slept well, Mom. How about you and Dad?" Derwin's tone was light, but there was an undercurrent to it, one that said, *Don't ask about things you don't want to know.*

Elliot chuckled and ate his cereal.

Myrna laughed. "Oh, your father and I slept just fine."

There was something about that laugh that hinted . . . Elliot's cheeks heated, and he stared at his bowl to avoid eye contact. "Derwin . . ." The very *last* thing he wanted to know about right now was somebody else's parents' love life.

Derwin sounded chagrined. "Forget I asked. Oh—Mom, mind if I make a few sandwiches to take on the drive today?"

A chair scraped on the floor, and Elliot looked up to find Derwin's mother heading for the refrigerator. "Let me take care of it. Are you sure you have to go so soon?"

"Afraid so. Elliot's helping me while he heals, but after that he may not be available. I want to go talk with Grady's sister, see if she was mixed up with anything that might've brought him trouble. Today, hopefully." Derwin finished his own breakfast, which was actually a bowl of last night's dinner. He stood. "I'm going to toss the bedding into the washing machine and pack the car."

Once he'd left, Myrna returned to the table with bread, mayo, and sliced roast beef. As she made the sandwiches, her gaze fell on Elliot. "Promise me two things, sweetie."

He almost choked on his bite, his eyes wide. Surely she wasn't going to say something about breaking hearts, was she? But she loved her son, that much he could see. "Yes?"

Her expression softened. "Promise me you won't let him get into too much trouble while you're with him. And second, if you ever need help or a place to stay, you come here. Understand?" She wiped her hands and reached for a notepad and pen on the counter. "I'm giving you our phone number and address. Just in case."

Elliot stared at her as she scribbled them down on the notepad, tore the sheet off, and handed it to him. Almost mechanically, he took the paper and stuffed it into the pocket of his jeans. He couldn't blame his blank look on the painkillers; he'd only taken half a pill this morning. "Why would you do this for me?"

She smiled. "Because I can see you are a decent person and that Derwin cares for you. Whatever your troubles, Elliot, you've got at least one family who will be there if you need help."

He barely had time to ponder that before it was time to hit the road.

CHAPTER EIGHTEEN

THE NEXT PLAN OF ATTACK

Two hours flew by as Derwin drove back to Nis, gunning the engine around the hairpin turns, and again when they hit the paved parts. Elliot said little, mostly commenting on the wilderness and asking what kind of men would want to work out there, dealing with demons on a daily basis. Once they reached the city, the guards waved them through the gates, and Derwin wasted no time in going to his place.

They made a quick stop to drop off the head of the *kasha* and get the bounty at the local police station. Derwin wasn't surprised when Elliot elected to stay in the car.

As they pulled up to park in front of the condo, a teenaged boy was sitting on the steps to his place—the same one who had delivered Elliot's clothes the day before. The boy glanced at Elliot, who frowned as he exited the car.

"Looks like I've got a message," he said, walking over to speak with the young man.

Derwin carried their things inside, debating whether to listen in or let Elliot be. If only he knew him better. Last night had been confusing: the sex had been great, of course, but between Elliot crying in his arms and the kiss afterward, he didn't know what to think. It was like the guy *craved* a real home, a real relationship.

That didn't mean Elliot would accept an offer of either.

Once he'd set the backpacks inside, Derwin hovered at the front door, wishing there was a handy window or something so he could see the expressions on Elliot's face. Was he pleased to hear from his Madame? Or afraid? After a minute, Derwin put away the leftovers from his parents, unable to stand still and unable to bring himself to open the door. Elliot's rib was only starting to mend, but he might decide to leave anyway. There was nothing to bind him here.

Time to call Grady's sister, Ceci. He hadn't spoken to her since Grady's funeral. Ceci was a heroin addict, and had been for years, so Grady had spent a lot of time arguing with her. She'd been an avid gymnast in high school. According to Grady, she'd started out on painkillers after she broke her ankle.

He punched in the number and wiped crumbs off the counter as he waited for her to pick up.

"Hello?" She sounded sober. Hesitant, timid, but sober.

"Hey, Ceci? It's me, Derwin Bryant. You know—Grady's boyfriend." Just saying the words made Derwin's stomach lurch, his heart clench. He powered through. "How've you been?"

There was a pause. "Derwin? You're calling me? Do I have a warrant out on me or something?" She gave a false laugh, her tone high-pitched.

Derwin groaned inwardly, hoping that she *didn't* have any outstanding warrants. Bob would be the sort to sign Ceci, and if she'd failed to appear for court, he'd owe it to Bob to take care of it. But bringing her in on a bounty would be beyond embarrassing.

"Not that I know of." He glanced over as he heard the front door open and steps approaching. Elliot appeared in the doorway of the kitchen, and looked at him uncertainly. Derwin tried to smile at him through his nerves. "No, I just received some more information about Grady's death, and I thought you might want to hear about it. Also, you might be able to help me. I'm thinking now that it wasn't a simple robbery." Giving her even that much was a risk, but he'd probably be able to tell if she was surprised or not.

There was a longer pause this time. *She knows something. She knows his secret, and she's not going to reveal it to me.* He thought she might hang up on him, but then she cleared her throat. "Really? The cops said this?"

Oh, he so wanted to talk to her. "No, not the cops. Just me, Ceci. Can I come by today? I need closure on this." Hopefully if Grady's secret had anything to do with her, she would trust him to keep it under wraps. He'd have to figure out how to introduce Elliot when they got there, because he *definitely* wanted Elliot's help on this one.

Elliot was trying to slip out of the kitchen, and Derwin waved a hand at him to stay put. *Need you*, he mouthed for good measure. Elliot raised one eyebrow.

"Huh, well, okay, then. Oh—you don't happen to have any money I can borrow, do you? Rent's due in a couple days and I'm short."

Derwin smiled. So she'd take a bribe from him for information? Same as she'd always bugged Grady for dough to buy her dope?

He could work with that. "You're in luck—I bagged a couple demons recently. Want me to bring lunch by too?"

She yawned; perhaps she'd just woken up. "Sounds good. Catch you in a few. You remember where I live?"

Derwin didn't, so he jotted down the directions, then said good-bye. Taking a deep breath, he faced Elliot. "I need your help."

Elliot tilted his head guardedly, and Derwin's heart beat a staccato pace, hammering in his chest. Had Elliot's Madame sent for him?

Leaning against the fridge, Elliot crossed his arms. "What do you need?"

Derwin stuck his hands in his pockets, before he started to do something insane like clean the already immaculate counters. "I'm going to interview Grady's sister. If I gave you an opportunity with her out of the room, would you be able to use your ability? After he died, I sent most of his old stuff to her. Some of it could be lying around. Or maybe you could check anything of hers that seems suspicious." Saying it like that, it sounded like a tall order.

Blowing out a breath, Elliot frowned. He dragged a hand through his hair. "What kind of person is this sister? What would be the worst that I might experience?"

Derwin held his nerves in check. That wasn't a no, not yet. "She's a heroin addict, so it probably wouldn't be pretty, but I doubt it'd be violent." He grimaced. "I mean I guess the worst thing you could see would be Grady's murder again, if she has anything from that day, but that's a really long shot."

Elliot growled under his breath. "I swear I'm going to find some way someday for you to experience what those visions are like. See if you make light of them then." He fell silent, and Derwin mentally kicked himself a few times. Whatever took place inside Elliot's head during visions, it hadn't looked pleasant. In fact, he'd been sure the young man had burst a few blood vessels, given how his body had spasmed and contorted when he'd seen Grady's murder.

Unease made the back of Derwin's neck prickle, as he imagined what Grady must have felt right before he died. Grady had been a good person, one whose death shouldn't be locked up in the police cold-case files. The grief still sent sharp pain through Derwin's heart every time he thought about him. While Elliot was fascinating in his own way, his walls set off alarms in Derwin's head. He was nice, but he couldn't compare to loving, affectionate Grady.

Meanwhile, Derwin could come up with all kinds of reasons why Elliot should help him. But only Elliot could decide.

Elliot sighed. "You're still paying me for these services, right? I have to make a living. Although I guess I owe you for the ER visit."

Since technically Elliot could have charged him for the "services" rendered last night in bed, Derwin shrugged. "Don't worry about the ER visit. But yes, I'm paying. Fifty per vision if it's not a horrible one? Is that reasonable?" He'd have to keep capturing demons to fund his investigation, but at least at the moment he was flush.

Elliot nodded. "Seems fair. Quadruple that if I'm scarred for life by something I witness." He stood up straighter. "Let's do this."

Ceci's place was halfway between Derwin's condo and the warehouse district with all the prostitutes and drug houses. It wasn't much of a place. Ceci shared it with her boyfriend, Bud Larsen, though Derwin hadn't met the guy. He wasn't there today, which was good on one hand and bad on the other—it would be easier to question Ceci, but Derwin had to wonder if Bud was the guy he should be investigating. If Ceci was an addict, chances were Bud was too, and he was probably into other things as well.

Derwin rang the doorbell three times before Ceci answered, wearing boxers, a stained tank top, and an untied flannel robe. It looked like there was gum stuck in her blond, matted hair, or it could have been something else. He didn't want to know.

"Oh gods, food!" She grabbed the bag from Derwin before he even had a chance to introduce Elliot. Ceci pulled out the French dip sandwich and bit into it, making happy noises. When she did glance at Elliot, she pursed her lips in interest. "New boyfriend?"

"Something like that."

She waved for them to come in and then staggered into the living room, which was half covered in old newspapers, paper plates with dried bits of food, and various drug paraphernalia. Derwin grimaced, swiping at a mystery pile of trash and hoping nothing was alive where he took a seat.

Elliot sat down gingerly beside Derwin, gloved hands clenched at his sides. His disgust bolstered Derwin's opinion of him. Whore or not, he'd managed to avoid becoming an addict. Into Derwin's ear he whispered, "I'm not sure I want to see anything here."

Derwin whispered back, "Hang on. Let me see if there's some worthwhile object."

They waited as Ceci devoured the first sandwich, then started on a second one. The grease rolled down her forearm, highlighting the white track marks. She opened up a beer and chugged it down. "Man, that was good. I've been eating crap the last two days." She hiccupped and laughed, wiping her mouth. Derwin's gorge rose.

She glanced between him and Elliot, and her eyes seemed relatively clear but haunted. "So, okay. You have money for me, right?" Such desperation in her voice. Derwin sighed, and pulled out two crisp hundred dollar bills, showing them to her before returning them to his pocket.

"I need you to answer some questions," he began, wishing he'd written them down. He opened the notepad app on his phone. "I talked to Lloyd Brunson, the convict I helped capture. The one the cops thought killed Grady." He shook his head. "He didn't do it. He was busy stealing a car at the time."

Ceci shrugged. "I know."

Derwin blinked, staring at her. "You know? How?" Why hadn't she told him?

She dug through the empty cups on the coffee table and picked up one with some kind of amber liquid in it. Beer, maybe. Derwin didn't want to know. "Okay I don't *know* it, per se, but Bud said he'd heard of the guy and couldn't come up with any reason he'd want to kill somebody—not his thing, you know? Stealing cars, now that I can totally believe."

A headache gnawed at the space between Derwin's eyeballs. He massaged the area. "And you didn't think to share information like that with me?" He expelled a breath. "Ceci . . . be honest. Was Grady into anything that might've gotten him killed?" Anger fought with grief, turning it sour.

She paused in raising the cup to her mouth, and set it down, frowning. For the first time since Derwin had walked into her house, she seemed sober. "I don't know. Me and him, we got into it sometimes. He found out my boyfriend was—well, let's just say he's my supplier. Grady and Bud fought about that." She blinked, and Derwin saw it, the sorrow she'd been trying to hide. She laughed, but it sounded forced, painful. "Grady was the good one. The one who got away from Mom and her drinking and me and the dope. He never did nothing illegal."

Derwin glanced over at Elliot, who remained silent, his face carefully neutral. He was probably wondering what he could accomplish here, since the house was such a mess. Too much crap to touch, and possibly none of it connected to Grady's murder. Derwin tried to think. "Just because he was lawful doesn't mean he didn't know about things. Was Grady keeping any of your secrets? Would Bud have had a reason to kill him? Remember, I'm not the cops, and I'm not going to rat on you or your boyfriend. Just what does Bud do, and what did Grady know about it?" It didn't make sense for Bud to have killed Grady, but Derwin didn't know about all of Bud's dealings. After all, Bud knew Lloyd. Bud could have killed Grady, taken the most sellable stuff from the house for drug money, and then tried to frame Lloyd. End result: no more angelic brother trying to take Ceci away from him.

She frowned again. "Well, Grady gave me money sometimes. I don't think that was a secret. And he didn't turn me over to the cops or anything. I don't know if he threatened to tell anyone about Bud dealing. Actually, it would have been worse to snitch on Bud's other—" She paused, staring at Derwin with wide eyes. His heart skipped a beat. So Bud had been hiding some kind of activity, apparently.

"What?" Derwin leaned forward. He flashed the money at her. "You said you needed help with the rent. What's Bud's other thing? I have ways of finding out, you know." While he didn't relish the idea of going to the cops to pull Bud's records—if he had any—it was an option.

Ceci shook her head. "Don't. He's got this poker game going, you know? That's all. It's illegal, and Bud's pretty protective of it." She scratched at her arm. "The money goes quick—it always did. But mainly it was money for food and rent that I asked Grady for. We didn't owe nobody nothing."

"What about the arguments you said Grady had with you and Bud? How mad was your boyfriend that your brother was interfering? Did Bud ever threaten him? Is that why you didn't speak up when the police went after Lloyd?" Derwin was going to get to the bottom of this. Maybe they'd have to find some of Bud's belongings for Elliot to read. But how would they know what items to check?

"It wasn't nothing!" Ceci exclaimed, thumping her fist on her thigh. Her eyes teared up. "We fought, sure, but family does that, you know? You think I would let my boyfriend kill my brother? You think I'd keep silent if I thought it happened like that? No way. Bud didn't like Grady knowing things about him, about me, but my Bud's not stupid. Grady let us be. I can't believe that Bud would do that to Grady, especially when Grady was helping me with money. I just can't believe that." She sobbed, a horrible, grating sound that instantly made Derwin want to plug his ears with cotton.

He rubbed his forehead in frustration. "Okay. I'm probably going to talk to Bud, because I'm trying to talk to everybody. But you say he's not the guy. Fine. So did Grady hang out with anyone else that I might not know about? Can you think of anyone else that might've done it?"

Ceci sniffled a few times and wiped her nose on her sleeve. "Nuh-uh. Like I said, Grady didn't hang out with criminals. Lemme see—he mostly hung out with you, and then there was Cole from his work. They went drinking sometimes when you were hunting criminals." Ceci chuckled through her tears. "Computer geeks, both of them. They liked to talk about video games." Her eyes went wide. "Oh! I know! What about Oren Whittaker? Grady's ex-boyfriend? That was some nasty shit, their breakup, before you came along. And Oren's not totally legit. He occasionally plays in Bud's games. You should check him out."

Derwin hastily jotted down the names in his phone, wishing he could remember Cole's last name. Mousy guy, he recalled. And Oren? There was a possibility. He hadn't been aware of Grady having contact with the guy before the murder, but if Oren knew Bud, he could have gotten Grady's address at any time. And Grady had told Derwin about his ex-boyfriend, how Oren used to beat him up.

"Are there other names that I should check out?" Derwin watched as Ceci finished off her beer and began digging around the stuff on the table. Looking for drugs, maybe. Now that she'd eaten and he'd brought up the painful subject of her brother, she would probably want to take her next hit. He had to work fast.

She paused. "No. I really can't think of anybody else. I mean, the two of you didn't go out much, right? He had his job and you, and that was pretty much it. Maybe talk to his boss? That's all I can come up with." She picked up a hash pipe and shook out something black and shriveled.

"I'm not staying here if she starts smoking that," Elliot said, standing. The sight of the pipe seemed to have made him nervous, and he was rubbing his hands on his jeans, though his palms were protected by the gloves.

Derwin stood as well, irritated with both of them. Elliot might not get how important this was to him, how much he needed some kind of closure on his partner's death, but Ceci was Grady's sister. Derwin hated how blasé she was about his unsolved murder. In fact, it was making him suspicious. "Ceci, do you still have the box of Grady's belongings I gave you after the funeral?" Chances were she'd sold a lot of the stuff. Still, he hoped she had kept a few items for sentimental value.

She winced, confirming his fears, but nodded. "I have a box of his things." Probably whatever she hadn't been able to sell.

"Anything recent?" He suddenly wished he'd held on to it all, every last sock. But it had been too painful, seeing Grady's stuff every day. He'd had to clean things out for his own sanity.

Ceci picked her way to the other side of the room, to a hallway closet. "Dunno. But you're free to look." She opened it and pulled out a large box that had seen better days, the corners supported by duct tape. She carried it over to the couch and dumped it on the floor, heedless of what might be underneath it.

Setting her hands on her hips, she peered at Derwin and Elliot.

"Give me my money. Then have at it."

Derwin handed her the money with a sigh. Afraid to see what was left, he leaned over and opened the box.

CHAPTER NINETEEN

SECRETS AND MORE SECRETS

Elliot sat nearby as Derwin gingerly picked through the box. His rib was starting to hurt again, and he was hungry. He didn't want to be in this stinking cesspit that Derwin's dead boyfriend's sister called a home.

The question was, where did he want to be?

Toby, who had been waiting on Derwin's doorstep, had come straight from Theresa's place. And Theresa had big news.

Apparently Roy Yoshiro had disciplined Crew Cut and his friends, enough so that they wouldn't be harassing anyone, at least not while they were wearing casts. Roy still wanted to see Elliot, like tomorrow. He was even willing to work around his injuries, which was a pretty big concession.

Elliot didn't want to go. He also didn't want to tell Derwin that whether he wanted to or not, he had to go. Otherwise Roy would not only go after him, but Theresa as well, and all her boys and girls. That couldn't happen, not if he could stop it. Guilt knotted Elliot's gut. Staying with Derwin was making him soft.

Derwin pulled out a few items and set them aside on the couch. There didn't seem to be anything of value, which didn't surprise Elliot. A few mechanical pencils, a notepad with some scribblings on it, an old empty wallet, and a small bottle of men's cologne. Derwin sighed as he set the box down. "I think that's the only recent stuff. The rest is from when he was a kid." He looked at Elliot apologetically.

Elliot stared back at him, a shiver going down his spine. "I'm not doing it here." Not a chance in the world that he'd let someone as volatile as a drug addict see his Oddity. His secret was worth money, and addicts could not be trusted where money was concerned.

He'd lost many of the friends he'd made growing up on the streets to that sad fact.

Derwin nodded and shoved the items back into the box, then picked it up and stood. "I guess that's it for now, Ceci. If I can just get Bud's number from you, I'll give him a call." He eyed her. "And if you can think of anything—*anything* that Grady might have known, any secrets he might have had, please let me know. He deserves justice." He headed for the door.

Only too happy to leave, Elliot stood as well, making it halfway to the door before Ceci's words slowed him down.

"Grady was always trying to help people out—Me, Bud, his ex-boyfriend Oren . . . everybody. I think that was his downfall. And when he wasn't playing the charity hero, he was working. That was his way." Her hands trembled. To a degree, Elliot felt sorry for her and her loss. Even in her addiction, she cared about her brother.

Depressing to think nobody would ever feel like that about Elliot.

"I'll check out the people you mentioned." Derwin opened the door and stepped out, Elliot close behind him.

Elliot waited until they were both in the car before speaking. "You think any of what she told you is the truth?"

Derwin sighed, shrugging. "Hopefully. I mean, he was her brother." As he pulled into traffic, he glanced at Elliot. "You've been quiet. You mind if I ask you how your Oddity works? Do you even know?"

It was a struggle not to feel insulted. "Yes, I know! Not every object triggers it. There has to be a powerful memory associated with an object for it to respond, like in your place with the bed and the chair. I can't just turn it on like a metal detector and choose what comes to me. And my palms have to touch, but I don't like taking chances." Maybe if he'd been trained in some way, by a more experienced Object Reader, he could have. But the only place to find those was in the police or military, and he wasn't about to go asking there.

Hurt flashed in Derwin's eyes. Elliot cursed himself. Every time the man tried to dig through Elliot's walls, he lashed out. He didn't really mean to. It was just such an ingrained response that he couldn't help it.

Derwin sighed. "Well, if you could try, we'll see what happens. But at least I know not to send you touching every damned thing in that house of hers."

Revulsion made Elliot swallow hard. "There is not enough money in the world to make me do that." Any strong memories there would be ones he didn't want to see.

Derwin smiled. "Cool. Then we'll try these objects, and I'll see if I can find anything else around my condo before we call it a day." He fell silent, the unspoken question in the air between them. *What message did you receive from Theresa?*

Elliot fidgeted. Honestly, Derwin deserved to know. Hadn't he saved Elliot's life? And confided in him about his old boyfriend's death, and his Oddity, and his dad . . . Elliot's hands clenched on the leather seats. He didn't need this connection to another person. It complicated things. Too many chances of getting hurt.

Maybe that was why he'd never taken any steps to get away from Theresa and the streets.

"That all sounds good." Elliot just couldn't hold back his next words, even if they shattered the nice illusion the two of them had created. "I have a client set up for tomorrow night. The Tatsu gang boss, Roy Yoshiro." He suddenly felt dizzy and had to remind himself to breathe.

On the steering wheel, Derwin's knuckles turned white, and a tic began in his jaw. "Do you really think you're up for that? I can still feel your pain."

Elliot chewed at a nail, tearing it with his teeth. "He knows about my condition. He's already taken care of those punks who beat me up. It's all part of the deal. My 'family' and his getting along." He gazed at Derwin and tried to shove down the apprehension and the unwillingness, tried to show that it was going to be fine, no big deal.

He just couldn't seem to muster the old bravado. Derwin had dug in too deep.

While Derwin looked like he wanted to say something, he kept his mouth shut and stared at the road ahead, just driving.

They reached the condo with the shadow of Roy Yoshiro looming over them.

It was almost worse, Derwin *not* arguing with him. Elliot had expected fireworks. Hell, he'd at least expected a barrage of reasons why he shouldn't keep the appointment. But the guy had either given up on him, or just didn't know what to say. He hoped it was the latter.

While Derwin scoured his closet for clues, Elliot waited in the living room, turning on the TV to fight off the silence. Was he even staying here tonight? He wasn't sure anymore.

He watched a news story about a merger between pharmaceutical giant Abbott Industries and a small start-up security and biometrics company, Immune, which sounded like a good marriage, according to the news people. Fifteen minutes later, Derwin returned from upstairs carrying a briefcase, a nice pin-striped shirt and tie, and a mouse pad. He set them all on the coffee table together with the objects from Ceci's place and sat down next to Elliot.

Elliot looked over the objects cautiously, then glanced up and was relieved when Derwin met his eyes. But all Derwin said was, "I'm going to record you, if that's all right?"

The businesslike attitude was a punch to the gut, but then, what had he expected? This was what they were, after all: client and provider. The fact that he was providing something besides sex this time didn't change the dynamic between them. Nor did the past two days. Derwin was probably handling this in the best way possible. If they weren't going to be more than business partners, they had no business behaving like lovers.

He tried not to let it eat at him, but it did.

Elliot took a breath. "Sounds good." Being involved with someone like Derwin was too complicated anyway. Money was simple. With it, he could achieve his goals. A motorcycle. A real apartment. Getting out of the sex trade someday.

There was no point in talking about his situation here and now. And yet, as he pulled off the gloves, Elliot couldn't keep the words from spilling out: "I don't have a choice, you know. About the appointment with the crime boss."

Derwin looked at his phone. "I understand. Let's . . ." He took a breath, unclenching his fists. "I'm not up for talking about it." He gestured at the objects, lifting his gaze to Elliot's face. "Please."

Elliot swallowed at the pleading tone, and nodded. Business time. He'd figure out everything else later. "I'll touch the stuff from his sister's place first." He reached for one of the mechanical pencils, half bracing himself. Holding it, he tried to open up to whatever wanted to come forward, but all he received were scattered images of writing that drifted in like a daydream. He turned the pencil over in his hands but got nothing more concrete.

Shrugging, he put it back on the table. "Pretty sure he handled it, but that's about all." He picked up another pencil, but no images came this time. After a few seconds, he returned it and took the notepad.

Something arose—a sense of urgency, combined with images. Jotting down words. A message? A phone number? Elliot struggled to get more, but like with the pencils, the memories weren't strong enough, or perhaps the items had been handled by too many people. Nothing had really stuck. "He wrote on this, but I don't know what." He gave Derwin an apologetic shrug and set the notepad back.

Next Elliot picked up the wallet. Images assailed him—Grady must've used it a lot. One memory pulled him in.

A guy with dark hair falling into his eyes and a paunch stood on the curb. He shook a handful of cash, and yelled, "You think you got rights, just 'cause you help out once in a while? You lay off us! Ceci's a grown woman! So fuck off with your high attitude!"

"She needs help! The stuff's killing her—I want to get her treatment." Grady was frantic; he was desperate. First his mother and now his sister.

The memory cut out. That must have been Grady trying to stop his sister's drug addiction. Which meant the guy yelling might have been Bud.

Elliot tossed back the wallet with a grimace. "Okay, that was weird. I saw an argument with some sleazy guy about Ceci. I'm thinking it was that boyfriend."

Derwin blinked, frowning "You mean Bud? Dark hair, doesn't shave too often?"

Elliot nodded. "Yeah, that sounds about right. He was shouting, and Grady was yelling about treatment. He might have been trying to get his sister into rehab."

"Interesting that she didn't mention that. We'll definitely bring it up when we talk to Bud." Derwin jotted the information down on another pad of paper. He sighed, gazing at the one item left from Ceci's box. "Damn Ceci. There was a lot more stuff." Derwin held out the cologne with a questioning look in his eyes. "This next, or the briefcase that he took with him to work?" All traces of anger seemed to have left him. Instead, there was raw pain and loss, vulnerability. Elliot wanted to pull Derwin's muscular frame into his arms and hold him, tell him it was going to be okay.

Instead, Elliot nodded toward the briefcase and mouse pad. "I'll try those first." Derwin handed the case to him, handle out. The instant he touched it, he was walking into a tall glass building, into the elevator, and then into a cubicle with a computer, accompanied by a vague sense of anxiety.

That was all.

He set the briefcase down. "I got a vision of a building, walking into an elevator, and then into a cubicle. Does that sound like where Grady worked?" Fairly mundane stuff, but the anxiety had been strong enough to leave the impression. "He felt nervous for some reason." At Derwin's frown, Elliot hurried to add, "I don't think that's worth a full reading fee. It was pretty weak."

Derwin waved a hand dismissively. "Don't worry about the cost. Just try to get whatever details you can." He rubbed his temples. "This is giving me a headache. And you need to take another oxycodone." He stood up and headed to the backpacks. Elliot waited for him to return, then took the medicine and picked up the mouse pad.

The vision came stronger this time. Foreboding and distress assailed Elliot. He was Grady, sitting at his computer desk, mouse moving as he navigated emails, reading through a conversation on the screen. *I should tell Derwin. I shouldn't tell Derwin. I can't believe somebody would do this!* Each thought was punctuated by movement of the mouse on the mouse pad, moving files, copying them into sub-folders.

And then Elliot was himself again, clutching the mouse pad and breathing hard.

Derwin grabbed his arm, an intense look on his face. "You got something," he said, and Elliot nodded.

It was interesting that he hadn't needed help coming out of any of these smaller visions. Elliot had spent so much of his life trying to avoid visions, he'd never gone seeking trace remnants like this. "He was chatting with someone online, sending emails. He had some kind of files on his computer. That might've been the folder I saw earlier. But I don't know anything beyond that." Still no names. No clues as to whether Grady had encountered the secret at work, or from his sister and her nefarious beau.

Pacing now, Derwin dragged a hand through his hair. "Gods, I wish I knew what he'd stumbled into!" He stood facing the TV, hands on his hips, as Elliot mentally prepared himself for the last two objects—the shirt and the cologne bottle. He picked up the shirt.

Nothing. Perhaps it had been washed too many times, or perhaps it had never held a strong memory to begin with. One more object to go.

"I think we're going to have to check out Grady's workplace. Abbott Industries." Derwin glanced over at Elliot.

"Abbott? That's where he worked? I saw them in the news just now." The pharmaceutical company merging with the biometric security start-up. A shiver passed through Elliot. But why should that be strange? Their customers probably only wanted their health information secure.

"You willing to come tomorrow?"

It was impossible not to hear the plea in those words, even though things stood on shaky ground between them. "As long as I get back here early." Elliot tried to figure out how much time he'd need to get ready for Roy. Still, if he was helping Derwin, at least he wouldn't be dwelling on the upcoming encounter.

Derwin nodded, his eyes hooded. "I'll get you wherever you need to go." He went silent as Elliot went for the cologne bottle. Was it Elliot's imagination, or was he holding his breath?

As his hand closed over the cool glass, Elliot knew the vision was coming. He braced for it, but then he found himself *sitting on the couch, only now the room was decorated for Christmas, with a tree full of blinking lights in the corner and a candle with a wreath on the table. There was an open gift box in his lap with the bottle of cologne. He couldn't speak, his throat closing up with love as he turned to Derwin, who seemed happy. "Thank you so much. It's my favorite brand,"* he—*Grady said. He took Derwin's hand, pulling him to sit down on the couch beside him, leaning closer to give him a kiss . . .*

And then Elliot was back in his own body, in his own time. He turned to Derwin, but the man was standing several feet away, watching him. Hurriedly, Elliot set the cologne down, and carefully reached for his gloves. His face was hot, and his heart was beating rapidly.

He could still feel Grady's emotions. Or were they his own developing now? It bugged him that he couldn't differentiate between the two. "Memory, but not one that will help solve the case," he said, his throat dry.

Derwin's brows drew together, and he stepped closer. Elliot clenched the gloves and scowled, warning him not to get near. The last thing he needed right now was more confusing signals. "What did you see?" Derwin asked.

"You giving him this present." Elliot's voice was steady despite his turbulent emotions.

Derwin dropped his gaze, but not before Elliot saw his flash of pain. What hope could Elliot have of ever matching such a happy memory, such a happy union? He'd always be trying to measure up to Grady's ghost. Elliot sighed. "I think I'm done for the day." With a grimace, he yanked on the gloves. The back of his head hurt, and he didn't know if it was from the concussion or the visions. Either way, he just wanted some solitude and rest.

With a sigh, Derwin knelt beside the couch as Elliot lay down, rubbing his forehead. "You did great. Can I get you anything? Oxycodone kicking in yet?"

The pain seemed to flow to spots just behind Elliot's eyes. Yeah, this was going to be the start of a massive headache. He groaned, closing his lids. "Water sounds good. Not sure if the painkiller is going to reach my skull, so I'm going to lay here awhile."

Apparently doing multiple visions in one sitting was a bad idea. He'd have to remember that. As for Grady . . . Elliot wasn't sure he wanted to know more. It was stupid to be jealous of a dead person, but there it was. He was jealous.

CHAPTER TWENTY

THE NEW BOSS

erwin set Elliot up on the couch with water, a blanket, and his medication nearby. Their investigating was pretty much through for the day. Derwin caught up on household chores while Elliot slept away the afternoon, woke him up to eat soup for dinner, and then watched as Elliot went back to sleep. Derwin toyed with the idea of dragging the young man up to his comfortable bed, but he felt more emotionally secure sleeping separately. It was time to take a step back, try to get a reality check. He went to bed alone, determined to get at least a few hours' rest.

Elliot was a whore. He traded sex for money, and that wasn't likely to change just because Derwin had rescued him from a gang fight and they'd had a few good nights together. Worse, he'd been booked by some high crime boss who Derwin didn't know, didn't want to know, and didn't want to think about.

Despite what it cost him, he'd used his Oddity to help Derwin, and for that, Derwin should be grateful. And that was all.

Those reminders didn't help the raging hard-on that kept sleep away, unfortunately. The drugs had taken the edge off Elliot's pain, but it never fully left, which meant Derwin was still getting a slow but steady stream of energy from him. That, together with Elliot's devastatingly good looks, was a recipe for disaster.

Derwin sighed, giving himself a squeeze as he tossed and turned. He was horny, but his anxiety was beginning to grow as well. Checking out Grady's old workplace would be no problem, but then driving Elliot to his so-called date? And what was he supposed to do with himself for the rest of the night? Derwin dreaded how quiet and empty the condo would feel without him. The last thing he wanted was to sit at home and think about what Elliot was doing, but he already knew that was what he'd do. If something bad happened, if he had to rescue the stupid waif again ...

Cursing, Derwin punched his pillow. Why couldn't he have let this be a simple fuck? Why did his sex life have to be so complicated?

He took a deep breath, and let it out slowly. There was an alternative plan tomorrow night. What he'd done every night that he couldn't sleep, before he'd met Elliot. He'd hunt. Demon, fugitive, it didn't matter. The hunt had gotten him through losing Grady, and it could get him through this as well.

Maybe eventually he'd stop caring about lost causes.

At six the next morning, Derwin woke to the hiss of the shower running in his bathroom. He yawned and stretched, amazed that he'd actually fallen into a deep enough sleep that the sounds of somebody entering the room hadn't awakened him. Either that, or he was used to Elliot and his movements now.

Derwin dressed unhurriedly, unsure whether he should keep his distance or take advantage of the little time they had left together. Best to simply go about his business. He went into the bathroom to brush his teeth only to find Elliot bent over, finger-fucking himself.

Freezing midstride, Derwin asked, "Do I want to know?"

Elliot grunted, pulling his fingers out and straightening as the hot water continued to spray over his naked body. "Prepping. Figure I'd get it done now since I didn't know our schedule today."

Derwin's mouth went dry, and suddenly his erection was straining at his boxers.

"Knew I shouldn't have asked," he muttered, squeezing toothpaste onto his brush. He jammed the toothbrush into his mouth and fought not to watch as Elliot bent over again. A morning fuck in the shower probably wasn't wise. Still, his body ached for it.

He managed to ignore Elliot for the next several minutes, concentrating on getting ready. They weren't visiting a jail or a junkie's house today, so they both needed to look presentable. Derwin pulled on some khakis and a button-down shirt his mom had bought him that he'd hardly worn.

By the time he was putting on his leather shoes, Elliot was out of the bathroom, wearing his usual T-shirt and jeans. Derwin frowned at him.

"What?" Elliot snapped, and Derwin blinked. The guy was mad at him now? Why?

"Do you own anything nice to wear? We can stop by your place if we need to," Derwin replied, careful to keep his voice calm and steady. He'd sensed right away that Elliot hadn't taken any pain medication this morning. Perhaps that was making him cranky. "Aren't you going to take your oxycodone?"

"What are you, my mother?" Elliot growled, but then he fell quiet, glancing down at his attire. "I have some black slacks. And that silk shirt you saw me wearing. I also have a few other shirts, but..." He chuckled, but it lacked humor. "I don't think they'd qualify as 'nice.' More like naughty."

He's nervous. That only compounded Derwin's worry for him. Derwin blew out a breath, nodding. "We'll stop by before heading to Abbott Industries."

Elliot nodded. His eyes held an apology, but he only said, "Sounds good."

They'd probably both feel better once today was over.

Derwin had the urge to strangle something as he pulled up to the warehouse, following Elliot's directions. "This is where you live?"

Elliot shrugged, opened the car door, and eased himself out. "It has a roof. And a bed."

Derwin took in the large building and connected loading dock as Elliot led him toward a small back entrance. Forklifts rumbled as they moved and there was the squeal of some hydraulic machine in the background. The air smelled of oil and seawater: not a pleasant mixture. Elliot produced a key, and they slipped inside the building to a narrow hallway lined with supply closets and offices, by the look of it. They reached the end of the hallway, where Elliot produced a second key and unlocked a closet door.

"Home sweet home," Elliot muttered, holding the door open for Derwin.

Elliot's living space was maybe half the size of Derwin's bedroom. Granted, he had a fairly big bedroom, but it wasn't an exaggeration to call this place little more than a redesigned storage room. There was a vanity with peeling paint and a cracked mirror, an old mattress with sheets and a blanket, and one of those plastic, build-it-yourself storage closets. That was about all the furniture in the room. On the other hand, the closet was stuffed full of clothing, and there were several pairs of boots and shoes lining one wall.

"Cozy," he said.

There has to be some way to get Elliot to move in with me. Even as he thought it, Derwin cursed himself. Why was he clinging on to hope like this?

"Cheap." Elliot took off his T-shirt and rummaged in the closet until he retrieved the blue silk shirt that Derwin loved. Buttoning it up only halfway, he then pulled out the black slacks, grimacing in pain. "Help me change clothes? I don't want to slow us up."

Derwin wanted nothing more than to rub his cheek against the smooth silk of that shirt, but he kept his body in check and helped Elliot take off his jeans, wincing at the bruises from the beating, still bluish but with tinges of yellow and green now. Was Elliot really up to seeing a client?

In short order they had Elliot dressed. The clothes from earlier were stuffed into a bag along with some toiletries and a couple pairs of latex gloves. Best not to dwell on what those were for.

Instead, he kept his mouth shut as they made the drive over to Abbott Industries on the other side of town.

Abbott Industries occupied several floors of a sleek skyscraper near downtown Nis, in the banking and computer technology sector. They had other sites as well, including buildings in the docking area of the bay and even on the fringes of the wilderness. But their main office was where Grady had worked.

Derwin managed to find a visitor parking space and signed himself and Elliot in at the front desk. When he asked about heading up to the programmers' offices, he was told to wait.

"My partner, Grady Tucker, was a programmer here," he informed the receptionist, a thin brunette with teeth that were too large for her face. "I need to talk to his old boss."

Glancing behind him, Derwin noticed Elliot gazing at a display of company awards. He didn't seem as nervous as he had at the prison. Still, he appeared out of his element. If he was planning on making a career doing readings, Derwin would have to coach him on how to present himself.

The receptionist gave him a fake smile. "I'll take you upstairs. Just a few moments, sir."

As they waited, Derwin tried to think out his strategy. It wasn't likely that anything in the boss's office would hold evidence—well, not as likely as the computer that Grady had actually worked on. He whispered to Elliot. "See if you can get any kind of reading from Grady's old desk. Third cubicle, second row to the right. Also, see if you can chat up some of his coworkers, and see if they noticed anything strange before his death."

Somehow he'd try to distract Grady's boss so that Elliot could work his magic. He doubted there would be strong memories in a cubicle, but maybe Elliot could get an image or two, as he had with the briefcase.

Elliot nodded, just as the receptionist approached to take them upstairs. As soon as they reached the correct floor, he groaned. "Hey, is there a bathroom somewhere up here?"

She pointed down the hall. "That way, sir." As Elliot headed off, she glanced at Derwin. "Did you want to wait for your friend? I believe our Informatics manager is available to speak with you."

Derwin waved a hand. "Nah. He can join us once he's done." He looked around: everything seemed like business as usual. People were typing away at their computers, occasionally peeking at him.

She nodded and led Derwin past several rows of cubicles, to a closed-in office with an actual door. No windows, but it was twice as big as what regular employees had. A figure emerged to greet them. Derwin blinked and then smiled as Cole, a short, slightly balding man wearing a cheap gray suit and tie, walked over. Adjusting his glasses, Cole smiled back.

"Cole Murphy," Derwin said, remembering his full name at last.

"How ya doing, Derwin? What brings you to this neck of the woods?" Cole extended a hand, and when Derwin took it, he shook vigorously, his jowls jiggling. Like Derwin and Grady, Cole came from the lower working class, and shared Grady's love of beer and hockey matches.

The receptionist returned to the elevator, and Derwin told Cole, "I'm following up on some new information about Grady's death. Is his boss in today?"

Cole's face clouded over. "Wow. I can't believe they still haven't caught anyone for that." He cleared his throat. "Actually, I'm the boss now—well, manager of the department, anyway. Mr. Willart left about six months ago to work for Immune."

Derwin blinked. "Aren't you guys merging with them?" At Cole's confused stare, he flushed, wondering if he'd gotten what Elliot had told him right. "It was on the news, I think."

Cole snorted. "Yeah. Everybody's all excited about it. They're known for fingerprint and iris recognition, but that's nothing compared to the stuff we're working on now with DNA testing." His smile turned sad, and he fidgeted with his glasses. "I miss Grady. I don't know if I can help, but I'd be happy to try. At the very least I should have a number to reach Willart."

Derwin followed Cole into his office. Cole had crammed a desk too large for the space inside, along with a dual-monitor computer and two file cabinets. Derwin tried to think of what to say to him, what to discuss. "So how is it being the boss?"

"Beats working overtime in a cubicle, I'll tell you that," Cole quipped, moving a chair for Derwin to sit, grinning. "Pays better too." He relaxed into his own overstuffed swivel chair: leather, by the looks of it. "Glad you stopped by, Derwin. This breaks up my day a little. It's been crazy."

Derwin closed the door and sat down, hoping that Elliot was having some luck on his search. "Oh? What's been keeping you busy?"

He'd intended to ask Mr. Willart about what projects Grady had been working on, if there were any secrets he might have had access to. Perhaps Cole would know.

Cole picked up a puzzle cube and started playing with it, rocking his chair. "Oh, the merger with Immune and all. We've started moving into these bio-engineered drugs, genetic testing, and stuff. And with that, you know, you're keeping files of your test subjects, pretty personal information. So I guess they figured it would be cheaper to bring in the Big Boys of security with Immune. Plus if they start to market things like genetic testing, they can include that security as part of the package to the consumer. Imagine a computer only your genetic markers can access. It's a brave new world for medicine and science."

"Oh," Derwin said, not sure how to respond to that. Again, it bothered him that Grady hadn't shared details of his work with him, the issues he'd had with his boss or coworkers. Maybe they hadn't had as good of a relationship as Derwin had thought. "Was Grady working on any of that?"

Cole waved a hand. "Oh no. The genetic testing wasn't even a sparkle in the CEO's eye two years ago. Um, let me think. Grady was working on data compilations, as I recall. Crunching the numbers from some of Abbott Industries' clinical trials on cancer treatments. Typical stuff."

"What about company secrets? Anything that could have gotten him in trouble?" Cole's foot was tapping under the desk. Had he always been the nervous sort? Yeah, he had. Derwin brought out his notebook.

"No, definitely not." Cole shook his head. "Really basic trials that we did all the time." He fell silent, and the air grew heavy with tension. Before Derwin could ask for further details, he felt a familiar buzz—Elliot was in pain again. He almost stood up, ready to rescue him if Elliot had been caught snooping, to see if something was wrong. But just as quickly, the buzz stopped. Derwin gripped the armrests of his chair.

He could barely concentrate on Cole's next words. "You okay? You went pale."

Cole didn't know about Derwin's Oddity, or at least Derwin didn't think he did. "I'm fine. Had a little touch of vertigo. Low blood sugar." He needed to keep Cole's attention on himself to allow Elliot to check Grady's desk. But what if Elliot had failed? What was happening out there?

Resolutely, Derwin continued. "You saw Grady the day before he died, correct?" It was better to concentrate on the questions, trust that Elliot could handle himself.

The chair creaked as Cole rocked back in it, clicking a pen in his right hand. "Um, yes. I think it was the day before. It's been a while. But I think we grabbed a drink or something." He clutched the pen to his chest. "I just never knew anything like that could happen. I didn't get to say good-bye, you know? Grady was upset that night." He shut his mouth abruptly.

Finally, a clue. Derwin leaned in closer. "What was he upset about? Did he say?"

"Yeah—actually, he didn't even have to say. Everybody in the office knew about it. Grady and Mr. Willart had this big fight that day, here, in this very office." Cole pointed at the desk, and Derwin wished Elliot was close at hand. Yet how would he have done a reading with Cole sitting there? Should he tell Cole about Elliot's Oddity? He wasn't ready to go that far.

"What were they fighting about?" Had Grady mentioned trouble with his boss before? Derwin couldn't recall. But then again, he'd been so occupied with his bond-enforcement shit that Grady could have been crying out for help, and Derwin might not have heard him. His heart gave a painful beat.

"I don't know—they had the door closed, and I didn't ask. But they were both yelling." Cole shook his head. "I wish I'd asked." He sighed, and Derwin wondered what Elliot was up to, if he was questioning the other analysts on this floor. Would others remember a fight with the boss?

"You know," Cole tapped at his keyboard, "one suspicious thing did happen around here after Grady was gone. Mr. Willart sent Grady's work up to his bosses, you know, the cancer trials. It wasn't long afterward that Abbott Industries made breakthroughs with blood typing and DNA that went beyond the cancer treatment.

We're working on a project now, something that might be able to test for all kinds of things." He pulled up a schematic, but it could have been in Japanese for all Derwin could make of it. "Maybe even treat some forms of Oddities."

"Oddities, you say? What do you mean by 'treat'? You mean like suppress?" A sinking feeling went through Derwin. He needed to tell his dad about this. It could spell bad news for all of them.

"I don't know. My department doesn't work on that. But Mr. Willart got big kudos. Probably helped him land the job he's at now. So it just got me pondering." Cole clicked out of the screen, frowning. "Grady didn't tell me about any secrets with his project. But that's what I know. One other thing I should add, though . . . I think his old boyfriend tried to contact him. You might want to check him out as well."

Another finger pointing at Oren. Still, talking to Willart might be a better bet. "Maybe. I talked to his sister. She also mentioned Oren." Perhaps that would be tomorrow's order of business. Or that and Mr. Willart. "Anything else? I'm trying to get some closure."

Shrugging, Cole spread his hands. "Wish I could help you. It was such a shock to everybody. He was real popular here."

"Right." Derwin sighed. The emotions this stirred up exhausted him. "If you could send me more information about the projects he was working on, that'd be great. He knew something. I just don't know what."

Cole nodded and rose from his chair. "I'll do my best. Should be able to get you a list by the end of the week, okay?" He glanced at the door. "Who's that?"

At that instant, Elliot tapped and peeked in. "Hey, sorry. I didn't want to disturb you guys."

Derwin had to hand it to him: he looked really innocent. His ungloved hands were demurely by his sides, and he wore an open expression on his face. Derwin resisted the urge to check Cole to see if he'd bought it. Instead, Derwin stood up with a grin and patted Elliot's back. "Elliot's my friend. Elliot, this is Cole. He and Grady were good friends."

Cole just nodded and smiled awkwardly. Probably he was thinking *boyfriend*. Elliot gave Derwin a sizzling smirk that could only confirm it. It was as good a cover as any.

"Yeah. I don't have a car, and I have an appointment later, so I tagged along." Elliot inched closer to Derwin, hand grazing his hip. Derwin didn't have to fake the blush that crept into his cheeks.

Cole cleared his throat. "Well, it was nice to see you, Derwin. Good luck on your investigation." His words were rushed and high-pitched, not at all like his normal tone. It was clearly a dismissal, which was fine with Derwin.

"Yeah—I might be back to talk to some other coworkers of his. Anything else that you can think of would be useful." Derwin stepped out of the little office, and Elliot followed close behind.

The ride down in the elevator seemed to take forever. The urge to ask questions was overwhelming, but Derwin managed to wait until they walked out the front doors.

What has he found out?

CHAPTER TWENTY-ONE

THE BIG BOSS

Elliot hated to crush the hope on Derwin's face, but it wasn't like he could lie. Still, when Derwin asked, Elliot held up a finger for him to wait, and didn't speak until Derwin pulled his car into the street, leaving the shiny glass façade of Abbott Industries behind.

"I didn't get any visions. After you left, I pretended to stumble and fall over the guy in your boyfriend's old cubicle, touched the monitor, the keypad, the mouse, the chair . . ." He shook his head, unable to hold back a smirk. "I acted super clumsy. But I think the computers have been used by too many people. I didn't get anything. Big companies like that—don't they sometimes move the computers around too?"

Derwin glanced over as he drove, deep lines showing in his brow. "It's possible. I didn't ask Cole about that. He was promoted about six months ago when Grady's old boss left the company. While I was questioning him, I think I felt you get hurt? I wanted to check on you, but I figured you were busy with your search. Really wish I could have gotten you inside that office; apparently Grady had a fight with his old boss the day he died."

Elliot winced. Perhaps he should have been with Derwin instead of in the stupid cubicle. Maybe he could have gotten a vision of the fight. But he couldn't have been in both places. "When I stumbled, it made my bruised calf flare up. The rib too. Um, as far as the boss's office goes, maybe later after they close we could slip in? I dunno. But I did talk to some of his other coworkers. One of them mentioned that fight. She said that they could hear the yelling all the way to the back printer." He grimaced. "She couldn't remember what they said."

Derwin sighed, nodding. "I'm glad you had a chance to talk to people. Cole said pretty much the same thing. Oh—and the project that Grady had been working on? His boss turned it in and got the credit. Something about DNA testing. And Oddities."

Elliot shivered. "Great. Like we don't have enough problems already." All they needed was for this company to sell that information to the government, and start some crazy scheme to wipe out the abilities of Oddities. Or control Oddities. He didn't know which would be worse. "You think that's what Grady knew about?"

"I wish I knew." Derwin sighed as they waited for a stoplight to turn green. "So where am I taking you?"

Elliot gripped the straps of his backpack. He felt naked without his gloves. "I need to change and do myself up a bit. Public bathroom, your place—it doesn't matter. Then I have to go over to City Central for the pickup. They'll come get me in a limo." It worked that way every time. Discreet pickup and drop-off meant no questions asked, nothing to taint Roy Yoshiro's public image. Only those closest to him in his gang even knew he liked guys as well as girls.

"Right. City Central—that's nowhere near home. But they've got facilities." Derwin's voice was gruff. His grip on the steering wheel turned white-knuckled. Elliot entertained the notion of rubbing his chest, anything to help relax him. At the moment, however, the gesture probably wouldn't be welcome.

So he sat quietly, reached into his bag for his gloves, and pulled them on. "That's fine. You can just drop me off." He'd done what Derwin had asked of him, and now Derwin was returning the favor. They were only business partners. Today of all days, he couldn't afford to let his mind go anywhere else. Bad enough that Roy would find him already bruised and marked up from the fight. If he suspected Elliot was thinking about someone else—hell, sleeping over at another man's house—Elliot'd be dead. Not figuratively, but literally.

"Wh—" Derwin started, and then pressed his lips together. At the next stoplight, he tried again. "Will you be coming back to my place after? Tonight?"

The question lingered in Elliot's mind. Suddenly he was angry—mostly at himself for becoming *attached*. For allowing Derwin to crowd in. He hadn't felt this unbalanced about a client since his first year whoring. "Probably not tonight." At best, it would be late when Roy was done with him, though the temptation of having some aftercare was strong. "Tomorrow. Maybe early." He rubbed his hands, leather against leather, the feel of it soothing him. Reminding him that it was his responsibility to keep up his barriers.

"What happens if you're hurt? What if you need help?" Derwin's voice was strained.

"If I need help, I'll call. I'm not stupid." This, of course, was assuming that Roy would allow him to call for help. But Elliot couldn't see any advantage Roy had in killing or damaging him. The guy liked his toys, and Elliot was just that: a fun toy.

Derwin glanced over at him, his eyes dark, almost black. "Really?"

Ignoring the knot in his stomach, Elliot nodded. He didn't want to do this. He *needed* to do this. Agonizing about it was useless. "Really. You questioning someone else tomorrow?"

If there was one thing that might shift Derwin's focus, it had to be the investigation. His dead lover always hung like a ghost over them.

Derwin was silent a moment before answering. "Maybe. I need to check in with my bail bond agency, see if there are new skips to track. But I'm hoping to talk to Grady's boss. Either that or Ceci's boyfriend."

Elliot thought of Derwin's bed. To rest after the appointment in Derwin's arms, cared for rather than huddled alone in his shabby hole, would be heaven. "I'll come to your place. After." He tucked a curl back behind his ear. "Dunno when that will be."

Derwin nodded but didn't speak. The station was ahead on the left, a solid gray block building with a network of driveways and railways leading into it. He pulled into the drop-off lane, and Elliot grabbed his backpack.

He looked over at Derwin as the car stopped. Derwin kept his eyes forward, hands on the steering wheel in a death grip.

Without another word, heart lodged in his throat, Elliot exited the car and shut the door.

When Roy's driver pulled up in the black limo, Elliot was ready and waiting. He still was wearing the blue silk shirt with the black slacks, but he'd gelled his hair back and added lip gloss, eyeliner, and just a touch of body glitter. After the driver opened the door for him, he smiled and got into the backseat, moving carefully so that he didn't jar his rib or the healing bruises. Roy wasn't in the car, which wasn't unusual.

The driver never said a word as he returned to the front seat and put the car in motion.

Elliot had debated between taking half an oxycodone, a full one, or none at all. Roy might want to share a bottle of wine, but he also might want to strap Elliot up to a cross and beat him black and blue. In the end, Elliot had taken half a pill, just in case. He'd remind Roy about the broken rib.

If necessary.

Twenty minutes later, they arrived at Roy's uptown condominium, where he engaged in his private pleasures. The driver pulled into the underground parking structure, then let Elliot out and directed him over to the bank of elevators, handing him a key card that would take him to the top floor. Elliot nodded, knowing that the driver would be ready to whisk him away once the appointment was over.

Gathering himself, Elliot took a deep breath and slid the key card through the slot in the elevator, then waited for the elevator to rise.

Only two condos occupied the top floor of this particular building. Roy's was on the left. After Elliot rang the doorbell, it was mere seconds before the door clicked open. He stepped in, removing his shoes to leave beside the door, alongside two other pairs—Roy's and his security escort's, who was never far from his side. Elliot's scuffed loafers looked pathetic next to Italian leather.

From beyond the gleaming white-tiled foyer came Roy's silken voice, with just a touch of a Japanese accent. "In the playroom."

Elliot set down his backpack, then fell into his role, sauntering into the playroom at the other end of the condo, a little smile on his face. At the bus station, he'd changed into a pair of white lambskin gloves, ones Roy had given him after he'd "confessed" to being a germaphobe. Roy thought they were cute.

The gang lord was lounging on a black leather recliner, one leg hooked over the arm, idly fondling a riding crop. He wore black silk pajamas, his black hair cut long with spiny bangs falling into his eyes. Roy was young and handsome, but Elliot knew better than to let appearances deceive him. Roy might look like a playboy, but he was a viper. He'd inherited much of his power from his father, who held an even greater position in Japan with the gangs there.

Swallowing, Elliot crossed to stand in front of Roy for his inspection.

"Tch," Roy muttered, shaking his head. He'd noticed the bruising along Elliot's jaw and temple, most likely. The man flicked a finger at him. "Undress. Let's take a look at the damage."

Elliot suppressed a sigh as he complied. He burned to know what Roy had done to those assholes responsible, but knew better than to ask. Right now, he was a walking, talking toy. Any exhibition of free will would break that illusion and invite punishment. With casual grace, he unbuttoned his shirt and let it slip down his torso and to the floor, then unzipped his pants to slink out of them as well.

The sharp intake of breath indicated that Roy had probably seen the rest of his bruises. This time when Roy spoke, there was fury in his tone. "Tell me what you remember of the incident."

Why should this make him more nervous than the man's typical appraisals of Elliot's appearance? Elliot tried to speak past the sudden fear in his gut, but it was difficult. "I don't know any of their names. There were five of them—their leader was white with light-brown hair in a crew cut. He had two friends I'd seen before, one tall and gangly, the other a guy with a scar on his face. And bruises." Bruises Derwin had given the guy in the first scuffle. "Those three were the ones who tried to drag me off for a freebie the night before. I don't remember the other two. I'm afraid I don't know who did what, but the leader, Crew Cut, used a tire iron. Pretty sure he's the one who broke my rib. Might've been the one who gave me a concussion also."

Roy stood and walked over, motioning for Elliot to turn around, his eyes narrowed. "I should have done worse than break his arms. Maybe I'll shove a hot poker up his ass—would you like to watch?"

Cold hands slid down Elliot's back, and he bit back a shudder. He needed to drive out the fear. He needed to concentrate on lust, on pleasure. While he'd never had problems before, tonight he longed to see Derwin's face instead of Roy's. It was making it hard to perform. In desperation, he imagined Derwin's firm, muscled body, up against his, the smell of him. The way a look from those dark eyes could make Elliot instantly hard.

Not once had Elliot needed to fantasize about someone else to achieve an erection before, but it worked: blood rushed to his groin, just in time as Roy's hands found him, rubbing him. Roy's breath heated the back of his neck. Elliot shivered and fought to hold on to Derwin's image. "Hmm?" The man had asked him a question. Elliot had to focus.

"Watch," Roy purred, grinding up against him, his own arousal pressing against Elliot's ass. "I could eviscerate him for you. And you could watch."

Meaning filtered through, and Elliot blanched, his gorge rising. Was Roy being serious? Elliot suspected he was. "N-no," he whispered, heart pounding, as Roy nibbled along his shoulder. "That's not necessary." *Just focus on pleasing him. Don't think about anything else.*

"I decide what's necessary!" Roy suddenly grabbed his balls and twisted, sending a jolt of pain through him. Elliot hissed. Just as abruptly, Roy let go and took a step away.

Elliot was quaking inside, but held still, trying to take slow, even breaths. He didn't apologize, but let Roy scrutinize him again, waiting for the next command.

After a moment, Roy huffed. "So. It seems I'll have to avoid your right side, and your left calf." He growled under his breath and motioned Elliot over. As soon as Elliot was within reach once more, Roy grabbed his hair, forcing his head back, and moved in close, nuzzling his throat. "I'll go easy on you tonight, boy." He chuckled, as Elliot tried to relax, tried to ignore the pull on his hair and the awkward position. Roy's grip was painfully close to the lump on his skull. "Good thing they didn't damage your face."

Submissive and coy. Right now, those were Elliot's best qualities if he was to escape injury. "Good thing," he agreed softly, swallowing. This was only his body. That's all Roy was playing with. It meant nothing.

Elliot was starting to relax when the touches suddenly stopped. With a snarl, Roy lifted Elliot up by his hair, until Elliot had to stand tiptoe, stretched out to the point of agony.

"You have a *mark*," Roy snarled. He let go of Elliot only to backhand him across the cheek.

Pain flared through his face and jaw, and Elliot found himself sprawled on the floor, dazed. He had only a few seconds to realize his mistake—the mark. *Derwin's teeth marks on his throat.* It had happened during that dance with Derwin, before he'd even told Derwin what he was. He was lucky the welts from their first session had faded or been obscured by the beating.

Roy hauled Elliot to his feet again, nearly wrenching his arm. "Who did it? That wasn't from my boys, was it?"

Miserably, Elliot shook his head. "No, sir. It was a john I picked up the night they harassed me." How stupid he'd been to accept this booking so soon after his play with Derwin. Of course, the original appointment had been for Wednesday; by that time the mark would have healed. But Roy had bumped it up because of the second attack.

The look on Roy's face was pure fury. He dragged Elliot over to the spanking bench and shoved him against it. "From now on, you will *not* allow other clients to mark you in any way! Am I clear? *You will be mine to mark as I see fit!*"

Inside, Elliot quailed. It was an impossible request; Roy must know that. But Elliot dared not say anything. Roy had broken Crew Cut's arms. He'd killed rivals, both inside and outside of his gang. There was no telling what he would do to some nameless whore without a family. Ignoring the prickle of tears, he nodded. Roy pointed at the bench, his face cold, impassive.

Silently, Elliot bent over the bench, hissing as the position pulled on his ribs, making it painful to breathe. He was doing this for the other homeless youths out there like himself, so that the rest of the Tatsu couldn't just take whatever they wanted, whenever. He had to focus on that. And, most of all, he couldn't think about Derwin. About the fact that, despite Roy's words, all he wanted right now was more of Derwin's marks on him, to blot out what was about to occur.

The blows began.

The good news was that Roy concentrated his efforts on Elliot's thighs and buttocks, never on his back or lower legs where he'd taken the worst of the beating. Still, he was ruthless with the crop, each stroke a cutting blow, leaving gods knew how many marks, how many welts. Elliot quickly abandoned any idea of holding back his cries, and sobbed in pain, begging for mercy.

Roy was not merciful.

The beating seemed to last for hours, until Elliot was wheezing and coughing, unable to breathe, fighting to keep from passing out. He didn't know what would happen if he did, if the Tatsu crime boss would allow him medical aid or watch him die on the wooden floor of the playroom. A stray thought came to him, that all this pain would have probably filled Derwin with power, and he laughed hysterically.

"Shut . . . up!" Roy backhanded him again. With that, the punishment was apparently over; Elliot was dragged to the bedroom, dazed and high on endorphins and adrenaline, which was good because they were combating the pain, but bad because he couldn't think straight and wanted to puke.

When they reached the bed, Roy threw Elliot down so that he lay prone, but then tossed him over to lie on his back. That movement sent pain flaring through the raw welts and cuts on his ass and legs, and through his busted rib. Elliot watched with morbid curiosity as Roy undressed, and it suddenly occurred to him that normally by this stage he'd be hard, but he wasn't. He didn't believe he'd be able to get it up, either.

He was almost relieved when Roy didn't give him a chance, holding him down and impaling him. Gods, at least he had prepped earlier, though it was a small comfort.

He sought refuge in his head, trying to pretend that it was Derwin inside him, Derwin fucking him. But the fantasy couldn't hold, not under such savage brutality. It felt like he was being ripped open.

"Look at me!" Roy demanded, grabbing his chin, forcing eye contact. Bent almost in half as Elliot was, each thrust only served to crush his knees to his chest, exacerbating his injuries. Tears streamed from his eyes, but he obeyed, offering no resistance.

Roy transferred his hand from Elliot's chin to his throat, pressing down, cutting off his air.

"You listen to me, rentboy. You're my plaything. I say 'jump'; you fucking jump, you understand that? I book; you come. And don't *ever* let me catch you with someone else's mark on you again. Got it?"

Elliot nodded. Black spots danced in his vision, and his heart was going to beat its way right out of his chest; he didn't do breath play, not ever, not in any form. Too dangerous. *He could kill me. I could die.*

Then, just as he thought his lungs would burst, Roy let go. Elliot drank in deep gulps of air, concentrating on that, hardly feeling the man pounding into him or the pain in his rib cage until with a curse, Roy came. Panic momentarily overcame Elliot's thoughts until Roy pulled out and tossed away the spent condom. Thank God Roy had used one—though probably more for his own safety than for Elliot's.

Roy collapsed on him, breathing heavily. Elliot held very still. Was that it? Or had this only been the first trial in an evening of terrible trials?

He tensed as Roy slid a hand up his leg, gently over his hip, and up the sensitive ridges of his ribs. Lips nuzzled Elliot's ear. Inside, Elliot retreated into a safe place, willing his body to react, respond without him.

"You know that I adore you, little E? I'm changing your name. Ecstasy," Roy whispered, and his cock stirred against Elliot's leg. His fingers circled Elliot's cock, coaxing him to life. "I forgive you. But just don't make me mad again. All right?" The sweetness in his tone belied the fiery welts on Elliot's ass, the stinging on his cheek.

Elliot dared to open his eyes. He had to know one thing. "So you punished them? They won't give me or Theresa's other girls and boys any trouble?" If he had consigned his body and soul to Hell, at least he could have that.

Roy nodded. "Besides breaking Chris's arms—the fellow with the crew cut—I also busted the bones in his friends' hands. They won't be troubling anyone for a while." He bent down to kiss Elliot brutally, teeth scraping his swollen lip. Tears burned in Elliot's eyes, but he swallowed hard, forcing them back down. Before, Roy had only booked him a few times; there had never been regular bookings, nor a lifetime sentence to serve the man. While Roy had complained about marks before, he'd never reacted like this. Never gone so far as to punish him and threaten his life. He quailed at the idea of going to

Derwin, telling the man no marks, no biting. No play that he actually desired.

Elliot returned Roy's kiss, but it was hollow, a burial of all his dreams. He'd never be free now.

It was going to be a long night.

CHAPTER TWENTY-TWO

BREATHING

On the drive home, Derwin called Connie to see how work was going at Bob's Bail Bonds; nothing much had come in since his last time there. Next he called Grady's old boss, knowing if he didn't do it right away, he might not have the presence of mind to do it later with Elliot's "date" distracting him and all. He set up a meeting for the next day, then left a message with Ceci's boyfriend to see him as well, at night during one of his poker games. Even if it looked like clues were pointing to Grady's workplace, Derwin needed to be thorough. No stones would be left unturned this time.

When Derwin reached his condo, he had to force himself to walk inside. Silence and emptiness greeted him, until an annoyed meow from Bickering broke the tension. Gratefully, he fed the cat, gave him a few scratches. Bickering arched against him, blinking grumpily. Derwin smiled. *Just you and me tonight, bud. Again.*

With Bickering fed, he wandered into the living room. Perhaps some television would be just the thing to occupy himself. His gaze fell to Grady's belongings scattered on the coffee table.

Pain, sharp and fiery, burned in Derwin's chest. Resolutely, he picked up the items and put them into a bag. Grady was gone. Elliot wasn't his, never would be his. Right now, Roy or whoever was probably peeling off Elliot's clothing, kissing the skin Derwin had so recently bitten and tried to lay claim to.

The burn in his chest threatened to cut off his air, making him wheeze. He kept seeing those intense blue eyes, their lost and helpless expression when he'd found Elliot in the gutter. Their introspection when he and Derwin had stayed at Derwin's parents' house. Their longing after sex, when Elliot had lain beneath him.

I won't be jealous. It's not my right. He wanted to slam his fist into a wall anyway.

It wasn't just jealousy that was churning in Derwin's gut. This was the fucking Tatsu gang, and even if Elliot's Madame had set it all up, even if this Roy guy was supposed to ensure Elliot's safety, that didn't mean shit. Gang bosses were notoriously vicious and temperamental. Elliot was young, but should have been wise enough to know that every single time he conducted business, he put his life on the line. Into somebody else's hands.

And that drove Derwin crazy.

Will it be worse if the guy hurts him? Maybe then Elliot won't want to go back. But what if he decides to stay with Roy? Permanently? He's already pretty much stated that a relationship with me won't happen. He wants to be free, to fuck as many men as he likes. And money, always the money. Roy could give him that. Make him a pampered pet.

Derwin recalled Elliot's coy smile and his sexy sway on the dance floor, knew how they must appeal to his clients. Why wouldn't a rich crime boss keep him around? And Elliot could shop at the downtown boutiques, eat lobster, never have to worry about where to sleep or what to eat again. Have every luxury he could ever want.

Derwin ground his thumbs into his eyes to stop the thoughts.

He set to washing the sheets and clothes, mopping the kitchen floor, vacuuming the carpet, while the TV blared some detective show. Images of Elliot crying, lying bloody in the street, moaning in pleasure, of his pale, naked body assaulted Derwin no matter how hard he scrubbed. So he paced the floor, breath hitching in his lungs, his body throbbing with worry and tension. This was all wrong!

When he ran out of chores, Derwin tried to watch TV for a while. The minutes ticked by, punctuated by the scrape of Bickering pushing his food dish across the kitchen floor and gunshots from a chase scene on the show where he had no idea who the villain was.

Inactivity was bad. Thinking was worse.

Derwin left the house before he even knew what he was doing, and took off at a run, trying to escape his imagination. Buildings swept by, but he barely saw them. How much time had passed since he dropped off Elliot? Was his date over? How late would Elliot be? He'd said he wouldn't be back this evening . . .

Just let him be okay, Derwin found himself praying, which was ludicrous, because he didn't believe in any gods and never prayed. The beat of his feet against the pavement was a steady impact, the run making his lungs burn, draining the stress from his limbs. He ran a full ten miles, until he had to slow down out of hunger and thirst. On the run home he ordered pizza, and chose takeout so he wouldn't have to sit around waiting for the delivery guy. Now it was more morning than night, with a pale glow in the east, but the streetlights were still on, and the air was cold with a salty breeze. A shiver went through him. What if Elliot had stopped by while he was out? The time had gone by quicker than he'd realized.

When he reached his condo, Derwin juggled the pizza and his keys, trying to unlock the door—except that apparently he'd forgotten to lock it when he left. And to set the alarm. Grumbling, he opened the door, only to nearly lose his pizza when Bickering shot past him into the night.

"Hey!" Derwin called, but to no avail. He cursed under his breath. Most of the time Bickering was happy to stay inside, but every now and then he seemed to get wanderlust. Derwin had actually been in the mood to pet the damn thing tonight. He shoved the door open and headed toward the living room, letting the door close behind him. Just in case, he did a quick cursory sweep downstairs and then upstairs, but he didn't see anything missing or any intruders. At least he lived on a decent street.

Satisfied that no one was in the condo, Derwin returned to the living room, sat on the couch, and clicked on the TV. He set the box of pizza on his lap, opening it to grab a hot slice. The first few bites tasted heavenly, but his stomach continued to twist and turn with apprehension. Derwin glanced at his phone. No calls, no texts. Chances were, it could be tomorrow afternoon before he heard from Elliot. If ever.

He groaned, setting the box on the coffee table. As if his upset stomach wasn't enough, he was starting to develop a headache as well. The room felt stuffy, airless. Derwin took a deep breath, dizzy with it all: the emotions, the worry. *This* was why he'd stayed home alone so many nights. This was exactly the kind of shit he wasn't ready to deal with again.

Want you. Need you.

The running had taken it out of him. He wasn't hungry anymore, just faint and sick. Derwin lay back on the sofa, worn out. He didn't want to face the night. Or the morning. He was tired of being alone.

Sleep would be his escape. Simple, dreamless sleep.

As his eyes shut, the smell of sulfur hit his nostrils. Alarmed, he fought to sit up, but it was as if his body was made of lead. His vision went gray, wavering. It darkened.

He passed out.

It was after three in the morning when Roy shoved Elliot off the bed and told him to clean up and get out. That was just fine, as far as Elliot was concerned. The last thing he wanted to do was cuddle with the guy.

All he wanted to do was clean off every trace of Roy and get over to Derwin's.

He showered quickly but thoroughly, inspecting the new bruises on his cheek and all the marks on his ass. Those would go over real well with Derwin.

Elliot scowled. He wasn't in a relationship with Derwin. So why should it matter to him what Derwin thought? It was his body. If he'd given it a little extra abuse lately, well, that was just how things went. He'd take some time to heal, and . . . get on with life. Keep on surviving.

Trying to be silent, Elliot slipped new clothes on, popped a pain pill, and headed toward the suite entrance. Though this was meant to be a free appointment, his cash was in an envelope on a little table by the door, as was Roy's custom. He counted it, feeling hollow inside. Apparently Roy had decided to pay anyway. Elliot had done his job well. The ache in his ass proved it.

Down in the parking garage, the driver was waiting for him, smoking a cigarette. While he didn't smoke (too expensive), Elliot was tempted to bum one just to see if it would help calm his nerves.

But upon seeing him, the driver grunted and stamped out his own cigarette, striding over to the car to open the door.

"Thanks," Elliot said quietly as he sat down in the backseat.

Part of him wondered if the man had noticed the new bruise on his cheek, but it didn't matter. Roy's driver had probably seen a lot worse. He might have helped to dispose of a corpse before. The guy closed the door and headed around to the driver's seat, climbed in, and started the car.

"Would you be willing to drop me off somewhere other than at City Central?" Elliot was dreading the long walk in the dark through the city to Derwin's place. He wasn't sure his body was up to it. "Anywhere near Highland and Fifty-second Street would be fine."

"I'll find you a restaurant or something near there," the driver replied. Elliot's heart beat a little easier. Not long now. He only hoped Derwin would let him in.

The place where the limo pulled up was more of a coffee shop than a restaurant, and it was closed, but Elliot didn't care.

"Thanks a bunch," he told the driver, and gently eased his backpack over his shoulder, wincing as he exited the car. The driver gave him a look that said Elliot was crazy, but remained silent, shutting the door after Elliot was out. As the car drove away, Elliot glanced around to get his bearings. Only two blocks to Derwin's. He could make that. It had to be close to dawn, by the brightening sky. Would Derwin be mad at him for waking him up?

Only one way to find out.

Elliot wanted to run, but his body wouldn't let him, so he walked as quickly as he was able, ignoring the hunger pains in his stomach and the rub of his jeans against the raw welts on his thighs and ass. It fucking hurt to breathe, even through the painkillers. He couldn't keep living like this. He needed to get off the streets, permanently. Maybe Derwin was still willing to help him with that.

When he reached the right street, he saw at least one light was on at Derwin's place. That was heartening. Maybe everything would be okay.

He stepped up to the front door and rang the doorbell. Then waited.

And waited.

Dread crept in. Perhaps Derwin knew it was him standing out in the chilly predawn. Maybe this was it. Derwin wanted him gone. Perhaps all the encouragement, all the words had been just that: words. Elliot breathed hard against a pain in his chest that was not due to his mending rib.

A cat meowed loudly and rubbed up against his leg.

"Hey there—" Elliot tried to remember the cat's name, but drew a blank. A wave of dizziness hit him; the pain pill kicking in, probably. The cat meowed again, head-butting his ankle and then scratching at the front door impatiently.

Well, if Derwin didn't want Elliot, he should at least want his cat. Elliot rang again.

Nothing.

Elliot tested the door handle. To his surprise, it was unlocked. He opened the door, ready to call out, when the smell hit him.

The noxious odor of a gas leak. Elliot stumbled, and the cat yowled and took off.

"Derwin!" Setting down his backpack, Elliot grabbed a spare T-shirt from inside it and tied it over his nose and mouth, and then opened the door wide to let the fumes out. How long ago had it happened? Was it an accident? Taking a deep breath of the outside air, he rushed inside.

Elliot checked the kitchen first—the oven door was slightly open and there was a shimmer of gas in the air. This didn't seem like an accident. He turned the knobs to shut off the gas. Nearby on the counter, the coffeemaker was plugged into an outlet timer connected to the wall outlet. The coffeemaker's cord was half-stripped, leaving copper wire showing. That couldn't be good—why would Derwin keep something like that? Goose bumps prickled Elliot's skin.

In an instant, it all clicked. The timer would reach zero, then power would flow to the stripped cord of the coffeemaker. *Boom.*

"Derwin!"

The T-shirt muffled Elliot's shout; he ran into the living room, beginning to gag at the rotten-egg smell of the suffocating gas permeating the apartment. Derwin was passed out on the couch. Grabbing him by the arms, Elliot shook him as hard as he could, ignoring his own pain. "Wake up!"

His heart leaped into his throat as Derwin blearily opened his eyes. "Wazzup? Don't feel good." He tried to rise but swayed sideways. Elliot strained to pull him up. Derwin's face was flushed. Was that bad?

"We have to get outside. Now." Elliot tugged insistently.

"Gonna puke," Derwin moaned, and took a step forward, and then another, lurching uncertainly.

"Gas leak—we need to go! Someone set a timer!" Elliot moved closer to wrap one arm around Derwin to help support him, even though it made his rib scream in pain. Understanding seemed to hit Derwin. He staggered, as if intoxicated, trying to hurry.

Elliot's heart hammered in his chest. "Come on. A little more. Get some fresh air." He prayed Derwin didn't collapse before they reached the door. He'd never be able to drag him out in time.

As they passed through the foyer, Elliot glanced at the timer on the kitchen counter. The little pointer seemed almost on top of the black mark that would flip the switch and kill them both. "Hurry," he pleaded, shoving Derwin toward the door.

They crossed the threshold as there was a tiny *click*. They took two more steps.

Then the gas ignited.

There was a flash, and hot air punched him like a fist of the gods, and they were flung into the street, Elliot falling on top of Derwin.

Derwin was unconscious, his face gray.

Behind them, the roar of flames filled the air. Elliot frantically searched Derwin's pockets. *Where's his phone? He's got to have his phone!* His hand closed around the cool rectangular object, and he breathed a sigh of relief, punching in the emergency code and holding it up to his ear.

"What is your emergency?" a female voice greeted him.

"Gas explosion," Elliot gasped, looking for the house number. He rattled off the address, then added, "There's injuries—the homeowner is unconscious, and before the explosion he was inside, breathing the gas." He swallowed hard, his heart pounding. "What do I do?"

The dispatcher's voice remained mercifully calm, though Elliot had to struggle to hear her over the ringing of his ears. "Are you out of the building?"

"Barely—we're in the street. Guess I should get us to the sidewalk," Elliot said, hitting the speakerphone button as he tried to get up. His legs still ached from Roy's session, and he suspected his back had taken more damage, possibly from flying glass. Blood was dripping from a cut he didn't remember receiving.

"No." The dispatcher's voice was firm. "Don't move him, and just stay where you are. The fire department and paramedics are on their way. Can you tell if he's breathing?"

Elliot's heart lurched. *Oh gods, he has to be. He can't die. I need him.* "I'll check," he said, voice shaking. Dimly he became aware of people standing nearby. One of them might have even asked him something, but he couldn't concentrate. He pulled off the glove from his right hand with his teeth, and laid his fingertips against Derwin's throat, hoping with all his being for signs of life. His pulse was there, steady and strong. Almost dizzy with relief, he bent close, trying to feel Derwin's breath on his hand, on his face.

It was difficult to tell with the ocean breeze and the hot wind from the fire behind him; nevertheless, Elliot was pretty sure he felt moist breath. "He's got a pulse, and I'm not certain, but I think he's breathing."

The welcome scream of sirens drowned out the dispatcher's reply.

As flashing red lights neared them, Elliot glanced at Derwin's home with a pang of regret. The lower level was in flames, but the fire hadn't reached the upper floor just yet. Around them, slivers of glass from the broken windows caught the orange light, sparkling. Car alarms blared as people emerged from the buildings around them, looking shocked and scared.

The headlights of a fire truck shone right in his face, and he couldn't see any more. On the phone, the dispatcher said something, but he couldn't focus. Paramedics ran up, and then tried to separate him from Derwin. He clutched Derwin's arm and refused to let go.

"Need to move you out of the street," one said, and Elliot nodded dully.

"Not leaving him," he told the man, but he shakily rose to his feet, as two others knelt and started taking Derwin's vitals.

"Take it easy," the paramedic said, checking Elliot. "Seems like you got a bit banged up as well. You were inside?"

Before Elliot could protest, one paramedic was taking his pulse as the other two placed an oxygen mask over Derwin's mouth and nose, and then lifted him onto a backboard. Elliot shrugged, knowing he must look bad with the bruises. "I was just stopping by. The cat was outside, which wasn't normal, and the door was unlocked. I smelled the gas." He grabbed the paramedic's arm. "I saw a timer in the kitchen connected to the coffeemaker with some stripped wires. This wasn't an accident."

The paramedic nodded and fitted an oxygen mask over Elliot's face. "I'll tell the fire investigators. I'm sure they'll want details. For now, breathe and relax. You can see your friend as soon as he's doing a little better."

At least that sounded encouraging, although Elliot dreaded further questioning. He wanted to ask more, but then the big paramedic herded him over to the sidewalk across the street. Elliot found his backpack, singed but intact. Shouldering it, he winced, his rib protesting, along with every other bruise and injury. He was so tired his legs were shaking. This was turning out to be one hell of a week. Elliot looked back at the ambulance where they were loading Derwin. A fresh wave of despair filled him. Another trip to the hospital. He couldn't believe it.

Somebody had tried to kill Derwin.

CHAPTER TWENTY-THREE

AFTERMATH

Derwin woke up in a hospital bed.

He yanked off the oxygen mask, wincing at the blinding headache and nausea that flared with his sudden movement. What the hell had happened? He dimly remembered falling asleep on the sofa, and then some kind of dream of Elliot waking him up and telling him to hurry and get out. And an explosion.

He peered down at his hands, which were lobster red as if sunburned.

Just as he was about to call for a nurse, a familiar voice began shouting, "I told you people already—I'm fine! I had a rough night. No, it wasn't the same guy, and now I need to see Derwin. And I'm not talking to the police until you let me in!"

Elliot burst into the room, his face smudged with something black and sporting a new bruise on one cheek. His clothing was singed and his hair was tangled, sticking out in odd places. Derwin's heart wrenched—he really did look like he'd been to Hell and back. *Was he hurt? But no—he's not the one in the hospital bed. Not this time.*

Elliot's blue eyes were almost glowing with ire, but once he saw Derwin, they softened immediately. He stopped and took a deep breath. "You're awake. Thank the gods."

Derwin sat up carefully, noting that he was still in his own clothing, which was good. The last thing he needed was a day or two in the hospital. His chest felt fine, so hopefully that meant he hadn't been breathing in smoke or superheated air. But he had so many questions. "What happened? Was there a fire at my place?" All the work he'd put into remodeling. The memories—he suddenly remembered Bickering, taking off into the night. "What about my cat?"

"Fine, last time I saw him. He ran off before the explosion, so he's probably hiding out in the neighborhood." Elliot raked a hand through his hair, shoulders hunching as he sat down at the end of the bed. "This wasn't an accident. I came over to your place—like I said I would, you know. It was maybe four in the morning and your front door was unlocked. As soon as I opened it, I smelled the gas leak."

It was fast becoming clear that Elliot was on the verge of collapse. His skin was a sickly, papery shade of white. He barely seemed able to keep his head up, and pain emanated from not only Elliot's rib but his thighs and his ass—not just on the surface either. He'd been used very roughly. Derwin clamped down on the rage that wanted to take over. He needed to listen.

"So I passed out because of a gas leak? Do they know where it was coming from?" A simple leak would have taken hours, days even, to build to the level that could threaten his oxygen. It would have had to be a massive leak, like one caused by somebody cutting the main line.

Elliot grabbed Derwin's hand firmly. "I saw the source when I walked in: the oven door was open. And I saw something else—you know your coffeemaker? It was plugged into one of those wall timers you use for lights when you go on vacation. The timer was set, and not only that, the wire to the coffeemaker had been stripped. It was about to go off and make the wire spark, and that's when I knew the place had been rigged."

Fear shot through Derwin. *They could have killed me, and anyone else nearby.* "So my condo? I remember running, and then an explosion. I guess it knocked me out."

"Yeah. We both flew halfway across the street." Elliot held up his hands, showing new scratches over the old ones that had just started to heal. "I don't know the details about your place yet. But I used your phone to call emergency services, and they got there pretty fast, so I'm hoping they saved at least some of your things." He made a rueful face.

A couple of detectives with badges hooked to their belts were hovering at the doorway, and Derwin realized he and Elliot were now in the center of their own criminal investigation. He squeezed Elliot's hand. "Hey, I'm alive, you're alive, the cat's alive. I'll figure out the rest."

Why had somebody tried to kill him, and why in such a remote way? Grady's death had been up close and personal. Why the change in methods? What the hell was going on here?

"Who do you think did it? Lloyd's in jail. And other than him, we only talked to your boyfriend's sister and his coworker buddy. You think Ceci told her boyfriend and he decided to kill you?" Elliot spoke rapidly, shooting the police officers a glare.

Light-headed, Derwin replaced the oxygen mask long enough to suck in a few lungfuls of air. "I also made arrangements to talk with Grady's boss today. And I called Ceci's boyfriend. Somebody's getting nervous that I'm poking around." If the secret that Grady had been keeping was this dangerous, that might better explain why he hadn't said anything. Maybe he really had been trying to protect Derwin.

"So what do we do?"

Then the police detective entered the room; Elliot fell silent. The detective looked vaguely familiar; Derwin had worked with a few cops in his time, but they often seemed like clones to him. He granted the guy a smile, hoping they didn't dig too much into his investigation. Police involvement was not something he wanted just yet, not when he was this close. Not when they'd been investigating the wrong guy for so long.

"Derwin Bryant? I'm Detective John Wentley, District Nine. If you're up to it, I'd like to ask you a few questions." The man glanced at Elliot before focusing on Derwin. "How are you feeling?"

Derwin took another puff of oxygen. "Alive." Was the headache tied to the lack of oxygen he'd experienced, or the lack of a decent sleep? He saw Elliot closing down, hugging himself as the other officer approached him. Those damn bruises on his face—Derwin just prayed nobody thought he was the cause. "Elliot—go ahead and tell them what you told me. It'll be all right." *Please let it be all right.*

"Sorry, but we need to speak with each of you separately," the other detective, a large fellow with Asian heritage, said, nodding toward Elliot. "Come along. Your friend here will be fine for the moment."

Elliot didn't appear convinced, but meekly followed the detective out, every step labored, and threw Derwin one last look that seared his heart. As soon as they were alone, he was going to find out what had happened during that damned date.

Detective Wentley pulled up a chair and sat down, then flipped open a notepad and clicked his pen. "So the EMTs tell me that they found you unconscious at the scene, suffering from oxygen deprivation and shock from the blast." He glanced up. "What do you remember?"

Derwin proceeded to tell the cop about his evening, from dropping off his "friend" Elliot for a date, up to eating a slice of pizza and falling asleep on the couch. He doubted Elliot would reveal that his date involved prostitution, though the cops would definitely want to know where the guy had been prior to arriving at his place at such an early morning hour. He only hoped Elliot was as truthful as he could be without getting himself into trouble.

"You didn't notice a strange smell when you returned from your run? Is there any chance you left your burners on?" The officer was busy writing stuff down.

"Not a chance. I haven't cooked at my place for a couple days. Didn't smell anything when I walked in, but I was preoccupied with the pizza." He suddenly remembered a detail. "When I got back from running, I realized I'd left my door unlocked. Anybody could have come in and turned my oven on. Plus, I understand there was some kind of a timer on my coffeemaker? I don't even own a timer. And that's not something I'd do, hooking it up to my coffeemaker. I work odd hours. I never know when I'll need a cup."

Wentley nodded. "You're sure you left your door unlocked when you went out to take a jog?"

Derwin struggled to recollect. He'd been in such a state, trying not to think about Elliot with that other man. And yet now Elliot was back, as if he'd never left. It all felt like a dream—or rather a nightmare, as far as his condo was concerned. "I don't remember. I was upset. Elliot—my friend—and I had gotten into an argument earlier in the evening. It's possible I forgot to lock it." And what an idiot that made him. Then again, he'd never dreamed someone would try to kill him. Even in his line of work, that hadn't happened before, at least not at home.

The scratch of Wentley's pen was the only sound for a moment. From beyond the room, Derwin heard people murmuring, as he waited for the inevitable question.

"Mr. Bryant, is there anyone who might want to hurt or kill you?"

"I'm a bounty hunter." The guy had probably pulled that up already. "I send fugitives to jail. So I have a long list of people who might want to do me harm." He debated adding further information. It was a risk, but what if the police knew more about Grady's murder than they'd told him before? "Plus I've been looking into the murder of my old boyfriend, Grady Tucker. I found out recently that the guy you had as the main suspect couldn't have done it, because he was busy stealing a car at the time. So maybe I've ruffled some feathers somewhere."

That earned him an intent stare. "Can you give me any names? The fire department is investigating the cause of the gas leak and the fire in your condominium. If it turns out to be arson, we'd like an idea on who to question next."

Yeah, here came the tricky part. "Unless you can give me file details about Grady's murder, I'd rather not mess with people I've talked with so far. Give me a couple days. Today I'm supposed to speak with two people who might know something." A thought came to him: even if he did reach Grady's old ex-boyfriend, the one Ceci suspected, it was unlikely that Oren would be willing to talk to him. "You could try Oren Whittaker. He was Grady's ex-boyfriend, and a son of a bitch from everything I heard. It's probably a long shot, but check him out. I'll tell you more as soon as I talk to these two people, I swear."

Detective Wentley scowled. "You realize you could be putting your life at risk. If someone is trying to kill you, they may try again."

Derwin nodded, waving that away. "I deal with dangerous criminals on a daily basis. Check my records over at Bob's Bail Bonds—they'll tell you. I've worked with the police before too; my dad's a correctional officer. Just give me two days. That's all I'm asking." His words were clipped with suppressed anger. If the police hadn't botched up the original investigation, none of this would have been necessary. He'd still have a nice place to go back to.

He didn't want to think about what it must look like. The last of Grady's things—they'd been on the coffee table. They had likely been destroyed.

Sighing, Wentley set aside his notepad. "Fine. Two days. I'll check out this Oren fellow. We'll get the results from the arson investigation and whatever we can dig up from surveillance cams in the area."

He gave Derwin a hard look. "But if you find out anything in connection to this, call me. If you think that your life is in danger, don't be the hero. Who knows; there could even be a dangerous Oddity behind all this. Let us do our job." He handed Derwin his card.

"Thanks. I will." Derwin searched for his cell phone to put in the detective's number. He suspected Elliot had it. Had the fire service brought anything at all out of his place? He checked his pockets. At least he still had his wallet.

After the detective left, it was several minutes before Elliot appeared in the doorway, scowling. All things considered, Derwin could take scowling. He was just happy that they were both alive. His head was starting to clear as his Oddity sped up his natural healing, and all he wanted was to get out of here and grab something to eat. Sleep would be fabulous too, but it would have to wait for the moment.

Elliot walked up and sat on the chair that Detective Wentley had vacated, groaning. "I need a nap. They kept asking me about my 'date.' I told them it was none of their business. I think they would have taken me in except for the fact I called 911 *and* rescued you from certain death." He chewed on a thumbnail, his skin pale and dark circles under his eyes.

"Yeah, about that. Thanks," Derwin said, setting aside the oxygen mask to buzz the nurse. "I mean it." When the nurse appeared, he gave her a hopeful smile. "Can I get out of here now?"

"Let me get your vitals." She took his arm.

As Derwin expected, they came out close to normal, which earned him a bemused look from the woman. She offered to fetch the attending physician for a possible discharge, then left them alone to go do so.

Derwin fixed his gaze on Elliot. "So. You came back to my place . . . after." He left unspoken his questions about how the date with Roy went, why Elliot had decided to come back. Instead, he asked the question he wanted answered first. "Are you okay?"

Elliot flushed and gazed down at his hands, scraped by this morning's ordeal. "I'm okay." He didn't elaborate, which was an immediate red flag.

"But?" Derwin didn't want to drill him.

A sad smile appeared on Elliot's face. "Yeah, but. I have a problem." He looked up, and there were conflicting emotions in his eyes, bravery combating misery. "Roy found the mark you made on me. That bite. From our first dance." He raked fingers through his hair.

"Uh-oh." Derwin didn't need Elliot to tell him that was bad. "Did he hit you? Is that where you got the new bruise on your face?" The sight of it made him clench his hands into fists. It also worried him. Pissing off a drug lord was really not a good thing to do, especially for someone as vulnerable as a street whore. "Is he still going to protect your friends? That was the whole purpose of last night, right?"

Fuck. If Elliot had suffered through sex with that guy, only to have it all be for nothing? Derwin would seriously have to kill Roy. Take on the whole fucking gang. And yeah, that was nuts.

Elliot ripped a thread from his jeans, causing a small tear. "Yeah, his deal's still on. Theresa will be happy." Unlike Elliot, who was clearly miserable. "He said if he sees a mark on me again, he's going to kill me."

Something black and ugly threatened to cut off Derwin's air, closing his throat. "What do you mean?" *Again*? As in, the asshole was going to book Elliot for more dates in the future? How the hell was he supposed to remain mark-free as a fucking rentboy, of all things? Particularly given that he seemed to have a kink for pain, and that shit probably paid better? It was worse than a slave collar; it was a damned noose to hang him by.

Elliot shrugged, plainly making an effort to appear nonchalant. But nothing could hide the pain he was in, and this time it wasn't all physical. "Guess he considers me one of his favorites. Lot of money to be made, at least. Right?" His voice wavered at the end, and he peered up at Derwin with abject despair in his eyes.

Derwin didn't waste time thinking. He stood and wrapped his arms around Elliot's smaller frame, pulling him in close. He wanted to punch something, yell, *That bastard's never laying a finger on you again!* More than anything, he wanted to beg and plead for Elliot to cast off his Madame, leave his hovel, and stay with him. The condo, a motel: it didn't matter. He didn't know if he could live with the consequences if something happened to Elliot.

Though stiff at first, Elliot slowly melted, relaxing into him and finally bringing up his own arms to tentatively wrap around Derwin. He took a deep breath that sounded suspiciously like a sob.

"I've got you," Derwin said in Elliot's ear. Just a few days knowing each other, and now both of them had had a near brush with death. He'd have to take better care of Elliot, keep vigilant. He wasn't going to fail again.

"So stupid," Elliot whispered against Derwin's sooty shirt. His voice shook, but whether in sadness or anger, Derwin couldn't tell. Maybe both. "I wasn't supposed to get myself into this kind of mess." He scrubbed at his eyes. "I'm supposed to be in control of my own life. Nobody else." His voice wavered.

"It's not your fault," Derwin said, unsure what else to say. He was actually amazed that Elliot was letting himself be held. How long had the kid sucked it up? Years, probably. Maybe as far back as life with his parents. Derwin pictured meeting Elliot's father—and punching him in the face.

Elliot gave a harsh laugh, shaking his head. "I don't know what to do."

There was really only one thing to say.

"Stay with me. Tie off whatever loose ends with your Madame, then come to the condo. We'll figure it out from there."

Elliot fell silent for a moment. Derwin felt the rise and fall of his chest slowing down, and held him more tightly. At least he didn't seem on the edge of tears anymore.

After a minute, Elliot tried to squirm free, and Derwin reluctantly let go. He ignored the emotions constricting his chest as Elliot dragged a hand through his hair. "I'm still working for you on this investigation, right?"

Derwin took a deep breath, his stomach turning a slow flip. "Yeah." He hadn't kept track of the exact fees, but he'd get the money, one way or another.

Elliot hugged himself. "I'll stay with you—for now. Until the job is done. Then . . . I need to decide what I'm doing next."

Was he actually considering leaving the sex trade? Derwin hardly dared hope. "Okay. That's fine." He winced, thinking about his condo. "We may be staying in a motel tonight."

Grim mirth showed on Elliot's face in the form of a smirk. "Motel's better than my hole-in-the-wall. We should go check on your cat, though. He'll be okay, won't he?"

Relief flooded Derwin. "Oh yeah. Bickering can take care of himself." He wanted to touch Elliot again, but he held back. Touching could come later. Whatever happened next, for now he didn't have to say good-bye.

Yet.

CHAPTER TWENTY-FOUR

FIGURING THINGS OUT

There wasn't time to find a hotel after the hospital finally allowed Derwin to leave, since Derwin had made plans to speak with Grady's old boss at midday. Elliot fell asleep while waiting for the nurse to bring the discharge papers, then again in the car as Derwin drove them to the business district. Considering that he'd slept maybe an hour or two in the last twenty-four hours, it wasn't surprising. Derwin had asked if he wanted to reschedule and get some real sleep. Elliot refused. The sooner they figured out who this fucking killer was, the sooner they could both feel safe.

Thanks to his new resolve to find long-term safety, Elliot couldn't face the idea of returning to the streets. He didn't want to call Theresa, though he knew she'd be waiting for an update. What would Theresa say when he told her about Roy, about the no-marks rule and the need to be available for Roy at any time? He had a sinking feeling that she'd be thrilled. A political marriage of sorts, guaranteeing the safety of her "children."

He felt dirty. Worthless. It made no sense. No appointment had ever made him feel like that, not even with the pedophiles when he was fifteen.

Of course, then the whoring had been a matter of not starving to death.

They stopped at a diner to eat, seeing that neither of them had eaten since the previous day.

"I had one slice of pizza before I passed out," Derwin said, before ordering a triple stack hamburger, fries, and a milkshake.

Elliot ordered a double cheeseburger with bacon. The world seemed to be floating, and his equilibrium was all shot to hell. If he could just get five or six solid hours' rest, then he'd be fine. Maybe the food would help as well.

"You okay?" Derwin asked, and Elliot had the sense it wasn't the first time he'd asked.

"Tired." His emotions were all over the place. Earlier while the ER nurses worked on Derwin, he'd been panicked, then giddy that he was all right. Now he felt like breaking into tears. "I'm feeling a bit lost today."

A shadow crossed Derwin's face. "Do you want to talk about it?"

Elliot shook his head. The last thing he wanted to do was relive last night's appointment. "Just trying to figure out stuff."

He appreciated Derwin's offer for a place to stay so that he could try to find something new to do for a living with no pressure. That wouldn't really be fair to Theresa's other charges, however. Plus if he left Theresa, he could wave her support good-bye, and he'd probably have a whole new set of enemies in the form of the entire Tatsu gang. Not a good way to start fresh. But what else was there to do if he didn't want to continue whoring? It wasn't like he could just leave town. Nor did he want to.

Derwin scanned the other patrons in the diner, most of whom were over at the main counter or tucked away in booths. He leaned closer, cupping Elliot's cheek. Elliot stilled, his heart racing. Derwin's dark eyes held him. Consumed him.

Elliot's breath stuck in his throat.

"It's going to be okay," Derwin said in a low voice, and closed the distance, his lips meeting Elliot's.

The kiss was slow, deep, and tender in a way that none of their kisses had been thus far. Elliot kissed back, hungry for it, desperate. He flashed back to that embrace in Derwin's childhood bedroom, the comfort the man had offered. Derwin made him feel safe.

Elliot could have gone on forever, just kissing, but Derwin pulled away. He glanced over at their waitress, who'd left the kitchen bringing plates laden with food. Elliot licked his lips as she set the plates down, wishing they were in private. The world felt solid again. He squirted some ketchup on his fries and dug in, nudging Derwin's foot under the table.

They ate in silence, gobbling down their meals. The chocolate shake tasted heavenly, and the sugar kicked Elliot's brain into gear.

One day at a time. That was how he'd take things. And one hour or one minute at a time at that.

Once he'd paid for the meal, Derwin checked his watch. "We'd better get over to meet with Mr. Willart." He sighed as he pointed at their clothes. "I don't care how we look. What I care about is if he was responsible for Grady's death. I want to see the look in his eyes when we confront him with it."

Elliot gazed down at his own ensemble. He'd changed back to the jeans and T-shirt before leaving Roy's place, but they stank from sweat and smoke. At least he'd washed off the body glitter. "This should be interesting."

The first thing Elliot noticed was that Grady's old boss worked at a building that looked similar to Abbott Industries: all glass and steel with fake plants in the lobby. Mr. Hank Willart was an associate director at Immune Biotechnical Security. Hank met them in the lobby, standing stiffly with a small frown on his face. A man in his fifties with little hair and large jowls, he wore a cheap suit and sensible shoes. "Derwin," he said, nodding. He glanced at Elliot but said nothing.

"Mr. Willart. Thank you for speaking with me," Derwin said with calm assurance, shaking his hand. "I hope you don't mind—this is Elliot Leed, a friend of mine. He's just tagging along."

By the frown lines, it seemed Hank did mind, but he only blinked, and avoided looking at Elliot. Maybe it was the bruises. "I'm sorry about your loss. Grady was an excellent employee. Come on up, and we can talk in my office."

His office was slightly larger than Cole's, but otherwise they could have been twins.

Elliot stuck close to Derwin, in the hopes that he could check out any objects that Hank handled on a daily basis, to pick up any dark dealings the man might have. Grady's coworkers had liked Hank overall, but that didn't mean anything, especially given the fight with Grady. As they all sat down, Elliot touched the phone receiver, the arm of Hank's chair, the picture of his daughter on the corner of his desk, his stapler, and even brushed his hands over the keyboard. Nothing.

Derwin glanced out at the rows of cubicles. "This looks familiar. So what's it like working here?"

Hank shrugged. "Same old, same old. Higher salary of course, and more people to manage. Instead of coordinating the reports on patient trials and drug clinical testing, now I manage those who keep us all safe from hackers who would do the world harm." He began going on about the technology developed by Immune, stuff that went way over Elliot's head. By the glazed expression on Derwin's face, he suspected Derwin wasn't getting much more than he was.

"Great," Derwin finally said. "So I'm talking to people who knew Grady, still trying to solve his murder. There's been some signs that maybe he knew a secret, possibly one related to his work. Do you happen to know what he was working on just before he died? Was any of it hush-hush, maybe potentially dangerous?"

Elliot watched Willart's face as Derwin asked his questions, but Hank only appeared bemused. "The cancer trials? Uh, no. I mean, not really. The records fall under federal regulations of privacy, so in that sense they're classified, yes. We can't exactly go around telling other pharmaceutical companies about prospective treatments or drugs. But not dangerous, no. Not unless he was trying to sell them to a competitor! Now that could be dangerous." A shadow passed over Willart's face, and he looked away. *Now that's a guilty expression.* Elliot nudged Derwin, out of sight.

If Derwin noticed, he didn't show it. "Cole's running your department now. He mentioned something about you and Grady having an argument—a fight? Can you tell me about that?"

Two spots of color appeared on Hank's face. He swallowed hard. "A fight? Surely he must be mistaken. Grady was a wonderful employee. I never had any problems with him."

This time Derwin did glance at Elliot, before turning back to Hank. "Cole wasn't the only one who witnessed it. I understand there was yelling." He didn't elaborate further, but let the silence stretch between them while Elliot debated spilling Hank's container of pens so that he could pick them all up by hand. He scanned the room for anything that the man might have brought over from his other office.

A framed college degree caught his eye, on the other side of Derwin, out of reach. Would that have recorded something?

"Ah," Hank said at last. He picked up his coffee mug and took a slow sip. "I think I might know what Cole's referring to. There was an aspect to the cancer treatment study that Grady . . . found objectionable. He didn't want to include certain numbers in his reports, and I told him it wouldn't be a valid analysis if he excluded them. As I recall, the debate grew quite heated. But I assure you, it was nothing sinister."

"Uh-huh." Derwin didn't sound convinced. He scratched his head. "You'll have to excuse me. I'm a bounty hunter. My job's pretty simple. Grady was ten times smarter than me, and I won't even pretend to understand what all you guys did. But you said it 'grew heated'? What does that mean? What numbers didn't he want to include, and why?"

Hank laughed nervously. "Well the treatments were coupled with genetic testing, you see, and a few anomalies emerged. Anomalies that hinted at certain types. You know. Oddities." He shrugged. "I can't imagine why he didn't want to include those findings in his report. It was actually an incredible breakthrough. It later led to Abbott Industries developing new blood-typing techniques and further DNA work." Hank rubbed at his temple. "Shame that he died before finishing the project. I did end up keeping that data in the findings. That would be the stuff that Abbott Industries is now capitalizing on."

Derwin perked up at that. "How is the company capitalizing on it? I think Cole mentioned something, but he wasn't specific."

Hank closed his mouth with a snap, regret in his eyes. "Ah! Well . . . it's government stuff, not really for public use. Basically, in trying to isolate genes that might predispose a person to certain cancers, we uncovered other genes. Very preliminary findings of course, but someday it might lead to the treatment of certain forms of Oddities."

Both Elliot and Derwin froze. Derwin cleared his throat. "Treatment, you say?"

Elliot was proud of the way Derwin managed to keep his voice steady. His own heart was pounding in double time.

By his slouched posture in the cushy office chair, Hank had obviously missed their tension, and waved his hand. "You know, some of the undesirable types—Incubus, for example. Might also lead to a better testing method to identify telepaths, empaths, etcetera. All of that came after your friend passed away. It's unlikely that he could have stopped such findings from moving forward. He was just an analyst, more involved with p-ratios in the main cancer treatment study, statistical significance, and whatnot."

This was the first hint they'd found that maybe, just maybe, Derwin's old boyfriend had come across something that people would kill for. The question was, who? An Oddity in hiding? A rival company? Elliot piped in with the question burning in his brain. "How valuable was that information?"

Hank took a moment to mull that over. "To another pharmaceutical company or lab? Millions." He shrugged. "That didn't happen, because they would have developed it, and it would have been a big news story. So it's useless to speculate. If your friend was killed for this information, it would have been used by someone else. Whereas Abbott Industries is currently the leader in both pharmaceutical and genetic research, largely thanks to the unique results of that study. So I can't see how this research would relate to Grady's murder. Plus I doubt he had contact with anyone who would see the value of it outside our company. Unless he had friends in competing companies?" He raised his eyebrows at Derwin.

Derwin shrugged, frowning. "Grady wasn't like that—not as far as I know. He was a bit shy, and he was lawful. But his computer was one of the things stolen from the condo. So I haven't a clue who he might have been in contact with." He rubbed his forehead, looking tired. "I don't know anything about this sort of stuff. Let me ask you this, Mr. Willart. You saw the data that Grady was working with, and recognized it was important. Did you guess how much it was worth?"

Elliot held his breath; that was like asking Hank if he had killed Grady to take the credit for his report. Yet Hank didn't seem concerned. He pursed his lips, his jowls quivering. "To the company? Oh, I knew it was worth a lot. And I won't lie—that report helped clinch my success in that company and later my job here. But it'd be insane to kill somebody for something like that. I mean, it's not like I personally made millions. It was just a little feather in my hat, nothing more." He shook his head sadly. "I'm afraid you're barking up the wrong tree here. I'm no corporate spy. I'm not bright enough."

The interview was drawing to a close. Elliot glanced at the framed degree again, wondering how he could get himself close without looking crazy.

Derwin nodded and sighed. "I see. Okay, one last question. Did you see signs that he was nervous before you guys had that fight? Make that two questions. Did he have any tension with his coworkers?"

Elliot stood up, stretching as if his back hurt, though it was more that damned rib. Cricking his neck, he paced the small office as Hank answered.

"I didn't see anything like that, no. You spoke to Cole already? If anyone would've seen it, he would have." Willart shook his head. "Grady was such a sweet guy. I just can't imagine he was having problems with anyone."

That seemed to deflate Derwin. He shrugged. "Yeah. I know."

It was the perfect opportunity. So Elliot touched the frame, as if inspecting the diploma.

He finally got something.

It came in a series of images: dancing around with the diploma when he first received it, setting the frame on the wall of his first office, the heartache of being fired from that job a few years later. Elliot swayed, barely managing to stay upright as he emerged again. No images of Grady at all. The frame must not have been touched or brushed against, or that fight just hadn't been emotional enough to stick to it.

Disappointed, Elliot sat down as Derwin and Hank concluded the interview. Derwin thanked the man for his time, and Elliot mustered up a smile when he stood. "Good luck with things," he told Hank, then followed Derwin back down to the lobby and out the main doors. Once again, he waited until they were driving before speaking. "Nothing. A few memories from his diploma, but nothing to do with Grady. I'm sorry." He felt worse than useless. He felt inept.

Derwin rubbed Elliot's shoulder as he drove. "Don't worry. Willart definitely knew things. I don't have a clue if he was the killer. All I can say is the more I dig, the more I suspect that maybe Grady really did discover something. Information that got him killed."

Elliot blew out a breath. "So what about the whole ex-boyfriend thing? And Ceci's boyfriend, the drug dealer?" He massaged his forehead. "You know, for some boring IT guy, your old boyfriend had ties to a lot of shady people."

"Yeah. I always thought I was the one with the bad connections. Maybe not," Derwin said with a sigh.

Not far from Ceci's place, Derwin pulled into a cheap hotel. *Good.* They both needed a nap, and Derwin's meeting with Bud Larsen wasn't until 10 p.m., during his poker game. Plenty of time for shut-eye and then dinner.

When they reached the room after checking in, Derwin stripped off his clothes immediately. "I swear I still smell of smoke," he told Elliot as he went over to the shower.

We both smell like it. But now that they'd reached somewhere quiet, Elliot was reluctant to get undressed. To let Derwin see what Roy had left on him. As Derwin stepped into the shower and began washing off, Elliot took off his shirt, wrestling with himself. He had no clean clothes, which bugged him. Even living in his hole of a place he managed to get laundry done—people didn't sleep with slovenly whores. He pulled his pants off and glanced at himself in the mirror above the vanity by the bed.

Even knowing what to expect, Elliot still winced when he saw the marks. As if the bruises from the beating weren't enough, now he had a series of welts running down the backs of his thighs and over his ass. And a nice purplish-red shiner on one cheek. Lovely.

"You coming in?" Derwin called from the shower.

"Yeah . . . just . . . don't freak out. Okay?" Elliot wanted to go crawl into a hole. He was too tired to deal with this shit. Too tired to untangle the mess of their emotions. Dropping his jeans on the floor, Elliot walked over to the bathroom, carefully avoiding looking in the mirror there.

As Elliot entered, Derwin inhaled sharply. Elliot closed his eyes, reached blindly for the soap, and hurried to wash himself, wincing as suds got into the road rash he'd received from hitting the street after the blast.

"It's not that bad," he said, mostly so that Derwin didn't get some crazy idea to go kill a gang boss. "Probably be gone in less than a week." He hoped, anyway.

Hands gently turned him toward the spray, helped rinse him off. Elliot tensed as lips grazed his cheek, but it was only a light kiss, nothing more. Frustration and despair burned in his chest, choking him, and when Derwin started to shampoo his hair, Elliot had to fight the urge to cry.

"It's okay," Derwin said softly, tilting Elliot's head to wash out the shampoo. Easy to let the water mask his tears; harder to keep back the sob that wanted to escape. Elliot took deep breaths.

"It's not okay," he finally said, once they were both clean. Why wasn't Derwin yelling at him? Why wasn't he making threats, getting mad, something? Hell, Derwin's mother had shown greater theatrics at that stupid bump on the head from Crew Cut's gang. Elliot opened his eyes, afraid of what he'd see.

The concern and the tenderness in Derwin's dark eyes was more than Elliot was prepared for. Hot tears leaked out only to be washed away by the water spray, and his cracked rib seemed to be on fire, crushing his chest. Or maybe that was just his shame.

Despite the hard set to Derwin's jaw, the man remained silent, only moving enough to turn off the water.

"I don't want to do this anymore." Elliot stepped out and scrubbed himself dry with the towel, shivering. He was aware of Derwin following and drying off beside him, but he didn't glance up. Exhaustion was making the room spin.

"This . . ." Derwin echoed, in a quiet voice.

Elliot fought against the despair. "This. Whoring. It served a purpose for a long time. But Theresa knew that I never wanted to get involved with the gangs. And now I am." He peered up at Derwin miserably. "I don't want to go back there. But if I don't . . ."

"We'll figure something out."

There was a bleak note in Derwin's voice. It only made Elliot's anxiety worse.

He shook his head. "You can't do anything. Not only does Roy run the Tatsu gang here, he's connected to the Tatsu gang in other cities. And in Japan. It's not like you can kill him and make it all go away."

Leaving Derwin to chew on that, Elliot returned to the bed, gazing in distaste at his dirty clothes on the floor. "Fuck it." He pulled down the covers and crawled into bed naked. The sheets felt glorious on his clean skin, even with the burn from all the welts and scrapes.

Derwin joined him. "So what's the worst thing that happens if you retire and don't see this client again? He puts out a hit on you? Is he really that possessive?" Firm hands slid over Elliot's body, drawing him in closer. If he hadn't been so tired, he'd be begging Derwin for another fuck. As it was, his cock only gave a halfhearted twitch.

Elliot rubbed his forehead. "I don't even want to think about it." He tried to turn away.

Derwin cupped Elliot's chin, forcing Elliot to look at him. "We'll figure it out," he repeated, and this time there was steel in his voice, a deadly seriousness.

The man is an Interrogator. He takes down demons and feeds on pain.

He could kill Roy Yoshiro. And then what?

Before Elliot could ponder that, Derwin spoke again. "You don't have to sell sex for money. You don't owe your Madame anything. Not anymore. You and I, we can find some other work for you. You might be able to help me on my hunts. Or use your Oddity. Or maybe Bob's Bail Bonds needs help filing. I know that we can find alternatives." He leaned in closer and pressed his lips to Elliot's mouth, demanding a kiss. Though Elliot's heart was pounding in fear, he couldn't help but kiss Derwin back desperately.

He broke away only when his lungs required air. "I hope so. Oh gods, I really hope so."

Less than a week ago, his life had been simple. If he hadn't gone to Club Demon, if he hadn't met Derwin and fought with the Tatsu boys, it still would be. And yet he couldn't bring himself to regret any of it. If he died tomorrow thanks to this killer or Roy and his goons, at least Elliot could say he'd had something real.

CHAPTER TWENTY-FIVE

GETTING DICEY

They ended up sleeping for two hours, and then had dinner at the cheap diner next door. During the meal, Derwin called his insurance agent, the police, Bob, and his parents. The hardest thing was telling his mother about Bickering, and how the cat had run off before the gas explosion and was lost. He noticed Theresa's number popping up after he hung up with his mom, but didn't take the call. What kind of hypocrisy was it to check on her boy after sending him off to a man like the Tatsu boss? What little regard Derwin had had for her was rapidly growing thin.

Even though it was looking more and more like Grady's death was tied to his work, they needed to check all the possible leads. So after they'd polished off their meals, Derwin reconfirmed with Ceci on where and when he could find Bud. He planned to stop by his condo for a change of clothing and a weapon or two before the meeting. The state of his place be damned. He didn't care if the smell of smoke clung to him again; there would be smoking at the poker game anyway.

When they arrived back at his condo, a cop was waiting outside and nodded once he'd established his identity. Apparently the arson investigation was still underway. Derwin tried not to examine the blasted-out front door or the plywood over the front window too closely.

The downstairs was a wreck.

He'd known it, expected it, and yet it was still a shock. The only good thing was that he was insured, which would cover the major appliances and furniture. Most of his precious belongings stored upstairs had only sustained mild smoke and water damage. He'd have to replace the bed, but the toy chest and its contents were intact.

However, the loss of his last few items from life with Grady tore at him. He called an industrial cleaning company to come scour the place. That done, he changed his clothes and offered Elliot a shirt as well, though he couldn't lend the smaller guy his jeans. The shirt hung loose on Elliot's slender frame, but it would do.

After stuffing more clothing into a duffel bag along with the small valuables in the house and a toiletry kit, Derwin headed back to the car with Elliot in tow. It didn't take long to drive over to Lucky Dog, the pub where Bud ran his weekly poker games.

It was too early for much of a crowd in the main bar; a few desperate souls sat on the wooden stools nursing their drinks, a football game showed on a tiny TV on a shelf, and two men were playing pool in one corner. Derwin crossed the room and nodded to the bartender. "Here to see Bud."

The bartender, a pudgy man with a stained apron, squinted at him. "Derwin? The bounty hunter?"

Derwin winced as all four men at the bar turned around to stare at him. It was possible that the bartender was just giving his patrons a fair warning, in case any of them had outstanding arrest warrants. Still, it was annoying. "That's me. Where's Bud?"

"In the back." The bartender turned around to grab a glass, apparently deciding to ignore Derwin and Elliot, so Derwin walked over to the unmarked door beside the bar. He knocked hard and opened the door. Immediately he found his path blocked by a giant of a man in a black tank top, with a full sleeve of tattoos.

"Bud Larsen," Derwin told the solid chest, before peering up at the guy. He barely received a glance in return, but the man stepped out of the way, allowing Derwin and Elliot to pass. The room was larger than Derwin had expected. A green-felted table occupied one end with several folding chairs surrounding it, but on this side there were additional seats and little tables with ashtrays. So maybe Bud's players liked to take a smoke, maybe do a line or two, and chat? Derwin didn't want to know.

"I don't like this," Elliot whispered in his ear. Derwin resisted the urge to take Elliot's hand. Bud knew his proclivities, but it wasn't wise to advertise them to everyone else.

"I know. Just a few questions, and we'll get out of here," Derwin whispered back. He tried to smile at the bouncer as they walked past, but afterward there was an itch between his shoulder blades, as if the bouncer was staring daggers at his back.

Bud was sitting at the card table, a cigar in his mouth and a foamy glass of beer beside him. Like Grady's sister, the guy might have been passably attractive if he'd kept away from drugs and alcohol. As it was, greasy black hair fell into his eyes, and a beer gut spilled over his jeans. Bud was a pretty big guy but not particularly fit. Derwin could easily take him. It was Bud's lackeys that concerned him.

Elliot stayed close enough that when Derwin stopped a few feet away from the poker table, Elliot bumped into him. Derwin tried to throw him a reassuring glance, but Elliot seemed focused elsewhere. Still, Derwin couldn't worry about that right now. While Bud might not have been a big powerful crime boss, he was still a drug addict, and addicts were unpredictable. "Hey, Bud. How's it been?"

Bud's pupils were slightly dilated, so he must have been inebriated from either alcohol or drugs. His voice gave no hint of that, sounding scratchy and irritated. "It's been. I hope you aren't gonna take long. I have a busy night ahead of me."

Derwin pulled up a chair and sat down. "It shouldn't. I just need to ask a few questions so that I can figure out who killed your girlfriend's brother." Put that way, he hoped Bud would do it for Ceci, because otherwise, he doubted he'd be allowed here tonight at all.

Anger flashed in Bud's dark eyes, and he took a swig of beer. "The fucker. You hear how he tried to boss his sister around? He blamed me for her being a dopehead, you know. I didn't introduce her to painkillers. The doctors were her dealers long before I came along."

"I heard," Derwin said in a calm voice, trying to keep things moving. "I guess you and him fought sometimes? Was it about you getting her drugs?" He needed to hear Bud's perspective on it, and see if it matched what Ceci had said.

A wariness came over Bud's features. "We argued, yeah. That's all. He wasn't too happy about me dealin', but his sister's an adult, and he didn't want to see her go to jail or anything." Bud fell silent, glowering. The vehemence in that gaze made the hairs on the back of Derwin's neck stand up.

Derwin crossed his arms, refusing to ease off. He glanced at Elliot, his signal to let Elliot loose on the place. If Bud wouldn't talk, maybe his place and his possessions would. "Where were you the night Grady was killed? That would've been May tenth, two years ago."

Bud sneered. "How the fuck should I know? No doubt getting stoned off my ass. Or I was here. Either way, I didn't do it. And you know Ceci will vouch for me." He waved a hand. "It wasn't like he'd just found out, you know. We argued about it a few times, but he let us be. He was paying his sister money—she told you that, yeah? You can check his withdrawals or something. It was cash. Why the fuck would I want to mess with that?"

Behind Bud, Derwin saw Elliot touring the room, gloves off, tentatively touching things. Elliot paused as he fingered an ashtray, grimacing. It was probably one of those smaller visions. Derwin itched to ask him what he'd just seen, but he couldn't reveal what Elliot was up to. He forced himself to smile at Bud and gave a shrug. "So she said. But I need to know the truth. She also mentioned you weren't too happy that Grady found out about your game here. Maybe you wanted to shut him up because this makes you a lot of money and he threatened to tell the cops. Or maybe you wanted to keep him from getting his sister away from you?"

Bud rolled his eyes, slouching. "I get what you're saying. But nothing like that happened. Grady wasn't stupid—hell, he was smarter than his sister. Or me. Or even you." He poked a finger at Derwin's chest. "Geeky boy like him didn't care about the politics of street life, drugs, gaming, and all that. He had higher ideals. He said so, one time to me. Asked me if I'd ever choose a more . . . what'd he call it? More 'stable' lifestyle." He snorted. "I laughed in his face."

Derwin shrugged. He could almost hear Grady's cheerful voice urging Bud to change his life choices. Grady had always been the type to give money to the poor, to try to talk to people and help them out of a bad situation. It sounded like Bud had made his list of lost causes. "So you weren't afraid he'd let slip anything about your suppliers? Or maybe the identities of your customers? Poker regulars?" He racked his brain trying to come up with questions that Bud might be able to answer. That damned folder still bothered him. "Do you keep files about your dealings? Computer files, I mean."

Bud looked at him like he was crazy. "First of all, I don't know how to use a fucking computer. But even if I did, I'd be stupid to put those on there! Might as well write a diary about all my transactions!" He gave a laugh, which turned into a cough. Bud took a long swallow of his beer. "You never want to make it easy on the cops. Hell, you think I'm stupid?"

With a sigh, Derwin shook his head. "This is just bugging me. Try to imagine if someone offed Ceci. You wouldn't investigate into why?" Elliot crossed to his side again, and placed his hand on the back of Derwin's chair. Glancing over his shoulder, Derwin saw Elliot's face go pale. Crap. Derwin returned his attention to Bud. "No, I don't think you're stupid."

Elliot cried out, as if in pain. "I didn't do it!" he yelled, startling both Bud and Derwin. "I wouldn't cheat you, Bud. You know I wouldn't!"

"What the fuck?" Bud rose from his chair, only just managing to catch his cigar as it fell out of his mouth. "Who are you? Do I know you?"

Derwin stood as well, whirling to face Elliot, who had gone stiff all over, his pupils blown wide. Clearly Elliot didn't even know that Bud was there, but it didn't matter. At that second, Elliot's eyes rolled up into his head. He staggered back as if struck, then collapsed, sprawled out on the floor, jerking about like someone was punching him. Perhaps they were, in whatever memory he was reliving.

"He's an epileptic," Derwin lied. He kneeled by Elliot's side. No way would he let Bud find out about Elliot's Oddity. He'd threaten the guy's balls if needed.

"He's a nutjob," Bud said, scowling. "Who is he?"

"A whore I've been watching out for." This time he might as well stick with the truth. Bud knew people on the wrong side of the law; it wouldn't take him much to verify Elliot's identity. Also, this way Elliot looked harmless, just a trinket that was currently amusing Derwin. "Don't mind him. I'm sure the spell will pass soon."

Bud didn't seem convinced. "He said my name." He signaled to his bouncer, and Derwin's gut sank. This wouldn't be happening if he hadn't brought Elliot.

"Yeah—I've been saying your name this whole time, haven't I? I asked for you when I came in here. It's not like it's a secret." He needed to get Bud back on track, and fast. "So talking about Grady. You gotta give me something."

"I don't gotta give you shit," Bud snarled, walking around the table to nudge Elliot with his boot.

"Don't hit me," Elliot moaned. Then his eyes opened. He stared up at Derwin and Bud in horror. "Oh man. What just happened?"

"Grab them," Bud ordered. Before Derwin could do anything, the tattooed bouncer had a grip on both of his arms from behind and was yanking him backward. Bud grabbed Elliot by the shirt and hauled him to his feet.

"Derwin?" Elliot asked in a small voice. Derwin tried to respond, but received a jab to his throat for his trouble. He coughed, glaring at Bud, as Bud pinned Elliot against the wall.

"Do I know you?" Bud leaned in. Elliot blinked stupidly, still obviously dazed by his vision.

"No—I don't think so." Elliot glanced over at Derwin. The questions were clear in his eyes, but Derwin couldn't answer them.

Bud gripped him by the chin. "Look at me when I'm talking to you! Have you been to one of my games before? Or maybe your pimp has?"

Elliot's eyes went wide. "No! We haven't met before. I'm just here with Derwin."

"Who's your pimp? Madame?" Bud shook him, and Derwin winced, feeling an electric surge from Elliot's still-healing ribs. He wanted to punch himself. He never should have brought Elliot to this dive. He was supposed to be protecting the guy, and here he was, putting him in danger. What had he been thinking?

Elliot didn't even show that he was in pain. "Theresa. We don't gamble. It's against her rules. Maybe you saw me on the street sometime? Or at a bar or party?" He seemed to be getting his wits back; he was smiling, pouring on the charm.

Bud studied Elliot with narrowed eyes. "Theresa," he said. Derwin couldn't tell if he recognized the name or not. "Maybe. What the hell were you saying about cheating me?"

"I . . ." The color drained from Elliot's face. Derwin knew he should say something, anything, but he couldn't think of what. Elliot gave a sickly grin. "I don't know; I haven't eaten much today. I think I was hallucinating, or maybe the drugs are catching up with me."

It was a good effort. But Bud clearly wasn't going to let go of his paranoia. "You're one of those Oddities. You read my mind." He yanked at Elliot, shoving him in Derwin's direction. Elliot barely managed to avoid hitting the poker table, and went sprawling on the floor instead. The bouncer growled as he let go of Derwin and pulled out a gun from a hidden holster. Derwin took a step forward and then froze at the sight. *Fuck!*

He glared at Bud. *You'd better not hurt Elliot.* If Bud didn't let up soon, he was likely to see another Oddity tear this place apart.

"Get out," Bud said, wiping spittle from his lips. "Just get out."

Derwin knew better than to push it. As soon as the bouncer released him, Derwin helped Elliot stand. Ignoring Bud's evil look, Derwin kept hold of Elliot's arm and pulled him out the door, inwardly fuming. Bud might have known more than he'd let on, but thanks to Elliot's vision, he'd never find out for sure.

As soon as they got outside, he rounded on Elliot. "What the hell happened in there?" He knew none of this was Elliot's fault, but the gods be damned! That had been a near disaster. Both of them could have been exposed, or hurt, or fuck it, even killed.

Elliot blinked as if stunned. "Excuse me? What the hell happened? I'll tell you what happened. A really bad fucking vision, that's what happened! I told you I don't like seeing that shit! Especially not around dangerous assholes like them!" He stalked off toward the car.

Derwin hurried to catch up with him. His heart was still pounding with adrenaline. "What did you see? Say that we actually got something there." Obviously Bud habitually roughed up people he didn't like. People cheating on him. Maybe people who knew too much.

Like Grady? Waves of guilt and betrayal swept through him, one after the other. It seemed like every interview was turning into a dead end, yielding nothing. No wonder the cops had given up on the case. Grady's secrets burned at him, and he was tired, exhausted, and yet jittery with too much energy.

He tried to put his hand on Elliot's shoulder, but Elliot yanked it off defiantly. Once they reached the car, they both climbed in without a word. Derwin looked at Elliot expectantly.

Elliot crossed his arms, staring straight ahead. There were dark circles under his eyes, and that damned bruise on his cheek, a big neon sign of how shitty a job Derwin was doing at protecting him. Just seeing that mark was infuriating. Derwin ground his teeth to keep his anger in check. "I'm sorry he roughed you up. You were kind of noisy in your vision." He turned on the car.

They were halfway to the hotel before Elliot said anything. "I was 'kinda noisy.' Yeah, considering I was having my face beat in and my fingers broken, I guess that makes sense." Fury didn't begin to describe the anger in his voice.

Derwin swallowed a lump of remorse, but he couldn't let go of his frustration. "Was it Grady? Was Bud interrogating him? Or someone else?" It had to be someone else. Grady hadn't ever had his fingers broken.

"Some idiot who came trying to make a few bucks by cheating. Bud was like an angry pit bull!" Elliot snarled, punching the glove box. "I told you I didn't want to have visions like that. Now he's going to come searching for me. You realize that, don't you? You're messing up my life!"

Just what Derwin needed: more guilt piled on top of him. The worst thing was Elliot was right. The more Derwin associated with Elliot, the worse trouble he seemed to bring to him. The scuffle with the Tatsu gang, which had led to the crime boss and his date, and now this? "You knew what kind of place that was when we walked in. I'm sorry it was a bad vision, but that was the risk. So did you learn anything? Is Bud the guy who was interrogating Grady in your first vision?"

Elliot was silent for several moments, obviously seething, and Derwin wondered if he'd pushed too far. They arrived at the hotel, but neither of them exited the car. It was a clear night outside. Inside the car it felt ready to storm.

Finally, Elliot answered. "I don't think it was the same voice. The voice in the Grady vision was educated. Not rough and drugged like Bud." He flexed his hands, as if making sure they worked. "Also, it seems like Bud beats people up a lot. It didn't feel like that with whoever had Grady. I don't think the killer was used to using force. He sounded scared. You know. Like he was panicking." He spoke the words in a flat tone, not meeting Derwin's gaze.

Disappointment hit Derwin like a fist to the gut. "So we went there for nothing." He was insane for continuing to pursue this. The cops hadn't figured it out. What had made him think he could? It was a sick obsession, and he should let it go. But he couldn't.

He opened the car door, glancing to see if Elliot would come with him. But Elliot didn't budge. Derwin fought the rising tide of anger.

Derwin huffed out a breath. "I'm sorry about Bud. I'm sorry you had to see more shit you didn't want to experience. When I stop to think about it, meeting him did help me. Every suspect that I can cross off my list gets me closer to the killer. To the truth." He still wished he could be certain that Bud didn't know anything, but that was on him, not Elliot. Maybe they'd gotten everything they could from Bud.

Elliot turned to him, eyes blazing, stark blue under the streetlights. "And then what? You hand your evidence over to the police, they arrest the killer, and you move on with your life? What about me? I get to keep every memory that I touch. I get to *know* what it feels like to have a knife slice my throat, or my fingers broken. What do I get out of it? What's my reward?" He punched the inside of the door this time, veins showing on the pale skin of his throat.

Derwin winced. The more he thought about his obsession with Grady's murder, the more selfish it felt. But Elliot had known how important this investigation was to him going in. What was he truly upset about? The visions? Or something else? "You'll be paid—"

"Money," Elliot scoffed. "For my services. That's all I am to you. That's all I am to anyone." He opened the car door and got out, slamming it shut behind him. Derwin's pain sense flared, and he knew Elliot's outburst was costing him.

The hell? When he'd met Elliot, the guy had cared about nothing but money. Derwin got out as well, following Elliot toward the lobby. "What's your problem? You say your life went to shit because of me? Sorry, but I've got news for you: Those gang members were going to drag you off whether or not I was there at that club. I stopped them. And I don't care how grateful you are to your Madame. She's using you."

"Like you?" Elliot glared back at him, then opened the doors and rushed through them, clutching his side. Derwin had to run to catch up with him. Hurt burned in his chest. *Is that true? It can't be true.*

He waited until they entered the elevator and the doors closed before continuing. "Relax. You had a bad vision. I get that you're upset. You have a right to be. But the fact that somebody tried to kill me means I'm getting close. I have to finish this, and then who knows? Maybe I can help you out. I'd like to help you out. For now, though, I have to keep going."

The elevator dinged, and they exited, heading toward their room. Derwin thought furiously. The last thing he wanted to do was spend an evening with a ticked-off partner. Elliot had every right to be pissed, but Derwin didn't know how to deal with his anger at the moment. It might be better to follow up on Oren Whittaker alone, and let Elliot cool off, give him some space.

He opened the door to their room and led Elliot inside, then turned around. "Get some sleep. It's not that late in the evening. I'm going to contact Grady's ex, Oren Whittaker, and get that interview done. I won't need you for that."

Elliot's eyes narrowed. "Why not? Isn't that the whole reason I'm here? The whole reason you've been helping me?"

Derwin closed his eyes, clenching his fist. He yearned to tell Elliot that the reason he wanted Elliot with him had nothing to do with his Oddity. But Elliot had made it clear that this arrangement was temporary, and Derwin couldn't afford to leave himself open to another wound. Not right now.

"Look," Derwin began, "I know you didn't get much sleep. And it's— You're not just here to help me. But we'll talk about that tomorrow. This interview should only take a couple hours. Once I get back, we can decide what to do next. Maybe I'll go to the police, tell them what we learned and see how it fits with whatever evidence they gathered." He sighed. "I don't know."

Elliot stood for a moment, staring at him. Derwin could see his chest rising and falling with deep breaths, as he seemed to gather himself. Finally, he nodded. "That makes sense. And yeah. I'm tired.

I'm fucking wiped out." He glanced over at the king-sized bed dominating the small room. "Once you nail this killer, what then? Do you and me go our separate ways?"

Was that regret in Elliot's voice? Hope? His chest tightening, Derwin plowed on, unwilling to ponder that. "That's up to you. I've told you before that you can stay, find other jobs." That first night he'd practically begged Elliot to stay. He still wanted Elliot to stick around, but he didn't think he could handle more nights like last night, waiting for Elliot to come back from one of his client calls. If that was how it was going to be, better to break whatever was between them now, before he fell any deeper.

Elliot looked thoughtful. "Okay." He yawned, then sat down and took off his shoes. "I guess we'll talk about this tomorrow."

Derwin gazed longingly at the bed, and at Elliot. To wrap himself around Elliot's lithe body, even just to sleep, would be heaven. For now though, he needed to get to the bottom of things before the past repeated itself. As long as the killer was loose, they were both in danger.

"See you in a few." He turned and headed out of the room.

CHAPTER TWENTY-SIX

REVELATIONS IN THE NIGHT

Elliot wanted to punch the walls. He wanted to scream with frustration, or break down and cry. He did neither. Instead he stared at the door that Derwin had just exited through and clutched the bed, shaking with the effort of restraining himself, cursing the fact he was so beat up, even breathing hurt. Earlier today things had seemed so perfect between them. He'd never slept so well as in Derwin's arms. So what the fuck was wrong now?

It was Grady. As long as the ghost of Grady haunted them, Derwin wouldn't think about anyone else. Shit, Derwin didn't care that Elliot had just had his *fingers broken*—okay not really, but in the vision it had certainly felt like it. And now Derwin was off again, to interview another gods-be-damned suspect. It was enough to make Elliot storm out and head home. Back to his hovel.

But Elliot had crossed a line sometime in the last twenty-four hours. He didn't want to return to that existence. Maybe he didn't know exactly what he wanted to do, but he couldn't keep submitting to the whims of mad men like Roy Yoshiro. Sooner or later, it would go too far. And fuck if he'd worked so hard to survive just to get killed off by scum like that.

So this stupid Grady case needed to be solved if he was to have any chance of a relationship with Derwin. Derwin thought there was something with the ex-boyfriend, Oren or whatever his name was. Elliot didn't think so. As far as they knew, nobody had tried to contact Oren until after the gas explosion at least. The more pieces Elliot gathered up in those little visions, the more they pointed toward Grady's first real love, his computer. The folders, which could be computer folders. The mouse, and chatting online with someone.

Somebody stealing Grady's laptop. They had talked about having Elliot read the computer desk earlier, but in all the craziness, they'd both forgotten, focusing instead on arranging meetings with people, questioning them. That made sense. Derwin was a people person, not a computer geek.

Hell, Elliot needed to go back to Derwin's place, to touch that computer desk and any components that might remain. The answer was there somewhere. And while he didn't want a repeat of the murder vision, didn't want to get lost inside another one of Grady's memories, taking that risk was the only way this whole mess might be finished.

With a longing look at the bed, Elliot put his shoes back on, grabbed his backpack, and left the hotel room. He had no bike, but lots of cash.

Hailing a cab, he gave the driver directions to Derwin's place.

When Elliot arrived at the condo, the front door had been fixed, though plywood covered the little kitchen window. There were no cops that he could see, but just to be on the safe side, Elliot headed to the side of the condo through the alley, where there was a bathroom window. The same window that Derwin said the killer had used to escape during Grady's murder. He went over to inspect it.

The glass had cracked with the force of the explosion in the kitchen, but remained intact. The alley was deserted, and the only sounds came from the TV in the condo next door and other night sounds of the city. Hugging the wall, he picked up a rock and, with one mighty swing, broke the window, wincing at the crash. His heart pounded as he waited several seconds, before carefully knocking away the sharp glass still left on the window sill, thankful for his leather gloves. Then he pulled himself up and into the bathroom, wincing again as broken glass followed him into the condo.

The glass crinkled under his shoes as he crossed the tiled floor. The house was dark, but there was enough light from the street to reveal the stairs leading up to the bedroom. He climbed, silence ringing in his ears.

Then something brushed against his leg—something *living*. Elliot yelped and jumped, before he heard the telltale mewl. He groaned, reaching down to pet the nearly-invisible gray-and-black cat. "Bickering! You scared me to death."

Bickering responded with a loud meow, and Elliot wondered when he'd last been fed. "Not sure where your food is, buddy, but I can at least get you some water in the bathroom. I'll bug Derwin to come feed you tomorrow, okay?" He continued up the stairs, feeling his way to the master bathroom in the pitch-blackness, and plugged the sink, filling it with water for the cat. Here it was probably safe for Bickering.

At the sound of running water, Bickering jumped up onto the bathroom counter. After a few seconds, Elliot heard him lapping up water. Poor thing.

Sighing, Elliot returned to the bedroom. He knew the room's layout enough to find the foot of the bed. From there it was only a few paces to the computer desk, and the evil computer chair. With his gloves still on, he pulled the chair out and set it away from the desk. He'd had all he was going to get from the chair.

Elliot removed his gloves. He set them on the bed and walked over to the desk, wishing he could turn on a light and inspect it further. Where the master bathroom had been like a tomb, at least in the bedroom there was some light from the streetlamp outside. He peeked under the desk—some of the electrical cords were still there, but he didn't think they would help, unless Grady had spent a lot of time messing around with them.

There was nothing for it. He'd just have to see what memories the desk held. Taking a deep breath and trying to stay relaxed, Elliot placed his palm on the top of the desk.

He was Grady. Sitting in his favorite chair, Grady typed quickly, alerted by the sounds downstairs that Derwin was wrapping up the cleaning in the kitchen. He had to hurry and finish before his boyfriend came upstairs. His heart raced, and dinner wasn't sitting so well in his stomach. This whole deception made him ill.

On the screen, his instant messenger showed the latest message from Cole. *What the hell were you doing, looking in my cached files?*

One of those files was open underneath the message window.

To Elliot it seemed like a garbled mess of numbers. To Grady it was data, important data about the genetic markers for a very specific cohort of test subjects in Abbott Industries' latest cancer trial. It appeared that in doing their genetic research to cure cancer, the company had discovered similarities in the genes of people with telepathic Oddities.

A way to diagnose an Oddity. Eventually maybe even a way to manipulate the gene, or purposefully breed for it.

What were you doing with that file in the first place? That's not your project, Grady typed back, thinking furiously. He'd stumbled across the cache after trying to open one of the cancer-trial documents at work and finding it already opened and locked for editing by Cole, which wasn't right at all. So he'd waited until Cole was on break, then checked his computer's trash can and his cached files. *Further, you made copies. Why would you make copies?*

The edges of Grady's—no, Elliot's—vision began to darken, and Elliot felt himself being pulled out of the memory. He desperately tried to stay, wanted to see what Cole wrote. But it was no use. Blackness crept over his vision.

Then he was back in a dark, empty room at a desk with no computer. The hairs on the back of his neck were standing up—had he heard something?

A hand closed over his mouth, and a cold blade pressed against his throat. His eyes flew open. The hand at his mouth slid down to yank one of his arms behind him, forcing him to step away from the desk.

"Don't move. Not a sound, or I'll slice your throat," a low voice whispered at Elliot's ear. Terror froze him. It was the voice from the first vision. The voice that had talked to Grady before he was murdered.

Elliot held still, though his knees wanted to give out. His pulse hammered out of control, and he only hoped he didn't piss himself. How much time had he spent in the vision? It couldn't have been long. Derwin was probably still trying to track down the ex-boyfriend.

After a moment, the voice spoke again. "What did you hope to find here?"

Elliot released a breath. There was just a glimmer of a chance. The killer didn't know about his Oddity. That could change at any second with him being ungloved, but right now it was an advantage. The killer didn't know how much Elliot knew.

What to answer?

"I left my watch here. I just wanted to slip in and find it before Derwin missed me." No point in lying about breaking in. If the guy believed he was the new boyfriend, or even if he knew that Elliot was a whore, Elliot might be discounted as ignorant. Maybe he could get out of this alive.

"I wish I could believe you," the voice commented, as the arms dragged Elliot back farther from the desk, toward the room's exit. That voice was familiar, yet different from the last time Elliot had heard it. He struggled to remember. "I'm afraid I can't though. You're a criminal, after all, with your line of work. You think you're smart, but you're just a little street whore."

Okay, so the killer knew who he was. Elliot licked his lips, not struggling as the figure steered him down the stairs, back toward the dimly lit bathroom with its broken window. The cops could still be out front. But what chance did Elliot have if he made a sound and the guy cut his throat?

Not a good one.

"Yeah, I'm just a whore," Elliot began, to gain time, to keep the killer occupied with anything other than the real questions. "Got a bit banged up, and I'm taking advantage of the man's good nature. Like I said, I came by to get my watch. I swear I won't say a thing about this."

"Still don't believe you," the man muttered. They'd reached the bathroom. His captor must have been thinking the same as Elliot: how the hell was the killer going to get him through the window like this? As he thought that, the blade nicked the side of his throat. Warm blood trickled down his neck. "Well this is a problem. If you're worthless, I guess I should simply kill you here."

Fucking hell.

Have to give him something. What? "He's getting closer to finding you, you know," Elliot said, and while his voice was shaking, he figured he was actually holding things together pretty well. He'd never been this scared before in his life. Not even those first terrifying nights alone on the streets could compare. "I may not know all the details, but Derwin's starting to suspect it had something to do with Grady's work." Revealing that was a risk. Somebody had tried to kill Derwin as soon as they started poking around there.

The knife trembled at his throat. He didn't have time to wonder if that was a bad thing or not, before his assailant whipped him around and slammed him against the wall of the bathroom. Elliot closed his eyes quickly, but he was too late.

He'd seen the killer.

A small whimper escaped Elliot as he opened his eyes and looked at the slightly crooked glasses and receding hairline of Cole. So it had been him all along. The best friend.

"What'd you do that for? I said I wasn't going to talk!" Elliot couldn't help glancing at Cole's hands. Sure enough, they were gloved. Cole had killed Grady because he knew too much. Was he planning to kill again?

Different knife. No gun this time, or at least not one he could see. What the fuck was going to happen now?

Cole's eyes went hard as he trailed the tip of the knife lower, ghosting over the hollow of Elliot's throat. "I knew I'd find you alone sometime. Your friends—the other whores—they were very helpful in revealing who you were and where you and Derwin were staying. I found one of them here earlier, trying to bring you a message." Elliot's gut tightened. He hoped Cole hadn't hurt anyone. The man had to be crazy.

"H-how long have you been following us?"

Grinning, Cole licked his lips. "After the two of you showed up at my office. I took some time off. Decided I needed to take care of loose ends before you guys ruined everything." Cole took a deep breath. "Tell me what you know. Why did he bring you with him when he came to Abbott Industries? Where were you while we were talking? I want it all, or you're dead, right here, right now. I'm not playing around."

Elliot's heart pounded in his rib cage as he tried to think of how to escape this, what to say. Did it matter if the killer knew what Derwin knew? The only thing that seemed important was to keep Cole ignorant of their Oddities. "Tha-that's going to take a while. He's been questioning people. Lloyd Brunson—that guy the police suspected, only apparently Lloyd was jacking a car at the time. Grady's sister and her boyfriend. You. Grady's boss. I was bluffing a little earlier. He doesn't know it's you, exactly. But everything he's uncovered points to Grady's work. It's the only possibility that makes any sense." *Please let that be enough.*

His stomach cramped. No matter which way events went now, he was as good as dead. The question was, could he somehow get a message to Derwin? Let him know what he'd learned?

Cole stared at him, studying him, and Elliot realized that he was trembling with fatigue. His body had taken a pounding lately, and this wasn't helping. For the first time ever, he wished he were a Telepath rather than an Object Reader. How the fuck was he supposed to tell Derwin about this? He didn't even dare glance away to look for a weapon.

Cole nodded slowly, frowning. "You're correct. This is going to take some time." He brought out a plastic baggie with a folded cloth inside. He held the baggie out to Elliot. "Open it. Unless you like the idea of bleeding out." The blade at his throat nicked him again, sending another drop of blood sliding down his throat to soak into the collar of his shirt.

With fumbling hands, Elliot opened the baggie. Immediately a strong chemical smell assaulted him. *Chloroform. Shit. Not good. Really not good.* He had a sinking feeling as he looked to Cole.

The man smiled grimly. "You know what's next. Hold it up to your face. Nice deep breaths. Better than dying, right?"

Cole had a point. What choice did he have? With a sickening trepidation in his stomach, Elliot brought the moist cloth up to his face. Immediately he wanted to hold his breath, push the cloth away, but as soon as he moved, Cole pressed his gloved hand against Elliot's on his mouth. Elliot struggled—he couldn't help it. As soon as he tried to take a breath, he felt the vapors start to work. Blackness rimmed his vision and his limbs grew heavy.

After that, he knew no more.

CHAPTER TWENTY-SEVEN

A DEAD END

What a fucking day. That was all Derwin could think as he drove through the night streets, trying to remember where Oren liked to hang out in the evening. He lived down south of the docks, in the most gang-infested part of the city. It was approaching ten o'clock, which meant that Oren was probably getting drunk somewhere or trying to get laid.

Derwin had kept tabs on Oren because he'd heard too much about Oren from Grady while they'd been dating. Like Grady's sister and mother, Oren had a substance-abuse problem. Only Oren also had an anger-management problem, and frequently Grady had been the target of his abuse. Grady had been smart enough to leave the guy after being hit a few times, but Oren had pestered Grady for months afterward, trying to patch things up.

As Derwin recalled, it had taken his open threats to feed Oren his own balls to make him quit. He was sure the cops had checked the guy out after the murder, but they might have botched it, as they had with Lloyd.

He turned onto a street with several dive bars, automotive shops, and stripper joints, looking for a place to park.

The hair at the back of his neck stood up, a sure sign of danger. Derwin scanned the area, trying to determine the source.

There was a man walking down the street, hands stuffed in his pockets. Right height and build, but it wasn't Oren. For a second, it looked like the bouncer at Bud's poker game, and a fresh wave of fear struck Derwin. Then the guy half turned under a streetlight to light a cigarette and Derwin got a better look. *Not the bouncer, then.* Derwin exhaled. *I wouldn't want to encounter that guy again. Gods, that was a rough meeting.* And Elliot's freak-out hadn't made it easier.

Derwin's heart beat faster just thinking about it. The young man didn't get how— But no, that wasn't fair. Elliot's agonized expression flashed through his mind. *His fingers were broken. He actually felt someone breaking his fingers. He told me the visions aren't just movies on a screen, but did I listen? No, I wanted answers so badly, I put him at risk again.*

And while Derwin had been ignoring the risk, Elliot had been suffering it. That meant fear. Agony. All the emotions, and all the physical sensations, from sexual ecstasy to torture.

If that wasn't bad enough, now there was somebody trying to kill Derwin, somebody who might decide to kill Elliot as well. The encounter with Bud had only proven that Elliot wasn't safe around Derwin. That was why he hadn't wanted Elliot along now. No good could come from him meeting Oren or Oren's nasty friends.

Only now Derwin was wondering if it had been wise to leave Elliot behind. Was he safe at the hotel? Or would it have been better to have him near? *I want him with me. Even when it's not the best for him, I still want him close. What does that mean?*

Derwin turned off the car, and an overpowering urge to turn back came over him. Cold shivers crept up from the base of his spine, and before he knew what he was doing, he'd pulled out his phone and clicked it open, expecting to see something, a text perhaps. That was ludicrous. Elliot didn't own a phone. He had no way to text.

So why were alarm bells going off in Derwin's head?

Derwin thumped the steering wheel. Here was the bar, and that might even be Oren's beat-up truck parked down the street, proof that he was inside, ready to be interrogated. Still, that nagging feeling . . . He'd ignored that feeling when he'd gone hunting for Jack. Then Grady had died.

Fucking hell. This had better just be my imagination. Oren could leave the bar at any moment and disappear to who-knew-where. If Derwin left now, he could be giving up an opportunity to find the real killer. He pressed his forehead to the wheel, biting his cheek. He couldn't get the image of Elliot's bruised cheek out of his brain. Or the horrible fear that he might return to the hotel to find the young man dead.

"Okay," he told his intuition, "you win." He was falling for Elliot, and it was time to face up to that. Time to let the past be.

Derwin turned on the car with a roar of the engine and began to drive back to the hotel.

Elliot woke to a blinding headache. His tongue felt like someone had rubbed it with a dirty sock. Swallowing with difficulty, he blinked as he opened his eyes.

He was tied to a bed. Well, more precisely, to a bed frame. The springs dug into his back, making him aware that he needed to pee and that his thighs still hurt from the beating Roy had given him. And he was thirsty.

With a sickening rush, he remembered what had happened, how he'd gotten here. Cautiously, he looked around. He was in a small room with metal siding: a storage shed perhaps. One door, no windows, with brooms, scrap metal, and trash lined against one wall. There were familiar sounds of the bay and the docks, though—the low hoot of a boat horn, the jagged whir of cranes and machinery. So he was somewhere along the coast, maybe not that far from his little room.

The only problem? He wasn't alone.

Cole Murphy had his back to Elliot, bending over as he went through a large duffel bag. Elliot didn't know what was in there, and didn't particularly want to find out. Hadn't it only been an hour or two ago that he'd had his fingers broken in some vision?

Elliot tried to move—he'd been securely tied with nylon ropes, the kind more likely to be found in a hardware store than around docks and warehouses. He bit back a moan, beginning to shake all over. Cole must have been planning this.

He forced himself to take deep breaths despite his racing heart. Based on what had happened last time Cole had tried to interrogate someone, Elliot would probably be killed, but he wasn't about to give up without a fight. He carefully began testing the ties at his wrists, working his hands around, seeing if he could get his fingers on any part of the knots.

Good thing he had small wrists and slender hands. While he had to almost twist his right hand backward to do it, Elliot was able to grasp the end of a rope through his middle and ring finger of his right hand. He carefully rotated the knot so that he could start to work at it with whatever fingers he could use, little by little. Too slow. He'd never be able to get his hand free before Cole realized he was awake.

Even as Elliot thought that, Cole straightened, picking out something from the bag before he turned around. Elliot cursed silently, letting go of the knot.

The delight in Cole's eyes was downright creepy. He seemed calmer, although he rubbed at his balding forehead, where a slight sheen of sweat showed. In his hands were a couple of instruments: a small paring knife and a lighter.

Nobody should look that happy while holding such items. Elliot shivered.

"Glad to see that you're awake! Now I'm afraid you'll have to let me have some fun. I didn't get to do anything with Grady. If you cooperate, it won't be all that bad. See, I'll make wounds, and then I'll cauterize them. That way I can do a whole lot to you, and you'll stay alive." He brandished the knife at Elliot. "What do you know about me?"

Bile rose to the back of Elliot's throat, and a wave of dizziness passed through him. "Dude, I'm just a street whore. Oh, and incidentally, the boss of the Tatsu gang told me last night that if any johns do anything to me, he's personally going to disembowel them. So this might not be a good idea."

Cole backhanded him. When the stars receded from Elliot's vision, he swallowed, cursing himself. Bravado had always been his best defense, especially when he wanted to curl up and cry. The man panted, rage on his round face. "You think you're funny! I don't have all night. Let's try this again: tell me what you know."

Elliot closed his eyes, hollow despair in his stomach. Would it be better to just spill it all? Or should he draw things out to give Derwin time to find him, maybe endure a few cuts before he started talking?

He didn't know how long it had been since Cole had knocked him out. Or if Derwin even knew he was gone.

Maybe Derwin would think he'd left and gone back to the streets.

All he could do at this point was pray that Derwin came looking for him. His gloves were still on the bed in Derwin's condo. Would he go there? *This is hopeless. There's no fucking hero coming to save the day. I really am on my own.*

"Yeah. I'll talk," he told Cole, shivering.

Cole regarded him with narrowed eyes, holding the knife at an angle, edge out. "You better not lie and waste my time."

Elliot laughed without humor. "What's the point? You've got me hidden somewhere, and nobody cares about me enough to look for me." And how sad was it that he was actually telling Cole the truth? He debated trying to work the knot again, then decided against it. Not while Cole's attention was focused on him.

Cole relaxed, lowering the knife. "That's right. I asked some of the prostitutes about you. They said you've been on the streets for years."

Elliot nodded, feeling every day of every one of those years. "Yeah. So you really don't have to persuade me or anything. I've got no stakes in this. You can put away the tools." Maybe Cole would let him go once he talked. And maybe his fairy godmother would burst into the room and give him a million dollars.

Cole sat down on a half-rusted chair at Elliot's left side, hand still shaking a little, but his jaw set. He placed the lighter on a little rickety table. Then suddenly he grabbed Elliot's hair, using his other hand to hold his knife against Elliot's upper arm. "Don't stall. Talk."

Elliot stayed very still. *Come get me, Derwin. Please.* "Well, the first clue that the murder was tied to Grady's work was the missing computer. You tried to cover it up by smashing the phone and taking the jewelry and the game console. Must've had your hands full getting those out. But considering how much Grady used his computer, it was a key clue."

That coaxed a laugh from Cole. "Yet the police never truly pursued that. Idiots!"

He's so sure of himself. Could Elliot make use of that ego? It was worth a try.

As he began speaking, he twisted his right hand again, trying to unravel the knot. "Like I said, Derwin talked to Lloyd Brunson, the one the police had questioned. He found out Lloyd was jacking a car on the day of the murder. So that didn't add up."

It was unbelievably hard to talk normally while trying to work the knot free, straining tendons and muscles that were never meant to be used at that angle. But thankfully Cole's eyes remained fixed on his face.

Cole sneered, brushing the edge of the knife up and down Elliot's arm, probably shaving off a few hairs in the process. "So he figured that one out. That Lloyd guy seemed like a good choice. I even tried to match his shoes. But alibis, you know. Can't do much about those. I had me a good one when the cops came—I went to the movies, then slipped out during the film. Kept my little stub, which was proof enough for the police. So why did Derwin come to the office?"

Elliot was starting to sweat; any second now, that blade might slice him. "It was a process of elimination. He wrote down a list of people that Grady associated with. Then he spoke to Grady's sister. From there he planned on talking to Grady's boss, you, Grady's ex-boyfriend, and also his sister's boyfriend, since she dates a drug dealer. He was just pulling at straws."

Cole's eyes grew hard. The blade snagged on Elliot's skin, and pain flashed through him as it cut in. His hand stilled. He felt a drop of blood sliding down his arm. All thoughts of escape were useless if he didn't survive the next few minutes. "Then he saw me at Abbott Industries. Talk. Tell me what he knows," Cole said.

Panic gripped Elliot, and he struggled to speak past the thundering of his heart. "He didn't learn much more than what you told him that day. We knew Grady was working on a special project, but that was all. Then that gas explosion happened at his house." He bit his tongue, not daring to accuse Cole of rigging that, and dying to know. If Cole hadn't tried to kill him, it meant Derwin had other enemies.

So when Cole chuckled, it actually lessened his fear. Elliot's said flatly, "You tried to kill him."

Cole grinned. "It seemed like the thing to do. Maybe I was a little early though—I heard you were the one to save the day?" The sneer in Cole's voice hinted his anger, his desperation. What the hell was so big a secret that Cole would kill not only Grady, but anybody else who got close to it?

"Yeah. Sort of an accident." What would have happened if Elliot had stayed the night with Roy? Derwin would be dead. He hoped Derwin could figure things out and stop this guy. Even if he was too late to save Elliot.

Cole's eyes narrowed. He glanced down at the trickle of blood on Elliot's arm, as if deciding whether to cut him on purpose this time. "Really. An accident? Right place, right time?"

Flushing, Elliot nodded. "I had another client, then I stopped by." All he could do was keep stalling. Keep hoping that Derwin would find him. He tried once again to twist his wrist around, and the rope scraped against the skin, making it raw. Just a little more, and he might be able to get the knot loose.

"Stop moving." Cole's voice was deadly serious, as his blade dug into the skin just above a major vein in Elliot's arm, drawing blood again. A drip, not a fountain, thank the gods. Elliot halted at once.

A moment drew out between them. What would it be like to truly die?

"Finish the story. So after you two survived, what happened? Did he learn anything else?"

Elliot's stomach churned, and he wondered what Cole would do when he finished. He wasn't ready to die, or to be sliced up into little pieces. "We learned more about Grady's cancer project from Grady's old boss, Mr. Willart. Something about DNA testing discovered during a cancer trial, about how to test for Telepaths and other Oddities. He said the information could have been profitable. He also said he and Grady fought about that data, that Grady didn't want it to be included in the report. He seemed pretty guilty, to be honest—" He shut up, afraid to say what he thought had happened. Grady had obviously been too good of a guy to abuse this knowledge, and he'd been trying to protect his boyfriend. But Cole must have found out about the results as well and decided to benefit somehow. Maybe he'd sold the secrets somewhere else, or maybe he'd worked together with Hank. After all, both of them had been promoted shortly afterward.

Cole leaned forward, gripping Elliot's shoulders painfully. The knife in his hand seemed almost forgotten, the blade brushing against the mattress and Elliot's skin. His eyes were wide, bloodshot, with a frightening intensity. "What else? Did Willart mention me? Did he suspect Grady knowing about that?"

"N-no," Elliot stammered, trying to stay calm. "He didn't mention you at all. He said the fight he and Grady had was about whether or not to include the weird findings. He said that after Grady died, he kept those numbers in and that's what led to Abbott Industries making new discoveries. He profited from it, but he didn't think anyone else had." Had Elliot just condemned another man to death? Or saved him?

Slowly, Cole drew back, scowling at Elliot. "You're sure? You're not lying to me, are you?" He waved the knife dangerously near.

Elliot took a deep breath before answering. "I'm sure. Willart seemed to think it was impossible that anyone had capitalized on it, since Abbott Industries is still the industry leader. That's what he said. I don't think he knew if you or anyone else was selling the info. We didn't know either." *But now I know. So now I'm toast.* Because that was the only logical explanation for Cole's actions. He had to have made some deal, somewhere, and Grady had found out. And then Cole had killed him.

Cole's eyes turned dark and cold, matching the cold pit in Elliot's stomach. He concentrated on breathing as Cole studied him, for how long, Elliot couldn't say. Maybe he was preparing himself to kill again. Elliot stared at the knife.

"So. You came close enough, anyway," Cole finally said.

Shivering, Elliot nodded.

CHAPTER TWENTY-EIGHT

MESSAGES

For Derwin, the first sign of trouble was the empty bed at the hotel.

"I knew it! Why don't I ever *listen* to my fucking feelings?" Derwin paced, wishing there were someone to listen, but there was no one in the cheaply furnished room. His heart was trying to pound its way out of his chest. Why had he left Elliot alone? He'd given Oren's name to the police, for crying out loud. They could have handled it.

He should have been here with Elliot. And now Elliot had vanished. The reality tore at his heart, making it hard to breathe.

Even more distressing was the fact that Elliot didn't own a phone. Derwin swore. The minute he found Elliot, he was getting that guy his own cell. He could only think of a few places that Elliot might have gone.

One: he might have left to get a drink. Or a client? But Elliot was still hurt and tired, so that wasn't likely.

Two: he'd returned to his shitty room at the warehouse. This wasn't as worrying, except if was true, it could be weeks before Elliot contacted Derwin to get paid. Derwin couldn't stand the thought of not knowing, of missing him and fearing the worst.

Or three: he'd gone to check on Bickering at Derwin's condo. He'd asked about the cat, after all.

Derwin didn't want to think about Elliot's last option: his Madame's place. All he knew was that he had to find Elliot, even if it took the whole night. What if he never saw him again? He couldn't bear contemplating that possibility, couldn't begin to deal with it. *I just found you. I can't lose you already.* Derwin left the hotel room, taking the elevator back down.

Derwin returned to his car. It made sense to check places he knew first. Fifteen minutes later, he was inside his condo, and what he found didn't ease his concerns. It was obvious that he'd had at least one visitor, by the broken window in the bathroom and the glass that had somehow fallen *into* the room rather than being blasted out by the explosion. Somebody had broken the window and climbed in.

Then he found Elliot's gloves on the bed.

At once his heart shot into his throat. He couldn't breathe. The past was there again—Grady's text, the frantic drive home, the blood on the carpet . . .

He searched the entire room. There was no blood here. He noticed a couple of faint impressions of hands on the dusty computer desk. Had Elliot attempted to do another reading? What had he learned? What had happened next?

Derwin vaulted down the stairs back to the downstairs toilet. He might not have a reading ability, but he'd been tracking criminals for a long time. Closer inspection of the window confirmed his theory. Elliot had come in this way. He'd also exited this way.

More concerning was the fact that there were signs that someone else had been in: drops of blood on the floor. A partial shoe impression in the midst of crushed glass that wasn't Elliot's small sneakers. Scents that were faintly detectable to Derwin's heightened senses: sweat and cologne, again not Elliot's.

Do I call the police? Will they do anything in time? Derwin wanted to scream Elliot's name in case he was somewhere nearby, that somehow he'd escaped and was waiting for help. That wasn't likely. There was a slight chemical tang to the air. He had a feeling he knew what the smell was.

Somebody took him. They drugged him with chloroform and took him. Why? Where?

Derwin examined the rest of the house. He found Bickering sleeping under the sofa, and had to coax him out to feed him. Derwin checked the alley and found tire tracks that seemed recent. But he didn't find any clues that could help him track Elliot down. He thought about calling Detective Wentley, but decided against it. What evidence did he really have that a kidnapping had taken place here?

He broke out in a sweat, his heart pounding as he returned to his bedroom. *Not again. I can't let it happen again.* Derwin slammed his hand into the wall a few times, trying to concentrate. He couldn't fall apart now. He had to focus on finding Elliot.

After more than an hour of searching the condo and racking his brain, he decided he'd drive over to Elliot's place. He'd check there, then with Theresa. And if he heard nothing by that point, he'd call the police.

Suddenly his phone rang.

For a second, Derwin panicked. He couldn't remember how to breathe or speak. Fumbling, he checked the number but didn't recognize it. He hit the Answer button and held the phone to his ear as if it would bite him. In a way, it did.

"D-Derwin?" It was Elliot.

"Elliot!" Suddenly Derwin could speak again. He could breathe. "Where are you?"

There was a pause before Elliot answered. "I'm tied to a bed. With a knife to my throat."

Derwin closed his eyes as the room started to spin. He took a deep breath. Elliot needed him. No time to pass out. "Are you hurt?" *Just concentrate on what's important.* He listened for background noise from the other end, some clue as to where Elliot was, but he couldn't hear anything. The kidnapper was staying quiet.

Seconds passed before Elliot spoke, and Derwin fought not to pace the room. "I'm okay. I told him what we know so far about Grady." His voice trembled with guilt. What had been done to him to get that information? *I'm not sure I want to know.*

Before Derwin could think what to ask next, there was a break in the line, as if someone had hit the Mute button.

"Elliot?" Fear made his voice rise in pitch. The killer/kidnapper had probably hurt Elliot in some way. Now he'd let Derwin know that Elliot was alive—so that he didn't go to the police? He needed to be patient.

Sound returned. "I'm here," Elliot said, breathlessly. "He says you need to come alone, or he'll kill me."

Derwin clenched his fist hard enough to crack his knuckles, driving his short nails into his palm. "Where do I need to go?"

Another pause. This time it was longer. Derwin bit his thumbnail, stopping only when the pain hit him and he realized it was bleeding.

Then Elliot spoke again, more subdued this time. Reluctant. "Harbor Street docks. One hour." His tone said he wanted to say more.

It was doubtful they'd be allowed to talk much longer. "I'll get you out of this. Hang in there. It'll be okay." *I'll fight through Hell and back to get you.*

Before Elliot could respond, the line went dead. Derwin collapsed into his chair, shaking all over.

Grady's killer has Elliot. Derwin took a deep breath and let it out slowly. Elliot wasn't dead. But he soon would be if Derwin didn't turn this thing around somehow.

The Harbor Street docks weren't that far from Elliot's place, but it was remote enough that it wasn't likely the killer was using that as his hiding spot. What was the likelihood that the guy would hand over Elliot and let the two of them go? Not good. He'd already tried to kill Derwin. This looked like another tactic to get him out of the way. They must have gotten too close to the truth.

Elliot's handprints were on the computer desk. If Elliot had suffered another vision, he might know everything. *"I told him what we know so far."* What *we* knew, not what Elliot knew. So maybe Elliot had the full story, but hadn't relayed all of it.

He needed an ace up his sleeve, something that the killer wouldn't expect. Yes, there was his Oddity, but what if the killer had one as well? It wasn't impossible.

Funny how Elliot hadn't been told to tell Derwin not to involve the cops. Didn't kidnappers always say that? Also funny that he hadn't mentioned coming alone *and unarmed.*

So maybe it was a risk, involving the police at this point. Somehow, Derwin got the feeling that this kidnapper/killer thought he was smart. Trying to stage a murder as a botched burglary. Using that homemade mechanism to cause a gas explosion. Making Elliot talk so that Derwin wouldn't hear his voice. But maybe he wasn't so smart after all.

Derwin prayed so. He took out the business card and called the detective, trying to ignore the uneasiness in his stomach. After four rings, it went to Detective Wentley's voice mail.

Frustrated, he almost hung up, but he forced himself to speak instead. Maybe the detective would hear his message in time. Maybe it wouldn't be like it had been with Grady: too little, too late.

"Detective, this is Derwin Bryant. You remember my friend Elliot? Somebody's kidnapped him. If you hear this within the next hour, I'm heading to the Harbor Street docks. Don't show yourself. It may be Grady's killer." He hung up, gripping the phone hard, hoping that he'd said enough. The detective might not even be on duty today. He might be busy with another case. And Derwin wasn't going to call the emergency number and get some nitwit who knew nothing—at least Wentley seemed trustworthy.

Derwin had tried. For now though, he was on his own. He went back upstairs to his closet. Good thing the call had come while he was still at his place; all his weapons were here. He strapped on an ankle sheath with his carbon-edged tactical blade, pulling his pants over it afterward to hide it.

Was there anything else he needed? His palms were sweating, and he couldn't decide if he was more scared or enraged. Had it been a mistake to contact the police? *They'd better not jeopardize Elliot.* Derwin grabbed the kid's gloves from the bed and stuffed them into his pockets. Though he had a gun in the car, he wouldn't wear it. He couldn't take the chance that the kidnapper had a gun to Elliot's head, or another homemade bomb. No need to piss the guy off until Elliot was secure.

He needed Elliot, and not just as a work partner, not just for his Oddity and abilities. While solving Grady's murder had seemed so important before, now it seemed stupid. He'd risked his life and Elliot's, for what? The truth? Revenge? And it was possible that instead of finding either, he'd lose his second chance at something great, at having someone else in his life.

Someone like Elliot. His smile, that cocky look when he knew he was so irresistible. His fire, and his bravery. His intelligence. Most of all, that vulnerability and hurt that he so tried to hide, the tender side that made Derwin want to hold him close and never let him go. So maybe Elliot might not be willing to leave his street life. At the moment, Derwin didn't care. He just wanted Elliot safe and in his arms.

Derwin only hoped he was in time.

CHAPTER TWENTY-NINE

CONFRONTATIONS

It was good to have a muscle car when you had to get somewhere fast. Derwin broke about half a dozen laws on his way to the Harbor Street docks, but he made it in twenty minutes. The sun was a red ball still on the horizon over the ocean, painting the rundown buildings, stacks of pallets, and other junk with crimson hues. He parked down the street, keeping his eye out for signs of the trap he was walking into.

The area was deserted. Whoever the kidnapper was, he'd chosen his location well. The warehouses here were abandoned, either because of worse-than-normal demon attacks, or maybe they had just been damaged in the last storm season. That only made the place more dangerous. The guy would have an easy time spotting Derwin. Perhaps he was waiting on a rooftop, rifle trained and ready to shoot.

Derwin checked the blade at his ankle one last time, and had to let go of the urge to take his sidearm. He pocketed his phone and stepped out of the car. Closing his eyes, he called on his heightened senses and listened.

There. Footsteps on gravel. Over toward the far side of the building. It was a good bet that the kidnapper had seen him. The question was, was there one set of footsteps, or two? Was Elliot with him? What would Derwin do if the kidnapper had brought him and had a gun to his head? Fat lot of good Derwin's abilities would do in that scenario.

Slamming the car door shut, Derwin didn't try to mask his approach. Stealth wouldn't help him here. He only hoped the kidnapper thought of him as an everyday run-of-the-mill human. A bounty hunter, yes, but nothing special beyond that. His best strategy was to surprise the guy.

He headed toward the warehouse, listening for anything unusual. So many things could go wrong here. He didn't know if the police would get his message in time, if Elliot was dead or alive, or if there was another Oddity waiting for him. Sweat beaded at the back of his neck, and a shiver went through him that wasn't just from the cold ocean breeze. *Can't think the worst. I have to remain calm.*

He was nearing the building when suddenly a voice warned, "Slowly, now. I've got my gun trained on you."

I know that voice, Derwin thought, proceeding cautiously. *It can't be!*

Derwin halted, peering down the alley between the warehouse and the storage yard beside it. A dark figure stood alone at the far end, one arm raised, aiming a Colt .45 at him. Even though it was dark, Derwin knew that silhouette immediately.

Cole Murphy. But Cole was a gamer, a geek—the idea of Grady's affable work buddy holding a gun was insane. Yet here he was.

"Cole. I'm surprised to see you here." Derwin's tone was ice. *You fucking bastard! How could you betray your best friend like this?* Willart had said somebody could profit from the information that Grady had discovered. Cole must have learned about Grady's project. "Was it about money?"

Grady's life for fucking corporate espionage. Derwin wanted to wrap his hands around Cole's fat neck.

"Money?" Cole laughed.

Derwin wished he could see Cole's expression, currently hidden in shadow. Was he scared? Confident? How dangerous was he? He could have been hiding a secret ability for years; it was always the quiet ones.

When Cole spoke next, there was fury in his voice. "Yes, money. Power. Respect. It's about all those things, and more. You have no idea."

Derwin's anger flared. "And that was worth the life of your best friend? Grady thought nothing but the best about you! You murdered him."

He crouched, ready to rush Cole, then stopped himself. He had to be careful. As long as Cole survived this, the Telepaths could read his mind to find Elliot. Cole wouldn't know the tricks to block them that Derwin was familiar with, thanks to his dad. But if the police didn't come, then it was up to him.

"Where's Elliot?" *Please let him be alive. Don't let him be dead already.* He took a step toward Cole.

"Don't move! He's alive, for now. If you do anything stupid, he'll be dead." The tremor in Cole's voice could be anger or fear. Was he bluffing? Derwin scanned Cole's form, but he couldn't see any detonator or other device that Cole might use to kill Elliot. So unless Cole had an accomplice, Elliot was alone. Hopefully somewhere close.

Derwin tried to sound casual. "You don't want to commit more crimes, do you? I mean if it's about money and power, I think the charges for murder and kidnapping might mess up your plans. Just tell me where he is. Or were you planning on killing both of us?" He didn't dare take another step forward. He needed some kind of clue about Elliot before the situation went to Hell.

Cole laughed without humor. "More crimes? I guess you don't know. Your new boyfriend is smarter than you. This is big. Much bigger than an imbecile like you can possibly comprehend. Killing you will be nothing." He cocked the gun.

Elliot could be out in the bay drowning right now. Seconds lost could be vital. "Tell me where Elliot is, or I'm going to grab that gun from you and blow your head off. I'm counting to five. One."

Not surprisingly, Cole pulled the trigger.

But Derwin had tracked Cole's shaking hand. As Cole fired, Derwin swerved, and burning pain seared across his biceps. Closer than he liked.

He couldn't let Cole get off another shot. Crouching low, he rushed him.

Cole gasped. "You're an Oddity!" He ducked back, knocking over a pile of crates to block the way.

By the time Derwin reached the end of the alley, Cole was gone. Derwin looked around. The docks were too exposed, and since Cole wasn't likely to climb up things and wouldn't fit somewhere narrow, he probably had gone into one of the warehouses. He still had the gun, though. Derwin ran to the closest door and tried to open it. The handle turned, but the door wouldn't budge.

What if he's got Elliot in there?

"Elliot!" He had to be inside, or somewhere near. Derwin slammed his shoulder against the aluminum door. Something inside scraped the floor—heavy furniture. *Or maybe Cole's trying to cut through the building.*

He would not escape. Not this time.

Derwin took three steps back, then rammed the door. Wood splintered on the other side of the door and he forced it open, and stumbled over the remains of a bookshelf stuffed with binders. The area beyond the doorway was dim, but he got the sense of a large space. By the light of the fading sunset, he could see boxes stacked high.

Running footsteps suddenly echoed in the near silence of the building. Derwin took off again, weaving his way through the maze of boxes. Cole huffed as he ran, making him easier to track.

Derwin rounded another stack and heard the shot just as cardboard and wood exploded by his face. *Not bad.* He had to be careful. Getting hit right now would really ruin his day. Elliot would probably kill him again just for fucking up. He spotted Cole at another door, struggling to aim the gun with one hand and turn the door handle with the other.

Derwin crashed into him, sending them both through the door to land on rough pavement, but Derwin hardly felt the scrapes. He grabbed for Cole's gun, forcing the barrel away from him. Cole got off another shot, and the muzzle burned Derwin's hand, but he refused to let go. "Where is he?" he shouted in Cole's face, his power surging in him.

Cole paled. Still, the only emotion in his eyes was fury, pure and strong. "I'm not telling you. You have no idea what you're messing with. I'll warn them about you. They'll find you."

"Who?" Derwin wrenched the gun away. He grabbed Cole by the collar, but though the man's breath hitched, he refused to answer.

"Stop there! Both of you!" Detective Wentley's voice cut through the red haze, but only barely. Derwin turned to see the detective raising his gun as he sprinted toward them, his partner close behind.

His timing couldn't have been worse. Disgusted, Derwin tossed the gun to the side, listened to it slide on the wet asphalt. He raised his fist and leaned in close to Cole. "You tell anyone about my Oddity and I swear you'll find demons in your cell, in your bedroom . . . everywhere. I'll let them loose on you until one of them kills you."

"Hands behind your heads! Mr. Bryant, back away from him slowly," Wentley instructed as he drew near, his gun covering Cole while his partner covered Derwin.

Derwin nodded and did as ordered, trying to calm down. Warm wetness trickled down his arm from the brush with the bullet, but there wasn't any pain. Whatever happened now, at least Grady would be avenged.

"He hasn't told me where Elliot is y-yet," Derwin told the detectives, struggling to get the words out. "He might be hurt." He didn't want to mention the other possibility.

Wentley nodded to his partner. "Cuff him." To Cole, he said, "You got anything to say? Just remember that anything you say can and will be used against you in a court of law. You have the right to an attorney. You look like a smart guy. I'm sure you know the drill."

Cole said nothing as Wentley's partner pulled him up and slapped the handcuffs on him. Instead, he glared at Derwin, who fought the urge to punch him in the nuts.

Derwin flexed his fingers. "We should search the area. I don't know what kind of condition Elliot's in. He said he was tied to a bed." While in some ways Wentley's calm professional manner was reassuring, the delays were making him want to scream.

Suddenly, Cole's eyes widened at something beyond Derwin's shoulder. All color left his face. He shoved against Wentley's partner, pointing at Derwin. "He's one of them! You have to help me. He's one, and maybe the other is too! Don't—"

Bang. Cole jerked backward as blood splattered the officer holding him. He slumped to the ground, a red hole in his forehead.

"Fuck!" Wentley whirled, gun raised, searching for the source of the shot.

Derwin spun as well, seeking high vantage points. A figure was running across the rooftop of an old mill across the street. Too quickly for a normal human. Twilight was fading fast, but he could still make out the figure as it leaped to the next rooftop, like a demon.

Or an Oddity.

He instinctively stepped forward, but the thought of Elliot pulled him back. If he gave chase, two things would happen: the detectives would see that he wasn't normal, and Elliot might die, wherever he was. He didn't need to pursue the shooter; Cole had killed Grady, and justice had been done. Grady could rest in peace.

But this meant there was more to why Grady had died.

"Fucking hell," Derwin muttered under his breath. He'd have to pursue this another time.

"Go after him," Wentley directed his partner as he pulled out his radio. The officer ran toward the building where the shooter had gone. Derwin knew they'd never catch the guy, but the gun might still be up on the rooftop. Hopefully with fingerprints.

Wentley quickly radioed in the situation, then rubbed his chin, contemplating their dead suspect. "You have no idea where he took your friend?"

Derwin wanted to smash something, yell, explode. He took a deep breath and let it out slowly, trying to settle the panic that trying to spread. "No. All I know is that it has to be less than twenty minutes from here, because that's the time it took me to arrive." He swiped at his sleeve, where blood was still dripping down his arm. He could barely feel it. "You mind if I search while you're waiting for your backup?"

Wentley eyed him cautiously. "All right. Don't stray too far. If you find him, call me." He slipped on a pair of gloves from his pocket and started to examine the hole in Cole's skull.

Derwin left him to it. He walked toward the seaside of the building, opening himself up wide, trying to feel for Elliot's pain. That rib was still healing. And there was the abuse he'd suffered at Roy's hands. Derwin would know if he came across those familiar injuries. *Where are you?*

He closed his eyes, searching with all his being for a clue, anything. Was that a scraping sound? Opening his eyes just enough to avoid obstacles, Derwin spotted a small building one lot over. Like the warehouse where Cole had tried to hide, it looked abandoned. Worth checking out.

Wentley's voice stopped him. "Hey, bounty hunter! He had a key in his pocket. Catch!"

Derwin turned as Wentley jogged over to toss him a key. The key was attached to a happy face with a bullet hole in its head. How appropriate. Wentley nodded, then returned to the body.

He kept walking toward the shack. It had a tin roof, no windows: perfect to hold someone in. He concentrated on feeling for pain, listening for a sound, praying for a sign.

There was a buzz in his head. Somebody's wrists were hurting.

Derwin paused; the connection faded. He focused harder, and this time he sensed more pain—an ache deep in the right side. That fucking rib. Not a sharp pain anymore, but bones took notoriously long to heal.

"Elliot!" Derwin shouted, running forward. He heard it louder now, a tapping from somewhere inside the building. The buzz intensified as he reached the door, then fumbled to get the key in the lock.

He pulled the door open.

CHAPTER THIRTY

CONFESSIONS

Elliot had been waiting for what felt like an eternity when the door opened.

He panicked, tugging uselessly at the tie holding his left wrist. He'd managed to free his right hand, only to find that the other knots were too tight. Cole had departed some time ago to kill Derwin. Was Elliot too late?

A figure stood silhouetted against the darkening sky. Tall and muscular—definitely *not* Cole.

Elliot's eyes widened, and his heart pounded. "Derwin?" Gods, if it wasn't Derwin, if this was some scary partner coming to finish him off, Elliot didn't know what he'd do. Die, most likely.

But then the figure let out a relieved moan.

"Oh thank the heavens," Derwin breathed, and yes, it really was Derwin, rushing forward to grab Elliot in a hard embrace, pressing his lips to Elliot's cheek. Elliot smelled his sweat, that unique spicy blend that was Derwin's, and just like that, all the emotions were up in his throat, choking him. He sobbed, clutching at him with one hand as Derwin fought to loosen his other wrist.

"I couldn't—" Elliot tried to speak, tried to apologize for not being able to escape on his own. He shook his hand uselessly, but then Derwin cupped his face, calming him.

"I've got you. Just relax. I'll get you free." Derwin reached down to his ankle and pulled out a long knife that was barely visible in the unlit room. Elliot shivered. He shouldn't be falling apart like this. Derwin was here. He was safe. Cole hadn't hurt him that badly—only a few cuts. He'd suffered worse in his job.

Maybe it was sheer exhaustion. Taking deep, shuddering breaths, Elliot held on to Derwin's shoulder with his right hand as the man sliced the ropes holding his left. As soon as that was free, Elliot gripped Derwin's other arm, pressing his face against the broad, muscled chest. Even when Derwin shifted to cut the ropes around his ankles, Elliot refused to budge. Derwin meant security. He wanted to feel protected. To get away from the killers and gang bosses and creeps on the street.

As soon as Elliot was free, Derwin gathered him up in his arms, holding him tight. "I'm here. You're okay."

Elliot nodded, but he didn't lift his head, his cheek brushing against the little patch of chest hair peeking above Derwin's shirt. He needed to be held firmly right now; otherwise he'd fall apart.

"Mr. Bryant? You okay?" the detective from the hospital called out. Elliot knew he should move away from Derwin and pull himself together. But he couldn't bring himself to do it. *No police. No more questions.* He sighed, burrowing in closer.

"I'm here. I've got him." Derwin's voice rumbled in his chest. His fingers brushed Elliot's cheek as he bent to whisper, "Are you okay? Can you stand up?"

Elliot sighed, holding on more tightly. It was stupid. He wasn't dead, and he wasn't injured, not really. But his body didn't want to obey.

A bright light flashed from the doorway. A flashlight, Elliot realized, as the beam moved over him, illuminating the cuts on his arm and throat, and the blood on his shirt. He closed his eyes. Didn't need to see it.

"I'm calling for an ambulance," the detective said.

"No!" Elliot's eyes flew open, and he glared into the light. "No hospitals!" If he had to go into another hospital room, he was going to shoot something. Possibly himself.

Derwin prevented Elliot from launching himself for the door by holding him down. "The cuts appear worse than they are." Derwin sounded calm, but the tremor in his voice and his fast heartbeat contradicted that. Derwin moved Elliot around just enough to inspect the new injuries. "Are you sure you're okay? What'd he do?"

Elliot shook his head. "Nothing much. Some . . . cuts." He looked at Derwin pleadingly. "I don't want to talk right now. Can we go?"

Home. That was where he wanted to go. But he didn't really have a home, did he? And Derwin's home was still uninhabitable. The hotel would do, though. Anywhere with Derwin was home.

"We need statements from both of you." The detective seemed tired. It occurred to Elliot that he should be wondering what had happened to Cole. He didn't care. Derwin was here. That was all that mattered.

Derwin rubbed Elliot's back in firm, soothing strokes. Elliot leaned against his shoulder, letting his eyes close.

"Can we come in tomorrow morning?" Derwin spoke for him again. "We're both recuperating—the explosion. And Elliot here was beat up by a bunch of punks a few days ago. That's where most of the injuries you see came from."

The detective didn't say anything, and Elliot swore he could feel the man's eyes roaming over him, making who knew what judgments. Opening his eyes, Elliot threw him a scowl, though he couldn't see the man's expression behind the bright glare of the flashlight. Didn't really want to anyway. Elliot struggled to speak, so that he wouldn't have to explain later. "He admitted it all. Killing Grady. Embezzling from his company. And setting the gas explosion in Derwin's condo to kill him."

The detective took a step forward. "He did? Would you be willing to have a Telepath confirm what you witnessed?"

Unease gripped Elliot's gut. The Telepath might also see what he'd seen in the visions. But what choice did he have? They'd probably make him do it anyways. Maybe he could convince the fellow Oddity to let that bit slide. A fresh wave of dread roiled in his gut. Glancing up, Elliot tried to read Derwin's face, to see what he thought of the idea.

Derwin studied him, then turned to the officer. "I can supply whatever the Telepaths need. Elliot's been through enough here. He wasn't even supposed to be involved in any of this." He looked down at Elliot, and his hand gripped Elliot's with a clear message: he'd protect Elliot, no matter what.

"We'll have to see. If we can find further evidence, we may not need confirmation." The detective nodded to the two of them, his face neutral.

Elliot took a deep breath. "Is Cole in custody? Can we go back to the hotel?" He was bone-weary; it was taking all his energy and focus just to talk.

Something dark and cold flashed in Derwin's eyes. "Cole's dead."

Elliot stared at him in shock. He didn't want to ask, but . . . "Did you?" Derwin must have killed him. What else could have happened?

Derwin clenched his jaw, looking away. "No, I didn't. Somebody was watching him. Probably whoever he was selling his secrets to. It was a professional hit: single shot from a high-powered rifle, from the rooftop across the street."

Horror washed over Elliot. "Professional?" He tried to recall if Cole had mentioned anything about the other party he must have been working with, the ones who paid for his secrets. Who would buy such information?

Corporations. Governments. Whatever it was, it had to be a well-funded, powerful entity.

"It's okay," Derwin insisted, but he didn't sound as sure this time. "I think they just didn't want Cole to talk."

Detective Wentley said, "We're going to be putting protection on the two of you, and we'll search Cole's home and office to figure out who he was working with."

So great, not only was there some professional killer somewhere, but Elliot would have to worry about law enforcement hovering nearby all the time, who might witness one or both of their Oddities.

Derwin's voice, soft in his ear, was the only thing that kept him calm. "That means he'll have a couple officers outside the hotel. That's all. Are you okay to stand? Shall we get out of here?"

Elliot nodded, leaning against him. Whatever other shit there was to deal with, it would have to wait. Cole was dead. "Let's go."

The criminal forensics team arrived before Derwin and Elliot even reached Derwin's car, which was still parked on the street nearby. Naturally the investigators insisted on checking both Derwin and Elliot for trace evidence. Derwin allowed it, but stayed close to Elliot from the snapping of pictures to the sampling of fibers, blood, and DNA—everything they took to prove what exactly had occurred here tonight. It was for the best to get out of here as quickly as possible. He was ready to release this whole thing back to the professionals.

He thought Elliot would balk when the men asked if he'd been sexually molested, but Elliot held out, stating in short, clipped words that he'd been threatened, tied to a bed, and cut a few times, but that was all. When Derwin saw the knife recovered from the room, he shuddered.

He gave his hotel's address to Detective Wentley. The detective took it all in stride, which helped cement him in Derwin's mind as one of the detectives he could trust. The police had their incompetent cops and their baggage from the city/state. Still, there were some like Wentley who could do the job well.

Once they were done, Derwin put an arm around Elliot and helped him into the car.

When they reached the hotel, Derwin guided Elliot up to the room and helped him undress.

"I'm keeping you locked in here with me for the next two weeks," he told Elliot gruffly as he noted yet more injuries on Elliot's pale skin. He had done a number on his wrists trying to escape, and it also looked like Cole had come close to nicking the artery in Elliot's throat. But Derwin didn't want to think about what could have happened. He only wanted to keep Elliot to himself until every last mark healed.

"Promise?" Elliot tried to smile, but it was a feeble attempt. His voice sounded watery, close to tears. His hands were trembling.

"Definitely."

They showered together—nothing sexual, just getting off the grime from the day. The blood. The tears. At one point, Derwin had to take the washcloth from Elliot's hands, afraid he'd scrub his skin raw.

Once they were both clean, Derwin grabbed a towel and helped Elliot dry off, as shivers wracked his thin frame. He hated how fragile this whole ordeal had made him.

He caught Elliot staring at his reflection in the bathroom mirror.

"I'm a mess, aren't I?" The bleakness in Elliot's voice cut Derwin like a knife.

Again, Derwin put his hands on Elliot, lightly gripping his arms. For some reason the contact seemed to calm Elliot. "You're going to be okay. You're tired, and you've been through a hell of a lot. But you'll be okay." He kissed the top of Elliot's head, standing behind him as they both gazed into the mirror. "I'm sorry."

Elliot blinked, a wrinkle forming between his brows. "What?"

Derwin waited until Elliot turned around to look into his face. "I'm sorry. For not listening to you earlier and basically brushing you off. I never should have left you alone here. I really thought I'd failed you."

The bleakness left Elliot's face, and some of the fire returned. "It wasn't your fault. Stupid me decided to be a detective and go back to your apartment. I should have waited."

"No. I was upset at Bud's place, and I took it out on you. You didn't deserve that. We're a team. When I heard you on the phone..." His voice broke. Those memories, that terrible drive home, finding Grady dead. "It would have destroyed me if anything had happened to you. You said to me that all you were worth to me was the money. That's not true. That's never been true." Tears burned in his eyes at the thought of losing Elliot. Was it too soon to fall in love? He didn't know. But it sure seemed to be happening to him.

Elliot looked down, rubbing at his raw wrists. "I knew you'd come for me." He gave a painful laugh. "So I guess that message got through. I was mad too." He swiped at his eyes. "I figured I could get a vision off Grady's computer desk, since nobody knew where his computer was. I was right. In the vision, I saw him exchanging instant messages with Cole, talking about that genetic-coding discovery that Willart mentioned. Grady knew, and so did the killer. Apparently Cole had gotten into Grady's work files, and Grady caught him. I didn't know it was Cole, though, until the vision was over. That's when he grabbed me from behind." He grimaced, growing paler, if that was possible.

Derwin rubbed his shoulders. "You're okay now. You're safe." Though he said the words, his heart chilled. So Cole really had been selling secrets to some other party, secrets about how to genetically test for Oddities. *"You have no idea what you're messing with. I'll warn them about you. They'll find you."* With Cole's last words, he'd told the shooter that Derwin was "one of them," an Oddity.

Did that message get through to Cole's unknown party?

Derwin couldn't afford to worry about that at the moment. For now, the most important person was right here. "He's dead, Elliot. Cole can never hurt us again."

Elliot nodded, snuggling in closer. He appeared exhausted, and Derwin couldn't blame him.

Gently, Derwin took a step backward, holding Elliot, guiding him. "Come to bed. Everything can wait until tomorrow."

Elliot didn't resist, walking like he was already half asleep.

They reached the bed together.

CHAPTER THIRTY-ONE

RESOLUTIONS

Showered and comforted, Elliot crawled into bed, welcoming Derwin's weight on him a moment later. He'd left his gloves off, but with Derwin nearby, he wasn't afraid of any visions that might come.

Derwin eased himself into position, his hips pinning Elliot's, and the pressure helped to center Elliot, ground him. "Do you want to sleep? Or—"

Elliot didn't give Derwin the chance to finish, pulling him close and bringing their lips together.

He wanted to crawl into Derwin's arms and never emerge again. To be safe, protected, loved. He kissed Derwin hard, their teeth clicking together, and tasted deeply of him as they fell into bed, limbs tangling. He didn't want to explain anything or say anything. Just to let their bodies do the talking.

He nibbled on Derwin's bottom lip, but it wasn't enough. So he bit down harder, until he tasted blood. Derwin growled, and where their bodies pressed together Elliot felt him go hard. A little payback for today was right, in Elliot's mind. Derwin had apologized for his words earlier, yes. But they had hurt.

Derwin placed his hands on the mattress, ending the kiss. "Easy, there. Are you still mad at me?"

Elliot made a frustrated grunt. His own erection should have been answer enough. "I want you. Need you," he groaned, nuzzling against Derwin as if he could climb inside him.

"I'm right here," Derwin said in a low, calm voice. He slid a hand up Elliot's thigh, up his side and then across his chest. Elliot moaned, arching into it, desperate. His cock was so hard; he'd never been this aroused by someone before.

Derwin's palm rubbed over one of his nipples. "Fuck me," Elliot gasped. His skin seemed to be on fire. Part of him suspected it was just a knee-jerk reaction to nearly getting killed. But then, sex had always been easy for him. This time it was much more than wanting a physical release. He doubted if Derwin knew that.

Derwin groaned. "Yes . . ." His mouth captured Elliot's again, and he plunged his tongue in, hips grinding against Elliot, their erections brushing each other. Elliot closed his hand around both of them, pulling on their sacs, playing. He could explore, and Derwin wouldn't hit him, wouldn't get mad or dock his pay. He could be himself. No roles.

He managed to give a few strokes to Derwin's cock, then Derwin was moving lower, teeth nibbling down the side of Elliot's neck that hadn't been nicked by the blade. He seemed to understand what Elliot craved at the moment, which was good, because Elliot didn't think he could articulate it. Derwin's hand joined his, pumping their cocks. Elliot whined, his hips thrusting. He felt ready to burst, but Derwin appeared intent on taking his time.

"I was afraid I'd lost you today." Derwin's words made Elliot's chest hurt for some reason. Maybe because it was so rare for anyone to give a damn about him.

Derwin brought up his hands to pin Elliot's shoulders to the bed, kissing a line down from his throat to the top of his shoulder, pausing now and then to lick and suck at the skin. Elliot's eyes rolled. He'd never been made love to like this. He gripped himself hard, trying to keep back his orgasm.

As Derwin's mouth licked a path to one hardened nipple, Elliot sobbed, and it wasn't all in pleasure. Could sex be cathartic? He didn't know. What he knew was that there was nothing in the world that could have torn him from this moment. He needed Derwin. And it went a long way beyond just hungering for that big cock up his ass.

"Don't want to be lost," Elliot finally responded, and even those words were an effort. Derwin's mouth felt so good, his teeth scraping the tight little bud, coaxing unreal sensations. Elliot was almost desperate for release, and they'd barely done anything yet. He gave up on trying to reciprocate as the man moved to lavish attention on the other nipple, causing him to squirm and moan. When he tried to stroke his aching cock, Derwin pinned him in place.

Raising his head, he looked Elliot in the eye. "You're never going to be lost. Do you understand? You've got a place with me now."

Elliot blinked. "What do you mean?" He tried to grab Derwin's hand and move it lower, to get some relief, but Derwin didn't let up on his hold. The funny thing about it was that it didn't hurt at all. Derwin knew how to immobilize a guy in a way that felt *good*.

Derwin kept his gaze locked on Elliot's as he licked a little pathway down to Elliot's navel before answering. "I mean," he said, kissing Elliot's stomach, "I didn't want you to leave from that very first night. And I sure as hell don't want you to leave now. I want to be *with* you. You know, as in a relationship. Whatever kind of relationship you can handle."

The fluttering in Elliot's stomach was only partially due to Derwin's mouth. He stared at Derwin; he couldn't help himself. *Relationship*? Did that mean what he thought it meant? As in boyfriend? What would it mean to have a boyfriend? Would Derwin be jealous if he still wanted to make money as an exotic dancer or something? So many questions, but his head just couldn't deal with them all. Right now his needs were simple. He'd untangle the rest later.

"Okay," he said, and if that seemed a little weak, then the fact that Derwin was headed for his cock excused him. He groaned as Derwin trailed the tip of his tongue over his length, all the way down to his balls. "Gods and demons," he moaned, spreading his legs to give Derwin more access, to give him everything.

He expected teasing, so when Derwin suddenly swallowed him, the muscles of his throat working around his cock, Elliot nearly lost it. He cried out, hips jerking, but Derwin's hands kept him pinned to the bed. Derwin went shallow next, tongue swirling around the head, and then took him deep again, sucking hard.

"Derwin, please," Elliot begged, scrabbling at Derwin's shoulders for some sort of purchase, some kind of anchor. It felt like his whole essence was here, and Derwin was going to draw it in, swallow it whole. It might not be a bad way to go.

Derwin drew off again and suckled on Elliot's balls. "Please what?" he asked, voice husky and tender. There was something different about him, now that the murder was solved. Where Elliot was all urgency, he was relaxed. Patient.

That wasn't what Elliot needed. "Please fuck me. I want to come with you inside me. Please—I can't hold on." The foreplay, which he normally loved, was going to kill him today. The pressure building inside threatened to tear him apart.

"Right." Derwin pulled back. Elliot wondered why until he heard the condom packet *crinkle* and saw Derwin reach for the lube. Part of him wanted to tell Derwin to screw it, fuck him without all that, skin to skin. But he was still a sex worker, and they should do the whole testing thing, and be safe. Maybe someday there'd be no need for protection. At the moment, he'd be satisfied with this. Elliot arched as Derwin's fingers found him, slicking up his hole with two fingers. He was still sore from the previous night, but that was okay. This was Derwin. He'd make it good, regardless.

"You okay?" Derwin asked, applying more lube. He pushed his fingers in deep, finding the spot that sent sparks shooting up Elliot's dick. Elliot gripped him harder, moaning, and nodded. It would have to do as an answer.

Derwin shook his head, smiling, his dark eyes warm and tender as he spread Elliot farther. "You're beautiful. Absolutely beautiful."

He kissed Elliot gently, his fingers gliding in and out, keeping Elliot close to the edge. Elliot rocked against him, loving both the pleasure and the burn, but most of all the kiss. No one had ever kissed him like this before.

Elliot panted, unable to catch his breath. He broke off the kiss, reaching for Derwin's cock, stroking him as Derwin pulled out his fingers. "Let me put the condom on you," Elliot whispered. He didn't know why it was important, but he wanted to touch Derwin now, not just lie there and take it.

"Be my guest." Derwin handed him the packet, and Elliot tore it open. As he slid the rubber on, Derwin's eyes held his, never glancing away. Elliot took a deep breath.

"This is different." It seemed like a stupid thing to say. But it *was* different from any other time he could remember. Giving Derwin one last stroke, Elliot guided him to his entrance, rubbing the bulbous head against it, eager for more.

Little laugh lines appeared at the corners of Derwin's eyes. "Yeah. It is. It's a good different, I hope?"

Elliot paused. He'd said he was lost before. Gazing into Derwin's eyes, he was lost again. Or maybe this was what being found felt like. "Yeah. A good different."

He couldn't wait any longer. Pushing his hips out, he pressed onto Derwin's cock, urging him with his eyes and his hips to thrust forward.

Derwin did so, and there was pure bliss on his face as his cock slid halfway in. Elliot bit his lip at the burn, telling his body to relax, that it was okay. Derwin seemed twice as big as when they'd last done this. Before the stretch could turn into pain, however, Derwin's hand was there, slowly stroking Elliot's cock, and everything transformed back to pleasure. Elliot moaned, as Derwin sank in deeper.

It wasn't enough. Elliot leaned up, sucking at Derwin's throat as he shifted his hips, trying to get more. When Derwin finally thrust all the way in, Elliot cried out, clutching at Derwin's back, his face buried against his throat.

"Love the feel of you," Derwin whispered, drawing out a little, then pushing in again. He provided a firm pressure with the fingers wrapped around Elliot's erection that both electrified and steadied him. "I know you're on the edge. Hold back and wait for me. It'll be worth it."

Elliot nodded, not sure his voice would work. Strange, how much he trusted Derwin. They'd known each other for less than a week, and yet it felt like it had been so much longer. Derwin would take care of him from now on. Something deep inside of Elliot knew that. Eyes closing, he groaned as Derwin began to fuck him slowly, hand stroking him in time. Elliot pinched his own nipples, basking in the sensations.

"Open your eyes for me," Derwin said, his lips brushing Elliot's collarbone. Elliot did so immediately. No golden glow to Derwin's irises right now, but the heat in them was searing. Suddenly the slow pace wasn't enough. All of Elliot's nerves were on fire, from the head of Derwin's cock brushing his prostate, the tip of Derwin's thumb on the slit of his cock. Elliot sucked in a breath.

Derwin slowed his hips even more, till he was just barely thrusting. His dark eyes seemed to swallow Elliot whole. "Say it." He gave Elliot's cock a firm stroke.

Elliot groaned. He knew what Derwin meant. By the look that Derwin was giving him, he knew. "You first."

This time Derwin thrust in hard, his legs shaking. Elliot gasped, his cock twitching. "I'm falling for you," Derwin said. Such simple words. Words that Elliot had never thought he'd hear directed at him.

It was too much. Crying out, Elliot grabbed on to Derwin like his life depended on it, his cock spurting as a powerful climax rocked him. Derwin quickened his pace, slamming into Elliot over and over as his orgasm went on. There was no finesse, no technique to it, just raw power as Derwin's cock buried itself deep in Elliot's core, sending jolts of pleasure through him.

Elliot thought that would be it, but he was wrong. Once the sizzle of pleasure died down a bit, Derwin eased his pace, still rock-hard inside him. Dazed, Elliot continued to hold on, just submitting to the larger man, letting his body receive. His cock wasn't even getting the chance to grow soft, as Derwin took his time, with deep, steady strokes. It felt incredible, every inch of Derwin's length rubbing sensitive nerves.

"Still with me?" Derwin asked in a low voice, smiling as he licked a trail along Elliot's collarbone. He kept his weight off Elliot with one hand, the other hand flicking over a nipple.

Elliot moaned, shuddering. "Yeah," he breathed, trying to hold on to coherent thought, or words, for that matter. He wanted to respond to what Derwin had said. About falling for him. "Me too," he rasped, and then realized that probably made no sense. He swallowed, stilling Derwin's hand for a second. "Falling for you, I mean. I think." How sad was it that he didn't know what it felt like to be in love? He just knew that right now, Derwin was the only thing in the world that mattered to him. If that was love, then yeah, he was there.

Derwin chuckled and kissed him, sucking at Elliot's tongue. Elliot couldn't believe that Derwin hadn't come yet. That he was so *calm* about everything.

With gentle pressure, Derwin shifted so he was behind Elliot, spooning him but still deep inside him, cradling him. His hand closed around Elliot's cock again, steadily coaxing him to more pleasure as they rocked against each other.

"You think?" Derwin whispered in his ear. Hopeful. Patient.

Just like that, it wasn't a question anymore. Who else had ever taken care of him like this? Had put up with both his moods and his rebelliousness? Elliot let his head fall back onto Derwin's shoulder, keeping one leg slightly raised so that Derwin could fuck him harder. He might be really sore after this, but oh, it would be *so* worth it. "Yeah. I mean no. I *know* I'm crazy about you."

No words came, because then Derwin was pounding into him, his hand fisting Elliot's cock, and fuck if he wasn't going to come again, and so soon. The pleasure surged up through his balls, and then with a cry, Elliot came, his semen splashing over Derwin's hand as he clenched. This time Derwin gave a low moan. He buried himself deep, and Elliot could feel the organ throbbing inside of him as Derwin shot his load. If his hold was a little too firm, Elliot could forgive him. Several pulses, and Elliot swore he could feel the heat of it, imagine being filled.

Afterward they both lay there, breathing softly and not moving. Elliot thought he might have dozed off for a few seconds, when he felt Derwin shifting, pulling carefully out. He whimpered in protest, but Derwin kissed him gently. "Shh. Just going to clean us up. Then I'm going to hold you like this, and we're going to sleep. Okay?"

He nodded. "Yeah. I'm sorry. I'm feeling a little clingy."

"Don't worry. So am I." Derwin petted his hair and slipped out of bed. He was back soon enough with a warm washcloth, which he used to clean them both. Then he pulled down the covers and resituated himself so that they were lying face-to-face, with his arms around Elliot. Derwin rubbed the bruise on Elliot's cheek with his thumb. "Are you going to be okay?"

Elliot hadn't been sure himself until that little gesture. And then suddenly, he was. Warmth spread through him, and this was probably the most comfortable he'd ever been in his life.

"Yeah. I will be."

CHAPTER THIRTY-TWO

NEW PURPOSE

Derwin slept about seven hours, and then watched Elliot sleep for another three. And then it was likely Elliot only woke because Derwin's phone kept vibrating. Everybody wanted to get ahold of them. Derwin assured his mother that everything was fine, but left the police and Theresa to wait.

He and Elliot got up leisurely, made love again, and then headed over to the police station. It took about six hours to give their full statements. Together with information the police had found at Cole's house and his office, the police anticipated they'd be able to close Grady's murder.

Cole had kept Grady's computer. Not particularly bright, in Derwin's mind, but maybe it had been a trophy, or memento. For Derwin's purposes, it was as good as a smoking gun.

The police had also found large sums deposited into Cole's account over the last two years. They'd hoped to find links to Cole's killer among his emails, but everything seemed to be encrypted and in code. It would take a long time to figure any of it out. The money had been routed through several dummy corporations and was similarly untraceable. Whoever he'd sold secrets to had hidden their tracks well.

So that left one murder solved, but another open. One thing that eased Derwin's mind was that the police discovered Cole had taken the last two days off, after that interview in his office. They found new tools in his house, tools that could have been used to tamper with Derwin's gas lines in his oven and to strip the wiring of his coffeemaker. That, along with Elliot's testimony that Cole had confessed to as much, cleared another mystery. Still, Derwin didn't like loose ends.

Somewhere out there were the people who had killed Cole before he could talk to the police. Those people, whoever they were, had at least one Oddity who knew how to use a sniper rifle.

Once the police interviews were done, Derwin drove Elliot to the hotel, stopping by to feed and check on Bickering. The cleaning crew would be in his house tomorrow, and in a few days, he'd move back there. What a relief that would be. He hated living out of a suitcase.

As soon as they reached the hotel room, Derwin sat down on the bed as Elliot flipped on the TV. Elliot seemed better than he had last night. Though he was paler, which was saying something, considering how alabaster his skin had already been, the circles under his eyes weren't as dark. The bruises on his face still made Derwin wince every time he looked at him, though. He needed to do a much better job of protecting the guy who was stealing his heart.

But at least the fire was back in Elliot's blue eyes.

Then Derwin's phone began ringing. He checked the Caller ID. Theresa. Again.

Derwin glanced at Elliot, who had clearly also seen the caller ID. Elliot's mouth tightened. Before Derwin could hit the Ignore button, Elliot snatched the phone off the coffee table and answered it.

"Theresa." Elliot's voice was flat, emotionless. It belied the fury in his face.

It wasn't hard to hear the other end of the conversation, not for Derwin. "Elliot, I'm so sorry."

Elliot glanced at Derwin. "Sorry for what? I did the job. The Tatsu gang shouldn't be bothering anyone for a while."

"Thank you. I really mean that. You know how tough it can be for my kids." At Theresa's words, the fury in Elliot's expression leeched away, and what was left made Derwin want to break the phone into tiny pieces. No nineteen-year-old should ever look so despondent.

Elliot took a deep breath and let it out. "It's why I did it."

There was silence on the other end for a moment. "Yes, Elliot. But Mr. Yoshiro . . . he sent one of his men here. He wanted to know where you were living."

And just like that, Elliot's eyes went wide in terror, and he almost dropped the phone. "Did you tell him? You can't tell him, Theresa. He says he'll kill me if anybody ever marks me again. I can't go back there. He *hurt* me."

"I know, sweetie." Theresa sounded tearful, but as far as Derwin was concerned, she had to be faking it. "I'm sorry I set the date up. I didn't have a choice."

By now Elliot had begun scratching at his knee through his jeans. Tight worry lines showed around his eyes, his mouth. "Did you tell him?" Elliot's voice had risen a notch. Derwin winced.

The silence was too much of an answer. How much would Elliot hate him if he punched his Madame in the face? "You know what Mr. Yoshiro is like. What his men are like. I had no choice but to tell him."

Elliot surprised Derwin by actually punching the couch, several times, breathing hard. Would he be the one to break the phone? His knuckles were white around it. "Which address did you tell him? The warehouse? Or where I've been lately?" His eyes met Derwin's.

Theresa sniffled. "Both."

Derwin groaned. Great. Now they had that to worry about as well. Time to buy more weapons. Maybe find himself a pet demon somewhere.

Elliot had grown still, and his voice was ice as he spoke. "I'm done, Theresa. I'm not working the streets anymore." Then he hung up.

They both waited a moment, watching, but it didn't ring again. Derwin gently took the phone from Elliot and set it on a side table, out of reach. He wrapped an arm around Elliot, and as he did so, a sense of stiffness crept over him. Elliot's rib was hurting. "You did great. She's not your friend. I know she helped you, but you don't need her." He had to be careful. Theresa had been the closest thing to a mother that Elliot had known for the past few years. There was still a chance, even now, that she could lure him back to the streets, and the gangs. "If she calls again, I can speak with her, if you don't want to."

Elliot sighed. "We should take pictures of the bruises and send them to her. That might shut her up for a while."

Derwin grunted, nodding. For several minutes neither of them spoke, letting the TV be the only sound. He wasn't sure yet how he was going to handle Mr. Roy Yoshiro, Tatsu gang leader. Maybe Detective Wentley would have some ideas. For the time being, though, they were hidden, safe in their hotel.

He ventured to ask the question that had been plaguing him for days. "So are you going to stay with me? Live in the condo with me once it's fixed up?" Last night Elliot had been traumatized. He'd been needy. But now he seemed calmer, and it was time to look forward and figure things out. "The alarm should be working by then. We'll have some cops watching the place, so I doubt Roy will try anything right away." Derwin had to work, of course. But maybe if they kept a low profile, Elliot's old clients would start to forget about him, including Mr. Yoshiro.

They'd take things a day at a time.

Elliot chewed on his lip and shrugged. "Perhaps." He glanced up, and Derwin caught a flash of vulnerability in his eyes. "I plan to lay low for a while. Yes, I . . . want . . . to stay with you. For as long as you'll have me."

Derwin couldn't hold back his grin. He never wanted to tame Elliot's feral nature, that wild nature he loved. Still, the fact he was willing to stick around was a step forward. "That could be a long time. One thing, though. I know I don't have any right to ask this, but I have to be honest about how I feel. I'm not going to be cool with you sleeping with other guys. I want to be the only one you have sex with. Are you okay with that?" He couldn't stomach the idea of another night like the one Elliot had spent with Roy. The sickening worry. The jealousy. He could admit that now.

Until Elliot took his hand, Derwin didn't realize that he'd been holding his breath. The smile on Elliot's face was calm and confident. "Yeah. I'm more than okay with that." He looked down at their joined hands, dark lashes brushing his cheek. "I think I need it, actually."

Derwin squeezed his hand. The past was falling away. Grady was gone, at peace, and the future stretched before him like an open road. "I think I need it too." He glanced at the borrowed shirt that Elliot was still wearing. "You think it's safe to stop by your place and grab the rest of your things? We could also stop by Bob's Bail Bonds. I could introduce you to Bob and Connie, the secretary. Like I said, you might be able to earn a few bucks filing for them."

"Later." Elliot let go of Derwin's hand only to slide his under Derwin's shirt. A pleasant shiver went through Derwin and his cock took notice. Elliot smiled his evil smile. The one that said he was about to pounce and subdue Derwin with that wicked mouth of his. "I want to talk about some of these tattoos of yours. And then I want to deep-throat you until I swallow your come."

Oh yeah. Derwin's libido was definitely waking up again. Everything else could wait.

Derwin groaned as Elliot helped him with his shirt, fingers ghosting over the ring of runes on Derwin's stomach. The shirt ended up on the floor, and Derwin ended up on his back with Elliot lying on top of him, their cocks rubbing together. Elliot traced the runes on his stomach. "Start with this one."

Derwin smiled faintly, tracing them along with Elliot. "Nordic runes. It's a protection spell, supposedly good for staving off possession by demonic spirits." He drew a line up Elliot's chest. "You like my tattoos?"

The look Elliot gave him was searing. "I like pretty much everything about you. The demon hunting scares me a bit. But yeah. Pretty much everything."

There was so much to explore in Elliot. Derwin flicked one of Elliot's nipples, watching his head fall back with the sensation. "I want to know all about you," he told Elliot, as he leaned up to kiss him. "Just give me time to do that. We'll see where things go." He chuckled. "I keep imagining you with pierced nipples."

Elliot laughed. "Maybe. Or maybe I should get protective runes."

That one struck a little too close to home. "I'm going to protect you. From now on."

"I know you will." Elliot smiled.

The trust in Elliot's eyes pierced Derwin's heart. Yep. He was definitely in love with Elliot Leed. Whatever challenges lay ahead, he'd find a way to make it work.

Dear Reader,

Thank you for reading J.T. Hall's *Murder Once Seen*!

We know your time is precious and you have many, many entertainment options, so it means a lot that you've chosen to spend your time reading. We really hope you enjoyed it.

We'd be honored if you'd consider posting a review—good or bad—on sites like **Amazon, Barnes & Noble, Kobo, Goodreads, Twitter, Facebook, Tumblr,** and your blog or website. We'd also be honored if you told your friends and family about this book. Word of mouth is a book's lifeblood!

For more information on upcoming releases, author interviews, blog tours, contests, giveaways, and more, please sign up for our weekly, spam-free newsletter and visit us around the web:

    Newsletter: tinyurl.com/RiptideSignup
    Twitter: twitter.com/RiptideBooks
    Facebook: facebook.com/RiptidePublishing
    Goodreads: tinyurl.com/RiptideOnGoodreads
    Tumblr: riptidepublishing.tumblr.com

Thank you so much for Reading the Rainbow!

RiptidePublishing.com

ACKNOWLEDGMENTS

This book was my first paranormal gay mystery suspense, and just saying all that hints at how much work and research was needed to get it right. I'd like to thank my partner, Tammie, for all the long hours she allowed me to spend at my desk pursuing my dreams, and for her valuable plot advice. I'd also like to thank the "House of Manlove" m/m romance critique group, in particular Heloise West, who helped me trim my wordy nature. And I'd like to acknowledge all the staff at Riptide Publishing, in particular Sarah Lyons, editorial director, and Caz Galloway, my editor. Last, I'd like to acknowledge Kanaxa for the lovely cover she created.

ALSO BY
J.T. HALL

The Oddities
Fraud Twice Felt (coming soon)

The Foreman (Part One of the Hard Hat Series)
The New Hire (Part Two of the Hard Hat Series)
Friday at the 7-Eleven
Vice and Exploitation

ABOUT
THE AUTHOR

J.T. Hall has been writing for many years under this name and others, and has appeared in magazines, anthologies, and online books. She earned her BA in creative writing from the University of Arizona, her master's in education from Argosy University, and works as an independent technical writer for state and federal programs. In her free time, she volunteers for the LGBT community and is active in the leather scene. She has a teenage daughter and a partner of over ten years. They live in sunny Arizona with three adorably cute dogs, three black cats, and a hamster who loves peanuts.

Social Media:

Visit J.T. Hall's blog at: thallwriting.wordpress.com

Facebook: facebook.com/profile.php?id=100005608068142

Twitter: twitter.com/JTHall7

Goodreads: goodreads.com/author/show/7035533.J_T_Hall

Newsletter, with announcements of new releases, sales, and special sneak peeks: eepurl.com/4TQCn

Enjoy more stories like
Murder Once Seen
at RiptidePublishing.com!

| *Friendly Fire* | *The Secret of Hunter's Bog* |
| ISBN: 978-1-62649-482-4 | ISBN: 978-1-62649-374-2 |

Earn Bonus Bucks!

Earn 1 Bonus Buck for each dollar you spend. Find out how at
RiptidePublishing.com/news/bonus-bucks.

Win Free Ebooks for a Year!

Pre-order coming soon titles directly through our site and you'll
receive one entry into a drawing for a chance to win free books for
a year! Get the details at RiptidePublishing.com/contests.